PRAISE FOR THE UNTAMED SERIES

"A fantastic dystopian tale. Highly recommended for fans of strong heroines and intriguing sci-fi worlds."
Pintip Dunn, *New York Times* bestselling author of the Forget Tomorrow series

"A YA *Mad Max*—thrilling and deep, with richly drawn characters and spot-on pacing. With the sequel every bit as good as the predecessor, Dyer's Untamed series is a must-read for dystopian fans."
T.A. Maclagan, author of *They Call Me Alexandra Gastone*

"Fascinating and intriguing."
A Drop of Ink Reviews

"Dyer is as much a poet as a dystopian scribe. Her images, at times surreal, at times brutal, propel you through the worlds of *Untamed* and *Fragmented* at high speed."
Marissa Kennerson, author of *The Family*

"Strong writing and well-rounded characters. If you loved *Untamed*, you'll want to pick up *Fragmented* right away to discover more about the world and the people Dyer has created."
Heidi Sinnet, author and librarian

"A kick-butt story with amazing characters and outstanding world building."
Readcommendations

"Highly recommended."
Dr. Jessie Voigts, *WanderingEducators.com*

"Dyer writes with an urgency and a rhythm that compels you to turn the page."
Sue Wyshynski, author of *Girl on Fire*

ALSO AVAILABLE FROM MADELINE DYER

THE UNTAMED SERIES

UNTAMED
FRAGMENTED

COMING SOON...
DIVIDED

THE UNTAMED SERIES
BOOK TWO

FRAGMENTED

MADELINE DYER

INEJA PRESS

Fragmented
Copyright © 2017 Madeline Dyer
All rights reserved.

Madeline Dyer asserts the moral right to be identified as the author of this work.

Second edition, January 2017
Published by Ineja Press

First published in 2016 by Prizm Books, a division of Torquere Press Publishers

Edited by Deelylah Mullin
Cover and Interior Design by We Got You Covered Book Design

Print ISBN: 978-0-9957191-2-5
eBook ISBN: 978-0-9957191-3-2

The author can be contacted via email at Madeline@MadelineDyer.co.uk or through her website www.MadelineDyer.co.uk

For Nana

SNAKES AND FIRES AND ANGRY Goddesses fill my dreams, and I wake to the feeling of feathers running along my shoulder blades. A spirit.

Get out. Leave us. Go.

The voice hovers around me, and I blink several times, half-imagine the words by my face, gaining substance, wrapping themselves in thick, outer shells. Wispy tendrils unfurl from each pod and reach out to me, strive to cling to my skin, but then something extracts the soft, singing bodies from their cages, pulls the words farther and farther away, until they've gone. Without their melodic centers, the armor disintegrates, and a moment later the lingering ethereal footprint of each husk disperses into dust, destroying all evidence that anyone—anything—ever spoke…until I'm certain no one did, and it was all my imagination.

I roll over—flaking mud from my clothes—careful not to disturb Corin's sleeping body next to me. The air tastes strange, like it's waiting for something, like it's humming with a slow-burning zeal.

I sit up and look down at Corin. He's a big man, broad-shouldered, tall, and he takes up most of the mattress we are sharing. His eyes are shut, his eyelids smooth, his expression peaceful as his chest rises and falls with the temporal security. For several moments, all I can do is stare at him, drink in his appearance. He looks so relaxed, so peaceful; it's almost possible to forget what has happened—all the blood, the losses, the deaths….

Yesterday comes back to me in flashes, and I inhale sharply, feel the air around me move. A glimpse of blood. A purple sky. A sharp knife. A gun, glinting in the light. A man with—

Something cold washes over me, pulls me from the broken echoes in my mind, and I sit up straighter, looking around. I shiver. The temple is cool, crisp, yet the air ripples. It starts off slowly—little, small movements—but then the momentum grows, and the atmosphere gets heavier, thicker, choppier.

The spirits move faster. I can't see them—they're invisible, because they're weak now, after the battle— but I can sense them, feel them. A biting frostiness that scatters icy particles over my shoulders. A flurry of movement against my bare arm.

My mother's Seer pendant around my neck feels heavier, bulkier than usual, but it's a reassuring presence. As if it can protect us from everything.

For a few seconds, all I can see in front of me are rapid snatches of my mother; how she looked yesterday when the slight wind lifted stray tendrils of her dark hair away from her face. How she still had those small scars on the side of her neck. How reflective her eyes were.

How Corin shot her in the leg.

I swallow hard and look down at my own legs, stretched out in front of me. They're covered in dirt, soft clay—like the rest of me. I look at Corin. We're both daubed in sludge, blood, mud. The back of my neck prickles. We…we—we *slept* like this… We didn't wash ourselves. I get a bad taste in my mouth, still can't remember arriving at the spirit temple. But we slept here. I try to recall my dream, but the angry Goddesses are only impressions now—a chalky silhouette, the shape of a head, and a lone arm—impressions that slither away like the snakes I think were there. The dying impression of a flame lingers a little longer in my mind, before fading into unease.

Spirits. I nod. Has to be. They took us there, knocked us out…made sure we got some sleep, some energy?

I look back at the pulsing air.

"Sev?"

I jump, turn at Corin's voice. He's awake, looking up at me. His eyes are pools of warmth that try to draw me in and swallow me.

Last night, he said he loved me.

"You okay?" He sits up, and his arms draw me close, away from the moving spirits, and I'm wrapped in the tangy smell of old smoke and mud.

I lean into him, liking the feeling of being close. Close to him, when the spirits are moving. I swallow hard, my fingers only shake a little. I manage to nod, but the action feels fake. Am I okay? I bite my lip. Nothing's *okay* anymore.

So, go! Leave! Get out, now.

Shivers run through me as I hear the spirit's words. It jogs something in me, makes me remember an earlier voice, movement, and words disappearing, their echoes disintegrating in front of me. My eyes widen… It wasn't my imagination? I sit up straighter. *Leave?* I hold onto Corin tighter, counting the beats of my own heart, and—

A spirit shrieks, cutting the air in two.

We flinch. Corin reaches for his gun from where it lies on the floor, a foot or so away. White light glints off it for a second, and I want to tell him it's futile—you can't shoot a spirit with a gun. But the moment he has the weapon in his hand, I feel better.

We stand up slowly.

More spirits scream. Scream because we're listening, echoing the sounds of last night's battle. Scream

3

because it's the only way they know how to grieve.

Get out, leave us!

It's all around us: memories and pain and shrieks and loss. I hear a soft whooshing sound, see a flash of gold as a chivra spirit—visible now—flies past us. I turn my head slowly, trying to see where the chivra went, but it's gone.

Something cracks and cackles behind us. I flinch. Corin reaches for my hand, and the gesture sends sparks through me. The air is colder—much colder—but it is alive, teeming, bursting. The wind's picking up, diving through the rectangular opening in the stonework, howling with the spirits. Something splashes over my right arm, and I taste rust, smell burning flesh. Corin winces as something invisible hits him, then he tries to shield my body with his.

I peer around his shoulder; ahead, the ripples in the air oscillate faster. Gusts of energy reach us in short, sharp bursts, and I step back, pull Corin with me. My shoes squeak against the stone floor, and a spirit imitates the sound. I jump as my back meets the cold stone wall of the temple, think for a second that it's another spirit.

"What are they doing?" Corin's voice is a low whisper, tense, and he looks up, flinching, as a flash of silver darts above us.

Eviction. They want us gone. The message is clear. They helped us in the battle, protected us overnight, but now our time's up.

"We need to go."

"Have you seen it?" Corin's dark eyes are intense with emotion. "Sev?"

I shake my head, lean against the wall. The Dream Land hasn't told me we need to go. I just know it. It's obvious. Obvious in the way the spirits are telling us, how they're crying for their own losses, tightening the air against us.

Except...except *I* don't want to go. I don't want to leave the safety of the temple. Out there, we'll be back in the real world. In here, we're safe…but not for much longer, I know that. Spirits aren't usually hospitable; we were lucky they allowed us to stay, protected us. But now they're turning, revoking their invite.

A gust of hot air urges me sideways, toward the exit.

"We need to see if they're still out there…" Corin frowns, starts to choke. "We need to see… We need to see if she's alive." But even as he says the words, I detect the weight in his voice. We both know the answer.

I nod, steel myself. I don't want to think about it, but I know ignorance is not bliss. The Enhanced Ones came for us, and—at the moment—Corin and I are the only survivors. My brother's dead; I saw him get shot. We need to send his body off, say the Spirit Releasing Words, make sure he gets to the New World safely—if it's not already too late.

And the same for Esther….

We have to find them both.

The spirit temple's opening is a small uneven gap in the stone wall, no door to speak of. Yet it had felt enclosed earlier, when we slept, hadn't it? But I can't remember. The brimming air pushes us toward the exit, nearer and nearer. Corin goes first, but he holds onto my hand tightly. So tight, I can almost feel his heart beating. With every step, the journey toward the door gets easier, and we walk faster; the spirits are eager for our departure.

Leave us! Go!

My eyes latch onto the gun as Corin tucks it under the back of his waistband with his free hand. Seeing it makes me wish I had a weapon. But I don't. Corin left his knife in Raleigh's chest when he stabbed him.

We reach the gap in the stone, see the early morning light. Corin steps out, then pulls me with him into the outside world.

Sheets of sudden rain smack against me, sharp and stinging. The wind yowls, grabs me with icy fingers. Corin's grip on my hand gets tighter. He pulls me forward, then stumbles before regaining his balance. Behind us, the spirits scream. The hairs on the back of my neck rise at the sounds of their power, their grief.

We stop once we're a good twenty feet from the spirit temple, and I look around. The air is hazy now, the rain lessening. So I concentrate on the sky. If I look at its moodiness, as its hues flit from orange to blue, to purple to yellow, and feel its weeping tears on my face, I don't have to look at the dead. I can almost pretend we're not standing above a battlefield.

"They've all gone," Corin says after a moment, "the live ones—they've gone. It's just their bodies, left behind."

I nod. I know he's talking about the Enhanced. Now I have to look. I have to see the corpses strewn across the landscape below us as though an unseen power simultaneously picked them all up and threw them down with such force their lives broke. I turn and look at the nearest hill—soft land rising out of the new basket of death—and I scan it for my mother's body. I can't see her. Then I survey the horizons. There are no signs of any towns; it's just wilderness. I don't know where she's gone. Where any of them have gone.

I look back at the bodies below us, cradled in the long-sunken land—there are so many of them. Even from here, rotting stenches fill my nostrils, the smells penetrating and pungent, as if they've been here for weeks, not hours. A living graveyard. One that stretches on and on and on. Logic tells me our enemy suffered more than us, because the spirits that joined in were generally on our side; there are hundreds and hundreds of bodies, and they have to be Enhanced. Raleigh had an army prepared. Our number was only four, when it came down to it. And we've got one confirmed death—my brother's. Half of us—or three-quarters, if Esther's still alive—survived, thanks to the spirits.

I squeeze Corin's hand, notice my arms are nearly clean from the rain, then my eyes focus on a shape three hundred feet away. My stomach twists. That could be Three's body. I gulp. My brother. Dead. It doesn't feel right. It can never feel *right*.

I look up at Corin. His expression is unreadable.

"Do you think it's safe down there?" he asks, his voice husky. "To look through the bodies?"

I stare at the fallen soldiers, somehow glistening under the morning light and the now-weak drizzle. This shouldn't have been the answer. This shouldn't be what the world's come to when the majority of people want to use chemical augmenters to alter and control their own feelings, appearances, and lives—and force the use of augmenters onto everyone else. We shouldn't be fighting to keep our own lives pure.

Pure. I am not pure.

I gulp at the memory. It's in the past. I have to focus on that. It wasn't my fault. But the echo—the feeling—of me unscrewing the lid of the vial and tipping the sweet, delicious augmenter into my mouth is beautifully strong....

But it's not right. I have to stay Untamed. I know that now.

"Sev? Should we go down there?"

"I don't know." At last, I look up at Corin. I'm tall for an Untamed girl, but he is taller, built like a true warrior: tall, strong, broad. Powerful. "The Enhanced have gone. I don't want to stay here long." I pause, trying to steady my breathing. A huge part of me wants to turn back, head for the temple again, beg the spirits to let us stay longer, beg them for safety...just for an extra day, an extra night. But I already know the answer. "We should look quickly, then leave."

He nods, eyes somber. I know he's thinking of Esther, his sister.

We start out for the scattered remains of humans, hand-in-hand. This is what our life is now: looking through bodies for our family and friends, and always being on the run, trying to find a safe place for the surviving Untamed—a place that doesn't exist. A place that can never exist.

I don't even know where we're going to go after this. The spirits won't have us back in their temple.

The ground is wet and slightly squelchy underfoot. We go to each body together. If we can't see the person's face—but the build and coloring of the individual matches either Three or Esther—then one of us nudges the corpse over, until we can. I can't help but notice no weapons have been left with the dead.

We keep doing this, over and over again. Five minutes. Ten. Twenty. Despite my earlier assertion that we should look quickly then leave, I know we'll keep doing it until we've found who we're looking for, or until we've checked every body. No matter how long it takes.

It's rhythmic, really. A routine. But I haven't actually thought about what we're going to do when we're confronted with their corpses. I don't think Corin has either. It's not something I want to think about. But I am, subconsciously. I imagine myself crying, falling down, fainting even? But it's not happening now, and it doesn't have to happen... I don't want to find Three or Esther's bodies. Yet I can't leave without confirming their fates, without saying the Spirit Releasing Words over their bodies, making all the signs of the Journeying Gods and Goddesses over them. Because I know neither Three nor Esther could have survived that—not without the spirits' help. And the spirits only took Corin and me to the temple.

After rolling over a particularly mutilated body with my foot—getting my only pair of shoes covered in congealed blood—Corin freezes. His face is ashen, and I follow his gaze.

Cold air wraps around me as I stare at the body.

It's *Corin*.

It looks exactly like him. This man's lying at an angle, his dark hair semi-obscuring a deep gash across his forehead. The red on his white, gaunt skin is blinding. I feel heat rising in my throat, and, after looking at the dead Corin's open eyes—the mirrors are still bouncing light—I have to look away.

I squeeze Corin's fingers tighter, appreciate the warmth of the man—the *live* man—next to me. "How?"

"They've cloned us all," Corin says. He pinches the bridge of his nose. "I suppose we leave DNA in their towns when we're raiding. Or it's their appearance-altering augmenters… Temporary clones like Marouska was? Shit. This is messed up. *Clones*." He shakes his head, and the early morning sun blinks in the flecks in his dark eyes. He looks down at the body. The body that's modeled on *him*. "They've made us into their soldiers…made us attack *us*."

For several minutes I can't say anything. I don't know what to say.

"Come on." Corin pulls me forward. "It's just another Enhanced."

But it's not. It's him. That Enhanced is—or rather was—identical to him…and if I lose Corin, I don't know what I'd do. The reality of our situation is terrifying. I don't want to be on my own.

"If we find them, we'll have to check their eyes. Check that they're not actually the Enhanced copies of them." Corin's hand shakes as he speaks, and I hold onto him tighter, as though my life depends on it.

We carry on checking the bodies. Corin never lets go of my hand. I am glad.

Minutes pass. Then hours. I hadn't realized how big the battleground was before. Or maybe the spirits have stretched it out, messed with the land. I turn back for a second, look for the spirit temple. It slices into the sky in the distance, so far away.

Corin squeezes my hand. We continue looking.

"Oh Gods." The words escape from my mouth before I can stop them. My eyes are already trying to examine the body in the distance… Female… Short, cropped, dark hair… A muscular build, like Corin's.

"Sev?" Corin's hand tenses, all the muscles in his

fingers going rigid against mine.

Then we're running.

It could just be a clone. It could just be a clone. It could just be a clone.

The mantra's shouting itself over and over again in my head.

But the closer I get to the body, the more sure I am. My spine tingles, my heart pounds. I can hardly breathe.

The young woman's lying on her side, her back to us. Dirt and grime and dried blood cover her pale skin. Her arm twitches. She's...she's not....

We reach her a second later. Untamed eyes. My neck clicks.

Esther. She's alive. She's still alive. Hope erupts from within me. If she is, then surely—

No. I saw my brother get shot. He's dead. We're not going to find him alive. We'll be lucky to find his body intact.

"Esther..." Corin says. His voice is strange, too quiet.

Then he throws himself down at his sister's side. I step around him and look down at her. Dark eyes, like warm chocolate—just like Corin's—watch me. There's still life in them—*Untamed life.* I know it's her—my Seer powers tell me that—but she's weak. Her face is divided in two by a long, bloody gash. Her skin's too pale. Far too pale and—

I choke as I see the bullet in her shoulder—a harsh glimpse of metal among torn muscle, bloodied tissues, shredded skin.

Bile rises in my throat. I bite my lip, look around. There are other bodies not far off; I don't recognize them.

Esther makes a gurgling sound as she rolls over onto her back with a blood-curdling scream. She looks at us, and I watch her absorb Corin's appearance, noting the obvious relief on her face, the way her shoulders sag slightly into the muddy ground. Then her face moves a fraction, until she's looking at me, and—

I know what she's going to say. I don't know how. But I *know*.

"No." I look at her, shake my head. "No… No, Esther, *no*."

Her eyes are on me, and she nods.

But she *can't* say those words, she mustn't. I clench my fists, feel the blood vessels over the back of my hand bump up.

I don't want her to speak. Esther *can't* say the words. It's impossible.

Blood drips down the side of her face. Corin tears part of his shirt off, tries to dab all the redness away, but the fabric soaks up the blood until it's bleeding itself.

Esther's lips start moving, and her eyes are still on me. "Seven, please, he's alive—"

I shake my head. He can't be. Half his face was shot off, and another bullet went into his abdomen. My brother's tough, but there's no way he could have survived that.

"He *is* alive." Esther shuts her eyes briefly, and her whole body shudders. When she opens them, I feel sick. "He was still breathing, Seven. I saw him, but—"

My spine clicks. Something strange happens to my legs, and I fall as she speaks.

"They've taken him. The Enhanced Ones have taken Three."

TWO

CORIN GRABS ME AS I fall.

But his arms aren't as strong as normal, and he can't stop me from meeting the ground. For a second, he tries to pull me up—his hands under my arms—but then Esther lets out a jagged gasp. Corin lets go of me, turns to her, and I crash into the mud for a second time.

Soft, too soft.

The sludge grabs me. It takes my feet first. I watch as it rises up over my legs, seeping into my shorts. It feels cold, like a spirit's clinging to me.

The Enhanced Ones have taken Three….

No.

My belt digs into me, sharp and hard. I stare at my long shorts. Can't even remember what color they're supposed to be. Navy? Black? Khaki? They'll be a neutral color, I know that. But they're just brown now. Dirty brown. My only pair. Ruined. And it seems important, I can't look away from them.

My shirt is the same—an oversized T-shirt, marred with mud stains and fresh dirt. My…jacket? I'm not wearing one. I frown, thought I had one on before…

in the battle? I can't think. My head hurts too much. My arms are bare, and I can see the new mud on them.

I'm covered. Covered in squelchy clay and dirt, and it's already drying—too quickly. Far too quickly. The spirits. It's got to be them. They're out here now—mostly invisible—and they're still active.

I look at Esther: alive, but with a bullet in her shoulder. The spirits must have been protecting her too, out here; she's not dead.

I take a deep breath, peel a layer of nearly dry sludge from my skin. Sharp pins dive through me.

"Seven, it's true," Esther says. Her voice is weak. She sounds like how my sister did when she got tonsillitis a few years ago: raspy, annoyed, tired. "I saw Three. He's alive, they've taken him—"

"No." I shake my head, pull more dried mud from my arm, wince as the tiny hairs there protest. "He's dead." I flinch as I bite the words, as if just by saying it I'm ensuring my brother's gone.

But I saw his face, I saw the gap where his left cheek should've been. I saw the blood, the mangled mess of tissues and flesh, the wild look in his eye—fear.

And I saw the second bullet plunge into his abdomen.

Nausea rises within me, and I struggle not to smell the putrid aroma of death. My hands splay out in the mud. I watch the gloopiness ooze between my fingers, over my nails. It reminds me of something, but I can't think what.

"Seven," Esther says, but I shake my head.

"They've copied us, cloned us," Corin says. He's crouching, and his back is turned. He's fiddling with the piece of fabric again, trying to adjust it so it's tighter around Esther's shoulder.

"And they've got appearance-altering augmenters," I say. "It wasn't Three you saw breathing." I nod. "Come on. We have to find his body, send him off."

"Seven, please… You have to go after him, after them."

My chest shudders.

Corin flicks his head toward me, his eyes dark. The wind starts to pick up, and the tattered front of his shirt flutters. "*Could* Three be alive?"

My shoulders tighten. I shake my head as a rush of something flies past me—I feel the movement against my back. A spirit.

"He *is* alive!" Esther's voice gets higher. "He is! I saw him… Seven, you *have* to go after him. Our village rescued you when the Enhanced took you to their compound, but you're not going to do the same? We *always* rescue each other. It *was* him—he was shouting your name—*Seven*, not Shania. Your Untamed name—it was him."

"The Marouska-imposter called me *Seven* too."

"But—"

I bolt upright, stand over them both. My fingers are burning shards. The wind wraps around me, along with remnants of rain. My clothes feel heavy.

"Esther," Corin says. "Leave it."

He takes out a lighter and a box of cigarettes from his pocket. I stare at him as he struggles to light one. We've just fought the Enhanced Ones, battled against and with spirits as they first fed from us, then helped us, had our numbers slashed and lost all our gear, *and* Corin's still got cigarettes with him.

Esther makes a gurgling sound. Her eyes start to water. With a jolt, I realize she's been shot in the same place I was, only…a month ago? Was it a month? I pull at my hair, then push it behind my ears. My arm tingles. After I got shot, Three checked my shoulder and said the bullet had missed the important stuff. It doesn't look like Esther's has.

I rub my nails up my arm, need to get rid of the dirt. Need to get clean. I look around, but there's no water. The land's just moorland, hilly, muddy. I can't see any valleys with water at the bottom.

I brush down my shorts.

"Khaki," I say.

"What?" Corin gives me a strange look.

I point at my shorts. "They were khaki."

Corin looks around. His lips are now pressed together so firmly the color's draining from them, and he holds the half-burnt cigarette between his thumb and forefinger. A trail of smoke lifts up toward the sky.

Corin coughs. "We need to get the bullet out."

Esther groans, her face paling. I thought she'd looked bad before, but now her skin has an eerie gray pallor. The exact same shade Kayden's face had been when he died. No. When he was murdered.

"Not here," I say. There isn't any cover. Just grass and mud and the odd bit of bracken. We need to get away, find somewhere we can hide, in case they come back. "We're too vulnerable here."

The Enhanced Ones have taken Three….

I gulp, a sour taste in my mouth. No, they haven't taken him. His body will still be here. Somewhere.

"Corin, get Esther away from here. I'll catch up." I turn away, look back out toward the other corpses.

"Sev, what are you doing?" Corin's voice is dark.

I flinch a little. "I need to keep looking, find his body. Three's body. The Spirit Releasing Words. They need to be said."

Especially when Death is around.

I shudder at the thought of seeing Death again—that cloaked man with glowing elbows. My mouth dries. The wind whistles past my teeth, makes an eerie shrieking sound. The memory feels almost like a dream, as if it can't possibly have happened. But it did. I saw Death, and he was angry because I was going to join the Enhanced. Because he knew I was a traitor.

The mask of betrayal hangs over your aura, like gold cobwebs rusting.

I duck my head a little. Water pours down the back of my neck, down my spine.

The day of your death is marked to end the suffering, but it is not today. A traitor's soul is never free. A traitor's soul is Death's soul. Remember that. Death will collect what belongs to Death. Death will not forget.

I swallow hard, don't want to think about my demise.

I rock my weight on the balls of my feet, look around again. *Three.* I need to concentrate on my brother. I'll find his body, send him off properly, make sure his soul gets to the New World. So long as I'm in time….

And the dog… My terrier… He'll be out here somewhere… I can find him too. Dead or alive. I gulp.

"Sev! It's too dangerous," Corin shouts after me as I head off.

I see him out of the corner of my eye, but he's not getting up; he won't leave Esther. I know that.

"I won't be long." I hug my arms to me. "Head north. I'll catch up."

I'm not sure why I say that. I don't know which way is north—or which way we should be going. There's nothing obvious in any direction, except for the spirit temple. Ahead and to the left, it towers, on its tor. We've come a long way down the slope, yet I… I almost don't remember moving… Everything's a surging blur.

Spirits, got to be spirits. They're still messing with my head. I can't even recall which way we came from to get here in the first place. Everything's just fading together, even the battle with the Enhanced Ones.

I hunker down as I walk, the rain gets heavier again. My clothes are sodden rags, molded to my body. My skin burns under them. Murky, dark water pools on the ground, between bodies that are the wrong size for Three. I splash through it, running now. Running fast. I concentrate on my breathing. Years of raiding on foot—and good genes—has made me an expert long distance runner. I know I can do this.

The terrain gets steeper, the water-laden grass is slippery. There are fewer bodies to check here. I power on, and then I stop, realize where I am. It's the place, the place where Raleigh—the leader of the Enhanced

Ones—tortured me. I was here, lying right in this spot—

My stomach twists. My eyes narrow.

No… No… No….

I peer through the rain, harder. The roof of my mouth tastes funny. I double-check where I am.

Oh Gods.

His body's not here.

Raleigh's body is not here.

But it should be. Corin stabbed him. Right here, this bit of grass. I heard the knife go into his chest. Heard Raleigh's last breath as it dragged on and on.

But Raleigh's body isn't here.

There's no one here, not on this mound.

I check again; my heart rate gets faster. But I can *feel* that is the place where Corin stabbed Raleigh, the place where Raleigh tortured me with his Seer powers.

Oh Gods. He's not… He survived the stabbing? I shake my head. His body's not here.

And all the other bodies *are* still here. The dead bodies. The live Enhanced Ones have all gone. My mother has, because she wasn't shot dead, just injured. I turn, look back to the right, to the place where Corin shot her—yes, she's gone. She's alive.

And Raleigh's gone too. A clue that he also survived?

My chest rises and falls. I clutch my Seer pendant until my knuckles burn. Still, it doesn't *mean* anything. I tell myself that, over and over again. Raleigh's their leader—they've probably carried his body back for a proper ceremony. That will be it. I nod.

I bite my lip, take a deep breath. I have to keep going. Need to find Three's body. Have to say the Spirit Releasing Words, call on all the Journeying Gods and Goddess, before it's too late.

But the earlier adrenaline and momentum's gone. I'm wobbly. My ankles feel soft, insubstantial. Like they're not mine. Someone else's. Still, I keep going. My brother's body needs sending off properly, if it's not already too late for him to safely reach the New

World.

After a few minutes, the rain begins to lessen again, until it's just a patter on the back of my neck. Doesn't make much difference though, I'm already soaked.

I jump over one ditch, then nearly trip over another body.

That's when I see her.

She's straight ahead of me, leaning over bodies. My eyes narrow. Dark hair, dark skin—

My breath catches in my throat.

No.

I slow down, then stop. I watch as the woman lifts one arm up, pushes her hair back behind her ears, then turns to the next body. She's doing the same thing Corin and I were. Looking for survivors.

My heart races. More water trickles down my spine. I open my mouth, my lips feel dry. Too dry. It can't be her. I know that. Every part of me knows that. And I know better now than to trust long-lost members of my old group who mysteriously, and very conveniently, turn up.

But she looks just like her….

The woman looks up, sees me.

Untamed eyes.

"Seven!"

And then Five's running, and I'm sprinting toward her, my head spinning, my legs burning, aching, hurting. I skid forward, spraying mud everywhere as I unsuccessfully try to jump over a body. My foot hits it, and I'm sent off at an angle, pain darting up my leg.

But I don't care.

My sister is here.

No.

I throw my arms out, skid to an abrupt stop. It's not her. Can't be her. I left her at Nbutai, during the attack. I drove away.

"Stay away from me!" I have no weapon so I hold my hands up between us, but my fingers are shaking because the sight of her makes my heart ache, makes the bridge of my nose feel all prickly.

Five takes a step forward, toward me, hands up in a surrender gesture.

"Stay back!"

"Seven, it's *me*."

She tosses her head, and the movement emphasizes the slightly hooked shape of her nose. The nose I know so well. She's the only one out of all my siblings who has that nose.

"Listen, Seven," she says. "I'm not really here. Two's channeling me from the New World—I don't understand it."

Her words hit me, and my gut squeezes. *The New World.*

She's dead. Confirmation. As dead as Two, another lost sibling.

She's dead—dead because of me. I swallow hard.

But her words mean she must have got to the New World, if she's with Two…and I doubt the Spirit Releasing Words were said for her by the Enhanced. And I know it should give me hope for Three, in case I can't find his body—but it doesn't.

I feel my face slacken. The rain's stopped now. Everything's just stopped, frozen.

"*Listen*," Five says. She lifts a hand up, and I see her nails are painted red, perfect. The polish looks like one Elf brought back from a raid for her, months and months ago. "Two's sending me here, because he needs to warn you. You've got to listen. Don't go to a black lake. If you see it, you run. If you go to this black lake, you'll die. But he's going to try and get you to go there. He'll trick you."

Two needs to warn me? A warning? I stare at Five, then look at the sky. There's no bison. This isn't the Dream Land. But the Dream Land is the only way to get warnings.

"Seven! Are you listening? Two's said if you go with him—"

"With Two?" I stare at her.

"No," Five says. "Not with Two. Just listen, will you?" She tosses her head, exasperation in her eyes. "With R—"

She disappears.

For a second, I freeze, heart pounding. I turn around, look back and forth. My eyes widen. Then I lurch forward.

The space where Five was? Empty. I stare at the grass, but everywhere is too windy and rain-beaten for a person's weight to make much of an impression.

I swallow hard. I look at the sky again. Still no bison. It wasn't the Dream Land. It wasn't a true warning.

I curse.

The spirits are messing with me, playing with me, trying to scare me. Hallucinations. They may have helped us before, but that was because they fed from us, got our energy—and even then, I couldn't control them for long. Spirits are volatile, dangerous; one moment they help you, the next they hurt you. Even the 'benevolent' spirits, that, alongside the Gods and Goddesses, make us into Seers and control the Dream Land, are still unpredictable and need to be watched. They can be good one moment and then suddenly revert, their behavior temporarily getting closer to that of their evil counterparts. And now the spirits around here are inventing stuff, making me scared, trying to convince me Raleigh's out there because his body's gone, and they're using my memories of Five to distract me, stop me from finding Three's body. Maybe they want my brother to be trapped between worlds, to not make it to the New World. They're trying to stop me from saying the Spirit Releasing Words.

Anger flares at how easily they tricked me. How easily I fell for it.

I brace myself, try to forget it, and look back. Corin and Esther aren't in sight. They'll be moving. I know I haven't got long. I need to find Three's body now.

THREE

"DID YOU FIND HIS BODY?" Corin asks as I rejoin them.

They haven't made it far. Corin's holding something in his right hand. A bullet. So he got it out. I glance at Esther. She's on the ground, and there's more fabric wound tighter around her shoulder and arm now. A small rucksack hangs off Corin's arm. Fabric spills out from it, getting soaked in a new bout of rain. It takes me a moment to realize it's clothes in the rucksack. The dead Enhanced Ones' clothes.

Of course Corin would collect them. Scavenging is the only way to survive.

I look back at the nearest body, look for a gun. A weapon. Anything. But, like with all the others, there's nothing there to find.

"Sev? Did you find Three's body?"

"No." I pause, catch my breath. "No, I didn't."

After that hallucination, I checked all the bodies as quickly as I could, running and skidding from one to another. Three's wasn't there. But it doesn't mean Esther's right. I might've just missed his corpse. Or my mother might've found his body and wanted a

21

proper send off for him, taken him to a river.

Corin reaches into the small rucksack, pulls something out, hands it to me. A small penknife. Holding it makes me feel a bit better.

"It was already in the bag when I found it," he says. "The blade is sharp. At least it's a weapon."

I watch as Corin picks Esther up, one arm under her legs and the other under her upper back. He should be carrying her over his shoulder, easier that way. I turn again, eyes smarting for no apparent reason.

"So he's alive then, your brother?" There's hope in Corin's voice, and I think Esther murmurs a little, though she keeps her eyes shut.

"No. He's dead. They've taken other bodies too."

"What?" Corin frowns. "Whose?"

"Raleigh's. Could be others too that have gone. They could be coming back to collect them all."

Or Raleigh's alive, and that wasn't a hallucination sent by the spirits to distract you.

I shudder, push that thought away.

Corin swears, then he's turning his back to me. "How the hell does he keep surviving? I stabbed him in the *chest* for the Gods' sake."

"Doesn't mean he's alive. Doesn't mean either of them is alive, just because their bodies aren't here," I say as firmly as I can.

Corin grunts. "Take the gun."

I pause a little, then pull it from his waistband. I stare at the Colt Single Action Army revolver and realize I haven't looked at it properly until now. It's not a model I've used in a while.

"Is it Raleigh's gun?" I try to remember the firearm Raleigh threatened me with.

"Yeah, got it from him after I stabbed him. Damn, I should've shot him too. Made sure."

"Corin, he's not alive."

Corin grunts. "But your mother's gone, and we know I didn't kill her. She's alive. And they've left their dead here." He grits his teeth for a second or two.

"Why would they take two bodies away with them?"

"Raleigh's their leader," I say. "They'd want his body for a ceremony or something."

Corin shakes his head, then indicates the dead around us. "The Enhanced don't send their bodies off, Sev—not that the Gods and Goddesses *would* let their souls into the New World… But they don't say the Spirit Releasing Words either. The Enhanced don't believe in the New World. It's just a wild, Untamed fabrication, to them." He pulls a hand through his hair. "The Enhanced have no reason to take dead bodies with them—and they don't. Look."

"They'd still do *something* for their leader's body," I say. "He's important to them. A burial or something. And my mother might want to send off Three's body *properly*…if she's not completely converted." If she still sees him as her son and not just another wild monster who died before he could be saved. "That's why their bodies aren't here."

I press my lips together, breathe deeply.

"Maybe Esther *is* right," Corin says after a long few minutes.

I turn slowly, stop. Something strange flits through my muscles. "You think that if I thought my brother was alive, I'd just be walking away? That I wouldn't be racing off to whatever Enhanced town is the nearest and trying to get him back?"

Corin shrugs. "We don't know where the nearest Enhanced town is."

I let out an exasperated sigh. "He's dead, Corin. They both are. Three *and* Raleigh."

But I can tell what Corin's thinking: that I'm wrong, that they're both alive.

We don't know where to go.

Corin asks me several times—probing to see if I've got any Seer knowledge, but I haven't. I know he doesn't like asking me. He's the leader, and I can tell by the way he says the question, with his brows furrowed, that he thinks it makes him look weak. Like he should know what to do because he's the leader.

So we just walk. And we keep going until the Spirit Temple's out of sight, until the battlefield is long behind. We follow the contours of the land, sticking close to the bases of the hills. After a couple of hours, our pace is slower, but the land's leveling out. The terrain is changing, merging into savannah. I wonder what we're going to do about food when I catch a glimpse of two ostriches in the distance. It's been years since I've had ostrich meat, and I don't even particularly like it, but it still makes me salivate. Corin doesn't appear to see them, and, just when I'm about to point them out, they've gone. I grit my teeth hard until my jaw aches.

"We need to keep going," Corin says sometime later, shifting Esther's weight. I've slowed down, my legs are aching. "We've got to find people soon. Esther needs medicine. And we need food." He looks at me, purses his lips. "If we could just find a town, one of us can raid it. *I* can raid it, get medicine," he quickly adds, his eyes darting away from me. "You can stay with Esther."

I feel my cheeks filling with heat. I know what he's thinking, how he'll never trust me on a raid again.

Lesson four: Never let yourself be Enhanced. Once it's done, there's no going back.

No going back? But I managed it.

But I know I'm not the same.

And the more we walk, taking turns to carry Esther, the more I can't help but feel contaminated.

We stop a couple of times to drink rainwater that seems to be clean, and we're well into the grassland by late evening. We find a few trees that are a little closer together. A little more secluded. It's stopped raining, but the ground's still sodden.

I stare at the trees. Acacia trees. But they're too close together for the savannah. It's not right. Acacias should be growing in the cracks of the dry ground, not here, where it's wet. And the savannah shouldn't be wet. Yet it is.

Still, the acacias have seeds, and we collect them. We normally use them in soups, or roast them, but now we eat them raw. Corin mutters about collecting some of the wood and boiling it, using the extract as a medicine—says his mother did it once, but he can't remember what it was for. In the end, we just eat the seeds and collect the young leaves and shoots. We can boil them later, for food, if necessary.

Corin says we should stay here for the night, so I look around as he heads to a nearby stream to get washed; he has a lot of Esther's blood on him. The light is bad, streaking through the branches and leaves, and I peer carefully, look for any movement.

It is *too* quiet, *too* still.

This land isn't right. It's all changed, and I know that before—when we were still traveling with Rahn and Three and the Marouska-imposter—we weren't this close to a savannah…even if it is a strangely wet one. It's got to be the spirits, in the battle. They changed the land, broke the rules. To help us? I bite my lip. Maybe. If they changed the land after the Enhanced retreated, it would make it harder for our enemy to find us again.

But it seems mad. Things like that *shouldn't* happen, I know that. The land around the battleground—like any land—is supposed to be solid, constant. And I think about our terrier, wonder where he's ended up. I see him now, hundreds of miles away, trotting over dried desert ground, then slowing, nose to the floor as he follows a trail. His tail will be up in the air, but he'll start whining after a while. His barks will get shorter, sharper. And by the time it's properly dark, he'll be frantic. Looking for us. Looking for someone.

Maybe the Enhanced will take him in…and give him augmenters too, make him into the perfect canine companion. No, that's silly. They don't give animals augmenters. But then we didn't think they'd ever use weapons. I swallow hard.

A few minutes later, Corin returns. His skin is flushed, and the smell of smoke wraps around him, wafts over toward me.

I gesture around us as I set the rucksack down. "What do you think of the land, how it's changed? Do you think it's the spirits?"

He shrugs, looks across at Esther. "Spirits can't be trusted. Not even the good ones. Not fully. They made us sleep at that temple for far too long." He pauses. "Works better for us though, if they really have changed the land. We don't want to be hounded by the Enhanced."

He sits down next to me, puts an arm around my shoulders. I lean into him. I know he's right—it is better for us. Because we both know if the Enhanced are near, are going to find us, then we won't all get away—if *any* of us do.

I concentrate on Corin's warmth as we watch Esther. She's lying in front of us, her skin emanating a strange kind of sickly glow. Her breathing is shallow. It's been a good few hours since she's made any sound or movement on her own. But she's still alive. And that's what I focus on. For now.

"Look, Sev," Corin says suddenly. His arm around me tenses. "About what I said…after the battle, up there…when I said I love you…."

I stiffen, blink several times, waiting for him to pull away, waiting for the coldness to bite.

But he doesn't move. His arm stays right where it is. His fingers rest on the top of my shoulder, tingling my skin. I clench my fist, my hand is too sweaty. My stomach feels strange, empty.

Corin clears his throat. It takes him a while.

"I meant it," he says in a voice that sounds strange,

forced—not at all natural. "It wasn't a spur of the moment thing because it was life or death. I do love you. I just… I only knew for sure then."

I turn to face him, feel the muscles in my upper arm twitch. He moves his head; in the half-light, I see his face perfectly. The lines that are more ragged each time I see them. The sunburn that looks angrier. The faint scars on the left side of his face look redder, deeper—the remnants of a wildcat attack when he was a child. I can still see the claws ripping into his skin now.

I chased the cat away, even though I hated him then. But it didn't matter. I just had to save him.

Corin takes both my hands in his, squeezes them gently. "Gods, I'm probably *in love* with you." His pupils are dilated, and he shakes his head. "I always thought that I'd be saying these words after I'd been in a relationship a while… After we'd…done things." His fingers feel thicker than I remember, make mine look more slender. "Don't say it to me though."

"What?" I lift my head a little.

"Don't say you love me because I've said it. Say it when you mean it… If you mean it." His eyes darken. "I'd rather you never said it, than pretended. I know you probably don't love me, not at the moment. My feelings are stronger than yours."

I don't know what to say, or how to feel, what to think. Other than he's still the same old arrogant Corin, assuming he knows how I feel, and his feelings have to be bigger than mine.

But he's right. I know that.

"You do like me, though?" His eyes narrow a little, but there's warmth in them.

I press my lips together for a second, try to get the courage. And I manage the words in the end. "I like you."

His touch makes me jump. Sudden heat as his thumb traces my jawline. I feel myself leaning in closer still to him, eradicating some of the little distance that had been between us. Part of me is surprised I'm doing this, that I seem to know what to do, but it's automatic—instinct. Corin's other hand goes to the small of my back, draws me in more. My eyes focus on his lips. Heat rushes to my face. I can see every pore of his skin, smell the smoke on him from that last cigarette, entwined with the musty scent of sweat. I stare into his eyes. His beautiful Untamed eyes.

Our lips meet, tenderly at first.

Then I kiss him deeper, shut my eyes, shut the world out as his mouth gets rougher, his breathing harder. He presses our bodies firmly together, and my hands end up on his shoulders, holding onto him. His are on my back, fingers catching on my shirt. I feel my heart get faster, hear my pulse in my ears as he pulls me onto his lap. As we kiss again, his arms tighten around me, that familiar cage. And...and this is Corin. *This is Corin!* The voice in my mind won't shut up.

Then he pulls his head back a little. Cold air rushes over me.

My eyes spring open. Corin's face is a few inches from mine, and the corners of his lips twitch. There's a strange look in his eyes. A look I haven't seen before.

"Are you all right?" My voice is odd.

He stares at me for a few moments, then nods, just watching me. So we stay here, like we are. Me, sitting on his lap. His arms around me, my hands on his shoulders. He offers me a smile. I return it. It feels so simple.

Then my pulse slows as I look past him, at Esther, completely motionless, but in a slightly different position from before—her head's turned away from us.

"It's late. We'd better take turns being on guard. I'll stay up first," Corin says. The rucksack's on the ground, and he reaches for it, opens it carefully. Then he pulls out a large fleece and hands it to me. "No point in us both being sleep-deprived. We don't know what tomorrow will hold."

FOUR

IT'S DARK WHEN CORIN WAKES me some hours later. He's got a burning torch now, and he holds it over my face. It takes several seconds for my eyes to adjust to the sudden bright light in front of me. The flames look too bright. Like they don't belong here.

Corin hands me the torch. I take it. A thick branch, with some sort of flaming wadding attached to it. I frown. I want to ask him where he got it from, how he made it, but then I stop. Of course, there are acacia trees around us—too many. And he has his lighter. It can't be difficult to make a torch.

I look up at the sky. Still dark, no signs of it lifting. It's probably the very early hours.

There's a loud *snap*. Like a twig. A twig underfoot.

Corin and I bolt up, turn to the left. I reach for the penknife—I'd put it in my belt before I went to sleep—and Corin's by my side, the gun ready.

"What's that?" My eyes narrow into the darkness, and I shift my weight a little.

I turn my head, taking in the full area. The hairs on the back of my neck stand up, and then I'm looking for big cats. Lions? They could live here.

Corin raises his free hand in the *silence!* gesture. He stares straight ahead, his gaze dark, penetrating. I inhale some of the smoke from the burning branch, feel my throat tickling, try not to cough.

I see them before he does.

It's the mirrors that give them away, the mirrors that steal and reflect the orange flames. Six—no eight—glints. My mouth slackens, and I feel something strange inside me. A twisting sensation.

And they're the people you wanted to be with.

I swallow hard. That was before. Not now.

Definitely not now.

I lift the knife up higher, toward them, pointing at them. I don't know whether Corin's seen them or not, but something stops me from saying the words. And that's stupid. I don't know why. I should be yelling at them, warning Corin. And Esther.

Oh Gods.

Esther.

Eight mirror eyes, so there are four of them. My heart pounds heavier. My mind whirls. Three of us, and Esther's injured, unconscious. And—

Corin yells suddenly, and then he's spinning around. I hear a gun go off—his gun?—as I stumble. The burning torch jerks out; it's in control, not me.

The four Enhanced men step through the trees. The trees that are suddenly so much thicker, bigger.

For a moment I can't think what to do. I just stand there, staring. The flames illuminate their faces, make their mirror eyes look orange and red and yellow.

"Take the gun!" Corin yells as he thrusts it into my face.

I do, but I drop the penknife, and then I'm scrabbling about among some white flowers—tiny dark gold centers, each with thirteen petals—trying to find it in all the dust as the burning torchlight chases me around. My eyes smart from the dust—dust that shouldn't be here, because it's wet—and I know I'm taking too long. My back is to the Enhanced, I'm leaving myself vulnerable to them. My father would be furious.

My head jerks up. They're lunging closer, mirror eyes flashing. Oh Gods. They're going to be on me in seconds.

There. Got it. I grab the penknife, then—

An Enhanced man smacks into me as I try to stand. I scream as I fall, dropping the torch, and fire a bullet into his abdomen just as I stab the back of his hand with the blade. He lets out a guttural cry, then blood splatters over my bare arms. I roll over, quick, heart pounding, see Corin scooping Esther up. He turns back to me, but I can't see him properly in the dark. Can only see the Enhanced because their eyes are reflecting what little light there is back at me in sharp stings, like bullets. One. Two. Three. Four—

Lesson one: You can never outrun the Enhanced Ones. They are better, faster, and stronger than you.

"Run!" Corin shouts.

I test my weight slowly on my feet, turning again, wiping the blood from the penknife's blade on my shorts.

One Enhanced is on the ground. The other three? *There*. Two are by the other trees, farther behind, and one—

I squeeze the trigger just as the fourth Enhanced man lines his shot up with Corin. But my bullet's wide. Far too wide. Worst shot I've had in a long time.

But the next one isn't.

"Run!" Corin's still shouting. He's pushing through branches now, suddenly farther away than I thought. He's disappearing, with Esther.

"Surrender yourselves, poor creatures," one of the men says.

Rahn's third survival lesson flashes into my mind. *They deserve to die. Each and every one of them.*

I turn on the Enhanced man, gun ready. Two cartridges gone, four left. I squeeze the trigger, and—

Nothing happens.

I try the gun again. I curse. It's empty. How? It

shouldn't be. There should be four cartridges left.

I throw it down. The penknife, it's all I've got.

They're getting nearer, their lips twisting into strange smiles as their hands reach toward me. Can't see their guns now.

A streak of lightning flashes across the sky. The movement burns through me, and I turn. Sweat drips from my hands. I'm starting to lose grip on the penknife.

"Sev, run!" Corin's voice is strained. It wraps around me, and I turn, and—

There are more of them. More Enhanced Ones. More than four. They're racing toward Corin and Esther.

"Run!"

I run.

Flames suddenly snake along next to me, keeping up as they burn through the ground. Heat smothers my legs. My khaki shorts are too hot.

The Enhanced are right behind me. I can hear them—pounding footsteps, heavy breathing.

I gulp in too much air—too much sooty black air. It clogs my lungs, weighs me down. Makes my arms shake. And the knife—the penknife's gone.

"Which way do we go?" Corin's voice is distant. I twist my head, trying to see him and Esther… Trying to see….

He's not here.

"Corin!" I scream.

I turn my head, quick. Behind, the flames are high, pulling up into the sky, trying to ignite the stars. The whole forest is on fire now. Smoke spreads along the ground, engulfing shrubs and trunks. Many leucaenas, going up in smoke. A bitter taste fills my mouth as I recognize the burning white flower balls of a leucaena species my father liked—white leadtrees, that's what he called them. And the acacias—no, there are no acacias here now.

A bitter taste fills my mouth. My head jerks up to the sky. Darkness. Inky, black darkness in a ring of fire.

Inky, black darkness that hides a shape.

The *bison*.

The sign of the Dream Land.

This isn't real.

Not yet.

My father's words burn through me. *Whenever the bison speaks to you, you pay attention. You've been chosen as a Seer for a reason. The future speaks to you. You must not ignore it.*

I swallow hard. My shoulders curl, I look back at the bison. He's getting stronger, standing out better from the dark sky now. His eyes are brighter, and I think of the time when he spoke to me, told me that I'm the key to the survival of one race—and that Raleigh will always be after me.

Because I'm the key. I'm the Seventh One—spirits told me that.

You're special, you're the seventh child of the light—so easily identifiable to us, but also to them. Be careful, Seventh One, for we'll help you. But others will want you. Others will destroy you. For there is no mistaking that you are the one. Your parents knew…they made it easy…easy for us to know… Easy for others to know… Be careful, Seventh One. Stay Untamed, and be careful.

The ring of fire around me gets taller.

A scream cuts through the flames.

A man's scream.

My heart goes cold. Power floods my legs, and I charge at the wall of fire.

Run, Seven. Go east. Find them, and go east. Whatever you do, go east.

FIVE

I JOLT AWAKE.

"What is it?"

Corin's turned to me in an instant, before I can even get a bearing on my surroundings. His eyes hover over me. It's not as dark as it was in the Seeing dream. It's nearing morning; the first glows of the coming sun are peeking through, lightening the sky. Corin didn't wake me up after a few hours, as planned.

"The Dream Land. Got to move now." I sound breathless, as if I really have just been running. "The Enhanced are coming."

I jump up, and all my joints ache. I'm stiff. Too stiff. I curse, then turn to the trees where I saw the Enhanced Ones appear. I stare at the wooded area, tension pulling through my body. Can't see anyone there now. And the trunks are different: they're farther apart from each other than in the Seeing dream, and maybe thicker too.

But I know how the Dream Land works. Little details aren't right, and they're the clues that it's a warning.

I look back at Corin, see his pupils dilate.

"How long've we got?"

I roll my shoulders as I look around. I wish he wouldn't ask me such stupid questions. He knows it could be seconds or hours. You can never tell with the Dream Land. But usually it's closer to the first option.

"We've got to go now."

Just like that, we jump into the routine that's been ingrained in us. Corin grabs the weapons, then hands the penknife and the rucksack to me. For a second, I think I'm going to get the gun too, but then he slides the Colt into the back of his waistband. After a moment's thought, he digs the lighter out of his pocket, holds it out for me.

"In case they get too close and you've lost the knife," he says.

I pause, then take it. This is big, I know that—for Corin to give me his cigarette lighter is massive. But now isn't the time to talk about this milestone.

"I'll carry Esther. You lead the way—you know which way we're going, right?"

"East." I pocket Corin's gift, then readjust the weight of the rucksack on my back. That's what the bison said, the last words of the Seeing dream: *Run, Seven. Go east. Find them, and go east. Whatever you do, go east.*

"East. Right." Corin turns and looks toward the lightest part of the horizon, where the sun will appear, chasing the first rays that are already here.

I follow his gaze. I'd guess it's about four in the morning. So Corin *has* let me sleep for a long time.

Corin pulls Esther up into a fireman's lift, leaving her injured arm hanging down his back. Even in the darkness, I see the strain on his face.

"You keep a lookout," Corin says as we start to walk, but he doesn't need to say that. I already am.

We tread over the wooded floor, small twigs breaking. The ground's not as damp now that the water's seeped into cracks. Mosquitoes are out though, and other flies buzz and whine. I bat several away, keeping my eyes on the trees around us. I hold the knife at the ready, searching for any movement. Several times, I mistake small branches swaying in the wind for the Enhanced, and adrenaline surges through me.

A bird screeches overhead, and I jump. Corin curses. I look back. He's starting to fall behind. Esther's not stirring at all. I swallow uncomfortably.

Something cracks to the right. I freeze. Corin takes another step behind me—I hear the sound of his feet on dried leaves—then stops. I raise my hand—the one with the penknife—and the hairs on the back of my neck feel slick with sweat. My breath comes in short, sharp bursts.

I peer into the darkness. Trees. Branches. Leaves. I pick out cobwebs, slightly illuminated by the little light edging the darkness.

Can't see anything else. I take a baby step forward, then another. Still looking, eyes going for the shadows, the dark spaces. My shoes are ridiculously noisy against the woodland floor as I move. Just another step so I can peer around a trunk.

"Is there anything there?" Corin's voice is low, barely audible.

I scan the trees again. Up and down. Side to side, eyes flitting from one branch formation to another. Corin's lighter presses into my thigh, feels solid. I look at the knife. A lone droplet of water glistens from it, like an eye, watching me.

"Don't think so."

Corin trudges forward. "Then let's keep going." He sounds annoyed. Or tired. Probably tired.

We keep going. The trees get thicker. My breathing gets shallower, I can't help it. My head starts to feel foggy, like I'm not getting enough oxygen.

We step over wide cracks in the ground, Corin struggling a little more than me. It's getting lighter now. I can clearly pick out the tree line against the sky a lot easier than before. I don't know whether that's reassuring or not.

Still, the sky gets brighter, lightening until the night has departed. I feel more confident in daylight. We both do. It's only natural. Can see farther.

"You sure it was a Seeing dream?" Corin asks sometime later. "There are no Enhanced about."

"Definitely a Seeing dream." I look around again, as if expecting hundreds of Enhanced Ones to suddenly jump out. But they don't. "We need to keep going. East. That's what the bison said. We should be glad we've been given a lot of warning. Could be worse."

Corin grunts, mutters something that's just out of my earshot.

We keep going east, and the strange savannah land with its copses transforms into thicker forest as more tree species pop up. The transition is too abrupt to be natural, I'm sure. It should take days to walk from one to another, not a matter of hours. Still the work of the spirits?

I press my lips together so tightly I can feel my pulse in them. After about another half an hour, the unease within me has grown. It *was* the Dream Land, wasn't it? I look down at the penknife. My fingers slackened around it long ago. I grimace. This is strange. In all the times when I've had Seeing dreams before, I'm sure there wasn't *this* much of a gap between the warning and the action. If I saw the Enhanced in the Dream Land, then I'd see the Enhanced pretty soon in reality.

I frown. Maybe we got away in time, missed them completely. Maybe they're back at our clearing now. And I know I should be pleased, but I can't help the way my knees feel weak, achy, or how my head pounds with the heavy air, as if something's going to happen.

Still, twenty minutes later, we've seen no Enhanced Ones. Not even any signs of them. Every few seconds, I scan the horizon for the lights of a far-away city or town, but it's hard to see past the looming trees, the many leucaenas all around me. The flowers of the white leadtree look smaller in real life, but the blooms are the same, and my eyes are drawn to them.

I freeze.

"They were in the Seeing dream." I point at the leucaena flowers. My arm is stiff, and my shoulder blade protests a little, makes the rucksack feel heavier. But there's not much in there, just some extra clothes and the acacia leaves and shoots.

"Coincidence?" Corin says. "Look, Sev, what if your vision was wrong? I don't like going east. We're just getting thicker into the woods. More cover, yes, but more places you can get ambushed. And more predators—snakes. I don't think we should go in deeper."

I pick my way over a fallen trunk that's half-rotted. Looks like termites have made their home in it. "But the bison said to go east. We have to go east."

We'd be stupid not to.

"Need to stop," Corin mutters sometime later.

I turn back to see him setting Esther on the ground. We haven't made that much progress since we last spoke; Corin was getting slower by the second. Esther's body flops forward. Her skin isn't a good color. Gray. Makes my stomach roll.

Corin looks at me as I near them. "Maybe you got it wrong. Or a false warning."

I frown. Seers don't just get their visions wrong. Corin should know that.

But then again, why should he? His mother wasn't a Seer. My mother was—no, she is. She's not dead. Just converted. Thinking about her—her current state—makes my legs feel heavier. Still, I don't sit. I look down at Corin. He's leaning against a thick leucaena trunk, his eyes half-shut. Looks worn out. Huge bags hang under his eyes. I study the rest of his face, note the heaviness of the sunburnt patches around his lips, the hard lines of his features, and how his scars seem more prominent. I feel a slight pull in my chest as I stare at him. A pull that I don't quite understand.

I turn away quickly, feel heat rush to my face.

Keeping a lookout—that's what I should be doing. My feet start to twitch as I turn. I scan, round and round, glance at Corin. His eyes are properly shut now. Alarm suddenly fills me. He can't sleep now! What if the Enhanced come along?

I shift my weight from foot to foot. But I can't wake him. He's knackered—exhausted. He let me sleep all through the night—well, until I woke. I owe it to him.

My throat feels strange as I swallow. Uncomfortable. I bat several mosquitoes away from my face, my ears, then give up. There are too many. And I can't use my energy up. I know that. I've been warned; something's going to happen, despite what Corin says. So I've got to stay alert and ready. Have to.

Still, nothing does happen. Other than some birds calling to their mates, and a swarm of insects flying past. Corin's still got his eyes shut, but I don't think he's asleep. That's something, I suppose.

After a few minutes, I check Esther. My fingers shake as I lightly trace her wrist, then her neck for a pulse. In the end, I manage to pick up a faint beat.

"Look." Corin's voice makes me jump, and I turn to see him pointing to the far left. My heart races. "Dima. That's the flower my mother was named after. Dimorphotheca Pluvialis."

I look. My lungs fill with cold, stagnant air, and I nearly choke; the flowers, they're the same, the same as the ones that were on the ground when I dropped the penknife in the dust in the Seeing dream. Thirteen white petals on each head, with a dark gold center.

My eyes widen.

And there are leucaenas here too.

"This was it." I look at Corin. "This was the place where I was… I think I went that way and—"

A scream cuts through the air. A man's scream. The

scream I've already heard. The scream I suddenly know—just *know*—can't belong to an Enhanced One.

My heart jolts.

Whatever you do, go east.

I run—run toward the east, toward the scream, toward the man...toward the Enhanced? No. My feet strike the ground. I feel sick with adrenaline. There's an Untamed man here. There's got to be. And he's hurt? I think of the Seeing dream, the Enhanced Ones I saw. They've got him... The Enhanced Ones have got him?

The Seeing dream wasn't about protecting *us*. It was about protecting *others*. Other Untamed.

It's a test. I breathe deeply. It makes sense now. Of course it's a test. It's the Gods and Goddesses and spirits testing me to see whose side I'm really on after my blips before, when I was mistaken, when I thought I wanted to be Enhanced. But I don't! I know now, and I have to prove it to them. They'll be watching.

I grab the penknife from my belt, feel Corin's lighter slam against my thigh. The movement reminds me of an augmenter in my pocket. I push that thought away, bury it—but I know buried things have a habit of resurfacing.

Never let yourself be Enhanced. Once it's done, there's no going back.

"Sev, wait!" Corin shouts.

I pause long enough to flick my head back, see him gathering Esther.

"Don't *go* to the Enhanced!" He's got her in his arms again and is catching up with me. Surprisingly quickly. But he doesn't understand, hasn't realized it.

I ignore him, plow ahead. I've got to go this way—the bison told me—whether the Enhanced are there or not.

My eyes smart with the sudden gushing of the sharp wind over me. And there's dust. I feel it against my legs, my arms. My foot catches something—the edge of a rock—and I veer off, nearly smack into a trunk.

But I get my balance at the last minute, lungs gasping, head pounding.

Light glints from the knife with every step. I look ahead, straining my eyes. There's a wall of trees. Solid. I don't recognize them.

"Slow down!" Corin hisses from behind me. He's close, still. "*Seven!*"

I skid on wet leaves, reach the line of trees.

The man screams again. A blood-curdling sound. My breath catches on the inside of my throat, makes a squeaky sound.

Torture.

They're torturing him. My hands tremble.

"Sev!" Corin's hand somehow lands on my shoulder, though he's still got Esther—can see his shadow, distorted by the trunks rising up. "Voices. *Listen.*"

I listen. After a few seconds, I pick them up, but can't make out words—my heart's going too fast, too loud.

Another scream. The same man? The Untamed man?

Or am I wrong? What if it is the Enhanced—just the Enhanced? But, no—I *know* there's got to be an Untamed man there too. And I know I'm supposed to act—the Dream Land showed me. The bison told me. I'm meant to be here, I'm meant to do *something*. And I *can* do something. If I wasn't strong enough— if it was a suicidal mission—the bison wouldn't have told me to go east. I wrench myself from Corin's grip. A strange confidence fills me—confidence that's unfamiliar, foreign.

I push my way through the trees, until there are less and less of them. Corin's still behind me, still managing to keep up, despite Esther. I stop at the last wall of foliage, grab another branch, using the penknife to lever some vegetation out of the way, and—

My eyes won't adjust. Everything's blurry, just a mass of colors, framed by greenery, leaves. My pulse drops, my head hurts as the mirrors ahead glint, marking my vision with murky red spots.

Eight figures. Men. Dressed in blue. No three are in black, but their clothes are tattered—mainly rags. I count them again, try to tally up the gleaming mirrors, trying to see—

Guns flash in the light. One man—one in black—is on the ground, his back to me. Think he's clutching at his leg, can't be sure. Was he the one who screamed? I silently beg him to turn around, so I can see his eyes, but he doesn't. Can't—too injured? But I need to know for sure, before I do anything. I need to know which ones are our enemy.

I lift my head higher, leaves scratching at my forehead.

The other men in black are in the middle of the group. The ones in blue surround them.

"This is your last chance," one mirror-eyed man says, and, somehow, I hear his voice so well, so clearly.

More reflectors flash as others nod.

And then I see the face of one of the figures in black. And I know, I realize the difference in their clothing. The Enhanced are in blue uniforms, the Untamed are in black tatters.

"Join us willingly," an Enhanced man says to the Untamed men. "Join us willingly or—"

A gun's raised—the metal flashes in my eyes, burning my retinas like the mirror eyes do—and then a bullet whizzes toward where we're hiding. Toward us. Going for Corin. They know we're here? My breath catches, and I slam my body into his. We both fall— onto Esther. I taste mud and grit. Corin's arms spring around me, hauling me over him, putting himself between me and the Enhanced. Then he's pulling Esther over to me too. She doesn't protest at all. Her eyes are shut.

Another gunshot. Loud. Resonates right through me. Just as the scream does. I flinch, try to see what's happening, but I can't. Corin places his hand on my lower back. Not sure if it's for comfort, or to keep me down low.

"Or we'll be forced to end your suffering a different way," an Enhanced One says.

The words wrap around me, and my heart stutters, every part of me still screams that the Enhanced aren't violent people—because that's what I was taught—despite everything I've seen and experienced, everything I know they've done.

Heart pounding, I raise my head. Try to see the Untamed men, try to work out what to do. Corin's already looking; I see his eyes darting about. I squish my lips from side to side, then frown, checking all the muscles in my face still work, just as my father once told me to do. I feel mud on my forehead, wipe it off. But the Enhanced aren't looking this way.

Corin lifts his head up again, eyes narrowing. I wait for his instructions, wait for his commands, his plan. But he doesn't say a word.

I look at him. I've still got the penknife—miraculously didn't stab any of us when we fell—but it's not enough. "Give me the gun."

Corin struggles with Esther in his arms, but doesn't make a move to give it to me. "No. It's too dangerous. They're outnumbered—even with us. It's a death trap."

"We've got to help them!"

The muscles around his jaw tighten. "No. We need to look after ourselves."

He turns slightly—probably trying to work out if we three can get away undetected—and I see the Colt. It's tucked in the back of his waistband again. Water droplets glisten from its handle.

I take a second to think of a plan. Then I grab the gun, and I run.

SIX

I LUNGE FORWARD, PUSHING THROUGH foliage. Can hear my pulse in my ears. Realize immediately I should've left the rucksack with Corin. Streams of sunlight divide my vision, and I crash into another branch. My hands are shaking, my eyes are on the Enhanced. And the Untamed.

"Stop!" I yell as I charge into view.

It's a large clearing. They are in the center. I count them quickly. Five Enhanced. Three Untamed—two are on the ground. Just as I thought.

My feet skid on loose bark and small stones as I stop, two hundred feet away. The rucksack slams into my back. I point the Colt at the group, look around, quick. Trees, behind and to the other sides. Blood—it's everywhere, in patches on the ground. My stomach tightens. There's salt in the air. I taste it. Behind the men, the trunks are thinner. Something gray, at ground level, farther back. A road?

My eyes latch onto three weapons on the ground nearby. Semi-automatic pistols. Lugers, I think. The Untamed men's weapons? Probably.

One of the Enhanced turns toward me. An

44

unnaturally tall man. The sunlight glints on his mirror eyes; they flash at me. I feel my chest tighten.

"Oh, another one of you. How delightful. Get over here."

The man points with his gun, behind him to where the Untamed men are. I look at the Enhanced.

"No. Let them go." My voice wobbles, I can't look away from his weapon. Lesson six—*The Enhanced don't believe in violence. Use that to your advantage*—is *still* wrong.

I focus the Colt on him. Feel the wind brush against the back of my neck, moving my hair, makes it feel sticky. I should've tied my hair up—but at least it's not in front of my eyes, yet.

The other four Enhanced men turn their guns on me.

My mouth dries. I feel my leg muscles tighten.

I've made a mistake.

I've made a *big* mistake.

Corin's right. We can't save them.

Corin. I turn my head a fraction, listening, looking. No movement behind me. He's not coming. He's staying with Esther. My lips tremble. Oh Gods, I've left them with no weapons. I've got the gun, the penknife, the lighter.

"There are more Untamed with you?" the Enhanced man barks, but I can't tell who his words are directed at.

The Untamed men are looking at me now. There's only one standing now, and he turns on me. The two on the ground lift their heads. The pool of red around them gets bigger.

"There's more of you? Get 'em out of here, woman! Tell 'em to go!" The Untamed man takes a small step toward me. His hair is in long braids, trailing from a receding hairline, and they whip around as he moves.

I swallow hard, grip the gun tighter. I force myself to look at the Enhanced. "I've got the area covered." I lift my chin up higher. "We've got guns on all of you. Let those men go, and we won't shoot."

"We wouldn't be doing our job if we just let these men go." It's a different Enhanced who speaks. I don't like his tone.

I step forward. And I don't know why. I should be running, running back to Corin and Esther. I need to get away.

But I can't leave the Untamed men here.

I shift my weight from foot to foot. "Let the men go, or I'll get my people to shoot." My voice is too shrill, and I wince. "I've got twenty stationed around this whole clearing. We can take you out easily."

Two of the Enhanced laugh. The other three visibly tighten their grip on their guns. The guns that are trained on me. I look from one to another again, checking. There are no weapons aimed at the Untamed men now.

Run. I try to mouth the word at the Untamed man with the braids, but he doesn't move. His eyes dart between me and the Lugers on the ground. Two of the Enhanced men stand between the weapons and the Untamed.

The barrel of a gun flashes as one of the Enhanced men moves, moves toward me. I grip my Colt tighter.

"Step over here now," he says, smiling. His voice is lighter now. "You haven't got any other people with you, sweetie. You're on your own, trying to be big and brave. Look, dear, you're even holding the gun wrong. You don't know how to use it. We can help you. You're just a child, and fear is controlling you. It's distorting who you are. You don't want to be bad, do—"

I pull the trigger.

One quick movement. Done before I even knew I was going to do it. A loud gunshot echoes around. My vision blurs, can't see if I hit him... Can't see if I hit anyone. Oh Gods, I hadn't even lined my shot up properly.

Someone shouts, and then I'm running. There's a *thud* to my left, more shouting, and I reach the Lugers. Grab at one, then turn. The Untamed man with the braids is behind me. I throw the Luger at him—no time to check the safety's on—and then—

"Woman!" the man with the braids shouts.

A bullet whizzes past my ear.

I throw myself down, nearly losing the Colt. Taste mud. Something smashes against my leg. Then liquid seeps against my skin: lighter fluid. The fumes clog my nostrils for a few seconds as I roll over, pull myself up. I curse, try to get the broken glass out of my pocket, but can't.

I look up. Four Enhanced men, standing. No, they're running, toward me. I clench the Colt tighter. It's got mud on it, it's slippery. I try to wipe it off.

"Get away, man!"

The man with the braids shoots at the Enhanced, but misses. His bullet explodes against a trunk. Fine wooden shards fly out.

"Surrender yourselves at once! This is—" one of the Enhanced men shouts, but he stops. Don't know why he stops. Can't tell.

"Violence is not the answer!" another yells.

I race forward. Toward the injured Untamed men on the ground. One's barely moving now. The other's trying to get up. I see the pain in his face, the way his muscles contort and stretch, and—

One of the Enhanced gets to him. I see the barrel of a gun press against his forehead. I hear shouting, so much shouting, and the Enhanced pulls the trigger. The Untamed man flops back, blood exploding everywhere.

My eyes water. I turn away, choking. Bile rises in my throat. I taste it, acid and badness and—

"Surrender yourselves, and no one else will die," the Enhanced man snarls. "Surrender now, and we will be kind enough to save you."

Suddenly, Corin storms into view. He trips over something, nearly falls, but doesn't.

"Sev, give me a gun!"

I scramble forward, retrieve the last Luger—don't

know who's got the other one—and throw it at him. It spins round and round in the air in a high arc. Corin grabs it, then shoots one of the Enhanced. I see the body fall, hear the sounds, the screams of pain he *shouldn't* feel. Blood splashes over me. Wet, slick.

Then Corin's racing forward, going for another Enhanced. Broken flashes of reflected sunlight stem from mirror eyes as I yank my head around. Another Enhanced man… No, a *woman*. My breathing speeds up. She wasn't there before.

She's—

My eyes narrow, then I aim my gun at her. I pull the trigger, blanch at the sounds of more shots next to me. Something splatters over my left ankle, sticky. I lunge forward. My breath comes in rapid bursts, so fast I start to go dizzy as I look. My arms and legs freeze up, like stone.

There are more of them. More Enhanced Ones are coming.

I count five new ones as they appear, and then Corin's screaming. The sound cuts through me, makes my blood boil. I whirl around, vision blurring.

There. He's there. He's—

I see the blood. Red, gushing. I stare at it. Stare at it so hard that I don't see him fall. I can only see the blood. My whole vision is red, like the burning sun above, and—

Corin.

My body jolts. I scream, turn around, fire the gun. Get two of them. And a third just before he pulls his own trigger.

"Corin!"

I'm running. My legs get too hard, too heavy, and then I've got the knife out, and I'm plunging it into an Enhanced man's arm without even looking. Just getting the blade in as I run past. I hear the scream, but, at the same time, I don't. I can't.

A hand grabs me. Fingers, around my ankle. I scream as I fall, but it's one of the Untamed. The one who's still on the ground, alive. I shriek, try to get up. But his grip is strong. Too strong. His fingers are like iron.

He yanks me back down just as a bullet flies over my head. I taste blood and grit and darkness at the back of my mouth, and I look up, look at Corin, lying there. Still.

Completely still.

I don't know if he's breathing. My chest caves in, sudden sharp pain. And I—I can't move. Can't. My body won't work.

"Surrender yourselves to us, poor Untamed creatures. Surrender before more of you get sadly hurt. You see, we shall win. We will always win, and we do want to save you, but you have to help yourself too. Don't fight us."

The Untamed man—the one who's still latched onto my ankle—grabs the Colt from me. I hear the sounds as he shoots, see his eyes light up.

"Call the rest of your pack, woman!"

I stare at Corin. Motionless. I need to get to him. I know that. Yet I can't move.

It's his foot. Corin's foot. No? His leg… I can't tell. I stare. The blood's just *everywhere*.

"Woman! The rest of your pack!" the Untamed man with the braids screams. Still firing. "We need help!"

And then the man holding my ankle lets go and shouts at me with words I don't understand.

"There's no one else." My voice is small. Too quiet, it's getting drowned out by the sounds of the engine.

Engine?

My eyes widen. My head jerks up. I listen hard, too hard. My ears won't work properly. But there's a vehicle coming. The Enhanced are shouting. And the—

A conversion team. That's who's coming. My stomach tightens, I start to feel sicker. Going to retch. Can feel bile moving in my stomach.

This is it. The end. The end of me being Untamed.

We're outnumbered.

You can never outrun the Enhanced Ones. They are better, faster, and stronger than you.

Outrun? But… I flick my head back. No. *Yes*. The Enhanced Ones here have *stopped*.

They're standing still. They're waiting. They're looking behind me. The engine gets louder, so loud. My left eye twitches. The vehicle must be massive…a heavy frame, a lorry transporting goods, transporting the Enhanced soldiers—the conversion teams.

And suddenly all I can think of is a huge lorry rumbling toward us, the vehicle's sides bursting with the vast number of people packed inside. And they're coming for us.

I look up. The Enhanced Ones' guns are limp at their sides. They're not looking at me.

I scramble forward, suddenly aware the Untamed man hasn't resumed his grip on my ankle. Something sharp digs into my knees, and pain flits down my spine. I crawl, put my hand in something sticky.

"Corin!"

I reach him, grab his hand, his wrist. A pulse. Need to find a pulse. My vision blurs, too many tears. No. No. No. This can't be—

But being dead is better than being Enhanced.

I'm shaking too much.

I turn around, look back. I know I'm leaving myself vulnerable to the Enhanced, but they still aren't looking at me. They haven't noticed I've moved.

"Corin, no…no…" I swallow hard, turning back. Got to find a pulse. Got to.

I'm muttering the words, over and over again. His wrist feels strange. It's bleeding… No, it's coming from his arm—no, higher up. He's—

"Corin!"

I try to stop the blood, but there's too much, and my hands are slippery with it; I can't apply enough pressure. Oh Gods. I need—the rucksack! I pull it off, slide the strap down my bad arm, pull the zip.

Material. Lots of fabric. I search through it, pull out a shirt, try to tear a strip off it, need to stop Corin's bleeding.

Fabric tears, grates on my ears. My fingers shake as I try to wrap it around his upper arm. But the blood soaks the cotton in seconds—how can there be so much blood?

Oh Gods.

More gunshots go off, the air's filling with them. Gunshots and ragged breaths and the sounds of the engine fog my ears, make me feel sicker. But I do it, I manage it—I tie the cloth.

"Corin?" I stroke the side of his face, down to the stubble over his chin, and I've smeared blood there before I realize just how covered in it I am. I swallow hard, feel my pulse quicken. "*Corin*?"

He stirs. The muscles across his face have slackened, relaxed.

"Woman!"

I see the Enhanced man coming toward me at the last second, see the knife in his hands, the knife that he brings down—hard.

I scream, roll over, somehow manage to pull Corin with me. Dirt fills my mouth, and then I'm scrambling back up, see the knife stuck in the ground, and the Enhanced—

I grab Corin's Luger. I shoot the Enhanced. He falls, eyes on me, but all I see in them is a girl with matted hair who screams and clings to a gun and the barely-moving man.

My lips taste strange as I press them together, breathing hard. Can't catch my breath. Heart rate's too fast, like it hasn't got time to pump properly between each beat.

"Sev?" Corin's voice.

Jolts run through me, and I turn. See his eyes on me, feel my chest weaken. A thousand feelings wash through me. Before I can think what I'm doing— think what I should be doing—I grab him to me, his head against my chest. My arms shake as I hold him, leaning over him, in the dirt.

Oh Gods.

"We… Where's the gun?" Corin's voice is a thick mumble. "Where are the—"

The sounds of squealing tires fill the air, burn my ears, and I'm crying, holding Corin against me.

The rumble of the engine is louder. So much louder. Too loud.

A lorry pulls into view. Two headlights coming toward us.

Then it turns and stops. There's a loud click, and the back doors fly open. Men jump out. They're Untamed. One, two, three, four—I start to lose track. My head feels too strange.

What the hell?

"Come on!" someone shouts at me. It's the man who grabbed my ankle. He's still on the woodland floor, but trying to crawl forward, dragging himself with his arms, a leg trailing behind. "Get in—quick! The Enhanced will be back!"

My head pounds. I look around, and that's when I realize the Enhanced are all dead, lying motionless. I count their bodies. Twelve. Dead—and then…then the newly-arrived Untamed are charging at the bodies, jumping on them, feet pounding them.

Bones crack, and blood spurts out; some of it gets me. I freeze, my stomach twists. And I watch them. Watch the men crush the bodies underfoot until they're unrecognizable. Just flesh and blood and broken bones and bits of fabric.

One man sees me looking. "There's only so much augmenters can fix."

My lips start to burn as I stare at the bloody masses. They're dead. They were already dead….

I have to look away. Look at Corin; he's watching the men destroy the Enhanced bodies too. All color has drained from his lips.

The Untamed man with the braids shouts to three of

the new arrivals. I catch the words *Yes, that's the woman* and *Get 'em in too* before my ears go fuzzy.

Then they're coming toward me. For me and Corin. My arms tighten around him. He's moving feebly, slurring words I can't understand. The men get nearer. My eyes widen. They're not taking him. They're not taking him anywhere. Not without me.

They stop in front of me.

"Come with us," one of them says. "Come on, you're in shock. He's injured. You need to get him help. We're offering it. You helped us, we'll help you. *Come on*."

Corin tries to sit up on his own, but ends up crashing back into me. He lets out a long moan, grabs my hand, squeezes it so hard my eyes water. "Get Esther. She's over there…the trees."

"There are more of you? And you did not call them to help us?" the man who grabbed my ankle shouts. He's nearly by the van now, leaning heavily on another man. I don't know how he heard Corin.

The other men are staring at me. Even the ones who are picking up the body of the dead Untamed man and taking him toward the lorry.

"You coming with us?"

"Get Esther…" Corin mumbles. His words sound thick, strange, not his voice. "Get her…."

"Esther. She's hurt, unconscious." I look at the men. "She's over there…somewhere." I point behind me, but I'm too disorientated, can't remember which trees it was I came through.

"Right," one of the men says, but I can't tell who. All their faces are just blurring together now. Maybe it's their tattoos. They've all got them. Intricate designs, animals, patterns, creeping over skin. The only man who looks different is the one with the braids. "Eelan, go and get this Esther woman. And you, help these two into the lorry. Be quick. The Enhanced could be back soon, with numbers. We need to be long gone."

SEVEN

IT SMELLS FUNNY IN THEIR lorry, and it looks like a cattle wagon: a twenty-five foot steel body, aluminum sides with breathing slats at the top, and metal dividers inside. My nostrils curl.

I look toward Corin. He's lying down, against the side of the vehicle bed, where two men lean over him, examining him. I watch as they tear off the bottom part of his trouser leg, then use the material to wrap his upper arm. The fabric turns a dark red color in seconds.

A gash across his arm. And minor cuts to his head. I try to step nearer Corin, but elbows shove me back. Not roughly though. Just like they didn't see me.

"Clear some space for the other woman," one man tells another. "Eelan's got her now. Can see him. Almost here. And make sure we're ready to leave."

My eyes blur as men bustle past me. I step closer to the wall, then press my back against it until my spine aches. Cold.

There are so many men, everywhere. And they're all Untamed. So many of them. I pick out their tattoos, and the more I look, the more of them I see. They've all got them—matching designs: silhouettes of animals inked onto necklines, creeping onto jaws—but the Untamed man who grabbed my ankle has got more.

Boxes are shoved up against me—big cardboard boxes and plastic crates—and I sidestep, then crash into another man. He turns on me. His eyes scan me. Then he grunts.

"She the one you were saying something 'bout, Manning?"

"Aye."

"What? *Her*?"

The new voice is a sneer. From a boy. Fourteen years old. Or fifteen. Something like that. I watch as he turns toward me. He eyes me up and down, his bottom lip sticking out, and then he makes a huffing noise. His facial features look too small for his head, and he reminds me of Finn, a boy I never liked at my village. Finn's dead now, and I feel wrong thinking badly of him.

"Aye, Mart. *Her*," the man with the braids says—the one called Manning? "If it wasn't for her charging in, Jed and I would be dead. Not just Iro." He steps closer to me, and I stare at the debris caught in his braids. Little pieces of sticks, dried blood, leaves. "Thank you, woman—what's your name?"

Before I can say anything, the boy—Mart—grunts, pulls at his red hair. "But she looks weak."

"Your name?" Manning points at me, ignores Mart.

I swallow hard. "Seven Sarr."

The injured man who grabbed my ankle repeats my name, but his accent makes it sound like *S'ven Sarr*.

I wince. For a second, I expect them to question me. *But you can't be called Seven! Seven is a number, not a name*. But no one does.

Manning smiles, then offers me his hand. "Elwood Manning, Zharat Chief." He tucks two braids behind his right ear. The skin there's all bumpy, looks infected. "This ignorant man is Mart, my son. Them men over there be Miles, Masterman, and Kai."

He points behind him, at another group of men, then another, and he's rattling off more names. I can't follow. Manning, oblivious, carries on. They're all men though. That's one thing I do notice. I'm the only female here. And I don't like the way some of the men are looking at me.

Manning nods. "And there's Eelan with your other pack member. Esther, you said her name was?"

I nod just as another man appears in the lorry bed. Esther is over his shoulder. He marches straight forward, shoves two of the men out of the way, then places her next to Corin.

Corin appears to be fully conscious now. He shouts something, reaching for her.

"What's the screamer called?"

It takes me a moment to realize Manning's referring to Corin. I tell him his name, but my voice sounds weak—weak, just like Mart said. I'm shaking, and Manning guides me toward Corin and Esther. Tells me to sit with them.

"Right." He turns back to the rest of the men. "Strap everything in place. We're leaving. I want the usual drivers."

The floor is hard and has some boards over it. I sit on it, feel splinters rubbing into the back of my legs. All around me, the men are fixing the dividers in place, reaching for huge straps and ties, securing all the boxes. Not that well though—several sway precariously.

"Sev." Corin reaches for my hand, pulls me toward him. He's sitting up now, leaning against the wall. His eyes are dark, and he's breathing hard, nostrils flaring. The cuts on his head have stopped bleeding. "What the hell did you think you were doing? You could've been killed. That was stupid, reckless, charging in there like that."

I stare at him. My chest rises and falls slowly. He glares at me.

"Have you any idea how differently this could've

turned out?" Corin continues, and I don't know how he can talk so much after what he just went through. "We didn't know they had a whole army coming for them. You had no idea when you went charging in there, leaving me and Esther with no weapons! You just went right against Rahn's survival lesson: *If attacked by the Enhanced, save as many people as you can, and get as far away as possible*—not *run into a bloody conversion attack*—"

"Hey—you should not talk to your leader-woman like that," Manning says. His voice is suddenly really close, and I turn to find him right behind me.

"*Leader*?" Corin glares past me. His grip on my hand gets tighter, then he lets go completely. "*I'm* the leader, and she disobeyed me, my orders."

"Disobeyed?" I shake my head, then point back at the men. "I *had* to help them."

Manning makes a sound that's remarkably close to a lion's roar as he points at Corin. "You ain't a leader, man. The leader's the most courageous, the bravest one in a pack. And she's braver than you, that woman. You didn't do nothing to help. It was all her. You came in, got taken out within seconds. We owe our lives to Seven, so you treat her with respect."

It sounds like a warning, the way he says it, and it makes the hairs on the back of my neck stand up.

Corin shakes his head. "There's a difference between bravery and foolishness." He leans in closer to me, eyes narrowed, and I see the full tension—the anger—within them. It makes me feel strange. "You could've got yourself killed."

I breathe out through my nose. "I *had* to help them."

And I know I'm right. The Dream Land showed me.

"Just ignore him," Manning tells me. "He's probably concussed. Injury does that to people. You can sit over here, with us, if you want." He points at a container.

"No, Sev's sitting with me," Corin says. He doesn't look at me though.

I stay where I am, watch the rest of the men push the

last boxes back into place. Then four men jump out. I listen to their footsteps as they move around outside. A few seconds later, I hear doors slam.

Manning hands out electric torches. Corin doesn't take the one that's offered, so I take it instead. The chief pulls the lorry's backdoors shut, and darkness descends for an instant before torches are flicked on. I struggle with mine for a few seconds.

The engine rumbles up—a loud, throaty sound that reverberates through me—and, a few seconds later, we're moving. The lorry lurches to the left, bumps over uneven ground, then speeds up. The engine gets louder, and the wind whistles through the slats along the top edges of the walls. I flinch at every sound.

I gulp, look up at Corin. But he's leaning over Esther, holding her. The circles of torchlight jump around a few seconds later. Blood starts to seep through Esther's makeshift bandage. For some reason, it makes my stomach curdle. I look away, and spots of bright light burn my eyes, then hover in front of me, like stamps over my vision, as I look around again.

My rucksack's here. One of the men must've brought it. It's covered in Corin's blood. And the clothes inside, they're falling out.

"Wait, did you say you were Zharat?" Corin says suddenly. His voice is loud—it has to be so we can hear his words over the roar of the engine.

"I'm the Zharat Chief," Manning says. Another man points a torch beam at him, and Manning lifts up his shirt, revealing a rather paunchy stomach covered in more tattoos: eagles and bats. I'm not sure what the action's supposed to convey, but, five seconds later, Manning lets his shirt fall back down, and the fabric bunches in his lap.

I sit up straighter, look around. I count the men. Twelve in here, including Manning and the dead man. The injured one—the one who grabbed my ankle—is only a few feet from me, lying on his back groaning with pain. And there's the boy too, Mart.

And the drivers. Was it four who got out? I struggle to remember. But that puts it at *seventeen* Untamed.

"The Zharat? As in one of the last big tribes of Untamed?" My voice sounds strange.

I stare at them. My skin starts to tingle. This doesn't feel right, doesn't feel real. It can't be real. We shouldn't be anywhere near their lands. Except we don't really know where they live. But we can't have just stumbled into them by coincidence.

Except it wasn't coincidence. It was the Dream Land. The bison showed me, told me which way to go. And the spirits helped, by altering the land after the battle? And was that why they wanted us to leave the temple, so we wouldn't miss them? My head spins, and I lean back against the wall. The sharp jolty movements hurt my spine.

Manning smiles. "You run-arounders always be so surprised when you find us. The last ones we found thought we was ghosts. They thought they was in the New World when we brought 'em back to our den." His laugh is too high-pitched, makes my mouth dry.

"Your den," Corin says. "Is that where we're going?"

"Aye." Manning sits down, stretches his legs out. "Takes a couple days to get to the Noir Lands though."

"The Noir Lands?" Corin's face turns fuchsia; the hue makes his sunburnt patches look more orange. He shakes his head, starts to cough, a hand flying to his mouth.

I stare at him. "What are the Noir Lands?" I start to say, but Corin's not looking at me, he's just staring at the Zharat. I don't think Corin's even realized I've spoken. I wrack my head, searching for information on the Noir Lands, but nothing comes to mind.

"Yes, we live in the Noir Lands," Manning says. "Safest place."

The chief turns and looks at the injured Zharat man, the one who grabbed my ankle. He nods at him, then turns back to me. The sharpness of his eyes reminds me of a porcupine.

"Now, woman, we can drop you off on the way, the three of you. Or you come with us, and our healers will help 'em." He gestures at Corin and Esther. "If you come with us, you join us. Permanently. We can't have no non-Zharat knowing where our den is. Understand?"

My mouth dries, and my next breath makes a squeaky noise. I stare at him, then look around. They're all watching me, all the men. All the *Zharat* men. I frown. The bigger forces of this world guided us to them, and now we're not only being offered medical help, but permanent residence too. I make the thank-you sign to the Gods and Goddesses and spirits, still breathing deeply.

Manning's waiting, staring at me.

"We need to discuss this," Corin says. "I need to think about this. I'm the leader of our group, not Sev. And we need to talk about this. Hell, the *Noir Lands*."

"No," Manning says. "No leader takes time to think, to discuss. Time doing that's what gives the Enhanced the advantage, time to sneak up. Time gets you converted, man. A leader makes quick decisions. Just like what this woman there did: made a quick decision, confused the Enhanced, got us the upper hand. We're only here now 'cause she didn't do no thinking about what to do, she just acted. A sign of a true warrior."

The boy—Mart—grunts, then mutters something about how females can't be warriors. Manning ignores him, just looks at me.

"Your answer?"

"Hey!" Corin says. He sticks his arm out, points at Manning. "This isn't the sort of thing that can be decided quickly. This is important, we don't know anything about you."

The injured man on the floor, the one who grabbed my ankle, raises his head. "We are the Zharat," he says. His voice is strange, comes in thick bursts that emphasize his heavy accent, makes him seem older.

And he does look older, in here, than he did outside. At least in his thirties. "We are the ones who are surviving. Not you run-arounders. You would be stupid to turn this offer down. And your other woman will die if you do not get her to our healers."

"Jed is right," Manning says. "She'll be dead with no help; she's close to leaving us for a journey to the New World as it is. Anyone can see that. She ain't got long. Wanna save her? Join us, and our healers will, aided by our Seers and the power of the Gods." He fixes me with that same spiky look. "I ain't asking you no more after this, woman. You joining us, or are we gonna drop you off on the other side of these woods?"

"We're joining you." The words come out of my mouth before Corin has time to say anything else.

I nod and look around at the Zharat men. Mart glares at me, pulling his red hair back from his face so I get the full power of his glare. I look away. My eyes settle on the injured man who grabbed my ankle, who stopped me from going to Corin, who stopped me from standing up into a bullet's path. Jed. That's what Manning just called him. I look at his leg. He's got bandages tied around the top of his right thigh now, but redness slowly seeps through them.

The Dream Land showed me these people for a reason, so we could save them from the Enhanced. So we could get away with them.

We're meant to join them.

Manning smiles, then nods at Corin. "You should get lessons from her on making quick decisions, man," he says, a hard edge to his voice.

I turn to Corin, but he looks away. I watch as a small muscle in his jaw pulses. I rub at the back of my neck. It feels stiff. I glance around at all the boxes, the gear, aiming my torchlight at the bulky shapes. There are a lot. Part of me wonders how they managed such a big raid without getting caught.

"Where'd you raid?" I ask. My eyes fall on a bundle of blankets near the back doors, and—with a jolt—I realize that the dead Untamed man is inside them.

"New Eber-Elrayi," one of them says. "Fifty-one miles from here, west."

Corin coughs. "So why weren't all of you here in the lorry? Why were you on foot near us? What were you doing?" His voice has a dangerous edge to it.

Manning stretches his legs out. "Coincidence, man. They dropped us off. We was dissecting a body. Over at the Gates."

"The Gates?" Corin says.

"Dissecting a body?" I sit up straighter, thinking of how they jumped up and down, broke the Enhanced Ones' bones back there. "Another Enhanced?"

There's only so much augmenters can fix.

Manning tilts his head forward, makes his gaze more severe. "Not an Enhanced. She had been one of us."

"And do you always destroy your own people's bodies?" Corin's frown matches the tension in his voice.

"No," Manning says. A slow smile crosses his lips, makes me edge closer to Corin.

"Only the ones who deserve it," Jed says. "The ones we want to make sure do not reach the New World."

I gasp. I can't help it. The men all look at me. Corin elbows me, but it's not in an irritated or annoyed way. Maybe it's supposed to be comforting.

"Why would you do that?" Corin asks.

"Her soul was damaged, man." Manning yawns. "Girl pretended to be a Seer, pretended she'd been in the Dream Land. We had no choice. If we left her body intact she would've damaged us all."

I freeze, then drag in my next breath too quickly. My lips taste salty as I breathe in. The air makes a raspy sound against the inside of my throat.

"What do you mean?" Corin asks. He glances across at me for a brief second.

Several Zharat men laugh.

"Any female Seer is a fake," Jed says, moving his

head a little. I see deep lines around his eyes, though his tattoos mask them a little. "Sent by the demon spirits to taint the real Seers, to trick them, to hurt them. If a female Seer lives among people, she will only bring destruction. They have to be killed. I am surprised you do not know this. Well, I suppose that explains why you run-arounders are so short on numbers if you trust and believe female Seers."

Manning nods. "Had to get rid of her, quick, for all our sakes. Burnt her at the stake, as Elmiro guided us, then cut her up. Sent her through the Gates." He shakes his head. "Just luck that we was in the same area as you, man."

"What?" Corin says. He sits up straighter, and his hand finds mine, by my side. He squeezes my fingers, and my palm tingles. "You're saying women can't be Seers? And you kill them?"

"Of course women cannot be Seers. It is unnatural," Jed says the words as if it's the most absurd thing that's ever been questioned. Then his gaze crosses to me, then Esther. "Why, are you saying one of your women thinks she is a Seer?"

"No," Corin says. But he answers too quickly.

I gulp, try not to look at them. My fingers burn in Corin's hand.

"Good," Manning says, and his eyes settle on me. "Else we'd have to kill her."

EIGHT

WE STOP SOME THREE HOURS later for them to send off the dead Zharat man's body. I'm still holding the packet of food Manning gave me two hours ago. I tried to eat it, but the texture just wadded against the roof of my mouth, and it tasted stale. I couldn't swallow it; I didn't seem to have enough saliva left.

"Ten minutes," Manning says as the Zharat jump out the van. "Not back within ten and you'll be left behind."

I look at Corin. After a few seconds, we both stand up, stretching. He's a bit wobbly, and he glances down at Esther. We're the only ones left in here now—even Jed, though injured, hobbled out.

I look out the lorry doors. One of the Zharat leans against a trunk nearby. His eyes are narrowed, watching us. Behind him, there are trees. We've parked in a wooded, shaded area. Looks like we're in the rainforest again. The air's humid. I think there's a river nearby, and that's where four of the men, Manning included, are taking the dead man's body. Earlier, I heard them going through all Spirit Releasing Words and other preparations for his send off. It seemed like a lot more than we do for our dead.

I have no idea where we are exactly, but the Zharat obviously know. I listened to some of their conversation earlier, and this seems to be one of their regular raiding routes—though it still didn't seem like they raid towns often. Only every six months or so for bare necessities. As they talked, I got the impression there are no Enhanced towns anyway near the Noir Lands, so they always travel far in their lorries, taking at least a week, there and back. It seems risky to me. If there are no Enhanced in the Noir Lands, why can't they be completely self-sufficient there?

"Follow me," Corin says under his breath.

His eyes meet mine, then he drops his gaze—studying Esther for a few seconds—before heading out of the lorry. He turns back, helps me down, then heads to the right.

The other Zharat are all to the left, smoking some strange-looking cigarettes. I can smell the smoke from here. Kind of spicy. My nostrils curl, and I think of Corin's lighter. The one that smashed against my thigh, though my shorts are now dry. I can't tell if they smell though, I'm too blocked up. I gulp, unsure whether to tell Corin about his lighter. He hasn't asked for it back yet.

"Nine minutes," a Zharat man calls after us as I follow Corin.

Corin keeps turning his head, checking how far away from the lorry we are. We can just about see the open doors and some other Zharat. I watch as he counts them several times, probably checking none have gone back in the lorry, alone with Esther.

We don't go far. Corin stops, steps close to me. So close I can smell his scent: sweat, mixed with something musky. A little cigarette smoke.

"Do you see?" He grits his teeth for a few seconds. "This is *exactly* why we shouldn't have gone with them. This, and the Noir Lands. If they find out you're a Seer, we're done for."

I push my tongue up against the roof of my mouth. It still feels dry. I look at Corin. He means *I* would be done for, not all of us. It would only be me they killed. But I know that thought isn't setting in; I don't feel scared. I just feel uncomfortable.

"Sev!" Corin grabs my arms, shakes me a little. "Are you not listening? This is serious—they could already suspect and—"

"They won't find out." I press my lips together. "I can hide it."

Can you?

"And what if you have a Seeing dream and need to warn us of something?" His eyes bore into mine.

That's something I thought of about an hour ago. "I'll tell you, and you can tell them."

For a second, Corin shows no emotion. Then his lips tighten. "I am *not* pretending to be a Seer."

The anger in his voice gets to me. It's the old anger. The prejudice toward Seers, the prejudice he used to treat me and my family with.

"Not even to save us?" My lips start to tingle. I squish them together again, but it makes the sensation worse.

Corin exhales hard, then releases my arms. The movement seems to hurt his injured arm.

"We need to get Esther better," I remind him. "That's only going to happen if we go with them. And you need medical help too."

"But they live in the *Noir Land*s."

I don't understand what he's alluding to, but I think of what our old leader Rahn said when I was young. *Everything comes at a price. Compromises and sacrifices are part of life.* I pause, then repeat my earlier point. "Corin, Esther needs help. They've offered it. We've accepted it."

Corin's jaw twitches twice. "No. We need to tell them now, we've changed our minds, and we want to be dropped off. There'll be other Untamed about who can help us."

"Really?" I raise my eyebrows. "Because we haven't seen any others, have we? We don't even know where we are now. And the Dream Land told me to go east. To find them—the Zharat. It's obvious. We're meant to go with them. The Gods and Goddesses and spirits have said that."

Corin jerks his thumb behind us, toward the Zharat men. "But according to them you're a fraud, not a *proper* Seer. No, it's too dangerous." He breathes out through his nose, hard. "And the Noir Lands too— no."

"What's wrong with the Noir Lands?"

"You've not heard of them?"

"No."

Corin pulls his hands through his hair. "But Faya was always talking about them, when we were little. The stories she told. The Bee and the Witch?"

I stare at him, waiting.

"The Old Man and the Chivra? The Skywalker?"

"Corin, I don't know those stories—"

"But you must. I was about six and—"

"So I was three years old." I shake my head. "Just get to the point."

For a second, he seems surprised at my blunt tone, but then his nostrils flare. "The Noir Lands are bad. They're full of spirits. Really evil ones. It's like the Turning—but every day, there. Babies get snatched. And people get…taken over. It's dangerous. People go mad, can't think rationally. And the land isn't normal—doesn't follow the rules."

I gesture around us. "But the land after the battle changed, didn't follow the rules."

Corin shakes his head. "It's more than that. If we go to the Noir Lands, we'll lose ourselves."

"And if we don't we'll lose Esther for sure."

"But you heard what he said. It takes days to get to the Noir Lands. And Esther's not going to last that long." He flinches. "There's no point in going. *We're* the ones who'll get stuck there. When Esther dies on the way, they're not just going to let us get out and leave. These people are demented."

"*If*," I correct.

"What?"

The wind picks up a little, and I swallow hard. "*If* Esther dies on the way. Not *when*."

"It doesn't invalidate my argument though. The Noir Lands are *bad*. And we both know what you're like when the going gets tough."

Heat flushes through my body, and I struggle to push it away.

But it wasn't *me* who wanted to become Enhanced again, I remind myself. It was because I got caught and temporarily converted; my memories of the augmenters and how it felt to be calm and safe—to have no worries—had been controlling me. And the Marouska-imposter had been feeding me small amounts of augmenters too, keeping me addicted. It wasn't really *me* who made all those plans.

But it feels like it was. Because I remember. I remember everything. How I was sure it was my decision. How maybe it was... How maybe the augmenters had nothing to do with it... Because the Enhanced Ones aren't on the run... They have food, shelter, water—

Stop it.

I swallow hard. I am stronger than that. Still, it doesn't make Corin's words sting any less.

Corin lets out an exasperated sigh, but he doesn't apologize. Of course he wouldn't.

"I don't think we're in a position to turn them down." There's a hard edge to my voice, and I wonder whether part of me just wants to go there to prove Corin wrong—no matter how tough it is I won't turn to the Enhanced lifestyle. A part of me needs to prove myself. Corin needs to know I'm strong. "Anyway, I've already said we're going. The Noir Lands can't be as bad as you think—probably just exaggerated in stories. Things always are."

Corin doesn't reply, so I reach for his hands, try to draw him in closer. He's reluctant at first, and I feel the walls go up around him, but he doesn't pull away. I take that for a good sign.

"Fine. Whatever." Corin grunts, then snatches his hands from mine before turning away.

I stay where I am, watching him trudge back to the lorry.

I follow half a minute later and climb in. Corin's moved Esther so she's lying across the space where I was sitting. For a second, I don't know what to do, and I just stand there, my feet numb. I feel silly, getting upset about this, but I can't stop my bottom lip from wobbling. I look around, then touch the crystal Seer pendant around my neck, absentmindedly.

"Nice jewelry." Jed's voice makes me jump. He's back in the lorry—I hadn't noticed—and is lying down again, but partly propped up on his elbows. I think someone's changed the bandages around his thigh because they don't look as red now. "Calcite crystals?"

I stare at him, my fingers clenching the pendant tighter. I nod slowly.

His eyes are on me, not on the pendant—on *me*. Direct eye contact. Jed's are darker than Corin's. My mouth draws into a straight line, and I bite my bottom lip. My throat feels tickly. I don't know what to say. What if he knows what it is? My Seer pendant... Oh Gods. I need to hide it, put it under my top. The Zharat Seers must have them—or something similar—so what if he's recognized it?

Any female Seer is a fake. Sent by the demon spirits to taint the real Seers, to trick them, to hurt them. If a female Seer lives among people, she'll only bring destruction. They have to be killed.

NINE

"YOU TWO MARRIED?"

Manning's voice makes me jump, pulling me out of my disturbed sense of being. No one's spoken much for the last few hours. Mostly, the men slept. I couldn't sleep though. I just kept glancing across at Corin, hoping he'd smile at me, hoping he'd see we really didn't have a choice. But, in all the time we've been traveling again, he hasn't looked at me, much less smiled.

But Manning's question makes him react.

"Sev and I aren't married."

"She married to someone else?" That's Mart, the boy. He looks at Corin. It's then I notice the boy's wearing a gold ring on his finger. A wedding band. I stare at him, trying to see him as older. But no, no matter how hard I try, I can't. Fifteen is the oldest I can place him at. Maybe sixteen, at a push.

"No," Corin says. "But she's my girlfriend."

And he looks up at me, at last. His eyes are softer than I'd been expecting, but his brow still holds tension. I wonder if he's got a headache.

Manning leans forward, looks at me. He's sitting

cross-legged in front of me—and his posture emphasizes his round stomach. Jed is next to him.

"How old are you, woman?" Manning's voice is slow.

"Seventeen."

"And you never been married?"

I shake my head.

Manning's lips twist together a little. "Never procreated?"

"Babies?" I raise my eyebrows. I shake my head. "No."

The men exchange looks. Jed sits up a little straighter. Manning doesn't say anything else, but I notice the way he regards me. The way all the men now look at me. And I don't like it. It makes my skin feel dirty, just under their observation. It makes me feel wrong.

Corin shifts over to me, puts his arm around me, pulls me closer to him. I turn my head to find him glaring at the Zharat. I swallow hard and try to ignore the way the Zharat men are still looking at me, like I'm a piece of meat.

We don't make any more stops for the rest of the day—at one point, a driver radioed through and said it wasn't safe to, which didn't make me feel better. Still, no one has said anything more about my unmarried, childless state, and that's got to be something.

"Best we all go to sleep now, before we enter the Noir Lands," Manning says. He looks at me. "Our den's on the far side. Opposite border."

No sooner has he said the words when blankets are handed out and the men are all moving, stretching out on the floor.

"Stay this side of me." Corin points at the small space between his body and the wall. The Zharat men are lying down on his other side, but their eyes are on me. I don't like it. "It'll be all right," he says, but his voice is thick.

I lie down slowly. My back hurts, and my mother's pendant burns against my skin. It's under my shirt now; after Jed seemed interested in it, hiding the pendant seemed like a good call. Corin puts his arm around me, and I listen to the sounds of the engine. My stomach clenches, a little painfully. The roof of my mouth tastes strange as I stare up at the ceiling of the lorry. There are a few cracks in it, and, along with the slats at the top of the walls, some light streaks through. But the light's getting darker. Nighttime? I suppose it must be. I've lost all sense of time today.

After a few minutes, I hear heavy breathing. Deeper, more even. I turn my head, and my neck cricks. Someone starts snoring. I frown. How can they fall asleep that quickly?

Small movement catches my eyes suddenly. Corin blinking. I lift my head up a little. He's staring at me. Still awake. That makes me feel better. His arm is still around me, and he squeezes my shoulder slightly.

I try to smile, but the muscles ache. I try to feel calmer, because this is what we're supposed to do, joining the Zharat; the Dream Land told me that. Still, I can't help but wonder whether Corin's right. Maybe we'd be better off trying to find other Untamed who can help Esther.

Or maybe there isn't anyone else left. Maybe that's why the bison helped us find the Zharat.

Or maybe they just needed rescuing.

I close my eyes, let out a shaky breath.

And I'm pulled into the Dream Land.

Light hurtles past me; for several seconds, I can't breathe. I stay where I'm standing, can't see properly. Darkness clouds my head for a moment. The transition—it's wrong. Not normal. I frown, look up at the sky. The bison's there. My breath catches in my throat.

I swallow hard. The Zharat? Am I going to be warned about them? Told that the Dream Land made a mistake last time, that we shouldn't have found them? Or we were just supposed to save them from the Enhanced, not go with them?

I stare at the bison, waiting. It's hot here. I look around. A desert. But not like the desert I grew up in. That was dry heat and sand. This is… I frown, nudge the ground carefully with the toe of my left boot. It's like orange clay. But drier than normal clay. Not sand though. And the air's different. Humid. There's vegetation too. Low-creeping plants, like what we had at Nbutai. But there are sub-alpine plants too.

There are dunes in the distance, on every horizon. But even as I look at the mounds of sand, they're changing. The land's shifting. The dunes get bigger, erupting up into the sky, reaching up higher and higher. Trees sprout at their bases. They're making a forest. Montane forest. And mountains.

Seconds go by. Then minutes.

It's getting hotter. Sweat lines the back of my arms, trails down my spine. It's not a nice heat. It's the kind of heat that tries to pull you down, the kind that—

Don't show him where you are.

The voice booms out from the sky—echoing around the landscape in a way it definitely shouldn't—and the words zoom back and forth, before getting caught in the forests in the distance.

I turn, fast. Look around. No one's behind me. No one. It's empty. There's no one here. Only me.

And the bison. His gaze is stronger now.

"What?" I shout.

The voice gets louder. *If he sees the land, he'll know. He'll follow. He'll get all the Zharat. Don't let him have that knowledge, don't let him have them. Stay in the lorry until you reach safety. If he doesn't know where the Zharat caves are, he can't find them. None of them can.*

My lungs start to burn.

Don't leave the lorry again, Seven. Not until you're there. He sees what you see. Don't let him see the way to the Zharat caves.

"*He?*" I shout. "Raleigh?"

I try to take a step forward. I need to run. I don't know why, I just suddenly do. I have to run. But I

73

can't. My feet, they're stuck. I'm sinking. The ground is moving. The clay is moving over my feet, holding me down. And then—then it's shaking, and everything's quivering, and a part of me doesn't want to know the answer to my question, doesn't want it to become concrete.

My heart pounds. I try to take another step forward, but the clay's higher now, halfway up my shins. It's sticky, wet, clammy, clings to my skin. And there's no way out—the rocks are still falling, falling in front of me, next to me, behind me. Building a wall. A wall so I can't see the land beyond.

The air gets drier still, feels grittier. It's scratching me. My face. Invisible claws.

I scream.

Your eyes, Seven! Raleigh has your eyes.

SPLUTTERING AND CHOKING, I WAKE. I bolt upright, pull blankets up with me. My head pounds, and I look around, expect to see him. Expect to see Raleigh.

He's not dead. Raleigh's not dead.

"Sev?" Corin peers bleary-eyed at me. It's lighter now. I can see the concern on his face.

I take several deep breaths, try to still my rapid heart. I splay my fingers out on the floor, then feel Corin's hand as he places it over mine. Our arms leap up in the air a little as the lorry goes over a pothole or something.

We're still driving. That seems important.

"What is it?" Corin squeezes my fingers.

I swallow hard, looking around for other signs of alertness. I pick out dusty shapes in the semi-darkness. The Zharat are still lying down. It's only Corin and me who are sitting up. But they could be awake. Could be listening.

My eyes latch onto Corin's again. "Nightmare."

Raleigh has your eyes.

My skin goosefleshes, and I shiver, then touch my

75

eyes, feel my eyelids, expect them to feel different. They don't.

Corin pulls me close to him. His skin is warm, a little tacky. My head bumps against his chest with the momentum of the lorry. We must be on a dirt road. Or no road at all.

I try to relax, try to stop the jittery feelings. But my legs tremble, and pins and needles run down my skin.

"Bison?" Corin's voice is a murmur, barely audible, but I detect the load within it.

I nod.

Corin's intake of breath is too sharp. I wince, drag in air that grates on my lungs.

The Jed-shape on the floor stirs. He's closer to us than I remembered. Much closer. He's switched places with Mart.

I pull away from Corin slightly, turn my head, check the Zharat again. Double-check Jed. His eyes are still shut. He's still asleep, I tell myself. Everyone's asleep, apart from me and Corin, because I woke him up. And I need to tell Corin more. Much more. My lips burn, almost in anticipation.

Raleigh has your eyes.

I gulp, don't even know what it means. I blink slowly, exaggeratedly. My eyes still feel the same. But Raleigh has them? I frown, feel slight pressure begin to settle in my temples. Sleep-deprivation. I recognize the signs immediately.

"We'll talk during the next stop," Corin says, dipping his head down so his lips are by my ear. "That soon enough?"

I swallow hard. Don't know. I mean, I wasn't shown an immediate conversion attack, was I? But isn't that the purpose of the Dream Land?

But it could be a conversion attack warning… If I go outside, Raleigh will know where I am? Where we are? I could trigger a conversion attack?

I nod at Corin.

"Let's go back to sleep," he says.

He pulls me back down with him, gently, and wraps his arms around me. I'm glad. It's safety, him—around me. I breathe in his scent. There isn't as much smoke on him as usual. I wonder if he's struggling with cravings for cigarettes, whether he'll get withdrawal symptoms.

Corin's eyes are dark, watching me. He sees me looking, manages a smile. But it's only a half-smile.

"Bad dreams?"

The next morning Manning's voice is loud, intrusive, and I don't like it; it makes me feel sticky. I grimace.

"Aye. That's the greeting. Bad dreams and screams—all you need to know about the Noir Lands. Unique, ain't it?"

"What?" I blink, see Raleigh's face, super-imposed onto Jed's. His perfect white teeth. The defined jaw Raleigh told me was the work of augmenters. What was it? Two a day that kept it that strong? I squirm, feel sick, look away.

The small slits of sky I can see still look dark. But it's a different type of darkness. I frown. It's dark, but it's light in here. Yet there are no torches on now.

I frown, remembering what Corin told me about the Noir Lands earlier—that it doesn't follow the normal rules. I look up at the sky again. Still dark.

Corin's starting to say something, but his words rush past me, and I can't make them out.

Jed smiles. I swallow hard, tell myself that it's just Jed. Not Raleigh.

"We are in the Noir Lands now. We will probably reach the den tomorrow." Jed folds his blanket up, then chucks it over toward another man who catches it. "Maybe a couple of days, depends how the spirits are feeling. Can get quite dangerous."

I frown. Dangerous. That's what Corin said.

"Our home is far, far into the Noir Lands. The Fire Mountain," Jed says, pride evident in his voice.

"You live on a mountain?" Corin frowns at them. "That's just stupid. Anyone'll be able to see you from miles off."

"We live *inside* the mountain. Underground," Manning says. "Don't insult our culture, man, or there'll be consequences."

Corin mutters something under his breath about these consequences, but the Zharat men leave it.

"How many people do you have?" I ask. I squeeze the edge of the blanket, tighter, tighter. I need to distract myself.

Jed's eyes watch my hands. "About two hundred. More when the next babies are born."

I can't hide my surprise. Two hundred. That's just—

"That's crazy," Corin says. "You're asking to be caught with that number."

"Like I said, man, we live *inside* the mountain," Manning's voice is a low drool. "And there ain't no Enhanced around to see us. They ain't ventured into the Noir Lands in decades. The Gods keep us safe."

Corin snorts and folds his arms. "So, do we get another pit stop here?" He glances at me. "Or is it a straight ride until your mountain?"

"Depends on the spirits," Manning says, voice hard.

His words don't make me feel any better.

A few hours later, Manning announces that we *are* stopping, that the spirits are being lenient. He doesn't think they'll attack us as they've let the sky go back to a normal color. I don't know whether that makes me feel better or not.

It's getting hot. Much hotter. The air is heavy with heat, and inside the lorry is like a greenhouse. Sweat lines my skin, and my clothes are damp with it. Corin's face is shiny, red. We must be near the equator now, or on it.

I watch as the Zharat men pass me, head to the door. I hear one of them shout about a water hole. I want to get out, but the bison's words drum through me.

Don't show him where you are… He sees what you see. Don't let him see the way to the Zharat caves. Even going over the words in memory unsettles me. *Don't let him have that knowledge, don't let him have them. Stay in the lorry until you reach safety. If he doesn't know where the Zharat caves are, he can't find them. None of them can.*

And it's Rahn's lesson two, after all: *Don't ever lead the Enhanced Ones toward the village, no matter how scared you are. Sacrifice yourself.*

Sacrifice? I gulp. No. The wording doesn't match the situation exactly here. I don't need to sacrifice myself….

"Sev." Corin's standing over me, holding his hand out. The look in his eyes is intense. "Come on."

I shake my head. I've already turned my back to the door, so I can't see out. So Raleigh can't see out. I swallow hard. "I don't feel like it."

Jed's still in here. He hasn't gone out this time. I heard him mumbling earlier, something about his leg, that it's got worse. Manning thinks it might be infected. Jed's watching me now. His eyes are too sharp, they flicker like serpents. I turn my head quickly. He can't know anything, can he?

No. I'm being paranoid. *Of course* Jed can't know. *If he knew, he'd be dissecting you.*

I shudder, push that thought away.

"But, Sev, you need to get some air," Corin says. "It's stuffy in here." His voice is tense, and I know he wants to talk to me about my Seeing dream.

"I don't feel well. I need to stay in here." I look up at

Corin, trying to catch his eyes, make him understand.

But he shakes his head, reaches for my hand. "Come on."

Jed coughs loudly.

"Excuse me?" Corin turns on him.

Jed shrugs. "I am wondering whether you are always this forceful and controlling with your girlfriend."

"Forceful and controlling?" Corin says.

Jed nods and stretches his right leg out a little more. He groans, and the lines around his eyes look deeper, make him look older—in his forties? I'm not sure.

"S'ven has said she does not want to go out, yet you are trying to make her," Jed says. "That is forceful and controlling behavior."

Corin glares at him. "You don't know what you're talking about."

"Maybe I do. Maybe I do not. But it does not seem like S'ven wants to go with you. It seems like she barely likes you."

"*What*?" Corin says. He's bracing his legs now, and I see the tension in his injured arm, how he's holding it.

I glare at Jed, and then try to get Corin to look back at me, but he won't. He's turned his body completely toward Jed now.

And Jed doesn't stop.

"S'ven, do you even like him? Or are you just with this jerk because he is the only man you have known, the only option you have had? He does not seem like a good choice to me. You know, you will have plenty of choice among the Zharat men."

I stand up, feel something like fire—something so unlike me—in my veins. "Stop it."

My eyes narrow at Jed. He doesn't know what he's talking about. I've known Corin most of my life. I know him well. And I care about him. I do—but I'm just not one to shout about my feelings. And I've got nothing to prove to Jed.

Jed shrugs. "I just do not like to see a woman being taken advantage of. Especially such a woman as you."

I ignore him, turn to Corin, my heart rate high.

He's standing there, looking across at me, frowning. I can see the tension in his jaw and the hurt in his face that he's desperately trying to hide. His fists shake.

"It's all right," I say, taking hold of his hands. I go onto my tiptoes, kiss him lightly on the lips. He's unresponsive, still glaring at Jed. I don't know why that makes my chest ache.

At last, Corin looks at me. "Let's go." He nods toward the open doors.

I turn, see pale gold sand and—

Raleigh has your eyes.

I turn back quickly, legs shaking. "I already said that I'm staying here. I don't feel well." My voice wobbles.

Corin's eyes narrow. He looks between me and Jed. "You want to stay with *him*?"

"No." I sit down—as far away from Jed as I can— and focus on Esther. She still hasn't stirred, but she is breathing. I check the rise and fall of her chest, twice. "I just don't want to get out. You can stay here as well, if you want."

Corin grunts. "I'll be right back after a cigarette, or whatever it is you men smoke." He fixes Jed under his heavy gaze. "Don't try anything. Don't even talk to her."

Jed snorts. "Jealousy is not a good trait, Corin. Did your mother not teach you to share?"

Corin says something very rude under his breath, then leaves. I glance at Jed, still half-lying on the floor. He catches me looking at him and laughs.

"Better not let him see you looking at another man."

I ignore him, focus on the sounds outside. Some of the Zharat are talking nearby, then I hear Corin asking for a lighter. There are no sounds of spirits screaming. That makes me feel better.

"Do you mind?" Jed says a few minutes later. I turn to see him holding up an empty bottle. "Need to pee."

I shrug, turn my head away even farther. I stare at Esther, still motionless, on the floor. I try not to listen, but really that's impossible.

"We will be there soon." Jed's voice makes me jump. I hear him screwing the lid onto the bottle. "We are making good progress, probably get there tomorrow. We have not had to take any diversions."

I don't say anything. I don't understand why he's even trying to engage me in conversation, why he's trying to annoy Corin, because Corin's going to be back here any second now.

"You will like our home," he continues. "Your disposition reminds me of my daughter, Jeena. She is twelve. You are older. But you have the same mind. Inquisitive, strong, quiet. Easily overwhelmed."

My shoulders prickle.

"Do not worry," Jed says. "You will be safe with us." He pauses for a second. "But, if you do not want to be with Corin, then that can be sorted. I would hate for any daughter of mine to be with a man she does not really want, especially when there is better being offered."

I turn my head away from Jed, my shoulders tight, and try to pretend that he didn't just say that.

ELEVEN

THE SKIES ARE GETTING DARKER, spirits closing in. That's what Corin tells me when he gets back in the lorry, along with the rest of the Zharat, and we continue on our way. The Zharat are worried, I can tell that. Manning's sitting with the two-way radio clasped in his hand, and he speaks rushed comments into it. A lot of interference and crackles blare out of it, but he seems to be able to pick out words.

Jed and three other men stare at a map. One of them got it out a box a minute ago. It's laminated, and I watch as they draw lines on it with non-permanent marker pens.

"We need to go 'round that way. We 'ave no choice. There are too many chivras gathered east—"

Manning cuts the man off by barking something into the radio, and the other men go quiet. He then looks at Jed. "Eelan says there be water spirits in the distance. Looks like kavalahs. This ain't good."

I blink hard, recognize the name. It takes me a few moments to think. Kavalahs are one of the evil spirit types; they want human interaction and to make deals and feed on as much human energy as possible.

Any human energy—and they don't care about the difference between us and the Enhanced, all they want is to be fed. I think I remember my mother talking about a woman who sought out a kavalah once, made a deal with the evil spirit. The kavalah fed from her every day, in return for getting the woman something. That's as much as I know. But it must have been something important, because giving the evil spirit her energy every day killed the woman within a year.

"Speed up," Manning orders into the radio. "We have no choice. They're less likely to attack a fast lorry."

A few seconds later, I feel the lorry speed up. Wind whistles through the gaps in the wagon.

Several of the Zharat look worried.

"But why they gatherin' now? The calendar says—"

"Aye. I know, man. But the spirits be gathering *now*."

"The Turning coming?"

"Shouldn't be. Too soon to the last one."

I frown, trying to remember Corin's words. Hadn't he said it was the Turning *all the time* in the Noir Lands? I can't remember. My head feels too groggy.

"The spirits are active. Unusually active."

"Probably that damn girl, pretending to be a Seer, angered them. Good job we killed her when we did."

I turn, look at Corin. The way he's sitting says he's tense, that he's going to have bad backache later. He hasn't said much at all. Part of me wants to lean across, put my hand on his arm, but I stop myself. His brows are furrowed, and he looks annoyed as he stares at Esther.

I want him to speak to me, to say something, but I don't know what to say. Jed's words still ring in my ears, and I can tell Corin is angry, that he feels threatened by the older man, but he's trying not to show it. I feel like I should reassure him, but I don't know how—and I don't want to do anything in front of all these men.

"If we head across, past the Old Lakes, we can get

in through the lower tubes," Jed says. He stretches forward, toward the map a different man's now holding, then groans, clutching at his thigh. "We should be getting close. What about the southern ones?"

"Not sure." One of the men stands up and—

The lorry hits something, lurches forward. The man flies forward, crashes into boxes. Something jolts into me, and I hit my head against the aluminum wall, see whiteness for a second.

"Sev?"

Corin's hand closes around my wrist, he pulls me to him. I look up, see—

Something crashes into the side of the lorry.

I pitch forward with the momentum as the lorry swings to the left, but Corin grabs me.

"What the hell?" Corin shouts, pulling me toward him as hard as he can. I hurl head-first into his chest. His arms go around me. "What the hell was that?" Then he's reaching for his gun. "The Enhanced?"

He glances sideways at me, his eyes searching.

I shake my head, breathing hard. But I don't know for sure… Just because I've had no Seeing dream, it doesn't mean… Or did I see too much of the outside before? Did Raleigh see where we were, work out where we're going?

Pain flitters in front of my left eye, and I flinch.

Manning laughs. "Put your gun away, man. You ain't shooting us, and you sure as hell ain't shooting no spirits and making 'em more angry. That one that hit us'll be angry enough."

A spirit? I try to sit up straighter, try to listen hard. I should be able to hear them. Spirits scream and scream. The sounds in each of the Turnings are horrible. I think back to the many nights I've spent undercover when the seasons were changing and the spirits were most active. I've spent *hours* listening to their fights, their frenzied battles.

But they were quiet when we spent the night in the

temple, quiet enough for us to sleep. They didn't start screaming until they wanted us gone. Or maybe that's only when we heard them, when they had enough energy again to be heard properly.

But I can't hear anything now, just the engine roaring and the humming in the air and—

The engine stutters. But it's just a one-off thing, and then we're accelerating again. I breathe a sigh of relief.

Corin shifts his weight a little, keeps his arm around me. I lean into him, but I'm too tense, can't relax. I drum my fingers against my thigh.

But it happens again: the engine stutters, five or ten minutes later. It lasts for longer this time, and I feel the momentum of the lorry slipping away.

Manning brings the radio to his mouth again, speaks into the little box. "Alban, what's going on? Why are we—"

The lorry slams to a stop, jolts to the left.

I scream, whack my head against something hard, see dark spots amid whiteness for a second.

"Sev!" Corin's by my side, falling, but grabbing me. He closes his fingers around my arm, yanks me up somehow.

I whirl around, choking, arms spread out, grabbing the wall. Boxes slide across the floor, throw up dust. Someone shrieks.

"What—"

The sounds of glass shattering fill my ears.

"Alban—what's going on?"

"They're…the windows…they're getting in…."

There's a pause, a long pause. And then a scream. A male scream.

Chills run down my spine. I look up, see purple swirls through the gaps in the wagon roof.

"Run for it! Only chance…" Alban's panting. Then we hear scraping noises. And another scream.

"Alban? Yanugh?" Manning grips the radio so tightly his knuckles go white. He's breathing hard, something drips from his braids. Dark red. Blood?

"Get out now… They're in the cab! Going to get in the—"

The radio cuts off, hissing.

Manning springs up, heads toward the door. No one says anything as he slides the bolt back. My heart hammers against my ribs. I feel sick.

Manning throws the door the rest of the way open.

The sky outside is deep purple, with smaller pockets of mauve, red, navy, and gaping gaps of blackness. The purple's stronger than what I've ever seen, and the black holes are eating everything.

I gulp.

The Turning.

It's the middle of the Turning. The most dangerous time. The most lethal time, as the seasons change, and the spirits—especially the evil spirits—become more active.

Something moves in the sky. A dark mass, and it howls, flies toward us. A spirit. And suddenly there are so many. My mouth dries, and I'm trying to move backward, trying to move away, as far away as possible. But Corin's in the way, and he's not moving. He's just a solid mass, like stone and—

A spirit dives down, toward us. I scream, and the men are shouting. And—

The spirit flies into the lorry.

I jerk up, arms and legs barely working. I crash into the side, with Corin. Then he leans forward, grabs Esther, wrenches her to us.

The spirit hovers in the middle of the lorry. It is grotesque, not one I recognize. Too many eyes. Semi-translucent. Lots of tendrils.

We're all pressed against the walls. Mart whimpers. Someone whispers how they wish Iro was here—the dead man?—that he could use his powers to help us.

And the spirit looks at us all, each in turn.

Don't look at it.

My heart's beating too fast, and my hands are clammy. People rarely see an evil spirit and live. I'm shaking, trying not to look at it, trying not to make contact with its many eyes, trying not to accidentally challenge it. I turn my head, see Manning still in the doorway. The light is strange; he's silhouetted, yet he shouldn't be.

Corin's hand suddenly closes around mine. He's shaking.

Everyone's shaking.

The spirit dives forward, screaming.

It crashes into the man next to Jed. And—

Too much happens at once. I can't make it out. I hear the screams, the crying. I see the man fall. I see the spirit leap onto his body, but I can't make its form out now. It's all just a mass of movement.

I see the man's foot kick out. And then—then his foot's gone. Just *gone*.

My chest tightens. My forehead burns.

"Run!" Manning screams.

Corin's hand jerks in mine, and then he's turning—turning toward Manning. I try to follow, but my legs won't work properly. And I can't move my head, can't look away from the spirit *eating* the man.

My eyes widen.

This isn't just feeding. This isn't what happened in the last Turning—immediately before the battle against the Enhanced Ones—when some spirits fed from us, so they could get enough energy to help us in the battle against the Enhanced—no.

This is—this is destruction.

This is bad.

This is carnivorous.

This is evil.

"Just run!" the chief shouts. "We've got a chance if we're quick! The Turning's only just begun. We've got to run for it. *Now*."

TWELVE

"WE CAN'T GO OUT THERE," Corin shouts. "It's the *Turning*. Shut the door!"

But the Zharat men are jumping out. They're just going. Running and jumping. I see Jed crawling to the doorway. Don't know how he's going to make it. Not outside, because… Because we'll be running.

But no one can outrun a spirit. We all know that.

Oh Gods.

And the spirit's still eating the man.

"Out now!" Manning shouts. "We know these lands. We know how to survive. Do as I say. Elmiro will help us."

I look around for this Elmiro man, but no one steps forward. And then Manning rushes at us. But no, he's not going for us. He's going for Esther, scooping her up, flinging her over his shoulder like she's a ragdoll. She screams—the first sound in ages—and her eyes flutter open. The fear in them grabs me.

"Hey!" Corin yells. "We—"

The second spirit enters.

A mass of red and green. It's small, but sharp teeth appear out of nowhere, all over it. I don't recognize it, haven't seen that type before, but there are so many. Thousands of different spirit types.

The mass of teeth goes straight for Corin.

I scream, throw myself in front of him. I crash into him. We fall. Sharp corners jab at my side—more pain—then I'm scrambling around. Dust billows into my eyes, scratches, claws. I gulp, rub at them, but just get more dust in them.

A dark shape moves toward me. The spirit? More? Can't tell. My chest tightens.

"Esther!" Corin shouts.

I turn, see boxes fall down. Something rushes past me, nails against my skin. Tearing. I shriek, and then—

The night is screaming.

I hunker down, or maybe I'm pushed down, I can't tell. I taste grit and phlegm at the back of my mouth, feel something hover above me. I roll over, try to get away, can't see a thing. Something hisses. A spirit?

There. A skeletal frame, dark, yet glowing. More hissing.

I crash into more boxes. Something moves in my right shoulder, a sharp twinge, reminds me of when I got shot there. White pain flits in front of my eyes. My skin tingles. Fingers. Spirits' fingers, on my back. Bare skin. My shirt?

Let me eat you, dear human.

The words jolt through me. I scream, trying to turn, and—

"Get out!"

Something inside me jars. I feel more fingers on my skin. Fingers that aren't fingers. The spirits. The Turning.

"Sev!"

Corin grabs me—his arms around my chest—and pulls me forward. I manage to find my feet, then we're by the open doors. He's shouting, cursing. Another spirit—a gust of sudden coldness—comes straight for us.

Corin aims his gun at it, fires. He misses.

But the sound—disorientating, too loud, and—
They rush at us.

Purple eyes and skulls and fingernails. I scream. Corin screams. My hands scrabble in the mess on the floor. Wet, blood. The smell of rust and bile. My insides heave. A skull hovers in front of me, blue tendrils dangling from its purple eye sockets.

Let me eat you!

I turn, step back onto the edge of the vehicle bed, then fall off. Land heavily on my right side. My mother's pendant slams into my chest, cold. I shriek, then Corin's there—right next to me, pulling me up. His gun goes off again, a hole in the night.

"Where did they go?" he shouts, pulling me forward. "The Zharat! Where did they go?"

My hair whips around, across my face, as I try to see, try to peer through the foggy colors and trees.

"That way!" I try to pull Corin along, but he's too big and my hand's too sweaty and my fingers are slipping. "Come on!"

We start to run, but our feet are sinking. The ground's too wet. It's mud, thick mud. The kind of mud that pulls you down. And there are plants, vines—things that grab me, try to stop me because everything's moving.

I focus on the retreating figures in the distance. Manning is struggling with Esther's weight, at the back of the group. Spirits are right by them, throwing their tendrils down and—

Corin's hand is ripped from mine.

I turn, eyes streaming, heart pounding.

"Corin!" I scream, but the spirits are howling, shrieking, and I can't hear anything else.

I drag more air in. Black dots appear in front of my eyes.

"Over here!" a voice yells.

A Zharat man—not Corin. He's suddenly close by and lunges for me, grabs me, and—

I see the spirit at the last moment.

Too late.

I scream as the heap of silver feathers hits the man. A flurry of movement, followed by howling. I cry out, trying to step forward toward him—to help him—but I don't know what to do, and—

The spirit tears a chunk from the man's torso. Clothes and sinewy muscle and redness and skin. Blood. Something white and hard and—

I inhale sharply, start choking. My eyes start streaming. Something brushes against my back, like fur. I whirl around—another spirit? But I can't see one…it's gone?

Or it's invisible and—

No. No. No.

Something hisses behind me, and I turn, heart pounding. I blink rapidly, see the silver spirit moving, see its teeth whirling around, and then it lifts up a few feet, and I see the man.

He looks at me, stares straight at me with hollow eyes. He's still standing—I don't know how—and his mouth is open, forming an eerie unison with the bloody aperture in his chest. His clothes are tattered around the edges of the gouge, frayed and broken. His lips are moving. With a jolt, I realize he's telling me something, but I don't know what he's saying. Can't make it out. A deep howling suddenly fills my ears; the spirit dives, going for him again, long teeth protruding like cast iron nails.

I try to turn, then duck as a wedge of the man's flesh—still covered in his tattoos of birds—flies through the air. It misses my head by inches, and a new streak of gold hits it, followed by an ear-piercing shriek. A flurry of movement, more spirits—streaks of blinding color and black eye sockets. A bright flash of orange.

Run!

But my legs are too heavy, and I can't leave the man, can't—

It's too late.

The spirits cover the man's writhing body as he falls to the floor, as his limbs flail, as his blood pours out, soaking the ground. And there's so much blood; the redness rapidly reaches my feet.

My stomach hardens, my breathing's suddenly too fast.

A second later, the assembly of spirits parts down the middle, dividing into two channels, and I see what's left of the man. Scraps of blood-steeped tattooed skin; the broken and scratched wings of birds that will never fly.

My chest hitches, my spine clicks.

Get out of here!

My body jolts, and I look around for the spirits—they'll go for me next—but I can't see them. The light's too bad, and they're hiding. All I can see is a thick, dark, pulsating fog around me that lifts and falls in waves.

"Come on!" Manning's shout is distant.

I try to see him, but there's no one here. Only the darkness as the world gets blacker and blacker. I turn and run and see land rising up ahead. A mountain. But the fog's changing, getting deeper, and I can't tell how far away the mountain is. And—

Raleigh has your eyes.

Rain lashes down. I try not to see anything, but the torrents of rain prevent it anyway.

"Sev!"

My chest thumps; he's alive. Still alive….

I try to move, try to pull my left foot out of the stickiness. It's gloopy, like tar. Like a black lake that wants to consume me.

Five. My chest tightens.

Don't go to a black lake. If you see it, you run.

But I am knee-deep in a black lake. And I'm sinking. My chin trembles, and my nostrils flare, letting in more of a rotting-flesh kind of smell. Sweat breaks out across my forehead, and I clench my hands into fists, feel my nails digging into the soft flesh of my palms.

"Seven!"

Suddenly another Zharat man is here. He grabs my arm, yanks me forward. My fists fly open, and I see blood in them.

The black lake lets me go.

We run.

"It's not far!"

Air rushes past me, and fingers. Lone fingers, on their own. I feel bile rise, and then I'm choking, gagging.

Let me eat you!

I surge forward, speed flowing into me.

And then...then there's a hole in the ground. Straight in front of me. And I can't stop.

I fall into the chasm—big, jagged edges of dark rock, leading down, down, down.

THIRTEEN

I CRASH ONTO HARDNESS AND rocks. Pain squeezes through me. I drag in air, but nothing happens—can't breathe. Gulp more air, but…nothing, nothing—

Then I start choking. I roll to the side as a shape falls next to me, a man. A Zharat man. And hands—hands are pulling me up.

I scream, try to get away from the spirits. But it's dark in here, and the ground's uneven; I can't see where I'm going, and huge nodules catch my feet. I stumble and—

"S'ven!"

I slam into a body. An upright body. Not dead. My chest rises and falls, too fast, can't breathe. Going to be sick.

"S'ven! Do not worry!" It's Jed's voice, and then he's patting me down—or at least, I think those hands are his. "The spirits will not enter the tubes."

I freeze, listen hard. Screeches and squeals fill my ears. From inside the—what? I look around. A cave. One of the Zharat caves? More screeches, and then a fluttering sound.

"Just the bats," Jed says. "They seek safety here too. Come on. Be careful in case a porcupine is sheltering at the side." He pauses, and I hear other voices, but farther away—the others? "The gorillas most likely will not be here. They stay away from the tubes in the Turnings."

Jed drags me forward, and I barely save myself from stumbling. I don't know how he can walk with his injured thigh, or see where we're going. I can't see a thing. It's just darkness—inkiness that fogs everything.

I turn my head, look back up, outside. The sky's purple. I can see it, and then Jed pulls me around a corner, cutting me off from that glimpse of sky. My right shoulder catches against something hard, and I grunt—it's my bad shoulder—but there are voices now. Lots of voices. Men's. And—and there's light again. I squint at the moving, luminous beam.

"Is there anyone else?" someone shouts.

"No," Jed yells. "We are the last."

No? No one else? *The last…* My chest stutters. What about…what about Corin?

I start to turn, but Jed's too strong. Far too strong—how can he even be walking, let alone this strong? And then—then we're with the other people.

A man shines an electric torch around, lighting up faces in jagged angles. I see Manning first. See him transfer Esther to another man and tell him to take her to the healers, that they need to be careful with her because she's weak and infected, and that she shouldn't be disturbed until she is better. Then everyone's around us, around me and Jed, and they're talking.

My heart pounds frantically. I feel sick.

"This way!"

Someone prods me in the back, rather hard, and I try to speed up as I look around, ahead, blinking against the harsh light, and—

Corin.

He's there, rushing toward Manning, and his shouts fill the tube, echoing strangely as he yells after his sister.

"You'll see her after the healers have finished, not before," Manning says. "I'll tell you when—"

Jed screams.

I whirl around. Spirits! Oh Gods, they've followed us in—we're trapped. Trapped. *Trapped*.

My vision blurs with the movement, and I can't process it, can't work it out, can't keep up.

Jed sinks to the floor, yelling. His face contorts under the dazzle of a torch. I look around, getting ready for the spirits, for the energy, the skulls. My heart pounds even harder, and I feel sweat drip down my back, sticking my shirt to my skin. I clench my fists.

"Murderer!" a female voice shrieks.

And then there's more screaming and movement, grunts and yells.

Extra torches light up and whirl around through the air, throwing streams of brightness everywhere, but I can't take anything in. I blink hard, nearly trip, but someone grabs my arm.

"Murderer!"

"Stop her!" one of the men shouts. I recognize his voice, but—

Someone crashes into me, and I start to stumble, but right myself. Then I see Jed, he's sprawled on the floor, groaning. Above him, is a knife. A big knife. And a tall woman dressed in green holds it, purposefully pointing it at Jed.

I try to shrink back, away from the woman whose face looks like an angry spirit, but there's nowhere to go, so I press my back against the stone wall and try not to breathe.

A second later, the woman turns on another man, but he backhands her, and she cries out in a tinny voice. Then there's more movement—movement I can't process.

"Clare!"

Manning's voice. He's suddenly beside Jed, on the floor.

The woman—Clare—throws herself down on Jed, screaming. Hair flies out. Blood sprays, splatters.

"You murderer! She didn't do nothin'! How could you? You're all murderers—"

I see the hand shoot out before I register what's about to happen. A loud *slap*. And then Clare's on the ground, on her stomach. More movement. I can't process it. It's the spirits—must be—they're still messing with me. I blink hard, try to clear my head. But everything's pounding inside it, and, in front of me, the torch beams are going everywhere—too disorientating—and I can't focus properly.

"Where's Miles?" Manning asks. "Jed. Get up, man. You're all right. Not gonna let a woman win, are you?"

Jed stands, shakily. I think there's blood coming from his arm, but it doesn't seem to be bad—not as bad as his injured leg. And now he's hobbling, groaning.

Clare jumps up with no fuss, glares at the men. Then she disappears into the shadows of the tube, and I'm sure I hear the words: *Just you wait.*

I go cold.

"*Did* you kill someone?" Corin pulls me away from Jed as he barks the question at the older man.

One of the other Zharat men pivots toward him. I recognize him vaguely as one who was in the lorry with us. "The girl we told you about. The fraud who thought she was a Seer. That was Clare's sister."

I swallow hard, try to turn away. My throat burns. They can't look at me, they can't see me, see what I really am. As if on cue, my Seer pendant burns my skin, burns as if it can rip through my shirt and reveal itself. I angle my body toward Corin.

"Come on, people," Manning says. "Keep going."

And then everyone's walking again.

The man who took Esther has disappeared… Or maybe he's still ahead, it's just too dark for me to pick him out. I think Clare must be in front of us now too, think I pick out light footsteps. The Zharat seem to be able to see better than me.

I reach a hand out, brush my fingers against the cave walls. Predominantly smooth, but sections resemble knotted rope in places. A snake of deep amber light flickers off it, catching the bumps at angles, making the texture seem deeper. The air smells strange.

Corin takes my hand. He squeezes my fingers, but doesn't look at me, stares straight ahead. As the torch beams move around, I see we're coming up to a fork in the passageway.

The Zharat men lead us down the left tube, where the air tastes fresher. I look up; there's a patch of sky up there, pale purple in color, and it makes the cave's ceiling look darker. Makes everything look darker.

"Is this volcanic rock?" Corin suddenly says.

We all stop.

"Aye," Manning says. "Our cave's a network of underground lava tubes at the foot of our Fire Mountain."

I look at the Zharat Chief. "*This* is a volcano?"

The air feels damp, and I can't see much. The torches aren't directed at the walls, and they make the darkness around the edges of the light seem greater. But I listen hard for a second, half expect to hear magma boiling and bubbling underfoot. But there's nothing. It's completely silent.

"Yes, we are inside a volcano," Jed says from behind. "Our Fire Mountain is a stratovolcano, so we are lucky to have a tube network here at all, let alone such an expansive one along the slopes—"

"You *said* it was a mountain." Corin steps closer to me.

Manning sighs. "The Fire Mountain ain't erupted in living memory. No signs of magma moving, the Gods keep it that way. They protect us. There ain't nothing to worry about, man. These be just like any other caves."

"Nothing to worry about?" Corin says, and the

inclination of his voice makes me sure he is raising his eyebrows.

I touch the rock. I think it might be some sort of basalt, but I'm not sure. Most of it is smooth, though I can feel where other parts have been chiseled away to widen the space; those edges are sharper. I wish it was lighter, so I could see it properly.

"We are very lucky to have these tubes to live in." Jed's voice is closer to me now, much closer, and his tone is more insistent than before. "This volcano structure—the mountain—rarely has tubes because this type of lava is slow and sticky. We are blessed to have them. They are a gift from Elmiro and the other Gods." He pauses. "I come from a land of smaller, flatter volcanoes; their lava is runnier, faster. They have a lot of tubes just under their surface. Of all the volcanoes in the Noir Lands, our Fire Mountain is the only one with tubes."

"So lava flowed through these tubes before," Corin says. "It could happen again." He looks up. "Or if the summit erupts, lava could come down through the skylights, even if it doesn't come directly through these tubes. This isn't safe."

"You wanna go back outside?" Manning snorts, and his light shines on Corin's face, makes his skin look orange—as orange as some of the spirits in the raging mass we ran through. "You run-arounders always be so worried. You think we ain't thought of this? If we ain't told you we was in a volcano, you wouldn't even know." He laughs, then fixes Corin with a hard look. "The Gods keep the magma far down, far below. Perfectly safe. Come on."

Corin doesn't move. "What about volcanic gases? We could get poisoned."

"We've lived here for *years*, and we're fine." The annoyance in Manning's voice is obvious. "Most volcanic gas is steam. There be occasional bad air in low points. But our tubes be well ventilated, and volcanic rock is porous. Gas ain't something to worry about."

"And the hot vapor is useful," Jed says. "It bursts out another tube, higher up. We do not live in that one. We have a grill over the entrance, and we cook from it. We are lucky that the Gods blessed our Fire Mountain and give us the resources we need to survive."

We keep going, deeper and deeper into the network of tubes, deeper into the mountain. The volcano. I sniff the air several times, expect to smell something bad. But I can't. It just smells…normal. And it's cold. Colder than I'd have thought, for a volcano. But it is essentially just a cave, I remind myself. It hasn't erupted in living memory—that's what Manning said. I shiver.

Up ahead, torches light up several objects arranged in a semi-circle at the side of the tube. I narrow my eyes as they come into focus: lumps of crudely cut minerals and a small child's doll with straw-hair. A wide grin has been painted onto the doll's red-dyed face; my mouth dries as I stare at it.

"You menstruating?" A man shines his light on me.

I blink, eyes stinging. "What?"

"You are female. If you're bleedin' then the Gods do not like females lookin' at their shrines. You need to pay respect, else they will punish us all. Same with the paintings down that corridor."

He points, and I just about make out another tube stretching to the right. It's dark down there, but not too dark for me to see that jagged lines have been painted on the walls. And then everyone else is moving again, and the torch beams are redirected.

"We'll call a meeting of our council," Manning announces a few minutes later.

We're in a wider tube now, at least thirty feet separate the walls, and the ceiling's a bit lower. Corin and several of the other men are stooping. Manning isn't though. For the first time, I realize just how short he is. Short and fat.

Then I notice the other people here, standing in the

shadows. Women, mainly dressed in bright colors, watch us with wide eyes, and children point. There are babies, but the babies are silent. Not crying. It's eerie, and I swallow hard, only to find I've not got enough saliva in my mouth, and the action scratches my throat, makes me cough. Through my watering eyes, I see Corin giving me a concerned look.

Manning waits until I've stopped before speaking again—but he glares at me first. "We'll discuss your welcomings. Call you up to us when we've got the details sorted. In the meantime, Nyesha will show you 'round the most-used tubes, get you fresh clothes, food."

He gestures into the shadows, and a woman dressed in yellow steps forward. She turns on a torch and holds it high above her head so the cave's roof is illuminated more than anything. I can't see her features that well, but her smile is wide. Immediately, I feel better.

"Do you want to wash first?" Nyesha asks as Manning and his men head off.

I nod, stepping closer to Corin. My arms feel strangely sticky with the dust that coats them. "You have showers?"

Nyesha nods. She looks about thirty, but her eyes have the youthful spark of a teenager's. "The Gods asked the Great River to flow through the end of the tube complex. We wouldn't survive without water. It is all on the lower level."

She heads off, and Corin and I follow her. He walks close to me, puts his arm around my shoulders, draws me nearer as we follow Nyesha.

"We need to talk," he says in a low voice.

I nod, swallow hard, then listen as Nyesha points out the different tubes we pass and tells us where they lead. She looks tired, and the torchlight accentuates the dark circles under her eyes.

I focus ahead. There are a few small crater marks on the walls. Little air bubbles, with their shells broken. And it all just seems so…so weird. Strange. Like none of this can really be happening.

Corin doesn't say anything as we walk, just nods as Nyesha explains. I can see him better now, even though the light's still not great. My eyes must have adjusted. Corin's expression is tight, muscles pulsating around his jaw. His gaze flickers down for a second, toward me. He nods, but I don't understand what he's trying to convey.

"Be careful on these steps." Nyesha points with the beam of her torch, illuminating uneven stone.

Crudely cut steps lead us down a level, and the air gets cleaner, but darker. That's when we hear the water. We speed up, automatically, though the floor gets steeper. We're climbing down, going far, far to the right. Corin's arm slides down from my shoulders, until his fingers wrap around mine. His touch makes me tingle.

"I can smell water." I can't help but smile. Fresh. Sparkling. *Water*.

I look up at Corin, then ahead. My eyes search the chasm. The light's strange in here. The lava wall in front of us has small gemstones in it. Pale blue, and orange. Some green ones that also look slightly mauve as we pass them. They're shining, catching light, and the sight of them makes my eyes fill. I don't know why, and I hide the tears before Corin can see.

"This way," Nyesha says, then disappears to the left.

We follow her around the corner, eyes searching. An electric lamp has been attached high up on the wall, and several torches are also propped up; there's more light than I'd expected, and the brightness seems almost intrusive.

We're deeper down now; above us must be the other tubes, the ones we were in before.

The roar of the water's loud. So loud my ears feel under pressure. Nyesha turns back, speaks to us, but I just watch her lips move, can't hear her. Nyesha points ahead, at the next corner, her smile growing.

Corin's fingers start to burn in my hand. We round

the corner together.

We see the waterfall.

I look up, trying to see the source of the water, but it's just gushing through the lava-rock ceiling—the ceiling that's suddenly really high—splashing down, turning a waterwheel, and crashing onto the smooth, black floor, where it trails off to the right and forms a healthy stream in a well-worn groove. There, the water flows along, fills the rest of the tube that veers away, getting smaller. There are two more waterwheels there, and wires snake off from them. A sliver of light shows at the end of the tube. With a jolt, I realize that's the outside world out there.

"The wheel shafts are connected to coil generators," Nyesha says, adjusting her bright yellow wrap-dress. Its color makes her dark skin glow. "They convert mechanical movement to electricity. The main parts of the caves are lit in the evenings, for a few hours. The rest of the power is used to recharge torch batteries." She pauses, and her voice is weary, as if this isn't the first time she's said these words. "We cannot have burning torches in here because of the air. They would steal our oxygen too quickly."

"What about smoking?" Corin asks. "Cigarettes?"

"We smoke outside." Nyesha turns and points to the waterfall. "We shower under there, under the wheel."

I bring a shaky hand up to my forehead, feel something in my chest wobble. I shake my head. Corin's hand slackens in mine, but I don't have the energy to grasp his fingers back. This place is just….

"Is the water safe?" Corin asks. "It's not acidic or anything, with the lava?"

"Not acidic." Nyesha shakes her head. "We have a lot of rain at this time of year. The rivers that form down the Fire Mountains provide the rest of the Noir Lands with water." She points at a waterfall, then directly above us. "The Great River flows down our Fire Mountain in the rainy season, but *this* lava tube has a separate opening. Directly up there. Part of the river falls down here, flows along there, and back out of the mountain in a small stream. It is fresh rainwater, and the Gods say it is safe."

"Unlike the ponds," another voice says.

Corin and I turn to find a young woman stepping through the waterfall. She's naked, heavily pregnant, and stares at us for a few seconds, before retrieving a towel from a basket not far away. There are several woven containers there I hadn't noticed.

"The ponds?" Corin asks. His eyes are on the floor, and his voice sounds a little strained.

The pregnant woman nods, wraps the towel around herself. "Some of the other tubes have dips in their floors. Little ponds form from water seeping in through the volcanic rock. Water in them ponds ain't that safe. It'll do in emergencies. But this water, from the Great River, won't burn." She stops and surveys us for a few minutes, then grabs a pale blue dress from the floor, pulls it on. "You the new arrivals?"

We nod, and then she's leaving. Nyesha watches after her for a few moments, then looks across at me. She points at two baskets by the wall.

"Help yourself. Clothes and shampoo." She looks at me for a second. "Wear only black or dark garments. You're not supposed to wear anything with a proper color until the day of your welcoming, when it's been decided what your color will be." She smiles.

"What about me?" Corin asks, a small hint of amusement in his voice.

"Men's clothes are dark. Neutral. Black, gray." Nyesha shrugs. "I'll be back in ten minutes to show you the rest of our home and get you some food, once you've washed. I need to feed my youngest."

"Thank you," I call after Nyesha as she disappears.

Corin turns to me. A strange smile plays across his lips, and I feel heat rushing to my face. I start to feel strange, giddy. This is just….

Too much?

I breathe hard, look around. We're alone now.

"Corin, I need to talk to you about the Seeing—"

He cuts me off, a finger to my lips. He points at the gushing water behind us. "Talk over there, while we shower."

"But—"

He shakes his head. "Less chance of anyone overhearing. We can't be too careful."

No one else is in here, but there's sense in what he's saying. Still, as we strip our clothes off, I wonder if he has another agenda for why he wants to hold the conversation under the shower.

Corin takes everything but his boxers off, then faces me. I'm a bit slower, and he helps me with my T-shirt as it gets caught on my matted hair. Where his fingers brush my bare skin, shivers run through me. I feel adrenaline rushing through my body, more and more. The way Corin's looking at me makes me feel different. Dizzy.

Corin takes my hand. "Come on."

We step under the crashing torrents. Warm water. No. It's *hot*. Corin groans as he stretches his arms out, then shakes his head.

A few seconds later, he looks at me. The water has plastered his hair to his forehead, makes his face look different. Stronger. The edges are harder.

"Talk," he says.

I look around for a few seconds, but there really is no one else here now. The falling water throws the artificial light around, gives the effect of movement, but there's no one watching. No one listening.

The Dream Land warning seems so long ago now, but I still shudder as I tell Corin the bison's exact words: *Raleigh has your eyes*.

The water beats down hard on the back of my neck, and my hair feels too heavy, like it's dragging me down.

Corin frowns, peers at me. I see the movement in his throat as he swallows. "What does it mean? How can Raleigh have your eyes?"

"I don't know."

"But he sees what you're seeing? *Exactly* what you're seeing?" A vacant expression fills his face for a few seconds. Then he snaps out of it. "So that's why you didn't get out at the last stop." He frowns. "But we ran here… You think that Raleigh could've recognized the scenery around here, from what you saw? That they could come here?"

I shrug. A new jet of hot water sprays onto my back. "I don't know. I didn't see much of the land. Couldn't, because of the spirits." And it *was* the Turning. The land sometimes changes during the Turning, then returns to its previous state afterward. "But the Enhanced probably know it's the Noir Lands the Zharat are in anyway."

But it doesn't make me feel any better. I rub at my arms.

"And the Noir Lands *are* vast," Corin says. He stares into my eyes. A stream of water trickles down the side of his face. "Think we should tell the Zharat? Think *I* should tell the Zharat?" He frowns at his correction.

I shake my head, send droplets flying. I don't know why I do it so quickly. But there's a certainty in me. "If it's a problem, the Dream Land will alert me." I hope.

Corin nods, then runs a hand through his hair. "Right."

He's trying not to look at my body. I can tell that; his eyes barely leave my face. Whether he's doing it to be courteous to me, I'm not sure, but a part of me feels disappointed. Doesn't he *want* to look at me? I look down at my own body. At my lack of curves.

I fold my arms. Then I realize that the movement has lifted my breasts up a little in my bra. Oh Gods. I look at Corin. His pupils dilate a little, and his gaze drops for a second. Two seconds. Three.

I look away, feel heat rush to my face. He'll think I did that on purpose. But I didn't. I don't do that sort of thing. Five did, yes. She was always telling me how to stand so I look more appealing. *Thrust your chest out.* I can hear her voice now. *And lift your head higher, show off your neck.*

"I…" Corin says. I see him swallow again, his Adam's apple moving. "We've forgotten the shampoo."

He ducks out from under the water, runs, and gets it. The shampoo is gloopy, but kind of fibrous, probably made from a root, like the ones we created at Nbutai. We froth some up in our hands, then work it into our hair. I try my best to forget he's here as I lather up the matted mass that is my hair, then try to wash out the suds.

"You need more." Corin transfers some of the shampoo into my hands from his, then works what's left back into his hair. Our eyes meet.

The intensity of his gaze is what gets me. Makes me stop. Makes me forget I'm covered in shampoo. Makes me just stare at him and admire how well-defined his body is. I know I've noticed it before, but not to this extent, not when there are shampoo suds running down his chest. His muscles look firm—so firm I want to touch them, and I'm suddenly taken with the most bizarre—and unlike *me*—urge to run my hands over them.

I swallow hard, alarmed at where that thought came from. I'm not like that. My sister was. She was always talking to Keelie about sex, sharing girly giggles and gossip—but not me.

But *I'm* staring at Corin now. And unexplained energy sizzles through me. The longer I observe Corin's broad shoulders, thick torso, and muscular legs, the weaker my knees get.

Corin stares at me.

I blink, and water crashes into my eyes, stings a little. I am standing under running water, very nearly naked with *Corin*.

Oh Gods.

The muscles in his neck tighten visibly. He moves his lips, as if he's going to say something, but doesn't.

Then he turns away.

I stare at his back. Can see the sunburn on his shoulders. Steam rises around him. The water seems to get hotter. Before I know what I'm doing, I'm reaching my hand out toward him.

My touch makes both of us jump. My hand, squarely in the middle of his shoulder blades. I press my palm flat against his skin. Feel the beads of water between my hand and his back move, and—

He whirls around. "Sev." His voice is low, far lower than I've ever heard. He seems to have difficulty when he tries to swallow again. His eyes widen, still on me, the desire within them obvious.

I feel my breath catch in my throat. This moment. It's important.

"Sev." He takes the smallest of steps toward me, then stops. A second later, his hands touch my shoulders.

Tingles run through me. Before I can register anything else, his lips brush against mine.

FOURTEEN

"PRAY TO ELMIRO."

The moment Nyesha delivers us to the Zharat council meeting, hands push Corin and me to the floor, onto our knees. More hands grab my head, force me to look upward. My eyes sting under the harsh light of a lantern, and the beams are reflected from mirror shards that are arranged in a semi-circle around another doll with a hideous face. But this doll has a dagger bound to its back by a long fibrous piece of sinew, and it's the dagger that I can't stop looking at.

We're back up on the top level of the Zharat caves now, apparently at the end of a tube that didn't make it out of the mountain, but the lava still drained away.

"Pray to Elmiro, the God of Security. Pray to him. Pray to him now," Manning barks the words at us.

Elmiro? I frown, it's that name again, the one I've heard a few times before from the Zharat... And Elmiro is a God? The realization weighs heavy on me. I've never heard any of the Divine Ones' names before. No one in Rahn's group knew them, and I didn't think there was anyone who still did. We thought the knowledge and the names from the ancient culture had been lost—even though we know the signs for all the Journeying Gods, we don't know *their* names. My father once told me the Gods and Goddesses don't mind us no longer knowing their names because they still want us—the Untamed—to win the war. They don't mind being referred to as a collective, or the smaller group of the Journeying Gods. I remember staying up one night thinking about it, wondering if our grouping of the Gods and Goddesses meant that their powers also became a collective force, that they were no longer individuals with independent abilities.

I turn my head as much as the hands will allow, look at Corin, see what he's doing. A man has hold of his head too, makes him look at the mirrors and the flashes of the lantern.

"Ask him for his protection, his safety here," the man holding my shoulders says. He presses down harder.

I look up at the wall, at the mirrors. The fragments are all different shapes and sizes. I swallow hard.

"Ask him!"

I press my lips together for a second, feel the back of my neck get hot under the man's breaths. "I… Please give me your security, your safety." My words get all mixed up, but the men let go of me.

Corin mutters something similar, and then he's free.

We stand up slowly, look from one to another. My lips tingle, and I straighten my dark T-shirt out, so it covers the waist of my black jeans. The doll's eyes watch me, and its gaze makes my stomach feel heavy. I only ate a little of the food that was offered after our shower—sweet flatbread and cold slices of baked yam—but now I wish I hadn't.

"You must learn our customs and fit in," Manning says, appearing from behind the other men. He gestures for us to sit down.

We do, cross-legged on the floor. Corin's knee touches mine. The other men—eight of them—sit with us, making a circle around the center of the room where there are coals and what looks like a metal bin of ashes. But they're stone cold, I can see that, and I remember Nyesha's words about how it's too dangerous to have a fire here, and wonder why they're here at all.

"That means no more being alone together," Manning says. "Nyesha should not have left you to shower alone."

"What?" Corin turns his head fast. "We're *together*, Sev and I. Of course we can be alone if we want to."

But several Zharat men shake their heads. I sit up a little straighter, get a sour taste on the tip of my tongue. I try to rub it off, against the back of my front teeth, but the bad flavor only spreads. And it keeps spreading, until it's all that I can perceive.

"These be our rules. It will upset the Gods if you disobey. If they be upset, they'll activate our Fire Mountain as punishment. We cannot have that," Manning says, looks at me, then Corin. "You ain't married. You mustn't be alone together. Seven's already above the age of marriage. We cannot have unmarried women here."

"All our women need to make babies. We must continue our people," another man says.

I clutch my arms to my chest, stare at him, feel my eyes widen until they hurt. I'm glad I'm sitting down already—that way I can't fall.

Manning nods. "We will hold your welcoming ceremonies tomorrow, make you Zharat officially. Two days later, Seven will marry the strongest warrior who fights for her."

I go cold, try to speak, try to form words, but my mouth won't work. Nothing will. I can't—I look from Manning to the next man. And they're—they're serious.

"*What*?" Corin slams his fist down onto the rock floor.

"You can fight for her," Manning says. "But you

112

won't get her. Seven rescued us, she's got high status now. A lot of men be talking about her already." He pauses. "But, man, you may take as many wives as you wish, so long as you win them. We have a number of girls turning fourteen within the next year who'll all be eligible."

"*Fourteen*?" Corin exclaims.

I stare at the Zharat blankly, my hands limp on my thighs. I'm still stuck on the *Seven will marry the strongest warrior who fights for her* part of the conversation. I turn to Manning, watch as he clasps one of his braids between his thumb and forefinger.

"This is *not* right." There's so much emotion in my voice—raw emotion—that my words shake. I feel sick, feel my insides squeezing together.

Manning just shrugs. "It's our way, woman. And it's us who be the Untamed who've survived; ain't that saying something? We need to produce children quickly. This be the best and most effective way to do it."

Corin stares at me, reaches across, grabs my hand. His eyes narrow as he turns back to Manning. "Seven is not marrying one of your men. She's *with me*."

Manning shakes his head. A few of the men around him glare at us. "No, man, she will marry the strongest man who fights for her, and she will bear his children."

My mouth dries, my chest tightens. Tightens until it's too tight, and then the corners of my vision start to blur and darken.

"But," Corin says. He looks around for a few seconds, then reaches for my hand. No. Not my hand—my stomach. He places his palm there, makes me jump. He's shaking. "She's already pregnant. With *my* child. I told you, we're together. To all intents and purposes, we *are* married."

I freeze, feel pressure in my ears. I want to turn, look at Corin, but I can't move. His hand is still on my stomach, but his fingers seem uncertain.

Manning's nostrils curl. "Warriors bring up other

men's children all the time. Makes no difference. But, with you as a father, I pity that child. He'd be spineless."

"What?" Corin pulls his hand back from my stomach, clenches it into a fist. His knuckles go white, so white that they seem to stand out more in this light.

"It was not you who came to our aid." Manning turns and points at me. "It was Seven. A child might inherit her bravery, but more likely yours. Bravery is usually a male trait. In any case, man, I know you're lying. She is not with child. You would've said before now if she was."

I squirm, but the movement hurts my right shoulder. I'm sweating, sweating so much that I'll probably need another shower straight after this. A proper shower though. I didn't clean my body as much as I should have because Corin was there. I felt self-conscious. And I *need* to get all this grime off.

Corin shakes his head. "This is ridiculous."

"Meeting's over." Manning gets up. "And the Turning's still going on—they can last for days here—so don't think about leaving unless you wanna die. You'd never make it on your own." But then he steps nearer, and there's a darker edge to his voice. "In any case, man, we can't have anyone out there knowing the location of our den. You show any signs of attempting to escape, and I'll kill you. Both of you, *and* Esther."

Suddenly, all eight men draw out long daggers. The flickering torchlight glints off them. My eyes widen. I then realize that neither Corin nor I have our weapons now—they've gone. Lost in the Turning? Or did the Zharat take them before then, when we were sleeping? I can't remember.

I swallow hard, trying to keep my eyes on all the knives at once. It's difficult, makes my head hurt.

"We're going." Corin stands up, pulls me up with him. My legs shake.

The Zharat move, daggers pointing at us.

"We're not leaving the lava tubes, don't worry."

Corin glares at them. "We're just leaving this space. You said the meeting was over, did you not?" There's a cool tone to his voice, a tone that makes me shiver.

Manning nods, and the Zharat men let us leave—surprisingly. Part of me expected them to complain about us going off together, but they don't.

I don't know where we're going, but somehow Corin seems to. He marches us forward, through the doorway with purpose.

"Don't worry," Corin says in an undertone, his arm around me. "We'll find a way around this. We will. *I* will. For the Gods' sake! You're not marrying some creep."

FIFTEEN

A WOMAN—ALSO HEAVILY PREGNANT—
shows Corin to an empty room. Or rather, she calls
it a room. But it's just a section of a wide tube that's
been screened off with furs, and there are many other
'rooms' either side. The partitioned area itself isn't that
big, and I can hear voices—mainly children laughing
and screaming—nearby.

I run my hands along the furs as I follow Corin in.
It's dark in here, but a little natural light filters in, and
there's a torch about ten feet away on the other side of
the fleece partition that sends some light in here.

The pregnant woman stands in the doorway for a few
seconds, looking at me. I know without asking she's
waiting for me to follow her. Even though Manning
let us leave the meeting together, his words ring in my
head, and I glance at Corin. I'm not supposed to be
alone with him.

"Sev's staying with me," Corin says, sitting down.
"You can go." His tone is a little more forceful than I'd
have liked.

The woman blinks a couple of times, opens her
mouth as if she's going to speak, then changes her

mind. We listen to the slaps of her bare feet on the rocky floor as she leaves.

"It will be all right," Corin says.

He reaches toward me, then pulls me onto the ground, next to where he's sitting. Someone's put together a mattress—of sorts: a wad of broad leaves, compacted together so it's a couple of inches thick. It's the only noticeable thing in the room, other than a toilet pot.

Corin's arm goes around me, and his fingers play with my hair over my shoulder. I start to feel strange, kind of dizzy, sitting next to him, so close—after that shower session—but I haven't got the energy to do anything now. I yawn.

"Do you think Esther will be all right?" I can't help the wobble in my voice.

I look up at Corin. He stares straight ahead, chews on his bottom lip for a few seconds.

"Manning said we can see her after their healers have done their work—he was insistent about that, not before. But he doesn't know how long that'll be." He moves his arm from around me, then stretches back on the mattress, groans a little. "I told you the Noir Lands are bad, that we shouldn't have come here."

My shoulders hunker a little. He's right. Corin didn't want to come here. But neither of us knew *this* would happen.

But anyway, it is safe here—isn't it? No Enhanced. And we're with Untamed people. Loads of them.

"Sorry," Corin says a few seconds later. "I'm just stressed. And I need to smoke or something but I'm not leaving you alone now."

I take several deep breaths. *He's* stressed. What about me? He's not the one who's going to have to marry a stranger. But I don't think it has fully settled in yet, that piece of information. I'm not shaky enough.

"What time is it?" Corin asks.

I shrug, and we hear the faint cry of a spirit shrieking.

"Late." That's about as accurate as I can be.

Corin grunts, and neither of us says anything more.

About half an hour later, a hand pulls back the drape from the doorway. Three women stand there. One of them is the pregnant woman from the showers.

"Seven must come with us," she says. "Manning's orders. She cannot stay here. We will put her in with the girls."

I start to get up, but Corin grabs my hand.

"No," he says. "She's staying here."

"But she must sleep—"

"She is staying *here*. Go."

I've never heard so much authority in Corin's voice before, and part of me is shocked by just how much force and power was in those five words. I turn to him, hear his heavy breathing.

"But—" another woman says. She seems to be the only one of the three who isn't pregnant. I look down at my stomach. A part of me wonders if I'll be pregnant soon. The thought does not make me feel any better.

"Go now." Corin stands up, flexes his fingers.

The women disappear, and more spirits outside scream.

He looks at me. "Don't do what they tell you," he says. "Stay with me."

I nod, wondering how easy this will be in practice. What happens when it's Manning and his men standing there? We can't win then. And we can't leave.

You show any signs of attempting to escape, and I'll kill you.

I draw my knees to my chest, curling up until my spine feels funny. The prickly feeling setting out across the bridge of my nose means I'm close to tears. Corin sees, and he sits next to me. Doesn't put his arm around me though, just stares straight ahead.

"It will be all right," he says.

I sniff, don't know how he can say that. It won't be all right. I know that now.

And now it's too late, the countdown has started.

We sleep on the leaf mattress. Or, at least, we try. Both of us lie there, side by side, under a thin blanket, but not touching. Every so often, Corin's breath catches, and he clears his throat loudly. I watch the flickering skylight for hours. When I do get to sleep, I dream of fire and magma. I'm being chased, and serpents' tongues keep getting me. Wherever they touch my skin, they leave huge welting marks, but they're in the shapes of letters. Jagged letters that construct words I don't understand.

And then—then everything changes.

I'm in a room, standing at one side. It's dark, but it's getting lighter. Like the sun is rising, but too quickly. Shapes start to appear. Bulky shapes. A bed, on the far side.

And a man in it. A man chained to it.

I walk closer.

I see his face. What's left of it.

My muscles tense.

I look at his forehead first. He still has the line of blood across his forehead. The line of blood that was the first thing I saw, when he fell. Now, that line of blood is dry, like it's been painted carefully on in permanent dye, and has become part of his skin. My jaw clenches.

Then I force myself to look at the rest of his face.

His left cheek is gone—I knew that—but in my memory, I'd pictured the injuries a lot better than they are. I'd forgotten how much tissue and flesh had been exposed. How you can see his teeth, like little marbles, and the edge of his jawbone, peeking through the gap where his cheek should be.

Something in my stomach shifts, and I feel bile moving, rising up, burning. I cough, and then I'm retching, turning away, insides heaving.

Blinding hot flushes pull through my body, and I reach out for something, anything to steady myself on. My fingers catch onto something—a metal bar—and I grip it, grip it until my knuckles burn.

It's too hot in here. The metal's too hot. I pull my fingers away, and then I realize what I've been holding onto: a trolley. A trolley full of devices and vials and….

I go cold.

Augmenters.

I turn back to my brother, heart pounding.

He's lying there, eyes open, staring. Eyes that are *Untamed*: clear, proper eyes. Eyes that—

I feel something strange wash across the back of my head, like silk, as I look at him. A lump forms in my throat, a lump I can't swallow. I stare at the chains around his ankles and wrists, follow them to the bedposts. There's a blanket over his stomach, folded so it covers most of his abdomen. I am glad. I don't want to see the wound there.

"Three?" My voice cracks, and I reach out for him, my fingers stretching.

But he doesn't react—not to my voice, or my touch—just stares straight up, not moving. I lean over him, try to ignore the injuries, until he's staring into my eyes, and I can see every detail of his face. Every detail that makes my stomach turn again.

"Three! It's me!"

My tears splash down onto his face. I am crying. Crying huge gulps. I pull at his hand, but his hand's just…heavy.

Heavy.

Heavy and *warm*.

I go cold.

No.

His body? No. Can't be… Why bring his body here, when they left so many? Why chain him up if he's… If he's here, he's got to be alive.

Esther was right.

My chest shudders, and I swallow down the rising bile quickly. Pain pulls through me, and I know I've made the biggest mistake of my life—one I'll never be able to forgive myself for.

Oh Gods.

I left him. Left him *here*. In the compound. And we always rescue each other.

Only I didn't.

I didn't even try to rescue Three.

I reach out again, needing confirmation. I press two fingers against the inside of his wrist, and I wait. I listen to the rushing in my ears, feel the pounding of my own heartbeat, and—

There.

I swallow hastily, but saliva goes down the wrong way. Just a trickle. But it's enough. I pull my hand away, and I'm spluttering, eyes streaming. Can't breathe. Can't get any air.

I move backward. Just a step at first. Then another and another. And I'm turning, running. I get to the door. I'm shaking, sweat covers me. And I can't get my fingers to work. My grip just slides off the handle, and I'm crying. Can't open it. Can't get out. But I need to.

I look back, and I don't know why I look back. But I do. And I see Three, my brother. And I see him chained to the bed, and I see his chest rise and fall.

Oh Gods.

Get out.

I flinch, feel something move inside me. And then I manage it: I grab the handle, and I yank the door open. It creaks. But I don't care.

I'm running. It's a corridor. A long hallway with a white marble floor and pale blue walls and a ceiling with too many fluorescent lights that watch me. And there are people. Figures walking up and down, near me, but I don't care.

And—

They're Enhanced.

I slam to a halt. Don't know how I missed their

mirrors. I stare at the nearest person: a young woman. Her eye-mirrors shine.

"How's he doing?"

The voice makes me jump, makes the hairs all over my body stand on end.

No.

I shake my head. No.

But it's his voice. It's *Raleigh's* voice.

He's behind me.

I turn, see him, see him walking toward me. No— not toward me, he's going for the door. The door to Three's room.

Raleigh's with two women. They're holding things. Implements. He nods at one of them, and I wait for him to see me, wait for him to pounce.

But he doesn't. He looks right through me, like I'm not here.

"Yes, his heart is stable now," one of the women says. "Dr. Andy did well. Good, old-fashioned surgery."

I keep watching Raleigh. His countenance looks more youthful than ever—mid-twenties at the most, as if he's somehow younger than he was the last time I saw him. But appearance means nothing, I know that. They use augmenters to stop themselves aging, take off the years, do whatever they want. It makes me wonder how old he really is, and suddenly I see him as an old man, wizened skin, hunched over, trembling.

And then the image is gone.

Raleigh steps into Three's room, and the two women follow.

I hear his words as clearly as if they're spoken in front of me. They resound through me, burn themselves to the insides of my ears.

"Start the facial reconstruction. We'll convert him after."

SIXTEEN

"BUT IT WASN'T A SEEING dream?"

It's dark, yet I know Corin is staring at me. Of course he would be, after what I told him. His words—*a Seeing dream*—pull through me, and I wish he hadn't said that. We're only separated from the next sleeping Zharat by the fur drapes, but what if one of them is awake? What if they hear? What if they kill me?

Maybe you deserve it. You left Three there. And you're not doing a thing to help. You're just holed up in safety.

I shake my head, claw at my skin. I'm soaked, soaked in sweat, and the air's too thick, too muggy. I can't breathe properly.

"Sev?" Corin's voice is soft. Reminds me of velvet. "Was it one?"

"I don't know."

"You didn't see a bison." His voice is low. But not low enough.

"I didn't look for one."

His clothes shuffle as he moves closer, puts an arm around me, pulls me to him. My breath catches in my throat as I rest my head against his chest.

"It's just a nightmare, Sev."

My neck clicks. "But it felt real... It felt...different."

"It can't have been a Seeing dream. They're for warnings of imminent danger that affect the Seer—that affect you. Us."

He's right. That's what Seeing dreams have *always* been for.

"But the one about Raleigh having my eyes was more of a general warning, Corin. And that other See—" I stop myself from saying the word. "That other *dream* I had wasn't about danger *we* were going to be in." I gulp, know I'm speaking too loudly.

Corin pauses. "No. But *that* one was still warning of imminent danger—a conversion attack. Your nightmare tonight wasn't."

I shake my head. "But Raleigh's last words!" *Start the facial reconstruction. We'll convert him after.* "Three's going to be converted. It's the same! It was a warning. A proper warning."

I start to pull away from him, need to get up. Need to get out of here, need to find Three. I try to remember the details of the dream, work out which town Raleigh's got Three in, but everything's blurring together. Mixing life and death and pain and hurt.

"Just calm down." A harder edge creeps into Corin's whisper. "It wasn't a Seeing dream, Sev. You didn't see the bison. It was just a nightmare. You said it yourself, Three's dead."

"But Esther—"

"You don't believe Esther," he says, "because you saw it yourself. He was shot—what was it?—*twice*." He squeezes my shoulder, but it's my bad one, and I flinch. It's been acting up more than usual since we had to run through the Turning. "It was just a nightmare. If the bison was there, the Gods and Goddesses and benevolent spirits would've made sure you saw it. Sev, it was just a bad dream, sent by *evil* spirits, playing with your grief."

I take a shaky breath. My lips feel strange, as if they're buzzing. Like I want to say something, but can't.

"It's just the stress of everything," Corin says. "The battle, the grief, and coming here. What Manning said about you having to marry someone soon."

His words bore into me. I stare at the dark drape ahead, feel pressure in my ears.

The marriage.

Oh Gods. I'd forgotten. How had I forgotten?

"Look, no one else is going to get you," Corin says a moment later. "Manning said we've got two days until the men fight for you. And I'll win—I'll do whatever I have to. And, Sev, nothing will change between us."

My bottom lip quivers.

"I mean it. All that talk of babies—I'm sure as hell not expecting to become a father anytime soon. So it *will* be okay." He pauses for a second, then places his hand over mine. "Nothing will happen that you're not comfortable with."

I find myself nodding, but it doesn't feel real. I wrap my hands in the thin blanket, study the murky impressions of my fingers in them. Then I stare at him, how can he be so sure?

"I mean it, Sev. I promise."

"You shouldn't make promises that you don't know you can keep. No one should." My voice wobbles. "What if you don't win?"

I swallow hard, and I know I'm only asking because I'm trying to distract myself. Distract myself from the *bad dream*.

Corin's voice darkens. "I will. Don't worry about that. Don't worry about anything."

The next morning, the music is loud for our welcoming ceremonies. Too loud. Drums and maracas.

I don't like it. I try to cover my ears as Corin and I walk toward the gathering room—the widest of the tubes—but I can't. The noise is too big, too definite. The drums are like a countdown…a countdown to my brother's conversion.

I swallow hard, feel sick. But it was just a nightmare. Because Corin's right, the bison wasn't there, so it can't have been true.

The Enhanced haven't got Three.

My brother's dead.

And I don't know whether that thought should make me feel any better or not. All it does is make my stomach feel uncomfortable; I'm glad I haven't had any food yet. I don't feel hungry at all, don't feel like I can ever eat again.

"It's all right," Corin says, but he doesn't sound like he thinks it's all right now.

The moment we get to the gathering room, Manning pulls us over to the side. His braids are greasier today—like he's oiled them—and his hairline appears to have receded even farther since last night. He's also holding the hand of a small child who looks vaguely like him, and two other young boys follow us at a distance. Their hair is the exact same shade as Mart's,

Manning's eyes narrow, flicker between Corin and me. "I hope this ain't a sign of things to come."

"What do you mean?" Corin keeps his voice neutral.

Manning glares at Corin, then at me. "Disobeying rules."

Three men step up around Manning, flanking him, and the children shrink away to the far side, where many more sit.

"I'll let it go once." Manning's eyes brush over me. Tingles run down my spine. "But this evening, and tomorrow night, Seven will sleep in the space for the unwed girls."

I feel Corin tense up next to me.

"But after that, she'll be with me," he says. "Just like she should be."

Just like she should be.

There's something about Corin's words—or maybe his tone, I don't know—that makes me shudder a little. Like I've got no say in this. But I know Corin has got my best interests at heart. The Zharat men haven't.

Manning's lips curl. "After that, Seven'll be married. She'll spend the nights with the warrior who wins her."

"Which will be me." Corin stands a little straighter.

Manning smirks. "I advise you not to be so flippant with me again, man. I could have you punished for spending the night together, but I won't."

"How very kind of you." Corin's voice drips with darkness.

Manning doesn't reply, just holds Corin's gaze for a while. I stand there, uncomfortable, shift my weight from foot to foot. A lot of people are looking at us now; they've stopped, formed small groups around the gathering room. Even the music has quieted down.

"If you disobey our rules again, we'll kill you," the man to the right of Manning says. He looks a lot like Manning: the same hooked nose. A brother, maybe. He bares teeth that have been filed into points.

Manning smiles before stepping nearer to him. The two men exchange words for several moments, and everyone else is silent. I look at Corin. He gives me a smile that I think is supposed to be reassuring. Manning and the other man step away from each other, and the Zharat Chief leaves, calls several small children to him on the way out.

The man with the pointy teeth turns his gaze on Corin. "You, get over there. And you," he barks at me, then points behind him. "Over there. We will start the welcomings soon, and you need to get ready."

Corin's arm around my shoulder gets heavier. Then we're pulled apart. Hands grab me—male hands—and force me away from Corin, steering me to the right, behind the men.

"Hey!" Corin shouts. "Don't touch her! Get off her—

don't touch her!"

I twist around, see him disappearing behind a new crowd of Zharat.

"Behave," a low voice snarls into my ear.

I nod.

The men take me to the back of the gathering room. The black rock here isn't as smooth underfoot, and there are huge boxes near the wall. A woman sits on one of them. I breathe a little deeper. Just the sight of her makes me a little more comfortable. She looks friendly, and she smiles at me—might be the first Zharat I've seen smile, after Nyesha. Maybe all the women are happier than the men. Then I remember Clare.

This woman has blond hair, clear skin, and a petite frame. She's probably about Esther's age, or maybe a bit older.

Then I notice she's got the beginning of a baby bump under her pale orange shirt, and it makes my chest tighten a little. All the women here seem to be pregnant or nursing, as if that's our only function as women. I swallow, uneasy.

"Get her ready." The man holding me shoves me toward the woman. "Find a suitable outfit for her. Manning's decided she's to wear the best red." He seems to relish saying those words, as if it's a big announcement.

Behind me, I hear several sharp intakes of breath and low murmurings.

The man grins as he leaves.

The woman smiles. "I'm Soraya."

"Seven," I say, a little wary. I try not to look at her stomach, then realize I'm subconsciously covering my own with my arms.

"I know your name," she says. The dark circles under her eyes make her face seem smaller. She turns her head, looks back out toward the rest of the room.

I follow her gaze, then search for Corin. Or any signs of him. But I can't see him. They've probably taken him far away—he'd still be shouting after me. I press my hands together in my lap; they're clammy.

"Come on," Soraya says. "You have to look good for your welcoming, else the Gods might not let you become Zharat. I've still got my dress from my ceremony. It's a sort-of red." She sizes me up, and the way she looks at me suddenly makes me think of my brother. She has the same look in her eyes as Three had when he was making radios.

I look away quickly.

"Yes," Soraya says, "the dress should fit. I've never been as high status as you, even when I was new here, but the color will do—I don't know if anyone's still got a full dress that's really bright red anyway, so the Gods will understand. But we can accessorize it. Adhylia and Keicha have both got some red ribbons they'll lend you, I'm sure. And my dress will look lovely on you. You've got the right figure. Though you're tall, aren't you? It might be a bit short."

The deep-orange dress is very short—though it has a high neckline that covers my Seer pendant beneath the fabric—and I don't think it's done up correctly at the back. Doesn't feel secure. There's also a stain—a stain that Soraya tells me is her blood—down the front, marring the ornate embroidery work and beading. But there's nothing I can do now because our welcoming ceremonies are starting. Anyway, it's not that noticeable. What's more noticeable are the neon orange ribbons in my hair—Soraya's face had dropped when she found she'd remembered the color incorrectly—and the fluorescent pink bands around my wrists that another woman, Olive, found for me. She told me it was important to emphasize my status to the Gods in my welcoming, but the red flower tucked in my hair is barely noticeable, and Olive seemed worried as she left.

Four older children are playing the drums now; they keep a monotonous beat going. There's a lot of light in here with the amount of bulbs that are rigged up across the tube's ceiling, and I don't like it. It's disorientating, and the brightness burns my eyes.

Huge red and black curtains hang along several walls, and furs and hides are spread over the center of the floor in a perfect circle. People—so many of them—thickly line the walls, all standing in silence.

"Welcome." Manning stands in the center of the circle of furs, his arms spread wide. He wears a long black cloak, and his braids look like the ends have been dipped in tar. Then he looks at me, takes in my appearance, and frowns. "Why ain't you wearing a red dress? That's your color—the best red, the brightest red, woman. Marcus said he passed on the message. Could no one find you one? There must be one…" He looks around then points at a woman who's wearing a purple frock. "What happened to the gown you had six years ago?"

She squeaks something back in a voice that sounds like it hasn't been used in just as many years, then steps back, allowing the crowd to swallow her.

Manning turns to me, disapproval written on his face. "You've gotta dress appropriately for your status, woman, else you'll lose it. You must wear something red all the time, but you must wear more red for the Gods, in the ceremonies. Make an effort. I'll make sure your status be apparent this time, but from now on, dress in your rightful color. *Red*." His eyes narrow, but, before I can say anything, he inclines his head toward the space next to him. "Stand there."

I walk over there, heart pounding. Everyone is watching. There are a lot of people squashed in, but I know not all the Zharat are here. Soraya told me that a lot will be preparing the feast, that it's a privilege to be told by the chief that you can be involved in preparation for a welcoming—let alone a double ceremony—and most of the children will be in the nursing chamber, out of the way. The Gods apparently don't like many children present in ceremonies.

I also asked Soraya about Esther, but the Zharat woman didn't know anything, other than that healers can't be interrupted. She was confident that when Esther's awake, Manning will tell me and Corin.

A quick flick of my head tells me Jed is the nearest person I recognize, besides Manning. Soraya seems to have melted into the wall. And Corin… I can't see him. I press my lips together, try to remain calm.

Manning smiles at me as I reach his side—but it is not a smile I want to receive. I stand a few feet from him. I look around. But everyone's quiet. They're all watching me. I try to think: am I supposed to do something? When Soraya sorted out the orange dress for me, she told me my part in the ritual would be self-explanatory, but now everyone's staring at me expectantly, and I don't know what to do.

Manning turns to me, and the tarry ends of his braids glisten under the bright light.

"Where's Corin?"

I feel my heart rate rise. What if he's gone, escaped? But he wouldn't, would he? He wouldn't just leave… He wouldn't leave me and Esther here….

"I don't know."

A man steps forward, and my eyes are drawn to the bison tattoo on his forehead. One of the Zharat Seers. I know I'm right, though I can't spot a pendant around his neck. No crystal anywhere that I can see… But it doesn't just have to be crystal does it? My mother said something about it once, but I curse silently, can't remember. I never paid much attention to her Seer talk before, because I only became one after she left—after she surrendered herself to the Enhanced to save Rahn and Corin. Hidden under my dress, my Seer pendant radiates a flash of warmth, and, for a moment, I'm terrified that this Zharat Seer has recognized me, that he knows what I am.

I hold my breath, then swallow hard.

But the man isn't looking at me. He has a small drum—skin stretched over a bone frame—attached to his waist, and now he beats it with what looks like a small bird's leg bone. But his rhythm is out of time with the children's, and the sounds grate on my ears.

"This be unfortunate, woman." It's the worst lie Manning's told yet.

My stomach clenches, my eyes water a little. I look around again, searching for Corin. But there are so many people in here now, and the only ones who stand out are Manning and the Seer.

A baby starts crying.

"Sorry I'm late."

I turn at Corin's voice, see him pushing through a group of blue-clad women. He looks a little sweaty, as if he's been rushing around.

Corin smiles broadly as he joins Manning and myself in the center of the room. His eyes meet mine, and—for a second—I'm sure he's trying to tell me something. But I've no idea what. I just concentrate on stilling my shaking legs, and trying not to fall over.

Manning turns and addresses his people in words I don't understand. There are nods. A few shakes of the head.

Then Manning turns back to us, indicates for us to stand closer together. We do. Corin's arm brushes against mine. I shiver a little.

"You must stand still," Manning says. He pauses between each word as though he's having trouble breathing. "Moving will fail your initiation. Both of you."

My heart races.

"Initiation?" Corin says.

"Stand still. We can't afford to have stupid people in our tribe."

I stand still. As still as I can. I look straight ahead,

then I pick out Nyesha from the crowd. She's wearing a beautiful yellow dress—where the color gets brighter as it moves to the hem—and she looks tense, her eyes focused on a spot somewhere behind me.

I listen, not daring to move. There's rustling. It fills my ears. Murmurs. And footsteps. I hone in on those, my breaths getting louder. More footsteps, closer now. I glance at Manning, then at the Seer, careful not to move my head, and—

A knife skims my ear.

I narrowly avoid screaming, force myself not to move just as another blade whizzes past me. Out of the corner of my eye, I see Corin flinch. But I can't turn my head toward him, can't check he's okay.

"Get down!" the Seer yells, and then he is a blur of falling movement.

I throw myself down onto the furs. But they don't help much. I crash into the stone floor. Pain in my chest and bad shoulder. I drag huge gulping breaths of ragged air in, tensing slightly. A moment later, I raise my head, listening. Footsteps again. But they're leaving, not approaching us.

Corin's lying next to me, also on his stomach. The Seer's on his side, watching us. His eyes are dark and beady. Like a hawk. A hawk who perpetually watches as he circles, never missing a thing.

Slowly, the Seer stands.

The Zharat start clapping. A low rumble.

I stay lying on the floor, my elbows poking out, in case I need to spring up at any second. I think Corin is in the same position, but I'm too scared to turn.

"Stand." The Seer's voice is loud.

Corin and I jump up in unison. I grab at my dress, pull the hem back down.

Manning lips peel back a little. "Well done." His tone is cynical. "You can take orders without questioning."

He beckons toward the crowd, and two men step forward. They are both holding knives. A woman follows them. She has a small bowl in her hands. I strain my neck to see what is in it: some sort of black liquid. Her hair is piled up high on her head, in loose plaits. She is dressed in a dark red hue that borders on brown. Both men wear loincloths. Nothing else. The sight of so much of their skin makes me uneasy, yet I know it's silly. I showered with Corin, and he was just wearing his boxers. It's not that much different.

But these men are huge. Their muscles bulge from them, make them look unnatural. And they're covered in tattoos.

"Sit down."

Corin and I do as instructed, and Manning addresses the gathering room in that strange language. I turn my head, look at Corin. He frowns a little, then straightens his expression as Manning turns back to us.

"You will have our sign on you now," Manning says to us. "And you will begin to learn the Zharat language tonight. The Seers say that the Gods have accepted you."

I start to nod, but the men with the knives are suddenly so close. One seizes my arm. His fingers are surprisingly short, chubby, and—

He stabs the knife into the inside of my elbow.

Sharp, hot pain fills me. I scream, but my scream cuts off as Corin's loud grunt fills the room. My head pounds as I turn to look at him. I see the blood, oozing across his arm. Across my arm. Down onto Soraya's dress. A strange sensation fills my ears.

The woman with the bowl steps forward, and the second man dips his forefinger into the bowl. Dark ink drips from his finger as he raises it. Then he smears it over my arm, over the fresh cut. I gasp, pain. Stinging.

"Hereby, Seven Sarr's welcomed to us." Manning sounds strangely enthusiastic about what he's saying. "She now be Seven Sarr of the Zharat. Seven's a highly ranked woman, of the *best red*, proven herself courageous and brave, worthy. A valued asset. She also be unblessed. Any men who wish to fight for her have two days, starting now, to make a formal proposal through me."

My breath hitches, but I try to remain calm, remind myself to breathe.

"Welcome, Seven Sarr of the Zharat!"

There's a loud cheer, and I don't know where to look. So I look at Corin and continue to as Manning welcomes him to the Zharat.

I can't help but notice that the cheer for Corin's welcoming is not as big as it was mine. But he doesn't look annoyed. He looks like he's barely noticed.

He turns, smiling warmly at me. Very warmly. So warmly that my skin begins to crawl. I frown.

Corin claps his hands three times. I frown, hadn't realized we were supposed to do anything more. I start to raise my hands.

"What is this?" Manning shouts. His face is red.

The Seer's suddenly by my side, trying to push Corin away from me.

"No, Sev!" Corin shouts.

I see him thrust his hand toward me. I see what's in his hand.

My head jerks up. I focus on his eyes. Warmth floods me. My mouth dries, my chest feels strange, too light. I can't breathe. The room's starting to spin, and all the Zharat faces whirl around me. Around me and Corin, and his hand with the—

"Marry me, Seven."

SEVENTEEN

THE RING IS SIMPLE, SILVER. One jewel. Pale green with a mauve aura. Like some of the ones I saw in the lava walls.

It's a Zharat ring. Somehow that seems significant....

He doesn't really want to marry you. He's only proposing because the situation has forced him to.

My next breath grates against my throat. I feel beads of sweat line the back of my neck, my spine, my legs. My Seer pendant feels strangely cold. I swallow hard, look up. The bulbs are pools of white light that try to blind me. My head fills with a jarring sensation.

"Sev?" Corin's eyes are urgent.

I look at the ring again, feel something strange within me. Something I can't put my finger on.

"Yes." The word jolts out of me.

Then—I don't know, the next few moments...well, too much happens. I can't take it all in. All I can do is stare at the ring as Corin slides it onto my finger. It's a little big, and it twists around so that the jewel is hidden from sight.

My chest feels strange, my Seer pendant burns.

Manning's shouting. A lot of the Zharat are shouting.

"We are now engaged," Corin announces. "So there's no point continuing with this warrior fight for *my* fiancée." His voice is loud, and it's as if he's speaking more to them than me. It's a public announcement. Not at all private or special like it's supposed to be.

I stiffen as there's another collective intake of breath. Somewhere in the distance, a spirit shrieks. The Turning, it's still going on. Manning said before they can last for days.

"*No,*" Manning says. "Seven's *not* engaged."

"But she accepted." Corin's grip on my hand gets tighter. "She wants to be with me."

I nod. "We're together."

Manning's eyes narrow. "Your engagement means nothing here." His brow seems to get heavier as he glares at Corin. "Proposals must be made through me. I told you, respect our traditions. Though I'll note your interest, and you can fight for her—I doubt you'll win though, man. Not with the amount of attention she be garnering."

Corin shakes his head. "It's not right that Sev can't choose who she wants to be with it. Not right for any woman. What if—"

"Seven will gladly wed the strongest suitor." Manning's eyes narrow even further. "He will be able to provide for her and her children the most efficiently. It is an effective system. Your engagement means nothing here," he repeats. He looks at me. "Take the ring off."

Shivers run down my spine. The back of my front teeth taste bad. And the Zharat mark on my arm stings.

"Take it off *now.*"

I hold the chief's gaze for as long as I can, before I do.

"Take this as a warning," Manning says in a low voice to Corin. Then he turns to the rest of his people— *our* people. "All *official* valid proposals and requests must be made through me, as always."

There's a murmur, several men nod. I start to feel

very sick.

"Good." Manning claps loudly. He speaks a few words in his language, then a few in ours. "We will now welcome Seven Sarr and Corin Eriksen. Let the celebrations begin."

The next few hours pass in a blur of dancing, drinking, and celebrating that I cannot get away from. Several times, I tried to get near Corin, squeezing between all the hands that kept grabbing me, but no one would let me near him. And then he seemed to disappear.

A woman now informs me that Corin went off in a mood after he asked Manning to tell him where Esther is, and Manning told him, in no uncertain terms, that he must not visit Esther until she's awake, and the healers have finished, and he's been given permission—and that Corin will be taken to his sister as soon as this is the case. Understandably, that made Corin angry. And it doesn't make me feel any better now.

I swallow hard, trying not to be overwhelmed by the atmosphere. I head over to the food tables, survey the options: celery, white potatoes, peas, beans, dried strips of meat that look like bushbuck. As I stand there, a woman pushes past me, sets new pans of steaming food down. It's orange, thick, gloopy.

"Yam pottage," she says. "Miran's just bringin' some more wholegrain sorghum. He's just gone out to collect it; it's been cookin' for a while."

"Gone out?" I echo her words faintly. "*Outside*?" Isn't the Turning still going on?

I immediately have visions of spirits tearing limbs from men, and it does nothing for my appetite.

The woman nods. "Aye. Outside. Up to the grill. Can't cook in these tubes, dear. We just do the preparation here, grindin' the sorghum, the mixin' ready for the bakin', the choppin', the butcherin'— that sort. The men have been goin' back and forth all mornin' to the grill. Won't let us women out in the Turning."

I stare at her. "But they're going out in the *Turning*?"

I see the spirits again, hear the sounds of glass shattering, see that man being killed, the blood. My stomach tightens.

"Aye. Not ideal," she agrees. "But Mannin' wanted the welcomings today so we had to have feasts cooked up. Anyway, on his last trip, Miran said the Turnin' looks like it's comin' to an end. They can stop pretty abruptly here nowadays."

She turns, heads back. I bite my lip, watch her get lost in the crowds.

In the end, I go for some sort of sorghum flat bread, thinking it will be a neutral flavor. I can't stomach anything strong at the moment. As I chew, I somehow get caught up in a conversation about how they only just managed to get the latest yam seed tubers planted before the *many* Turnings began.

The old man nods, smiling a semi-toothless grin. "You have to get 'em tubers in the mounds at the start of the rainy season, you see?" He wrings his hands out in front of him. "And the rainy season's always worse for spirits. My grandson nearly got caught out once, nearly got trapped too far from the tubes when the sky turned purple…."

After a while, his words seem to drain away. It's noisier now too, so busy, more drums. I push through the crowds, need to find Corin again. But there are people everywhere. I head into a new room, see Nyesha on a bench in the corner, breastfeeding a baby. But after a quick surveillance, I see Corin's not here.

I set off back down the tube, in the direction I think leads to the area with the drape divisions, where most people sleep. I take the second branch on the right. I pause for a second, my eyes lingering on the nearest torch. Its flickering light is therapeutic. I take a deep breath and keep going.

But the more I walk, the longer the tubes seem to get before they branch off and the more certain I am that I'm going the wrong away.

The pounding music becomes a distant hum, but the ground beneath my bare feet is hot and still pulses. I keep walking, taking the next right turn and then the following left. But I should have got to Corin's room by now, I am certain. Biting my lip, I turn back and look down the tube. It looks darker than it did when I came up here; the torches are growing dimmer, and everything's melting into shadows.

I keep going. Logic tells me I can't be lost in these tubes forever, but my head tells me something else. Still, I keep walking ahead. I *should* turn back. I *should* try and find the gathering room… But I don't. I keep walking.

A few minutes later, I hear voices ahead—loud voices, shouting—and I falter. Their tones are deep and gravely. Male voices. I feel adrenaline pouring through my body. They're close. Very close.

I want to turn back. I should turn back. I need to turn back.

Then I see them: eight Zharat men, each wearing very little clothing, showing off their muscles and tattoos—not that any of them have many of each. They're heading straight for me, eyes lit up with interest. I recognize one as Mart—his red hair is obvious—but that's it.

I lift my head higher, place one foot in front of the other, don't meet their eyes. I force myself to keep going—need to seem confident—and hope that they won't stop me, that they'll let me continue on through the tube.

"Come and join us, *Sev*!" one of them shouts. He's holding a cup, and dark liquid sloshes over the sides.

"Let us welcome you here *properly*."

Several laugh, and Mart shouts something I can't make out. I shudder, keep walking.

Can't show fear. Mustn't show fear.

I concentrate on my breathing.

Six feet away. Five feet away. Another one yells something at me, but it's in the other language, in Zharat. I glance at their faces. They're leering at me. I clench my fists by my sides, trying to mask my shaking.

"Come on, Seven. Come with us. If you're good, we'll even feed you."

More raucous laughter.

Others join in. The shortest one makes a gesture at me; he's the one who's the most clothed, but even his garments don't cover much. I look away. But my pace has slowed.

And now they're right in front of me, spreading out, blocking my way.

I stop, realize I should've run when I had the chance. Oh Gods. I look around, but there's no one else here. Just them. And me.

"Seven! Come and play!" One of them yells at me, his face contorting as if he's in pain.

"Take my ring as well!" Mart yells.

"Aaaaand mine!"

They grab me.

I kick out. But there are too many of them. Another hand's on my back. I turn and hit at the man behind me, but he just laughs, and my movement's too slow, clumsy. Automatically, my hand reaches for a weapon in my belt… But I'm wearing the dress, the dress that's too short. And there's no weapon.

Oh Gods.

I scream, lunge forward, feint to the right, step backward. But there are too many of them. I see a pair of teeth getting closer, snapping, snapping, and I'm reminded of how my terrier tore a chunk out of Raleigh's arm.

The men's hands pull at me.

"Oh, Seven, you're so beautiful! Look at her!"

"Can't see much," Mart says, and his red hair drips with grease. He suddenly looks more like Manning—he is the chief's son, isn't he?

"Get the dress off."

They push me up against the cave wall; cold stone presses against my back. I try to turn, try to get a kick in somewhere, but I miss. I'm too slow, too weak. One of them gets my hands, forces them above my head. Eyes leer at me.

I feel skin against my leg, and I jerk my knee upward, aiming for one man's crotch, but he moves, laughing. More hands push my dress up. I scream loudly.

"Oh, look—you're not as brave and courageous now, are you?" Mart says, and his eyes fill with mock sympathy. "Poor, little—"

"*S'ven*!"

"Hey!"

The men all turn, and I see the other people coming. Men and women, a child?

And then the man next to Mart grabs me, his hands around my throat. He shoves me into the wall again. Something sharp cuts my back. I struggle, eyes watering, try to pull his hands away from my throat. But can't. He's too strong. And my arms—they're too heavy.

I gasp, his fingers dig into my skin. Nails, sharp. Pain. I choke, spluttering. A string of phlegm flies from my mouth. Can't breathe.

"Leave her!" a female voice shouts.

And then more are shouting. And male voices—ones I recognize.

The man lets go of my throat, but a hand suddenly grabs me around my upper arm, pulls me to the right. I scream. Stumble, fall, and it's—

It's Jed.

And Manning. And others. Others I don't recognize. Women, who don't look happy.

Jed lets me go, then strides forward, limping badly. His staff is gone. Then he punches the nearest man.

The man falls, sprawls backward.

Manning grabs another man by the arm, shouts at him. Others are fighting.

"Take her back." Manning points at Jed.

I turn to Jed, shaking. He smiles at me, his dark skin shiny with perspiration.

"Come on." He holds his hand out, and I smell alcohol on him. But it's on everyone, that smell. It's on me.

I go with him, chest pounding.

"Are you hurt?" His voice is thick.

I shake my head, speed up. Can hear Manning shouting at the men.

"Come on," Jed says. "We will get you sorted."

EIGHTEEN

JED HANDS ME A CUP of something warm, once I've finished changing into the red T-shirt and dark pair of jeans he found that are both roughly my size. He turned away when I put them on, and I was glad, but the fear that he somehow might've seen my Seer pendant before I made sure it was safely tucked out of sight is high.

"I am sorry those are not red." He indicates the charcoal denim of my jeans as we sit down on the floor, facing each other. "But I have asked for some red clothes to be made for you. Some day-dresses. They should be ready soon. I did not realize we were so short, but like with any clothes they get holes and need repairing. And, if a high-status woman dies, it is not unusual for some of her clothes to be sent off with her so the Gods know her power and take her directly to the New World. That must be why we are running out of them."

Jed's eyes are still wild, but his overall expression is calmer. He presses his hands to his injured thigh for a few seconds, grimaces. But the action makes me feel better. He's hurt, so he can't hurt me.

"It's fine," I say. I feel more comfortable in jeans anyway.

We're in a small room off one of the lava tubes. And it's a proper *room*, with proper walls—I almost can't hear the music from here; the near-silence makes me feel calmer. Calmer than I should.

We're alone. The thought sends chills through me, and, for some reason, I think of Raleigh. That doesn't make me feel any better.

I flinch.

Jed's drawn the drape across the doorway, enclosing us in the space together. Something tells me despite what Manning said about their rules, if he heard I was alone with Jed he wouldn't make half the fuss that he had when it involved Corin.

Corin. I bite my lip a little. He won't like that I'm here alone with Jed. Jed who was so antagonistic toward him.

"Are you sure you are okay?" Jed looks at me, eyes scanning.

I nod, take a sip of the drink. It tastes peppery, but after a few minutes my head's not hurting as much. In fact, all the pain starts to go. My skin tingles, a little numb, but it feels better. I drink some more of the peppery water.

Jed watches, his expression neutral. I look at his eyes, so dark, and the deep grooves around them; the tattoos there look paler now—grayer—and smaller as if the animals have shrunk. I study them. Lizards. An antelope. Goats. The animals disappear under his collar.

"You've got lots of tattoos," I say, then I feel silly for stating the obvious.

Jed smiles, then pulls his sleeve up, revealing more ornate patterns. "Tattoos are a sign of our power. Our status. Only, unlike most men here, I do not feel the need to constantly wear skillfully knotted rags that show off my tattoos and reinforce my status. Manning neither." He pauses. "Everyone knows he is Chief, and he only shows off his torso tattoos if his status needs to be emphasized or displayed to newcomers. Manning and me, we only take our clothes off when it is important. Only the men who are less secure in their own power wear less clothing all the time. Intimidation. Their method of dominance."

I nod, then frown. "I haven't seen any women with tattoos."

His smile gets deeper, rivals Nyesha's. "Tattoos are a symbol of *male* power. Female power is marked through the color of their clothing—that is why us men wear dark or neutral tones. Girls usually inherit a starting color from their mothers, when they are six years old—before that, girls may wear what they like." He pauses. "The colors are ranked in their hierarchy based on the bands of the rainbow. Red is the highest, violet is the lowest. And the brightest red indicates the highest female status—*you*. That is why Manning was upset earlier—you were wearing an inferior color, and it would have indicated a lower status to the Gods, dropped your rank—and in your welcoming ceremony too! But Manning asserted your status to the Gods—so do not worry. Just remember, he cannot do that again. And not in day-to-day life. You must dress appropriately."

I frown, thinking of the yellow wrap-dress Nyesha was wearing the first time I met her and how I've not seen her wear another color. I lean forward. "So I *always* have to wear red then?"

Jed nods. "You must always wear something red over your heart. Most women wear day-dresses of their color *all* the time, but shirts are acceptable too. Just make sure your other garments are always dark—grey or black—so you are not introducing another status-color as well, as that would weaken your position, and your rank would subsequently drop. It is very hard for a woman's rank to increase. That is why women must guard what they are given."

I nod. "Right. So a red dress, or a red shirt and dark

clothes…" Then I frown. "Do any women try and wear a color that indicates a better status? I know I can't if I'm already red, but…."

He shakes his head, anger suddenly in his eyes. "No. If a woman does that, and her new rank has not been authorized, her greed will anger the Gods, risk them activating our Fire Mountain." A slight pause. "Be careful though, S'ven. Some women may be jealous of your status. They might leave out clothes of a lesser hue for you, in the hope that you would wear those garments and your rank would become that color."

I frown. That hadn't been what Soraya had done, was it? Tried to trick me into losing status?

"Don't worry, Soraya is kind," Jed says, as if reading my thoughts. "She did not do that on purpose, I am sure. And you still had the red flower in your hair. That helped." He reaches forward and touches it, then pulls it out. "Your status is safe. Manning made sure of that. Just make sure you protect it from now on."

His eyes widen as he tucks the flower back in my hair.

"You have an inquisitive mind, S'ven. Like my youngest daughter, Jeena. But you also look like my oldest, Zoe." Jed looks away. "She and my wife were killed in a hunt two years ago…and then my son died a year later, fell down the mountain… My youngest daughter, Jeena, is the only one left. I have been affected badly by grief. Lost a lot of myself. For a second, back there, with those men, I thought you were Zoe."

He tries to smile, but I get the feeling darkness is trying to overwhelm him now.

"Tell me about your family," he says.

I shudder, feel the air around me go cold. "My father's either dead or Enhanced. Same with my siblings." I swallow hard, try not to think of Three… and how I've left him with the Enhanced. *No.* "My mother's Enhanced."

Jed nods. "Then we have something in common. My

parents both converted when I was seven years old."
There's darkness in his voice now that I don't like.

I look up. "They didn't take you with them?"

Jed shakes his head. "It was my father… I can
understand why he did not want the girls, but I
thought I was important. He named me after him…"
Then he looks at me. "The Zharat renamed me when
they found me because I could not bring myself to say
my name when it was his."

The look in his eyes gets sharper; he's staring
at my chest. No. Not my chest, at the shape of the
Seer pendant beneath my T-shirt. I pull my knees
up quickly and rest my chin on them, blocking the
pendant from his sight. He asked if the pendant was
calcite crystals before. But he can't suspect what I am
because he hasn't tried to kill me.

"It was as if he knew something—knows something,"
Jed says. "I still hear his voice. My father's voice. He
tells me things, and I know I am going mad… But I
still follow what he says… He must know stuff, and
I want to hope that he is trying to tell me what will
happen, that he *does* want to save me."

His words make me feel even more uncomfortable,
because I don't understand what he's talking about,
but something stops me from asking.

Jed coughs. "I would never leave my children like
that…out in the open. We were lucky the Zharat found
us…" He turns, a far-away look in his eyes. Then he
takes the now-empty cup from me, places it next to
him. "They will not get away with it—those men who
tried to hurt you. Manning will punish them. Even
Mart, his son. But the men will blame it on the drink
and the party. They always do." His eyes darken. "It is
safer for females not to walk around here alone."

His words hang between us, and I swallow hard.

I want Corin. But the walls are heavy, shutting me
away from him. My chest hitches. More nausea. My
legs are shaking.

"Come on," Jed says. "I am supposed to collect the

next food from the grill. I believe they are cooking the freshwater crab now. They got them from the lakes a few days ago. We will go and get them."

I stand up, shaking. "But what about the Turning?" My words are slow, a little groggy. I blink hard.

"It is coming to an end," Jed says, sounds certain. He reaches into the shadows and pulls out a rucksack, then he slings it onto his back. A moment later, he grabs a thick stick, uses it to help him walk with more ease. "The spirits will be going back to the skies. And we are not going far. The Gods will protect us as we are getting food for the welcomings, and a lot will be left for them tonight. Come on."

My skin burns as I follow him, and my chest gets tighter and tighter.

Words begin to whisper their way to me, but they don't feel right, and I can't think, can't understand them. Everything feels different, as if I'm floating. Yes. That's right. Or swimming. I picture a leaf floating carelessly down a stream, start to smile. Part of me wants to laugh. I frown. I don't know why.

It doesn't take us long to get to the entranceway that leads up the mountain to the grill, and I listen to the *click click click* of Jed's stick all the way. It's a different entranceway from the one we came in through. This one is nearer to Jed's room, and there's a man sitting at it, cross-legged. Fresh air blows against my skin, makes me shiver, but it's a good kind of shiver.

"Bring me some food," the man says to Jed.

Jed says something back, but his words blur in my ears. Then he steers me through the entranceway, a hand lightly on my upper back.

I start to slow, drag my fingers against the rough volcanic rock. There's something…something somewhere…something that's trying to tell me….

I frown. But then the breeze pulls through my hair, lifting it. It feels good. Fresh.

I step outside, after Jed.

Click. Click. Click.

The sky is still purple in places, but it's the remnants of the Turning. No shrieks fill my ears, and I hold a hand up to the weak sun, trying to see any lingering spirits. But there are none. It's just cloudy with a hint of purple, low sun intensity. It is safe. The Turning has ended quickly.

"It is this way." Jed uses his stick to hold back foliage, points uphill with his right hand. He sways for a few seconds, but doesn't lose his balance.

I follow Jed up there, my eyes glossing over. I stare at the plants. Something tells me I know their names, and I search for them. But thinking makes my head hurt. So I just look at them. Most are moist, broad-leaved plants that creep low. But there are taller ones too.

And thistles. Nettles. Yes, those names come to me.

The air is humid, thick. And the light is bright, even looking at the ground. I take a few steps forward, eyes still on the ground.

I turn around, look, can't see much. We're on the side of a mountain, not that far up. The ground is surprisingly dry. Sandy and dry. Weathered volcanic rock? I stare at it. It shouldn't be that dry—not after the rain, the Turning. I frown.

But the more I stare at it, the more my eyes blur, as if I'm looking through water. I touch the back of my neck. The skin there is hot. I take a deep breath of fresh air, feel a little better.

I focus on the trees ahead. I recognize them… And—

And my sister is there. By the trees. Standing by the trees. It's Five.

My eyes widen.

She shakes her head.

Don't go up there.

And then—

Then she's gone.

I stop. Feel a little sick. I touch my forehead lightly. My skin is lined with a thin layer of sweat. I swallow hard. The spirits are still messing with me.

"Come on," Jed calls. He's walking fast for someone with a stick. Very fast.

Or maybe I'm slow.

Yes. I *am* slow. My legs are heavy. But as I walk they get lighter. We get into denser foliage, follow the path up as it winds.

"It is just up there." Jed points ahead. "See, it is—"

Raleigh has your eyes.

I flinch, go cold. Feel thousands of pins diving into my skin, everywhere. My chest tightens. My eyes widen a little, and I try to fight through the fog in my head, try to remember....

I see him.

I see Raleigh.

He's sitting in a plush, green armchair, watching everything I see on a giant screen. I see his lips twist into a smile, hear him murmur something about his *darling butterfly.*

I swear loudly.

My body jolts.

Raleigh.

Don't ever lead the Enhanced Ones toward the village, no matter how scared you are. Sacrifice yourself.

I go even colder. My breath comes in short, sharp bursts.

Raleigh. My eyes.

How did I...?

How? I touch my head. The drink... I had alcohol at the party... But that—oh Gods. I shake my head, and a fraction of pain rebounds back.

The ground. Oh Gods. Got to keep looking at the ground.

"S'ven?" Jed must've stopped, I can't hear him walking now. "What are you doing?"

My arms jerk out a little. Oh Gods.

Run! Get back to the cave!

And I do. I turn, and I run. And, trying not to look at anything else, I pray I haven't compromised the Zharat's safety.

NINETEEN

"WHY DIDN'T YOU TELL ME earlier?" Corin demands the moment I tell him what happened with the men.

But I haven't told him about my walk outside with Jed, and a part of me is glad; Corin's angry enough. If he knew I'd put us all in danger… I swallow hard. If I've compromised the safety of the Zharat den, then I should tell him. I *should* tell all of them.

I shudder, focus on the wall behind. It seems to shimmer, and I shake my head, try to get my eyes to work properly again. We're back in the area we slept in, and seeing the leaf mattress makes me feel funny. I think of tonight, of sleeping. Will the Gods and Goddesses and spirits call me into the Dream Land? Tell me off for going outside—or worse? Or warn me that Raleigh now knows where I am? Could he really find me—find us all—just from what I saw, what I showed him?

"So, that Jed guy rescued you." Corin's lips press into a thin line for a few seconds, and I hear the faint hum of the beating drums. The party's still going. "You should've come and found me straight away.

Not hours later."

It's not hours later, I want to say, but something stops me from speaking. My lips maybe. I touch them with my fingers, press into the soft flesh. They feel different, more rubbery.

Corin looks into my eyes, and the intensity in his jars through me. My hand drops to my side.

"Sev? Are you okay? *Did* they hurt you?"

"I'm all right." I nod, but it's too hot in here. I pull at the skin on the back of my neck, but I can't get hold of it properly between my thumb and forefinger. It's too sweaty.

"What is it then?" Corin's voice has a hard edge, and he reaches into his pocket, produces a lighter—a new one—and a cigarette box. He curses when he finds the box is empty.

Just tell him!

And I want to. I really want to—I know what it was like before, when I didn't tell him I was thinking of joining the Enhanced, and how that betrayal has come between us—but I just can't bring myself to say the words now.

So, I try to reason with myself. If I tell Corin, he'll be angry, but he'll probably say we can't tell the Zharat until we've got proof the Enhanced are here, because Manning will ask questions and suspect I'm a Seer. Corin will want to keep it a secret until then, to keep me safe—and a secret is what I want it to be now. Whether I tell him or not, it will have the same outcome: the Zharat won't find out we *could* be in danger. They'll only find out later, if we *are*—if I know for certain. And, if that point comes, I'll have to hide— or leave—to protect my own life from the Zharat.

I look at Corin carefully. He's frowning. He'd be worrying more if I said anything—he'd be stressed. And it could be for nothing. I don't know that Raleigh even saw anything. If he did, and they *are* coming to convert us, the Dream Land will warn me tonight—I hope. And it took us days to get here, so the Enhanced can't attack before I have the chance to have a Seeing dream. Or if they are close, the Gods and Goddesses and spirits will make me faint or something, summon me to the Dream Land that way.

So, I decide if I get a Dream Land warning, I'll tell Corin everything. There's no point making him worry more than is necessary.

"Sev?" he prompts.

I shake my head. Again the rock behind him shimmers. I swallow hard, try to pretend that the wall isn't moving. "Nothing."

"Well, you're certainly not walking around here on your own."

He leans forward, pulls me closer. His touch makes me jump, makes my heart go all fluttery. My head rests on his shoulder.

Tell him.

I flinch. Corin notices, holds me tighter. "It's all right."

It's all right. I hate those words.

I stare at the wall, watch it go out of focus. I take a deep breath, let the air fill my lungs, but it doesn't help. It still feels like something's wrong. I frown. I can think clearly now—not like before, outside—but I still don't feel right. I try to remember how much of the drink I had at the party. It wasn't that much, was it? My scalp tingles.

I pull back from Corin, look up at him. "Teach me. How to fight. Now." My voice wobbles, but only a little.

I swallow uneasily; I know I'm trying to distract myself, so I don't have to think about how stupid I was going outside, how I've put us all in danger—or *why* I went outside. And I *need* to stop thinking about it, else I'll blurt it out to him and make things worse.

Corin raises his eyebrows. "Now?"

I nod, look around. "We've got time. What else have we got to do?"

A muscle in his neck twitches. "I can think of quite

a few other things we could do, things that don't involve me fighting you."

"Corin, please?" I wince, aware that I sound desperate.

For a second, I think he's going to refuse, but then he holds his hands up.

"Okay. But are you sure you're up to this? You don't look that good."

I swallow the lump in my throat and try to ignore everything going on in my head. "Teach me, Corin. *Now*."

After a few seconds, he nods.

Corin likes teaching people; it makes him feel important. Living in the same village as him for years has taught me this, and it doesn't take long for him to slip into that role. He stands up straighter, holds his head higher, and reels off a set of instructions. I try to follow, as best as I can, but there's something off about me. Like I just can't concentrate properly.

Because you've put everyone in danger.

I force myself to push that thought away, but it only makes me feel sicker.

"No, you're doing it wrong." Corin shakes his head. "How do you not know how to punch properly? I'm sure Keelie taught you."

He takes hold of my clenched fist, wraps his fingers around it. His touch makes my skin tingle, makes my head feel like it's floating. I look up at him, realize suddenly that I want to kiss him and...and do more. I feel blood rush to my face, my ears rapidly going hot. I swallow hard, feel silly. This isn't like me. It must be the alcohol; it must still be in my system.

Corin—oblivious—continues. "You have to aim upward, like this." He pulls my fist toward him, demonstrating on himself. "And keep your elbow in line—most of the power will come from your elbow. If you twist your wrist like this, you're more likely to sprain it, do more damage than good."

I nod. His eyes meet mine for a second.

"And you've got to be quick. Don't hesitate. Just go for it."

I nod again. The skin around his lips looks less sunburnt. I look away quickly, eyes focusing on the lava floor. It's surprisingly clean, looks shiny. And the shininess makes me feel even stranger. Like the shiny floor doesn't belong here, because I don't belong here.

"Try again."

Corin has me try several more times—on him. I don't like hurting him, and I can tell he knows I'm purposefully not putting all my energy into the swings. But I line my arm up, work out *how* I'd put the energy.

"Okay," he says after a while. "How about getting away from someone who's already got you under their control?" He presses his lips together for a few seconds, until the color's drained from them. "Lie down."

I rub the back of my neck. His words seem to be getting quieter. Then I realize what he said. "What?"

"On the floor," he says, and I have to listen really hard to hear him—even though there are no other sounds. "Like you were when Raleigh was…torturing you. I'll be him—well, not him. Just some guy. See if you can get away from me."

My eyes widen. I know the answer to that. Corin's not just *some guy*. He's strong. He's built powerfully. He's male… And there's something different about me, something wrong. I can't think, and I can't hear properly. But I refuse to focus on that now as I size up his broad shoulders, watch how the thick bands of muscle ripple around his neck.

I lie down. On the floor. The lava floor digs into my back, next to my spine. Corin kneels over me, his knees either side of my hips. He places his hand on my shoulders, presses down lightly.

"Shove me away."

I push back, but he presses harder. I try to turn, manage to get a bit of leeway, but he moves. I feel his foot go across my shins, and then he's holding my legs down easily. Automatically, I kick out, but my movement is slow, groggy. My spine arches a little, and pain shoots through me from a ridge in the lava floor. I try to roll again, try to move, but can't. His weight holds me down.

I try again, but he shifts his weight, his position. His knee pushes my legs apart.

"Sev." He's amused. "I haven't got hold of your hands. What have we just been practicing?"

My mind clouds over, feels fuzzy. I don't know how he can sound so normal—I don't feel normal. Yet Corin's voice isn't even strained in the slightest. Huh, and I thought most men were the ones with the strongest hormones.

But no… That can't be why I'm distracted. No. It's because I'm worried. Because I've put us all in danger. I went outside. Raleigh has my eyes, and he could've seen. There could be a whole army of Enhanced Ones mapping their route to the Fire Mountain right this moment.

Oh Gods.

I breathe out quickly. Punching. Right.

I raise my arm up, but Corin grabs that hand before I can even draw my elbow back.

"Too slow. You've got to be quicker." He shakes his head. The light from the lantern starts to play with his eyes, and I see little shapes appear in them. Cats and dogs and goats—like the Zharat men's tattoos. I blink, and they're gone. "Sev, there was no energy in that…" And then his voice just trails off—or at least the sound does, because his lips are still moving.

I watch him form the words, squint at him. Then he stops, looks at me like he's expecting a reply.

I frown. "What?"

He raises his eyebrows. "You're not even trying with me."

"I *am*."

My head pounds, I struggle to breathe. The sounds

of distant children screaming and laughing fill my ears. My eyes focus on Corin's lips. I wonder if his lips feel like mine do, if his are tingling. He must have had some of that drink as well.

I want to touch his lips.

The realization dives at me, and I freeze for a second, wonder if I said it out loud… But I can't think. Heat rushes to my face, then down my neck. I feel it, like it's a rash spreading over my body. I squirm a little, try to shake my head, try to clear it, but I can't move it.

Corin stares at me, the look in his eyes is different now, like he's realized what I'm thinking… Like he's thinking it too.

He's so close. I gulp, and I'm suddenly very aware of where we're touching. Corin's hand is on my hip, but I don't remember him placing it there. And his knee is between my legs. He's leaning over me. There's a strange look in his eyes, a look that makes me feel dizzy, makes my head feel too heavy, too—

Someone coughs behind us.

My head snaps around. Three women stand in the doorway. One is Soraya.

I freeze, feel my blood still. I look up at Corin, his face inches from mine.

Oh Gods.

"Well," Soraya says. "Manning wants you in the washing zone—that's the bit near the waterfall, but you go down the other tubes to get there." She pauses. "But if you're busy, we can come back in, say, ten minutes. Could tell him we couldn't find you quickly… He's only going to start teaching you our language anyway." She gestures toward the other two women, then pauses, and winks at me—actually winks. "Though, I would suggest you do whatever it is you're doing on the leaves. This floor can absolutely kill your back."

The washing zone is where they wash their clothes. It's another cave room, fairly near the waterfall, and there's a big pool of slow-moving water. I watch the water there, the surface swirling round and round like an elaborate story. The light plays off it, creates more patterns, and, for a second, I think the patterns are talking to me. Then I shake my head. That's stupid.

Soraya is here, and she grins. A small child appears behind her, eyes wide, but confident.

I turn back to Corin.

"Are all their washing facilities this amazing?" He steps closer to me, his arm circling my waist.

"There you are."

We look up. Manning heads toward us. His long black cloak makes him look even shorter. A flicker of irritation crosses his face as he sees Corin's hand curved around my hip. But he doesn't say anything.

Manning leads us over to the far side of the washing zone. Several women are busy here packing wet clothes into a basket. It's then, as I watch them folding up the brightly colored garments, that I realize *only* the women here can lose their status. The women's clothes can be taken away, downgraded. The men's tattoos can't.

The women call out to two men who are on the other side of the pool, washing something. There aren't many people in here, but several fold-up chairs have been set out. They're the kind that have been manufactured. Probably mass-produced—which means they were taken during a raid. I frown. Raids are for absolute necessities: food, water, fuel, medicine. Not fold-up chairs.

Still, I suppose the Zharat must be good at raids. I think back to just how many boxes and crates were in that lorry. Boxes and crates that got left behind. The spirits have probably taken the stuff by now. The image of a chivra sitting on one of these fold-up chairs suddenly fills my head. I struggle not to laugh and have to look away.

The light on the water catches my eyes again. It's too bright, too sparkling, as if thousands of tiny lights have been sewn onto the water's seams, and every little wave or movement causes a beautiful display.

I step nearer to its edge—so close—and start to smile, feel my head get clearer.

"Sev?"

Corin's voice grabs me, and I turn back, see his mouth form more words, words I can't understand.

I shake my head, press my fingers to my face. My touch burns, I frown. I step back, eyes still on Corin. He's speaking, speaking words at me, and the others are too, but it's like before when Corin was speaking and I couldn't make out the words. The words are just…gone. Like they've been taken, before they can get to me, and all I'm left with are their outlines. No filling.

I raise my arm up, but the movement sends a jet of pain through my shoulder. I gasp, feel my body start to crumple, and—

I hit the water.

The cold grabs me first, then the warmth. No, it's *hot*. Then the—

This water isn't normal. It's stinging. Burning.

I start to choke, but somehow push myself deeper. Panic starts to rise in me, and I try to turn, try to move my arms and legs, but I can't….

My lungs squeeze….

The water's *wrong*.

Something tugs on my foot, and I sink back, see a dark shape, floating… The shape starts to move. It's no bigger than the girl who was with Soraya. My ears pop. Is she in here too? Distorted sounds fill my ears, and I—

I see it.

I see it come out of me. Just a gold wisp, at first. From my stomach. A gold wisp that gets bigger, pulls at me, slithering, its body curling. And a part of me wonders how I'm just staring at it, how I'm *breathing*, how I'm—

A *spirit*.

It's like a snake…a snake slithering along. But its head is pointed. Sharp lines define its contours, and it reminds me of a perfect chunk of quartz.

I stare at it.

The snake spirit rushes at me. Darkness and movement and—

I scream. Water fills my mouth, my throat. Burning, in my chest. Fire, too hot. I try to turn, can't see a thing. Everything's getting darker. Too dark. Too much, and—

The thing comes at me again, suddenly right in front of me. I breathe in water, more water. Too much water. There's only water. Sharp, stinging water.

My body jolts. It's a kavalah spirit. The type that try to make deals with people, so they can feed from them every day. I freeze, look at it. Kavalahs mess with your head.

And people make deals with them.

The snake grabs me. It's big. Massive, fills the water, wraps around me, squeezes me, tries to get back inside me, tries—

I choke, cough, but there's only more water. Hissing, in my ears. Oh Gods. Need to get out… Need to….

My throat's closing up. Muscles spasm. And the pendant… My mother's pendant, it's heavy, drags me down. For a second, all I can think about is that Seer's pendant, because he *must* have one. All Seers must, unless the Zharat are different… Yes, they must be. They're stronger, stronger than me and my mother? Or it's their bison tattoos….

Let me back in.

My body jolts, and then there's a net. Rope.

Something wraps around me. I try to see it, but can't. I kick out, but my legs aren't… My arms….

You're weak. Let me help you. It'll be all right.

I try to get away from it all, but I can't. My lungs are on fire. I can't breathe. Can't—

I try to see where the kavalah has gone, but everything's a murky gray, like there's an opaque film over my eyes. I kick out, but I'm disoriented— can't remember which direction the water's surface is, and….

My mouth opens, the water dives in.

The pain goes away.

Everything goes away.

TWENTY

I AM STRAPPED TO A bed. Huge buckles. There's no mattress on the bed, and the wooden slats of the frame dig into my spine.

"Such a pretty one, aren't you?"

My body jolts, but the metal straps pull me back. They're cold, sear my skin.

Raleigh steps closer, until I can just about see his head in my peripheral vision. I feel bile rise, sticking to my throat as he smiles.

It's all right now. The water spirit's voice is here. I turn, try to see it—my neck clicks—but can't.

"Oh, Shania."

I turn to Raleigh, feel something clicking and whirring inside me as I look at him. As I look at my reflection in his eyes. He smiles.

"Such a beautiful little one, aren't you? My darling butterfly."

I gulp. My mouth dries. He reaches forward, a finger on my face, traces along my jaw. He presses, exerting the smallest of pressures. Then he smiles. His teeth are whiter than I remembered.

For a second, Raleigh's face changes. His skin gets a

couple of shades lighter, and his eyes lose the mirrors, become brown. His features get blunter, and then he's Jed. But no, the changes don't stop. They keep going, skin darkening now, darkening more than Raleigh's skin is, and he's—

Three.

I'm trying to sit up, trying to reach my brother, and then—

Raleigh returns, laughing.

Pain whips through my body. I don't scream though, don't know how I don't.

"Are you ready?" Raleigh asks.

"For what?" My voice is a croak.

"To give me what is mine."

I see myself in his eyes again: my Untamed face. Makes me feel calmer, somehow. I think.

Raleigh leans backward, until I can't see him properly, just his shape. I hear the sounds of a case being opened and then metal scraping metal as something's pulled out.

Get out, Seven. Get out now. Get out while you can.

I don't know where the voice comes from. It's different.

"Oh, don't look so scared, my dear butterfly."

He's back, stepping closer. So close I smell the liquor on him. My nostrils curl.

He raises his hand. There's something clenched in his fist. Metal, thin. It takes a moment for my eyes to adjust, for my brain to recognize it.

I go cold.

Raleigh grins. Light bounces off the scalpel.

"Come on, Shania. I want them properly this time. Give me your eyes."

TWENTY-ONE

RALEIGH LEANS OVER ME. I scream, but, no—his face is changing. His skin pales, his hairline shoots back, and braids dart out behind him.

"You awake, woman?" Water drips from Manning's braids onto me. He's breathing hard, and his face is crimson.

I let out a small squeak and bolt upright, nearly clashing heads with him. I scramble backward, and my vision blurs for a second.

"Sev?"

Arms start to encircle me.

I scream. But it's Corin—his arms stop me—and I slam against him. He's soaked too. Still, I turn. The snake spirit, it's still here. I can feel it. And I'm trying to tell him, trying to tell them all, but my words are getting stuck. And they're all talking, ignoring me. I catch the word *hallucinations* and then something else that I don't understand. But they're the ones who don't understand. We're in danger, that thing, that snake spirit… It was here. Still here. It's got to still be here.

And Raleigh! I whimper at the nightmare, my

imagination—still fresh in my mind—and pull my head around. But everything's moving, and I can't see.

"It's all right! It's gone now. You're okay, Sev."

But I can't stop shaking.

Manning peers at me. "Do you remember it, woman? Who sent it after you?"

I shake my head, feel my neck click, and he barks the words at me again. I try to block his voice out, lean into Corin, but Manning's face just gets closer and closer.

"This be serious, woman. *Who* sent it?"

I feel Corin's body tense up, and I try turning my face into his chest more, but I can't move properly. I catch a glimpse of Soraya behind, her face pale, ashen.

"Back off," Corin says, and he's pointing at Manning. "Can't you see what state she's in? Your questioning can be done later."

I blink. My lashes are wet. No, all of me is. I take a shaky breath. The pounding in my head has gone. And I can hear, I can hear all their words, so clearly.

"*No,*" Manning says. "Someone's sent a kavalah to her. I need to know how long it's been in her system, messing with her soul."

His words pull through me, make me feel sick. I'm right next to the water's edge. I turn, heart pounding. Peer into the water. It's clear. Crystal clear. Not darkness, no murkiness, no colors. Can see the bottom, unlike before.

The Noir Lands are bad.

I shudder.

"Someone sent a kavalah to her?" Soraya's voice has a strange undertone to it. "So, Seven hasn't made a deal with it?"

Manning shakes his head. "She was fighting it, in the water, woman. If she'd bonded with it for a deal, she wouldn't have had no chance of fighting it, knocking it out her system like that." He turns to me, and water drips from his braids onto my face again. "Good idea, that was, throwing yourself in the water like that. Certainly got it out. Now, woman, have you felt unwell? How long? I need to know how long it was in you, what damage it's done."

I nod, try to think. All that time, when I felt strange—when I went outside because I forgot the bison's warning—that spirit was inside me? Feeding from me? And someone's *sent* it after me?

Raleigh.

I inhale sharply. He's got my eyes. And that spirit… That must be how he's doing it? He's made a deal with the kavalah spirit…and it's been *inside* me. For how long? Since the bison warned me? My stomach twists. All that time—and I only felt different, felt *it*, toward the end.

I don't get any warning before I throw up—all over Manning.

"It's all right," Corin says. And he's pulling me away, onto his lap, smoothing back my hair.

I drag a hand across the back of my mouth, taste bile and acid. My breaths come in sharp busts.

But it's okay. The spirit's out of my system now. I swallow hard. So Raleigh hasn't got my eyes any longer. He can't have. Not now that it's out of my system, gone.

But I *still* went outside. I *still* showed Raleigh what it looks like outside the cave.

I go even colder. He must've seen, mustn't he? But the Dream Land would've said… No. I haven't slept yet, not since going outside. I could still get summoned to the Dream Land tonight, in my sleep. But even as I think the words, I'm sure I won't be. Because I was unconscious in the water and when they got me out, wasn't I? And that would've been the perfect time for the Dream Land to summon me, to tell me—*if* anything needed to be told.

Manning stands up, and my vomit drips off him, makes long stringy patterns. My eyes start to glass over as he pulls his cloak off, thrusts it at Soraya.

"How long have you felt unwell?" Manning's voice

is dark.

I blink hard, lean against Corin, feel my chest shudder. "Since those men… Mart… Shortly after that."

Manning's eyes narrow. "A few hours then." He shakes his head. "I will kill him."

"Who?" Corin looks up.

"Mart."

"What? He did this?" Corin's arms get tighter around me.

No, I want to say, it wasn't Mart. It was Raleigh. But I can't. I can't say the words. I can't make it real.

But an innocent boy will die.

I swallow hard, and my fingers wrap around Corin's arm a little tighter. I wrinkle my nose, try not to smell my vomit.

Manning flicks his hand to my left, and then I realize the other two men are here. "Go and get Mart. Bring him to me. And get all our Seers down here. I wanna make sure that kavalah's gone and ain't hiding in the tubes."

Soraya blinks several times. "But if Mart's made a deal with it, it'll come in here every day to feed from him—and carry out his work."

"It won't if he be dead, woman. Mart's the one feeding it, controlling it. Not her."

Corin makes an irritated noise deep in his throat. "Doesn't Sev need to see a healer or someone?" His arms are still around me, and I listen to his heart.

Manning shakes his head. "She'll be fine, after rest, man. It'll just have given her hallucinations. No permanent damage. But we need to check where that spirit's gone, get it out if it still be lingering." He shakes his head, and his braids drip more water. He points to one of the men, tells him to get the Seers now.

Hallucinations?

Raleigh's face fills my vision for a split-second.

"Don't worry, woman. The kavalah knows you're too strong for it now, it won't try and get you again, even when it be looking for a new human to bargain with." Manning turns to Soraya. "Seven needs to rest, recover from the spirit attack. Take her to the girls' room, woman. She'll be sleeping there for the next two nights anyway."

By the morning, my head is clear, and I don't feel as sick. The Dream Land didn't call me, so Raleigh can't have seen anything—can't have been using my eyes when I left the tubes—else he'd be on his way, and the Gods and Goddesses would've told me. I breathe a sigh of relief. I don't need to tell Corin about going outside.

I get up slowly, realizing I'm the last one awake. The other girls are talking in low voices. I try not to think of yesterday as I sort through the pile of red dresses at the foot of my sleeping area—yet I can't help but wonder whether Raleigh will send another kavalah now the first one is out of my system, or how soon it will be before the bison warns me again.

A few minutes later, I pull on one of the dresses—though I long to wear a T-shirt and jeans again—and follow the girls out into the main tubes. Jed is already there. I hear the *click click click* of his stick immediately, and I make sure my pendant is safely hidden. Thankfully, the Zharat seem to like high necklines on their dresses.

I watch him for several moments. He looks like he's having trouble moving; the bandages under his jeans must need changing, redness seeps through the denim.

"S'ven." It's Jed, stepping closer now. He nods at me, at my dress. "Are you all right? I heard about the water spirit." Concern flashes across his eyes, then he yawns. "Do not worry, it has gone now. Mart has been dealt with."

Dealt with.

I nod, feel shaky, try to pull my dress down, stretch a crease out of it. The material is thick and heavy; I think the dresses have been made from one of the red curtains that hung in the gathering room for the welcomings.

"Come and sit down," he says, pointing to the side of the tube. "You should still be resting, so soon after an attack."

He switches to the Zharat language and addresses one of the girls. She nods, runs off, and returns with some food no less than half a minute later. She hands it to me. Slivers of meat and some sort of bread. I catch her side profile. She looks like Jed.

"Is she your daughter?"

Jed nods, rubs at the skin under his eyes. "Jeena." For a second, something crosses over his face. Then it's gone. "She looks so much like her mother... Sometimes I wonder if it is all pointless, raising children if *we* are all going to die."

His words jolt through me. I lean forward. "What do you mean?"

"My father was a Seer of Life. He knew how this war will end, who will survive."

His eyes go dark for a minute, and I frown, then look up as violet movement catches my attention. It's Clare, the one who called Jed a murderer before. She sees us sitting together, and her eyes narrow. She raises one hand, mimes a gun. Then she points at Jed, eyes darkening, before leaving.

I stare after her.

Violet. She wore green before. She's lost status.

The hairs on the back of my neck rise. I look at the wall. There are horizontal marks, drawing across from one side to the other, with a layer of lighter-colored lava between them.

Jed coughs, apparently oblivious to Clare's short

visit. "Shortly after my father was made a Seer, he was told it: how it will end, how the war ends. The augury, he called it. The Dream Land augury. A message of the far future. A promise. He said other Seers of Life would know it too, but that he could not tell ordinary people. Everyone thought he was more important than our other Seers. He lorded it over them, all because he was a Seer of Life. Well, I suppose he still is."

Jed spreads his hands wide, and I stare at the thick skin over his knuckles, the small scars. He sees me looking and turns his hands over.

"It must be the Enhanced," Jed says quickly. "The augury must say that only they survive the war. My father was making sure he was on the right side. He would not give up the Dream Land if he needed it, if the Untamed were to be the surviving side."

"Give up the Dream Land?" I can't help myself, the question's blurted out before I can stop myself.

"Of course." Then, seeing the look on my face, he lets out a bitter laugh. "This is the problem with you run-arounders. You have lost the ancient knowledge, the reasons for why everything is. You know why Seers were created?"

"To warn the Untamed of conversion attacks."

Jed grunts, half-nodding. "Yes. Well. Sort of. The Gods, sometimes aided by the benevolent spirits, choose some Untamed humans to give divine powers to, and access to the Dream Land, to help win the war, because they are angry that man is throwing away his individuality, joining a mass of robotic creatures. So they favor the Untamed, give powers to special ones to show their support, give us the advantage. That is how men become Seers. And we only get visions if we are in danger—that is how we know we are safe here, no visions.

"But if we get converted, the Gods block our access to the Dream Land—some Gods take longer to block the person, but they always do…eventually. Too risky in the end if they do not. The Dream Land has to stay

Untamed. If an Enhanced Seer got into the Dream Land, he would probably destroy it because it is one of our only advantages."

I swallow hard. I took augmenters, I wanted to become an Enhanced. Yet I've still got access to the Dream Land. I look at Jed. Does that mean I have one of the more lenient Gods or Goddesses guiding my Seer powers? Or was it because I hadn't actually *joined* the Enhanced fully, only making plans to go to one of their cities? Maybe once I'd got there, my access would've been blocked.

"Still, he will have his other powers." Jed glances at me.

I try to keep my face blank. Other powers. Like Raleigh's power—torturing. I go cold.

Jed coughs. "The other divine powers cannot be revoked. So my father still has his Seer powers. Just no visits to the Dream Land."

No visits to the Dream Land.

I frown. My chest tightens, and the Zharat mark on my arm throbs. What about my mother? Even though she didn't want to become an Enhanced, she got herself converted to save Corin and Rahn *and* because she knew an Enhanced One would get to me in the battle. She became Enhanced to help us all, to ensure that person was her, to ensure I could get away and remain Untamed.

Still, my mother's an Enhanced Seer.

I want to ask Jed, but I know mentioning that my mother's a Seer would be a bad idea.

"You know," Jed says. "It is nice to talk to someone about this... Us Zharat are not supposed to speak of the ones who converted. Same with the dead. Still, I do not know how I am just supposed to forget about my father, when I know he converted for a reason, to save himself, and that he did not care enough to take me or my sisters with him." He turns more to me, angling his body toward me. "Sometimes, I wish the God of Life had never showed up to my father. Maybe if it had been a different God who made him a Seer, things might have been different."

My mouth dries. "What? He saw an actual God?" I get a strange tight feeling in my chest.

Jed nods. "Of course. All Seers meet their God. That is how we know they are true Seers. Not fakes." A far-away look crosses Jed's eyes. "My father became a Seer at eighteen—quite late. He was very proud. Said the God of Life met him a few weeks later, told him he must never tell any others about the auguries, that others could use the information badly." His eyes darken, and he clenches his hands into tight fists. "I just wish he had told me for sure that that was why he left. Or why he did not take me."

Jed gets up and looks down at me. The light in his eyes changes.

"Anyway, I should not be discussing this with you." He points at his injured thigh—or at least, I think he does. "It is the painkillers, making me more lenient. Women should not ask about Seer matters, S'ven. Remember that. I am nicer than the other men, but you must try to fit in." His expression darkens. "If you do not, it will only bring bad things for you."

I try to pretend that it doesn't sound like a threat.

TWENTY-TWO

"WHAT? YOU ACTUALLY BELIEVE THIS?"

Corin stares at me after I've finished telling him what Jed said, an amused look on his face.

"It's obviously stories, Sev. No one actually sees Gods or Goddesses."

I squirm a little. The air's too hot. I don't like it, but at least we're the only two here.

"It's just going to be their lore, their culture," Corin says. He's wearing a tight black T-shirt and baggy gray jeans; he looks good. I feel stupid in my curtain day-dress compared to him.

"But what if it isn't? What if it *is* true?"

Corin raises his eyebrows. "You're actually contemplating this, even when the Zharat refuse to accept that women can be Seers?"

I sigh. "But I haven't seen a God or Goddess. What if they're right—women aren't proper Seers?"

Corin snorts. "Given how many times you've saved us from attacks, I'm not even going to answer that."

I lean forward, lower my voice. "But I still haven't *seen* a God or Goddess. I don't know which one of them made me a Seer, gave me these powers."

"And you're not going to," he says. "Because this is a load of shit. I'll tell you what, it's probably hallucinations that the Zharat Seers get, makes them think they're seeing Gods." He gestures around. "Or volcanic gases messing with their heads. This isn't real, Sev. And don't doubt yourself. You *are* a Seer. All this is just stories. They're trying to explain things we don't know about. Things we're not supposed to know about. Seer stuff is stuff of the Gods and Goddesses. And the spirits too. We're not supposed to know how it works, no one does. But it's human nature to fill in gaps, to invent stuff, and that's what the Zharat are doing. And—"

He breaks off as an old man seemingly appears out of nowhere and rushes toward us with surprising speed. Then Corin stands up straighter and puts his arm around me.

"You two." The old man points at us with a long finger that shakes. "Chief says Esther has just awoken, that you can see her. I'm to take you there. Follow me."

For a second, Corin stares at him, mouth open. Then he scrambles forward, pulls me along too.

The walk is long, and we weave through many tubes. I lose track of the way after the fourth or fifth turn and concentrate on walking as quickly as I can, avoiding the many toddlers who run the tubes in gaggles, laughing and shrieking. A couple of older children walk behind them, and they nod at us as we pass.

Some minutes later, the old man stops at a low doorway and pulls back the drape to one side, then indicates for us to go in.

Corin goes first, I follow.

Esther is lying on a heap of blankets and furs. Her head turns as we enter. Manning is seated, staring down at her. The look on his face makes my skin crawl. Esther smiles at Corin and me, then turns her gaze—quickly—back to Manning.

"I have been welcoming her to the Zharat," Manning

tells us, and he pats the pale green scarf that's draped over Esther's neck. "She, too, is now one of us." He pauses. "I will give you some time. But," he adds, gesturing toward the shadows of the room where I now notice a small man stands, "my attendant will remain here."

Manning leans in close to Esther and murmurs something to her for a second. Then he leaves the room. Corin and I step up to Esther's bed. She struggles to sit up a little, and Corin helps her.

"What did he just say to you?" he asks.

"Nothing." Her eyes narrow, and she shifts her weight a little.

"How are you?" I look at her right shoulder, where she got shot. It's carefully bandaged now, and there's no sign of blood.

Esther grimaces. "Better, I suppose."

Her skin is pale and gaunt still—reflecting a greenish tinge from the scarf—but there is some warmth in her cheeks. Although her eyes have a little life in them—a spark of hope—they've sunken back into her face, making her look deflated somehow. But her hair is clean. Not greasy at all, as if someone's washed it recently. Manning? I frown a little. No, he's the leader of the Zharat. He wouldn't have time.

"What's the last thing you remember?" I ask, just as I see the Zharat mark on her arm. It's lower down than the one on mine.

Corin frowns at me, as if it's a question I'm not supposed to ask.

Esther takes her time thinking, and Corin frowns at me again. But he doesn't say anything.

"It's all mixed up," she says. "Little bits here and there…merging into one another." She pauses. "I got shot, I remember that. And I was with Three. He was carrying me… Then I was on my own… And he was…" She coughs; her body shakes. "I remember you two though. You, Corin, you pulled the bullet out. That hurt." She attempts to laugh, but the sound is weak, makes my throat tighten. "After that, there's not really much. Just little bits. I saw the sky, the Turning. Then heard you talking, but I can't remember what you said... But that man—Manning—he saved me."

Corin's gaze snaps upward. "What?"

"There was a spirit trying to get me. The Turning. I thought I was going to die. Manning... He saved me from it." She smiles broadly.

Corin nods a little gruffly, then asks her about her health and the healing process. The two of them talk for a long time. I begin to feel more and more like an intruder on the siblings. Esther shows obvious surprise when she learns Corin proposed to me.

"I had to," Corin says, and his eyes dart up, meet mine.

Had to. I try not to let the words affect me. He *had* to... He didn't *want* to.

"Manning's been really nice to me," Esther says after a while.

"*Manning?*" Corin's voice is edged in darkness.

Esther nods. "He's been looking after me. And telling me about the Zharat, teaching me their ways. He says that women aren't allowed to ask many questions to a chief, but he doesn't mind if I do. He said there's a spark about me, that I've got...charisma."

Corin makes a noise in the back of his throat that's halfway between a snort and a cough. "Stay away from him."

His words aren't quiet, and I glance across at the Zharat Manning left in the room. He hasn't reacted to Corin's words. Maybe he didn't hear them? But it's wishful thinking, I know.

Esther struggles to sit up. "Stay away?" Her voice is high. "That's a little hard when he's the only one who's been coming to see me, the only one looking after me."

I narrow my eyes. "You were awake?" My voice is quiet. "You haven't just woken up—today?"

She shakes her head. "It's been just over a day. I

think. No, maybe longer. I was sleeping a lot. And Manning was here at one point, because I was having nightmares, and he said he'd watch me, keep them away."

Corin curses, then lowers his voice. "He told me that I'd see you as soon as you were awake, that the healers couldn't be disturbed. We were only just told we could see you. We thought you'd only just woken up."

The three of us descend into silence, and I look uncomfortably toward the small man in the shadows. Manning lied. And he held Esther's welcoming ceremony in secret. I shudder a little, then I look at Esther carefully. I want to ask her something, but I'm not sure what exactly. Or how.

"Have you been looking for Three?" Esther's voice breaks into my thoughts.

I look away, feel sharp pain in my chest. I take several deep breaths, then look up at the skylight. It's perhaps the biggest one I've seen, and this room has the freshest air. I gulp.

Corin glances at me. "It wouldn't do any good."

Esther turns on me. "*What*? You didn't try and find Three? You *left* him?"

He's dead.

The words burn me, and I want to say them, to tell her, but now I can't. Not after that dream. Not after I saw Three lying on the bed, chained up, at a compound.

But that was just a nightmare, I remind myself. Corin told me that.

"We had to—" Corin begins, but cuts himself off.

Instead, Corin busies himself with getting a lighter out of his back pocket, then a cigarette—not a proper one though. A crudely made Zharat one. I wonder if he's going to smoke it in here, go against what Nyesha said. Even though there's lots of fresh air here, and the walls are thick—and we're nowhere near the magma chamber—we're still *in* a volcano, and I don't know how dangerous it might be.

Esther stares at us. "You didn't go and look for him? Didn't go to any Enhanced towns? Not even the nearest ones?"

"The land had all changed," I mutter, but I sound pathetic.

I drop my gaze to the floor, feel my face burn.

"Then we've got to go now! We've got to find him!" She leans forward, tries to swing her legs over the side of the bed. "We need to tell Manning and—"

Corin places a hand on her shoulder. "No. Three is good enough dead to us. Get your head around that, Esther. Sev has." He glances at me for a half a second, then returns his gaze to her. "Don't make this any worse than it already is."

But Esther turns on me. Her eyes narrow until they're fine strips of accusatory light. "You abandoned him, Seven. We never do that—we *always* rescue each other. *We* rescued you. But you haven't—not for your own brother? You *left* him. Your only remaining sibling… And you're not even trying to get him back?" She shakes her head. "So much for family. So much for loyalty—how else are we going to survive as Untamed? You *left* him!" Her face darkens. "This is your fault. He'll be Enhanced because of you."

I try to look away, but I can't. I know she's right. It is my fault. But there's nothing I can do now. We can't leave the Zharat. Manning made that clear when we joined. And I'd never find my way back on my own.

No. Raleigh may not have my eyes any longer, but I *have* to stay here anyway. I can't leave. They'd kill me.

And Three has to stay there. Wherever he is. Enhanced.

Because of me.

TWENTY-THREE

THE NEXT MORNING, I DON'T want to open my eyes. I don't want this day to be happening; the day of the fight, the battle for me. But it is. And it happens too quickly. Everyone's up, shouting and running about. Small girls watch with excitement, and lots of the women give me narrowed-eyed looks. I try to ignore them as I eat small pieces of flatbread and celery, wincing at the taste.

"You are lucky," Nyesha tells me later as she fixes my hair into what she says is a suitable style for the wedding. Apparently, the ceremony will happen straight after the fight—that's the norm. "Manning's had thirteen requests for you. Thirteen proposals."

Thirteen.

I swallow hard, try not to show any emotion. If I don't react like it's happening, then it can't affect me when it does.

"And Yoliv's applied to be your husband," Nyesha says. "He'll probably win. He killed three men during the last battle. He always gets the women he wants. We'll be sisters then."

"What?" I pull away from Nyesha, letting my hair

fall back across my face. "He *killed* men?"

"Don't worry, he's nice."

"*Nice*?"

Nyesha nods. "And you'll see the all your suitors during the fight." She gestures at my hair, then holds up some red beading and a length of fine silver-link chain. "Come on, let me finish this. And you wanted that crystal in your hair too?"

I nod. My Seer pendant. The neckline of the dress Nyesha sorted out for me is too low to hide the crystal. But she said she could work it into my hair after I told her it was a prized possession of my mother's—risky, I know.

"It's very pretty." Nyesha wraps the sinew cord around her fingers a few times, holds it up against the golden beam that falls from the skylight above. "I can attach it to the silver chain, wrap it around, like this."

As she finishes my hair and secures the pendant into the elaborate twists, I can't stop shaking. And then, all too soon, it's time to discard the red top and jeans I covertly acquired this morning from the washing zone and pull on the vivid red, satin dress Nyesha tells me was her mother's—one of the ones she wasn't sent off in when she died. This gown is a lot longer than the one Soraya gave me—nearly floor-length—and it has shoulder straps. Earlier, Nyesha told me the color had faded to a dull pink—and even an off-white in several places—since it was last worn over thirty years ago, and she'd re-dyed it for me, for my wedding, after it became apparent there were no red dresses available for my welcoming. Apparently, one of my new day-dresses won't do for a wedding—not fancy enough.

I pause as we're about to leave.

"Is…" I flex my fingers. My new hairstyle's already starting to pull at my scalp, and I can feel the telltale signs of a coming headache. "Do men normally die in these fights?"

"They try to avoid it," she says, then clicks her tongue, "because it's silly given our number. But some men just won't back down. They won't admit defeat, so they fight to the death."

They won't admit defeat. I think of Corin, of how proud he is, how arrogant he can be. How he's told Manning he's going to win.

Oh Gods.

He's not going to back down.

He's going to be one of them. One of the men who die.

I stand up. Then I gather the long skirt of the dress and run out the room, ignoring Nyesha's exclamations. I power through the tubes, my bare feet hitting the stone hard. But I don't care. I turn the corner, and take the next right, but I'm not certain of the map in my head.

Still, I get to his room quickly, and I make good time.

I duck under the drape and blink hard as my eyes adjust to the dim light. I look around. There are blankets stacked in the corner. A broken arrow lies on the floor, next to a bow.

Corin stares at me. He looks alert, strong, ready. Then his eyes take in my dress and hairstyle, and I've never felt so silly.

"How are you feeling?" His voice is warm, strong. "Still recovering okay after that kavalah attack?"

I nod, but keep my eyes on him. He asked me this yesterday too, but I cut him off by telling him what Jed had said about Seers meeting Gods. "I'm almost back to normal. And I feel *a lot* better knowing Raleigh's not got my eyes any longer. I feel freer." I press my hands together; my palms are clammy.

"Raleigh?" Corin frowns. "I thought it was Mart who sent it?"

I shake my head. "No. It had to be Raleigh—it was how he was getting my eyes. Makes sense." I try to smile, but I'm speaking too quickly. "But at least he's gone now. I'm not putting the Zharat in danger."

Corin nods.

Then I take a deep breath. I didn't come here to talk

about Raleigh. I need to focus.

"You need to step down." I say the words as firmly as I can, looking Corin in the eye. "You need to say you don't want to marry me."

For several seconds, the look on Corin's face doesn't change. But when it does, it changes as quickly as a tropical storm descends on a jungle. His eyes darken, the corners of his mouth turn down, shadows fall across his face.

"I—what? *Seven!*" He grips my upper arms firmly, his fingers pressing into my bare skin. He starts to laugh, then stops. His eyes are wide and are full of confusion—and a hint of betrayal. "No."

"You have to!" I tell him. "They'll kill you! They will! You have to step down. Tell Manning now, come on, let's go! We can—"

I start forward, try to pull him with me, but he stops me.

"No!" Corin shakes his head. "We can't! They—we can't! Sev, you barely know any of those men! They're strangers. All of them! You have to marry someone, so it *has* to be me… Don't worry, I won't get hurt—"

"But you will!" I shout. And I'm shaking my head—as if the movement will shake the tightness out of my hair, my body. "Corin, please. They'll *kill* you."

His jaw tenses for a moment. "I'm not giving up on you. I'm not, so don't even say it again." He presses a finger to my lips, then wipes away my tears with the back of his hand. His eyes are lighter when he looks up at me. "You can't mean this," he says. "You can't want to marry one of them more than me." He shakes his head. "Sev, they'll expect you to *be* their wife. I won't. I told you before that, with me, nothing would happen that you don't want. I mean that."

I look at him so hard it hurts me. I take hold of his hands with both of mine, testing the familiar feel of their weight. The skirt of the gown swishes as I move slightly. "Corin, *please* step down."

"I'm not letting them get you—"

I gulp, got to make him see sense, need to. "They're not that bad—"

He cuts me off by shaking his head. "Don't delude yourself, Sev. You've seen them. You know what it's like around here. Men have already tried to attack you once. We have to stick together. It has to be you and me."

I bite my lip, can't bring myself to say anything more. Not when he says *you and me* like that.

"Look, I've got to get ready. I'm not going to hand you over to those men, okay? I'm doing this. I'd rather die than see one of them hurting you."

I don't remember moving from Corin's room, but I must have, because now I'm in a lower tube called the Old One's Arena, watching my suitors line up in the middle of the battleground circle. And all the Zharat men look more threatening, more foreboding than I remembered them. Corin's dressed the same as them—just wearing a stylized loincloth—but he looks like a gazelle compared to the mountain lions who are sizing him up. And I never thought I would ever be likening Corin—of all people—to a gazelle.

I stare as another man—one fully clothed—joins the queue of suitors, stands behind Corin, next to a huge lantern that throws shadows over them both.

It takes me a moment to recognize the newcomer, and I gasp as Jed's eyes meet mine. He smiles.

I look away. I wipe my sweaty palms on the dress, hoping that Nyesha won't mind the marks on it. I swallow hard; there's a lump in my throat as I look around the room, try to steady my nerves. The Old One's Arena is a large dungeon-like space within one of the tubes. Railings have been rigged up in a circle, and they keep us—the spectators—away from the fighters. Someone's hand presses against my upper back.

"He's got no chance."

Esther. I'd recognize her voice anywhere. I turn, meet her accusing eyes. She stands right behind me, dressed in a long, pale green dress made of flimsy, floaty fabric.

"They'll kill him, Seven," she says. "And it will be your fault. Corin's risking everything for you. But you don't care, do you? As long as you're okay, you don't care about anyone else."

"Esther, I—" But I break off, don't know what I'm saying. I feel like I don't know anything anymore.

I turn back to survey the arena. Corin and Jed look like the weakest men of the lot. Both stand with their feet shoulder-width apart, their arms locked by their sides, their hands clenched into tight, meaningful fists. Corin's face is full of concentration, and the way his eyes are locked straight ahead, and the angle of his lopsided frown, suggests he's thinking hard. Planning something. Whatever strategy he's got, I hope it's good.

Jed's posture lacks the tension. He looks more relaxed, comfortable. He's done this before, knows what to expect. But I'm guessing he wasn't injured before. He hasn't got a staff now, but even I can tell he's favoring his bad leg.

Several of the other men are warming up: flexing their muscles, stretching their legs, bracing their backs, showing off tattoos.

Then the fighting begins. Suddenly. Just like that.

I'd expected it to have some sort of structure. But it doesn't. The men just run at each other, punching, kicking, shoving. Nails draw blood. Bloodied noses appear.

And everyone around me is *cheering*.

Men wave their fists, children are reaching over the barrier. A woman to my left screams so loudly my ears start to ache. And *still* she carries on screaming. Her face gets dangerously red, her eyes are watering, a muscle in her jaw is throbbing. Her cracked lips are stretched, almost to breaking point, as she bellows words I can't make out. Something splatters over my bare arm—her saliva. I recoil back, but there's nowhere to go. More people press against me from behind, standing on the hem of my dress, yet forcing me forward until the rails dig into my ribs. I scream, try to push back, but no one's listening to me. Everyone is watching the fight.

And they are loving it.

Somehow I manage to turn around, and the rail presses across my spine, makes my muscles ache. I swallow hard, wipe more sweat from me… But it's so hot in here… Too hot… Oh Gods. I want to touch my Seer pendant, but my fingers are like ice because I know I mustn't, mustn't draw attention to it.

Ether's retreated to the back of the room. I can just see the top of her head, with her short, dark hair sticking up. She's leaning against someone. Manning?

A scream behind me cuts my breath short, and then the crowd pushes against me, right up close. The railing crushes against my spine. Pain. I can't breathe. I need to get out of here.

A gong sounds loudly, somewhere above me, makes me jump. And I know—just know—one of the men is down. The first one.

People scream either side of me. And then Clare's at my side, blond hair wild. Her eyes are narrowed but urgent.

"It's the perfect distraction," she says. I almost miss her words with all the noise around us.

"What is?" I blink several times.

Her eyes narrow into fine lines as she focuses on the fighting men. "Yes… I'll kill him… They'll think it's another man's doin'. They won't know it's me." She holds up her hand, shows me a small knife poking out of her fist. She smiles, and there's something about her stance that reminds me of Raleigh. "They're all fightin', not payin' attention to us. I'm a good aim. Even if I don't hit Jed, I'll hit one of them."

My eyes widen as I stare at her. She could hit Corin. "You can't!"

Clare lifts one shoulder a little, and the material of her violet dress swishes. She's taller than me, and her clear blue eyes look over the top of a lot of heads. "I didn't think you were so weak. Can't you see? We need to teach them a lesson. We're not weak. And women can be Seers, just like my sister was."

I flinch a little. But she can't know what I am. She can't. Because if she's worked it out, then surely the men must've too.

Or they will.

I hear a battle cry behind me—but the fury and intended intimidation is mixed with agony. The scream echoes above us all, ringing and ringing on and on, until the next one sounds.

"Esther!" I look around for her again, but now she's gone, and everyone's moving. And I can't do anything. Oh Gods.

Another gong.

I narrowly avoid throwing up. Someone near me has. The smell is pungent as it curls into my nostrils, mixing with body odor and stale sweat. I look down at my feet—my bare feet—and cringe as I imagine myself standing in something bad.

Gong.

The sound resounds around me, fills my ears. I can't breathe, can't think… Don't want to think.

I hear someone shouting, but can't make out the words. It's the Zharat language… But they shout again, and now I'm not so sure… My head's mangled up. I can't concentrate, can't think.

He's dead. Corin's dead.

I flinch. No. Can't be. No.

Two more gongs, in quick succession. Five men down. Nine to go.

I push away, toward another group of people,

squeeze between two men, force my way through. But I can't. Can't get far enough away. People keep pushing me back, and I'm turning—turning without realizing—because I keep ending up back at the rails.

The bridge of my nose prickles. My bottom lip trembles. I clasp my hands together, try to remain calm. Need to remain calm.

Gong.

Gong.

Gong.

Others are moving. Three men, supporting something between them. I glimpse bare flesh. Torn skin. Blood. Not something, *someone.*

"It's Yoliv!" a voice cries.

My vision blurs. If Yoliv is… Corin… He's… I gulp, still staring at the injured man. He's not dead.

And as I stare at Yoliv—for minutes that stretch on and on—the next five gongs ring loudly, one after another, hardly any space at all between them.

The final two. I can hear their grunts. They don't sound strong. They sound weak. The crowd is quieter now, more hushed. I want to turn to see who the top two men are, but I can't bring myself to move.

Seconds turn into minutes. Minutes turn into hours. Somehow, without trying, I've finally made it to the back of the crowd, and I lean against the wall, my palms pressed flat against the cold stone.

My chest tightens. I have to look to see if Corin is….

So I turn. And I barely register moving. And people are parting the crowd, letting me back through, and it isn't a struggle at all. It's so easy, and—

Corin. I see him. See his brown hair. See him as white light shoots out from Jed's hand toward him. A flash, burning.

I go cold.

That light… No. I shake my head… I've seen someone do that before: Raleigh. He sent a flash of white light toward the Untamed people from my village when they were rescuing me from the Enhanced Ones' compound.

It's the same light. Jed is using the same power.

Oh Gods. That's not fair.

But Jed hasn't got the bison tattooed on his forehead—not like….

I frown.

Yet it makes sense. That's how he's still there. That's how he's beating them.

People are cheering.

My hands go cold. Corin's not going to win. Corin *can't* win.

Gods, it's so obvious. So obvious now.

Jed's a Seer.

And he's going to kill Corin.

TWENTY-FOUR

THE FINAL GONG CRIES OUT.

The room goes quiet. Eerily quiet.

Then people move.

Someone claps. The clapping grows louder, pounding away, over and over at my skull.

I run forward, see Esther, reach out for her. But she moves, steered away by Manning.

Manning. I focus on him. He's walking forward. People are moving out of his way, dividing before him. He's walking toward the open space.

I can't see Corin.

He's dead, Seven. Jed killed him.

I flinch, pull at my hair—need to relieve some of the pressure in my head—and drag some of the beads out. I drop them on the floor and check that my Seer pendant is still secure in my hair.

Someone touches my shoulder. An old man grins at me. His eyes are bulging, his lips are blue. And then another man reaches for me, squeezing my shoulder, bowing his head toward me.

And the clapping's still going on. Louder. Louder.

A man shouts for silence. He gets it.

Manning smiles and points. "The winner! This man's proven himself worthy of being blessed for marriage with Seven Sarr of the Zharat, formerly of the Unknown Lands! Scream for Jed Zalinsky of the Zharat!"

My shoulders tighten. I don't know what to do. Can't… If Jed is here, that only means one thing: Corin is injured.

Or worse.

"Seven, you need to go up there, to the altar." Soraya's voice fogs my ears, and I stare at her blankly. She reaches forward, then she's doing something to my hair for a moment. Fixing it? A bright smile. "Go."

She starts to push me along, and then I'm in the arena, and I'm standing with them. With Manning and Jed, and Manning's reaching for my hand and he's already got Jed's and—

I feel sick. My head pounds. I start to gag.

The wedding.

"Stop!" Jed's voice. "I don't want the ceremony today." He's looking at me. Eyes firmly on me.

I shudder, don't understand.

"What?" Manning says.

"I want another month."

My head starts to spin. That's… He's buying us time? Me and Corin? My head pounds, the pain gets worse. I don't understand. He's just won the fight.

"It is too close," Jed says. "I cannot walk properly yet. I need another month, until the official ceremony. I want to be at my best for our presentation to the Gods. But we will live together before then."

Live together?

And Manning nods. Just like that. "Your marriage will take place at the next full moon."

I gasp, start to choke, and then things happen. A lot of things. Things that just blur over me, past me. Things that won't go away. I think I see Corin's face— bloodied and broken.

But then there's darkness all around me.

I'm falling, crashing… Something crawls over me, then prickles against my left side. Short, sharp pricks.

"She's fainting!" someone cries.

And then there's nothing.

I don't know what's happening. But I'm being led away, a few minutes later. By Jed. My hand is in his. And I've got a ring on, but don't remember it being slid on my finger. Don't remember much… Not since I fainted.

The shock of it, that's what someone said. That's why I fainted.

Jed's hand shakes.

But mine shakes more.

I try to turn, to search for Corin. But there are too many people. Too many faces swarm around me. And they're shouting. Everyone's shouting *something*.

Jed squeezes my hand, and my fingers crush up around the ring. Brief pain. I look up to see him grinning down at me. He has a cut under his left eye, and the skin over his collarbone has been broken in several places. I wonder whether Clare threw that knife in the end—and wish she had—then look away, feel my face burn.

I don't know if Corin is still alive.

Your marriage will take place at the next full moon.

I can't remember who said the words. Manning probably. But they're echoing over and over in my mind. Can't get them out of my head. They're torturing me, spinning round and round, tormenting me.

Your marriage will take place at the next full moon.

"Come to our room, S'ven." Jed's voice is low, and his breath pushes against the side of my face like an insistent mosquito. "Come on, wife."

Wife-to-be. I want to correct him. But I can't. I can't do anything. My body won't work properly, won't obey me. And it all happened so quickly. I shake my head. It can't be real. Not yet.

Jed Zalinsky. The name feels strange, and part of me wonders if I'll have to become Seven Zalinsky. My mother kept her name—and my father became a Sarr when they married—but something makes me think that Jed won't be taking mine.

A group of men pass us, shouting rowdy, rude remarks. Jed pushes forward, not saying anything. The bottom of my dress snags on something, but I can't stop to unfix it; the fabric tears.

"This is it here," Jed says a few moments later, but I know it is. He took me here before. His room.

Jed reaches out and holds the heavy drape back—I now notice it's got a dark tartan pattern to it, unusual—and gestures for me to go first.

But my feet are too heavy.

"It is okay," he whispers, "it is only me."

I don't know how those words are supposed to be comforting.

Jed takes my hand in his, leads me in carefully, as though I am fragile and might break at any moment. I don't know why that annoys me so much, when that's exactly how I feel.

Jed lets the drape fall back behind us, plummeting us into pitch black. I look around; try to remember where everything is. There's a bed somewhere behind me, a table to my left? Or was it over there? I press my hands together for comfort, but all I can feel is the ring.

"It is all right." Jed's voice is too close. "You will remember the layout soon."

"You're a Seer," I blurt out, heart pounding, and I don't like the way my voice echoes. But he didn't say anything before—when he talked about his father being a Seer of Life, he never said *he* was a Seer too.

But why would he?

There's a long pause, and I strain my eyes, try to see him. Try to see the bison tattooed on his forehead—even though I *know* it's not there. I shake my head. It must just be that one Seer who has that tattoo. Maybe he's more important—might have been a Seer for longer?

"It has been two years." Jed's words are edged in danger.

"What?"

"I am a Seer of Innovation. But my Seer powers and the Dream Land access were blocked—by grief. Not that we need the Dream Land here; we are never summoned, we are safe." He pauses, and I feel the rush of his breath against my face. He's closer than I thought. "But it feels good to have my Seer powers back."

I swallow hard. He's pleased to have his Seer powers back because he used them to fight?

Because he used them to win you.

Jed touches my shoulder, and I jump.

"The bed is just there." His accent is even stronger. "In case you want to sit down."

Panic starts to rise within me.

He laughs: a raucous sound. I clench my hands into tight fists. They twitch with energy. I think about punching him and running—but I know I won't be able to. My body's locking up, doesn't feel like it's my own.

"S'ven." Jed's voice is strangely soft. "I have no interest in having a sexual relationship with you."

"What?" I blink several times, wish I could see him. Don't understand what he means, what games he's playing. "But you've just... I'm supposed to *marry* you."

I think he nods.

"I know."

I stare at him. My eyes are adjusting now, and I can make out a slight contour in the darkness, a contour that I think is the edge of his face. "But you're not interested in me?"

"Do not sound so surprised. You are not that attractive."

My head whirs, and I don't know why those words make me feel like I do. Then it occurs to me: Jed and Corin were the last fighters left in the ring. Jed and Corin. *Corin*. And Jed doesn't like Corin.

My next breath catches. "You did it to stop Corin from winning me?"

"I am not a petty teenager, S'ven."

I shake my head. "So, why? Why did you do it? Why'd you stop Corin?"

There's a slight pause, a pause in which I hear just how heavy his breathing is.

"To keep an eye on you."

I go cold. I draw my lips into a firm line. In my hair, my Seer pendant starts to radiate heat; my fingers itch to touch it. But I force myself not to move. Jed's watching me, I'm sure, like he's waiting for something—for me to do something, say something. Confirm it.

I hear his clothes rustle as he steps closer. His hands land on my shoulders, make me jump.

"S'ven. Do not speak a word of this to anyone." He squeezes my shoulders; his grip is too hard, too firm. "No one can know about this arrangement, they must think we are together—together in *all* the ways—else I will lose status, and I will not be happy. Bad things happen when I am not happy. Understand? Good. Come on." He lets go of my shoulders, then grabs my hand. "We will go and find others."

I am only too eager to go back out into the tubes where there is light. I try to clear my throat, but I can't seem to work the muscles there.

Oh Gods. Somehow, he knows.

There's only one reason why a Zharat Seer would want to keep an eye on me: to get proof.

To get proof, before he kills me.

Jed knows I'm a Seer.

TWENTY-FIVE

I EXPECT JED TO SAY something—a hint at least of what he knows, a few words to scare me, make me nervous—but he doesn't. He doesn't say anything, just delivers me to the gathering area, then hovers behind me, leaving me wondering how long he's known for...since he asked about my pendant in the Zharat lorry? I swallow hard.

There are a few people chatting, and I catch the end of a conversation; how the girls who went fishing at the Old Lakes this morning are unusually late returning. They were supposed to bring fresh fish for the wedding supper, but at least that's not happening.

Jed prods me forward, then departs abruptly. Doesn't say anything. For some reason, that makes me more nervous.

I pull a hand through my hair, my fingers curling briefly around my pendant. I look around for a face I know, then cross my arms over my chest, wish I was wearing anything but this dress.

"Seven." Soraya approaches me.

Immediately, my chest lightens.

"I'm sorry." Her words are light. "Arranged

marriages suck when you don't get who you want, and I know that wasn't the outcome you were hoping for. Come on," she says. "You want to check on Corin?"

I nod, and then we're weaving through several tubes, descending deeper into the mountain. The whole way, I feel sick, and just when I think I'll have to stop—because I can't breathe and everything's moving too fast—I see him.

Corin's lying on a blanket in the middle of a small room, off to the side of the tube. He's awake, fully clothed now. I can hear his words—he's asking for a lighter. Two women are dressing a wound on his leg. I can't see how deep it is, but the bedclothes—and everything else around him—are stained with blood. Both his arms have already been bandaged, and his grip on the cigarette in his hand doesn't look strong.

Esther stands by him.

"Go on," Soraya says, gives me an encouraging smile. "I'll head back to the gathering room, cover for you if Jed comes back and asks where you are."

"Thank you," I whisper.

As I approach, Corin turns his head. His eyes meet mine, and emotions wash between us. I try to slide Jed's ring off my finger as subtly as I can, but it gets stuck. I leave it there, block that hand from Corin's sight.

Esther turns and sees me, scowls. I reach for her as she nears me, but she glares even harder.

"I suppose I should be grateful to you that your husband didn't kill my brother."

I freeze, feel every muscle in my body tighten. Tighten until it's too much, until there's too much pain. *Corin*. He—he's really hurt. And Jed did this.

A new wave of anger fills me.

"Shouldn't you be with your husband?" Esther's tone is cynical, and I don't understand. This isn't my fault, and I want to yell that at her. "That's what Manning says. We have to obey their customs. And Manning knows what he's talking about—he's the leader of the *biggest* Untamed group." Her lips pinch together.

I try to stay calm, end up wiping the sweat from my hands onto the back of my dress. The stupid ring catches the fabric. "Jed is not my husband."

Not yet. And he never will be. Because Jed will kill me. Kill me for being a Seer.

I swallow the lump in my throat, push past Esther, and kneel next to Corin. I reach out with my right hand to touch his arm.

But he shakes his head.

"Don't." His sweat-soaked hair falls over his damp forehead. He struggles to push it back, his arm jerking. He grunts several times, pain in his eyes.

I pull back my hand, feel the bridge of my nose prickling. The two women attending Corin get up in unison; I listen to their light footsteps as they leave. And then Esther's moving around the room. She stops by Corin's other side, looking at me with those accusing eyes.

This is your fault, she mouths.

Corin moves his head a fraction, and my eyes snap back to him.

"I'm sorry, Sev." His eyes are now completely devoid of emotion. He looks defeated, weak; I've done this to him. "I'm sorry, I failed."

I shake my head. "No, you didn't! Corin, he's a *Seer*. He was using his powers against you… Like how Raleigh did with me. There was nothing you could've done."

And I want to tell him. I want to tell Corin what Jed said… That he's not interested in a physical relationship with me—because I know if I tell Corin, it will make him feel better. But I can't; Jed's words ring in my ears. *Bad things happen when I am not happy.*

I try to keep calm, try to keep my breathing even, regular. But the waves inside me are rallying, pushing, shoving. And I've got to say something.

"Jed knows," I whisper. "He knows I'm a Seer."

For a second, I nearly choke. But it's okay, I *can* tell them that. There's nothing to stop me saying *that*— and no other Zharat are within hearing distance.

Corin's gaze jerks to me. His face pales even further, and he drops the cigarette.

"So?" Esther says.

"Don't you know what they do to female Seers?" Corin shakes his head, and I hope Esther can work it out. I don't want him to say the words. If he says the words, it makes it real. Too real.

Just like how you said the words that Three is dead? And he is, isn't he?

He is. He has to be. That was just a nightmare.

Corin looks at me. "You're sure? You're sure Jed knows?"

I press my lips into a thin line, then nod. It's the only explanation.

Neither of them says anything for a long, long moment.

"Has he said anything, tried to hurt you?" Esther asks. But her tone's still off, her voice isn't friendly.

I shake my head, but there's something about Esther's question that gets to me. According to the Zharat customs, Jed should have killed me already. I don't understand why he's waiting for proof. The Zharat are all action. It doesn't make sense.

My hands are behind my back, so Corin can't see the ring, and I grip them together hard.

Esther snorts. "You're overreacting." Then she scowls, her eyes disappearing under her dark brows. It's an expression I can't recall seeing on her for a long, long time. Even when I'd just been rescued from the Enhanced compound, and augmenters were still in my system, she was fairer than this.

"But he definitely knows?" Corin looks at me.

"I think he's waiting…" I look around again, check that no one else has entered. "He *must* be waiting for me to visit the Dream Land. Giving me the benefit of the doubt? Then he'll… Then he'll kill me." And I hate saying the words, because those words make me sound weak, like I'm not going to do anything, like my death is a certainty.

But I need to do something. Jed hasn't killed me yet—for whatever reason—so I *can* still act.

Corin swears, clenches his fists. The scabs on the back of his hands burst, fresh blood oozes out. "Gods, this is so messed up."

He breathes deeply, and Esther glares at me, as if it's all my fault. Maybe it is. I was the one who said we'd all come here.

"We should leave," Corin says slowly. "The three of us. We have to. We can't stay here. You can't marry that man." He meets my heavy eyes with his own, then sits up more. "We should just walk and keep going."

I nod. He's right. We have to leave.

And I can leave. The kavalah's gone now—so Raleigh won't have my eyes any longer—so I can't be putting anyone in danger by going the outside. And though I'm sure Raleigh's trying to find another way to use my eyes, something inside me insists that when he succeeds the bison will warn me. Just like he did last time, because I couldn't feel the effects of the kavalah for the first few days. The bison still told me, warned me.

And I *have* to leave. It's safe for me to go. I must.

I turn to Corin, feel the adrenaline fire through my body. I'm doing something. I'm taking control.

"Can you walk?" I eye his leg doubtfully.

"But the Zharat won't let us leave," Esther says. "Manning told me that. We can't leave."

Corin turns on Esther. "So you're not even going to try? You'd rather Sev be forced into this disgusting marriage, killed for being a Seer? That man is…" His voice is fraught with emotion. "It'll be you next, Esther. As soon as you're back to full health, they'll marry you off too. And the Gods only know which man will win you. It could be *anyone*." His expression hardens, and I can't help but think Manning will want

Esther. "We've got to leave. We've got to leave *now*. Sev's already in enough danger as it is."

After a few seconds, Esther shrugs. And—

And the darkness comes back, creeps and crawls over me, prickles my left side. Like… Like before, when Jed won—

I blink, throw my hands out, try to grab onto something before I fall.

"Sev?"

Corin… But I can't see him… My heart's too fast… Can't see anything… Or feel… There's nothing.

Just darkness. So much darkness. Darkness and—

There's nothing here to see, Little One.

A new voice. But…but not a voice.

"Sev? Esther—help!"

I hear him, his voice—strong, pure. Try to latch onto it, see his voice: beautiful gold threads, threads that pull me back.

I open my eyes, groggy, head pounding, find that I'm cradled in Corin's lap. Somehow, he managed to sit up and catch me? I stare up at him for several seconds, then try to get up. He stands with me, eyes wide.

"What happened?"

I touch my head gingerly, as if expecting blood. "What?" I stare at him—he's asking *me*?

"The Dream Land?" he says. "That was like when Katya fainted when we were…."

The Dream Land? I swallow with a little difficulty. "No. It… It wasn't." I shake my head. My vision blurs a little; for a moment, I think I remember words. Something—someone—spoke to me… Didn't they?

I frown, but the more I try to recall the voice, the less I'm certain of…until I'm sure there isn't anything to remember.

"You okay?" Corin asks.

I nod slowly. "My head feels foggy…like…I can't think properly." I grimace and rub my temples.

"Right," Corin says. He looks at me, dubiously,

then at his sister. "Well, we still need to get you out of here. Might be low blood sugar or something making you faint. We can find food outside. Yams, whatever. Esther, go and look at the nearest entranceway. See if there's anyone about."

Esther stands slowly. A second later, she heads for the exit. She's thinner than she used to be. A lot thinner. The green dress emphasizes it.

"It'll be all right, Sev," Corin says, pulling me close to him. I breathe in his scent. Slightly musky, and some strange smoke. He doesn't smell right. "We will get out of here. I'll make sure of it. You don't need to worry."

I nod, breathe deeply, and try to believe him.

Corin wraps his arms tightly around me. The familiar cage. Safety. Security. My heart quickens as I stretch up onto my tiptoes. A part of me is surprised as I initiate the kiss. His lips are harder than I remembered, and I feel him splay his fingers out against my upper back, bringing me closer still.

I keep the kiss short, try not to shake as we pull apart. We'll be outside soon.

Raleigh has your eyes.

I try to ignore the way the Dream Land warning echoes in my mind—it's wrong. That kavalah's no longer inside me, Raleigh's no longer got my eyes. And I have to go. If I stay here, they'll kill me.

Corin nods. "We'll finish that kiss when we're outside. When we're free of all this shit." His hands slide down my bare shoulders, my arms, and his fingers play with mine. "Ready?"

TWENTY-SIX

THE NEAREST EXIT IS DOWN a narrow tube. Esther isn't sure Corin will fit through it, but, as the tube is completely empty, Corin and I think it's the best option.

"Manning won't be happy when he finds out." Esther clicks her tongue.

"But we'll be long gone when he does. He won't be able to punish us then. We'll be safe." Corin coughs, gestures for me to step in front of him.

I do. I've got jeans, a yellow shirt, and leather shoe-wraps on now—they were in the corner of the room, with more bandages. Even though the Zharat won't be happy about the color, I feel better wearing the shirt than Nyesha's mother's dress, though the fabric rubs roughly against my left side—the prickly pain is still there. As if I've been bitten by insects or something. Maybe from the red wedding dress. I make a mental note to check for bites when we're outside.

The engagement ring is in my pocket now, and my mother's pendant is back around my neck, the crystal hidden under my shirt.

"And what about the spirits out there?" Esther says.

She's still wearing her dress. "Manning said there are always some about. And we won't have the chief to protect us from them."

I shake my head at her, in disbelief. "We don't need Manning. We've survived all this time without him."

"Not in the Noir Lands." She gestures around us. "This is the hardest place to survive, and look how many Untamed Manning has kept alive. We'd be stupid to leave."

I ignore her and go first, stooping. My height isn't ideal, and my neck cricks as I bend, but I'm skinny—I get through.

The darkness is disorientating. My hands brush against the walls, cold. I blink into the gloom; my brain starts to make out murky shapes ahead.

I push on ahead, and the space narrows even more.

"How long is this tube?" Corin's grunting hard. I can tell he's in pain, more pain than he's letting on.

I turn back, trying to see him, but can't.

"I *said* we should go to a better entrance." Esther's voice is shrill. "I *said* that. What if the Zharat come up behind us, realize what we're doing? We're not going to be able to move quickly, or talk our way out of this. They'll kill us."

She's right. Corin swears. We've trapped ourselves in.

"Keep going, Sev."

My chest burns. I feel my way ahead, hands on the damp stone. Something slimy washes over my fingers. I shudder.

"What was that?" Corin's voice is fast.

"What?" I come to a complete stop again.

Voices.

I inhale, try to turn, try to see Corin and Esther. But can't.

My stomach twists, and then Esther's hand is on my arm, pushing me forward. But the space is just too dark. There's no light at all.

Oh Gods.

"They're down there! They're trying to get out that way!" The voice is loud, shrill.

I freeze, feel sick. How do they know, how do the Zharat know we're trying to escape? They can't... Unless they heard us... Heard us saying that we needed to escape... And everyone knows we can't leave....

Oh Gods.

"We can't change the plan now," Esther hisses. "Keep going."

I do. I place my left foot in front of the other, pull myself forward, trip on something. My hands slam out onto the walls, and I grab at slime that squeezes through my fingers.

"They're right behind us, shit!" Corin grunts.

My breath comes in heavy gulps that rage through me. I start to feel lightheaded—or at least, I think I do, but I can't see. Can't see a thing. Can't see if I'm blacking out.

I hit my arm on the wall, pain. The tube continues to narrow. I try to speed up, but can't. The space is too small. Oh Gods. Corin's not going to get through here.

And the voices get louder. Shouting? I don't know, can't tell. Everything sounds fuzzy. My ears are too hot, they're burning.

But the voices are behind us—that much I know.

"Stop!" the voice cries. Male.

My stomach clenches.

Mart. It's Mart voice.

Mart. But he's dead... He's supposed to be dead. Jed said he'd been dealt with.

For something that wasn't his fault. I swallow hard.

"Keep going!" Esther's pushing at me, her nails are sharp. "It's just around the corner."

I try to keep going. There's a corner? I blink, can't see a thing. How does she know? Or can she see? Is it my panic that's blocking my vision?

Oh Gods. Need to calm down.

"You must stop now! Stop now, and we will not kill

you."

Kill us? I gulp. Oh Gods! But they're going to kill me anyway. Jed will have told them I'm a Seer, and that's why I'm trying to escape—because my cover is up. Oh Gods. They all know.

I'm shaking, shaking too much. But I push myself farther on, hands on the walls, have to duck even more. I'm crawling, on my knees. The ground is wet. My jeans are damp.

And the voices….

And then—then I slam into something hard. It takes me a moment to work it out, to realize that this is the corner. I stick my hands out either side, feeling for a way.

There. Right. I turn, pull myself down, whack my head on more rock, and—

I see light.

I blink. It's blinding. Too bright.

But it's light.

I surge forward. The voices get louder. I want to look back, want to check—*Corin*—but I can't. I have to keep going.

And I'm on my stomach, and my arms are aching. But I pull myself along. Something cold drips onto my neck, and I shudder. But I'm looking at the light. The little patches of light.

And—

My mouth dries.

No. No. No.

I stare at it. I stare at the metal bars. Beyond, I can see the sky—blue—and vegetation. Some sandy rock.

But there's a foot-high grid, in the way. The type of grid I know won't swing open.

My lips burn. How didn't I notice? How didn't Esther notice? And then a part of me wonders if she knew it was there—because she never wanted to leave… Could she have warned the Zharat?

No.

What am I thinking? Esther wouldn't do that. She's

one of us. I shake my head, stare at the grid. I'm almost at it now, right in front of it. In front of the metal grid. I pull myself farther along the tube, on my stomach, toward the bars. I reach them, shake them, try to move them, but I can't. I pull myself up until I'm crouching by the bars, my whole body pressed against the cool metal frame, leaning against it, hoping my weight will make it give.

But it doesn't.

And the Zharat are getting closer.

Esther's right behind me, starts saying something, but I can't make it out.

Pain shoots around my hip as I try with the grid again. I cry out in frustration. My left eyelid twitches, and some sandy soil blows against me from outside, gets in my eyes. Sharp stings.

Get out.

Nausea races through me.

Get out now, Seven.

There's a rushing in my ears, and I turn, trying to rub my eyes with the back of my hand. We need another exit—but the Zharat are too close, I can hear them.

"Stay back!" Corin shouts. "Sev, get out!"

But I can't. I can't do a thing. I was right—this isn't the type of grid that swings open. This is the type of grid used to block an exit.

We've trapped ourselves, like herd animals backed into a pit.

And they're going to kill us.

I turn slowly, maneuvering my body in the small space, my face pressed against the rough rock. Behind me, Esther's shaking, pressed up against the side of the tube, as if her posture will make her smaller or make the space bigger.

I look past her, see Corin, his face pushing through the shadows, the darkness. He's having difficulty—the tube walls are either side of him, and he breathes hard with every movement.

He's almost at us, but then he yells out and twists to

the side, throwing his hands forward. Somehow, I see his fingers as they try to get a grip on the floor. Behind him, movement and light—a torch. The flickering beam and Corin's foot lifting up—no, *being lifted*.

"Get off!" he yells.

My mouth dries as I see fingers wrap around Corin's ankle. Then he's dragged backward.

TWENTY-SEVEN

"CORIN!"

My scream fills the space, and then a beam of light burns my eyes, makes me turn my head.

"Get back over here now—and we won't kill any of you."

The voice is low, gritty, male, and I can't see who it belongs to—everywhere I look, I see the impression of the torch beam, burned into my retinas. But the words are a lie. I know that. They might not kill Esther or Corin, but they'll kill me. Manning made it clear they kill female Seers.

Oh Gods.

I swallow hard, feel mucus at the back of my throat.

Corin shouts, then I hear scuffled sounds. A moment later, the voice barks again.

Esther retreats, just about managing to turn around in the small, low space. I follow her, pulling myself along on my stomach until the space widens, and then hands grab me, pull me roughly toward them. My heart thumps. The side of my face catches on rough rock, and I wince, but the Zharat don't stop—they pull me to my feet, force me onward.

I try to see how many of them there are, but I can't make them out properly because torches throw light everywhere. The men are just shapes, shapes that snarl and dig their fingers into my arms as they drag me along.

Shapes that will kill me.

My throat tightens.

Somewhere ahead, Esther whimpers.

"Keep going," a whiny voice says, and the words are right next to me. Sudden heat brushes my neck. My arm jerks out, my hand touches a body, I scream.

And then—

Then something goes over my head.

I freeze and try to take a breath, but I only suck the gritty fabric closer. I try to breathe more shallowly, but he's holding the fabric too tightly over my face, and I can't see anything. It blocks out everything, even the torchlights. My chest burns. I turn, smack into something hard. Fear rises up in me.

Shit.

The fabric across my face scratches. The sudden blindness is horrible, more than if it was just the darkness around me. Because this is a barrier, a physical barrier. It makes me feel sicker, and I feel something moving inside me.

Oh Gods. I remember the waterboarding—the cloth against my face, the vomit stuck against my lips. I shudder.

I try to listen, try to think. I need to think, have to think.

Corin. Where is he? He's not shouting now. There's no sound from him. Or Esther. There are no sounds from either of them, not at all.

The bad taste in my mouth gets deeper, spreading down my throat as the intensity rises. Sour and bad and old.

"Walk," the man barks at me. I feel his hands on my shoulders, cold, like splinters of ice that scratch my soul, bestrewing frost over my being, freezing me. I shudder, but I walk.

He guides me forward. The stench of stale sweat drops over me.

"Keep walking, faster," the man holding me says.

I keep walking. No choice. Oh Gods. My head whirs. I start to feel strange. My movements become mechanical. I know I should be thinking about how I'm going to escape from this. How we're all going to escape.

I trip over something—a rough bit in the ground? Think we're at the end of the exit tube. We turn left, and the air gets heavier.

The man prods me in the back. A sharp dig. My tear ducts burn. I speed up, and then, a few minutes later, there are steps to climb. And more. Then we turn left again—down another tube? I'm not sure; I've lost all sense of direction.

The air gets colder still. I shudder. Then my foot lands in something wet, and I wince. The soaked leather of my shoe-wrap makes a *slap-slap* sound on the ground as I walk.

Someone breathes heavily.

"Down here," a voice says a minute later, and then there are more steps, leading down this time. Sharper ones, uneven.

I count them as we go down. There are eighteen. Dread fills every step I take.

If you're deep enough, no one will hear your screams when they kill you.

I flinch—don't know where that thought came from—and nearly stumble.

We keep walking. I hear more voices, more of the Zharat.

A few minutes later, they tell us to get in the cage. Then I'm pushed forward, and I trip over something, throw my hands out, hit the floor.

I hear the sounds of metal against metal, a big clang. Then I'm pulling at the textile material around my head. My fingers catch on string—they tied it?

When?—and my breath comes in shallow bursts as I try to work the knots out.

It takes me ages—ages while the Zharat must all just watch me, and I don't understand.

I get the fabric bag off, throw it to the side. Harsh light floods my eyes, and I blink rapidly, at last see the metal bars on three sides of me—they stretch from the floor to the ceiling. The fourth side of the enclosure is a lava wall, rough, lumpy-looking—and in front of it is Corin. I rush toward him, and his arms go around me, locking under my ribs. We're breathing hard, then we're both sliding down, grasping at each other and meeting the hard stone floor. I turn my head, but the light's too bright still, and everything's spinning.

It takes me a long time to make out the figures on the other side of the bars. The men, the women. *Mart.* I see him, feel my muscles tense.

Then they leave.

Corin shouts something, then peels himself from me, gets up. He runs to the metal bars, throws his weight at them. They don't move. The gate is secured with a padlock. It's a big one, and the electric lantern on the far wall—about four feet away from the cage— lights up the metal. It glints, smiles. Something about it reminds me of the Luger I had a long time ago.

"Where's Esther?" The question shoots out of me, makes me feel sick.

I turn, look around again, and so does Corin. But she's not here. It's just us. Just us—alone, but Manning doesn't want us alone together, does he? Or maybe they've only got one cage…and they're going to kill us anyway….

I clap a hand to my mouth, and then Corin's yelling. Yelling and yelling.

The Zharat don't come back.

A few minutes later, Corin turns back to me. "Are you hurt?"

He moves closer. He doesn't sit next to me though, just stands there, breathing hard. His hands are clenched into tight fists, and I pick out a vein on his neck that's pulsing. His forehead is bleeding a little, and I think of all the injuries he sustained in the fight for me only earlier today—yet he's the one asking me the question. I don't even know how he's standing.

I shake my head, then draw my knees up to my chest. I need to think. There's got to be something I can do. Corin's already tested the metal bars. I look toward him, then touch the back of my head. I swallow hard. There's a lump at the back of my throat that tastes like yam pottage.

Corin exhales, doesn't speak.

And I don't know what to say, so I just stare at the shapes in the lava, imagine them as different animals. A lion. An antelope. A gorilla. I should feel scared, I'm sure. I scratch at my neck, look across at Corin. They're going to kill me for being a Seer. But what about him? He was helping me escape. And Esther? I swallow hard, don't like where my line of thought is going.

I press my lips together. They taste salty.

We hear the footsteps long before the Zharat reappear. Three of them. Manning, Jed, and Mart. Now their eyes are on fire, and if there was anything friendly about them before, there's nothing left now.

I stand up slowly.

Manning steps up to the cage, the other two flank him, a few feet back. The Zharat Chief holds a gun, and he tosses another one at Jed, but Jed's reaction is slow, and he nearly drops it. Mart smirks.

Corin points at Mart. "I thought you killed him."

Manning shakes his head. "He ain't the one who sent the kavalah after the woman. None of us was— Jed traced the kavalah out of the cave, found the life-energy it had already obtained from its human wasn't Zharat. So it ain't Mart who sent it." Manning's eyes flicker to me; there's something dark and dangerous in them. "Though she deserved it. *Traitor*."

I frown and look at Jed—he told me before that Mart had been dealt with. I press my lips together, feel sicker still. And now Manning's saying Jed knew Mart wasn't involved, that no Zharat were. Why would he lie about Mart?

My mouth dries, tastes scratchy. I try to distract myself by staring at Manning's gun, try to work out its make and model, but I can't see it properly. I don't like the light in here, it's too bright. I'm dizzy enough already.

"You've got to let us out," Corin says. "This is mad. And where the hell is Esther? We weren't even trying to escape. Just exploring, and we got stuck in that tube—why have a tube that narrow? It's ridiculous. I don't know what the hell you—"

Manning points the gun at him, lining it up through the bars, and Corin freezes. My mouth dries. My throat tickles. I stay where I am, brace my legs, try to think of something to do.

"Don't lie. We know you're spies for the Enhanced Ones." Manning's words drip with venom. "Do not deny it. We *know*. And we will kill you both."

"*What*?" Corin exclaims. I think he's forgotten about the gun. Or he's not bothered anymore. He points a finger at Manning, and the gesture reminds me of Rahn. "Are you mad? Spies?"

Manning's eyes narrow. "If you were just trying to escape, man, you'd have gone for an entranceway. You were going for that grid. To pass messages out to the Enhanced."

I stare at him. This isn't about me being a Seer? My gaze jerks to Jed. He hasn't told them?

"No, we *weren't* going to pass messages on because we're *not* spies," Corin persists. "We were exploring."

I stand up straighter, and a weak, humming noise fills my ears. I flinch. It sounds like a swarm of flies. I look around, can't see any. Strange.

"I heard you," Mart says, and his eyes are narrowed, on me. "I heard you planning a conversion attack." He points at me. "You were speaking into a radio, organizing it. You're the one in charge of it."

"What?" I shake my head, heart pounding. "No! I'm not… I wasn't!"

"Don't lie your way out of this," Mart snarls.

"He's the one who's lying," Corin yells, then he limps right up to the bars, right up to Mart. "I know you don't like Sev, and you're holding a grudge against her since you tried to attack her. Manning, this is stupid. We are not spies. I'm telling you—and where the hell is my sister?"

Manning just smiles. "Esther's safe. She's a good woman. I know she ain't no spy. You was using her. She won't be punished."

"What?" Corin exclaims. He looks back at me, mouth dropping open.

"Yes," Manning smiles. "We know what you are." And he smiles across at Mart, pats him on the shoulder. Mart's lips curl into a dangerous grin. "Our executioners be on the way."

Executioners?

And we're being killed because we're spies, not because I'm a Seer. The whole thing seems ludicrous.

I glance at Corin. His face has paled.

"You can't actually believe this," Corin says. "We're not spies—let alone spies for them!"

For a second, I think Manning's face is going out of focus…then I blink again, and it rights itself. Pain flits across my forehead.

Jed makes a slight gasping noise, and Manning looks at him.

"Search the cave," Jed says, eyes on me. His voice is slow, like he's drugged. "Just in case the enemy is here. And look for the radio she has been using."

"Just kill them," Mart says, pointing at my face. "*She's* a spy. And Jed's right—we'd better do a search. It was a proper conversion attack she was planning, and it sounded like Enhanced Ones are definitely in here."

"I wasn't planning a conversion attack!" I glare at him, but then the humming in the air gets louder and more irregular, all crackly and abrasive against my ears. I rub my bare arms with my hands. My skin is sore.

"You… Don't kill them… " Jed shakes his head, gasping again. "You need to…" He trails off, then starts talking fast in the Zharat language.

I start to feel strange. My vision blurs again, but the left corner's lifting up, tilting. No. Can't be. But it *is*. I shake my head, frown, then feel pressure all around my temples. I touch them gently, try to massage them.

Interference. That's what I can hear. It's everywhere. Crackling. Hissing.

I look toward Corin, blinking hard. For a second, I see two of him.

"Jed?" Manning says, and his tone makes me jump. His voice sounds strange, like he's underwater. Or like I'm underwater. One of us is.

My heart rate soars. I think of the kavalah, feel my temperature rise. Oh Gods. Not again—he can't have got my eyes again… But before I didn't feel strange like this until the kavalah had been in me a while… And what if this one was already in me, when I saw out the grid?

But I didn't see much. Barely saw anything. It was just…generic. Nothing to identify this place. Just sand and rock and vegetation and—

The crackling around me gets louder, and I shake my head from side to side.

Nausea pulls through me, my gaze catches Jed's. He's staring at me, his expression blank, his eyes defocussing. Oh Gods. He can see it. He can see the kavalah in me.

"Jed, man? What is it?" Manning's voice. Angry. Too angry.

My Seer pendant burns savagely, suddenly white hot against my skin. I inhale sharply as the pain circles me, and Jed grunts. I press my hands to my sides, then feel something in the pocket of the jeans. I pull it out—a ring. The ring. The engagement ring. I drop it back into my pocket quickly.

Then I realize it. Whatever's happening to me, it's happening to Jed too. And I know, just know, it's happening to all other Seers. It's a Seer thing—nothing to do with a kavalah or Raleigh! And I don't know how I'm so certain, but I am.

And Manning and Mart will see it happen to me. They'll know. They'll know I'm a Seer.

Then they'll kill me.

Jed raises his arm. "The others—check the others… The other Seers…now!"

And he looks at me, directly at me, and his eyes are the clearest things I can see. They're the only shapes that are strong in here. The only things that aren't moving, blurring.

He knows. Confirmation. I'm a Seer, and he *knows*.

Yet I'm still alive.

He doesn't want me dead?

Jed coughs, bending over. He twists around, and then he's pushing Manning and Mart away. "Go and check the others, now!"

The air's getting too hot. It's smothering me. I try to bat it away, but can't. My hands won't work, and my movements are too jerky. I'm not in control.

"Sev?" Corin's hand is on my shoulder, and I twist my head as I try to see him. But his face is falling away from me.

"*Go*… Check the others now…" Jed cries. Out of the corner of my eye, I see him pushing Manning and Mart farther away still. "A God is *dying*."

Manning and Mart go. They just disappear.

A God is dying.

I look at Jed. He sent them away. He sent Manning and Mart away. He's protecting me? I don't understand, but it seems important. And I'm sure the reason is close, it's obvious, but there's too much other stuff and the air's murky and I can't work it out because I can't breathe, can't get enough oxygen, and my head's pounding. Pounding. Just pounding.

A God is dying.

I start to choke. Saliva goes the wrong way. I gag, feel Corin's hands on me. I try to turn.

The pain sets in.

Needles, they scratch my eyes. Pull at my ears. Soft flesh, tearing.

Screaming. Screaming. Screaming.

I feel my body stiffen as though it isn't my body, but someone else's. I feel everything harden—my lungs, my liver, my heart.

The last thing I see is Jed falling to the ground: how his body just collapses, the amount of foam that spews from his mouth, and the way his eyes roll backward, unseeing. And then there's nothing left. Nothing left for me to see—only darkness.

And the darkness stretches on forever.

I open my eyes to see the sharp edge of an axe two feet above me. So sharp. A fine line. I stare at the blade. It's—

I scream, roll over just as the axe comes down. Someone shouts something—Corin?—and then everything's a blur of movement and darkness. And there's not enough light in the caves, and I can't see properly.

My thighs protest as I stand—sharp, burning pains—but I make it to the side of the cage; my back presses against cold metal bars. The man with the axe advances toward me.

An executioner.

Behind him, on the other side, I see Corin fighting with a second man—another executioner, wielding a bigger axe and—

"Corin!"

A blur of movement as the axe moves toward Corin, but then he moves faster, and I hear his breathing—heavier.

"Lie down," the man in front of me snarls, and my gaze jolts back to him. I recognize him distantly—I've seen him about in the cave, but that's all I know. He readjusts the weight of the axe in his hands, grips the weapon higher up the handle. Light glints from a ring in his left brow. "It will be easier if you lie down."

"Sev, no!"

I try to stand my ground, but I'm shaking. The man and the axe get nearer. I press myself farther into the side of the cage, until the metal bars push painfully against my spine. Until it feels like I'm going to break.

"Lie down."

I look behind him, my chest rising and falling too quickly. Clench my fists, consider going for a punch, remembering what Corin taught me. But the axe is in the way. It's massive.

Oh Gods. I'm going to die. I'm really going to—

A gurgled noise fills the air, makes me jump.

My gaze jerks to the left...to Jed. On the floor, outside the cage. He's sitting up, wiping white frothy stuff from his mouth.

The executioner's still looking at me, still talking, telling me to lie down.

"No!" Jed yells. His arm flies out at an awkward angle, and he winces. "Do not kill her." Jed leans on the bars. "Do not kill either of them!"

The executioner turns back to him. "But they are traitors."

"No, they are *not*," Jed says. "She is my wife, and I do not want you killing my wife. And him—" Jed spits at the ground as he points at Corin. "Keep him alive. *Both* are to stay alive."

My executioner looks like he's going to protest, but Jed raises his hand. And I just stare at him, at Jed. He doesn't look good, sways slightly, and his eyes are bloodshot.

"That is an order, Renan. An *order* from a *Seer*."

I stare at him. Jed's protecting us—still...even though they all think we're spies...and he *knows* I'm a Seer? And he's not killing me....

Unless he really doesn't know?

I push that thought away; he *knows* I'm a Seer, definitely. What other reason could he have for wanting to *keep an eye* on me? And he sent Manning and Mart away, so they didn't see how I was affected by the God's death.

The God's death. I shudder. I don't understand.

I swallow hard. Jed has to know I'm a Seer. And he doesn't want anyone else killing me, because he wants to kill me himself.

"Why?" I ask, the sound drawing out. I catch Corin's eye. "Why save us? Jed?"

Jed's eyes seem to get darker as he walks toward the cage. "I would not ask that question," he says. "Not unless you want me to realize how mad I am because I listen to voices inside my head." He touches the padlock, and it unlocks—his Seer powers, got to be. Then he yanks the door open. "S'ven, just go!" he shouts. "Go back to our room. I will be there shortly, and I expect you to be wearing your engagement ring when I get there. And if you try to escape, mark my words, S'ven, I will kill you *and* Corin *and* Esther."

I swallow hard, don't want to go—don't want to leave Corin here. But something tells me disobeying Jed would be a very bad idea. And he can't be about to kill Corin, can he? Not when he just saved him....

"It's all right, Sev," Corin says. But he doesn't look certain.

"Go!" Jed yells. "I won't hurt him."

I go, heart pounding.

I get to Jed's room quickly, look around. The first thing I see is that there's an extra mattress in here now. It makes the room look smaller, more cramped, but relief floods through me. Then I pull the ring out my pocket—partly glad it's still there—and put it back on, try to pretend my stomach isn't churning.

I stand in the corner and wait, wishing I had a weapon, some way to protect myself. I don't know how long I'm in here for, but, when Jed arrives, he smiles strangely as he hands a cup and a bowl to me.

"You must be hungry, thirsty. Eat. Drink, S'ven."

After a long moment in which I try to work him out, I sit down on the nearest leaf mattress, and take a sip of the drink. It's that peppery flavor again. For a second, I feel uncomfortable, associating it with how ill I felt before. Then I tell myself to get a grip. It was that snake spirit that had made me feel bad before, or the alcohol. Not the drink Jed gave me.

I drink more, and I feel fine. *There*, I tell myself, but I don't move onto the food.

Jed points to the bed at the side of the room. "I will sleep here. I did not mean to scare you, S'ven."

I nod, but his words hang between us. I wait for his next sentence to be about me being a Seer. But it's not.

He just smiles. A smile that makes my skin crawl. A smile that makes me wrap my arms around myself. A smile that makes me sure there's something off about Jed, something I don't understand. Something bad.

But how can he be bad when he's letting you live, a female Seer? When he stopped them from killing you? When he stopped Manning and Mart from seeing how the dying God affected you?

I don't know. But I don't like him.

Jed sits down, looks at me. I swallow a bit more of the drink, a little too hastily. It seems to be getting hotter.

"I know you are not a spy," Jed says. "And I have searched for this radio you apparently used to plan the attack, and it does not exist. It was all Mart's lies. I have just been to Manning and made sure he knows of your innocence too—it will take a while for word to spread around, though. And I took Corin to get his head looked at—apparently he banged it hard on the way down there, when he was blindfolded. But he is okay." He shakes his head. "It was all Mart, his plan to get you killed for treason—pretending you were spies. He can be childish. I will have words with him, but you will have to watch out for him. He does not like you, thinks you tried to get him killed by blaming the kavalah spirit attack on him." He brushes his clothes down. "And the cave has been searched. Mart's story does not hold up. There are no Enhanced Ones here."

My body jolts a little, out of my control. I lift my head, find his eyes are on me. His look makes me go cold. Again, I try to work out why he's protecting me—a female Seer.

Because he thinks women can be Seers?

I clasp the back of my neck, feel pain in my head.

"Do not worry," Jed says. "I will protect you and look after you and honor you. I will never leave you."

I grip the cup tighter. My lips buzz. *Why*? My eyes narrow. Jed's lying. I know he is.

"But nothing can be done about your status now."

"What?" My word is a whisper.

He points at me—at my yellow top. "I told you what would happen before if you wore an inferior color. You become it. Dropped two whole ranks down the rainbow. Yellow is now your color."

There's something dark and heavy about the way he says the words, something that makes me shudder.

"We should get some sleep. I will be out hunting tomorrow." He pauses, and I hear his sharp intake of breath. "I do not want you to go outside."

"Why?" My voice is uncertain. He knows? How can he know? Have the Gods and Goddesses told him that our enemy had my eyes before and that they'll be trying to use them again? Or has he been warned that Raleigh's *already* done it again, that he's got my eyes once more, and that the Enhanced can track the Zharat through me for a second time? But, if that's the case, why hasn't the Dream Land told me that, warned me, like last time? Or am I going to get that message tonight?

And surely, *if* Jed knows I'm such a liability—that I could lead the enemy here—then he should just kill me right away to protect his people? Not keep me alive....

Jed's face darkens. "My wife—my *last* wife, Elle... she was killed during a hunt. A lion got her. They come up into the montane forest... I do not want you getting hurt. Stay in the caves. You will be safe here."

I swallow hard, feel a little sick. But why does he want me to be safe? He's not interested in me romantically—he made that clear. And he should hate me, should want me dead.

"We shall sleep now." He gives me a strong look. One I can't decipher.

I take off my shoe-wraps and lie down slowly, stiffly, still clothed in my damp jeans and yellow top, complete with blood and dirt. I brace myself as Jed places a blanket over me, then he lies down on his own mattress. A few minutes later, I hear the cries of a far-away baby.

"I do not want you talking to Corin anymore," Jed says suddenly. "You are supposed to be *my* fiancée. We have an appearance to keep up. You do not want to make me unhappy."

It sounds like a threat. And the words ring in my ears for hours afterward, and I fill in the rest of the threat: *You do not want to make me unhappy...else I'll tell Manning what you are.*

I swallow hard, turn onto my side. It takes hours for me to fall asleep, even once the far-away baby is quiet. Jed has kept the lantern on its lowest setting, so weak light filters out. He can't creep up on me in the dark. I stare across at the plates on the floor as sleep starts to overtake me. My food is still there; I can smell it.

My eyelids get heavier, and I don't want to sleep. Mustn't leave myself vulnerable to him....

But what if I need to go to the Dream Land? I need to sleep, in case the Gods and Goddesses and spirits need to give me a vision, warn me about Raleigh. I know that.

Sleep takes me, and I swim through darkness that drags me down. I wait for the Dream Land to materialize around me, wait for the bison.

But there's nothing. I just sleep. No Dream Land warnings. Nothing.

Because it's safe here, with the Zharat, a voice tells me. *Safer than you've ever been before. And you'll get used to the way things are run around here soon.*

And because I'm not called into the Dream Land, it makes me feel better. Raleigh hasn't got my eyes again, and he still isn't on his way, so he never saw the land outside when I went out that first time. And he didn't have my eyes earlier today, when I saw through the grid. If he had seen either of those times, the Dream Land would've warned me.

We really are safe here—and the bison told me to find the Zharat. We're meant to be here.

And it's that thought that terrifies me so much.

TWENTY-EIGHT

THE NEXT MORNING, JED LOOKS awful. Like he hasn't slept at all—the thought of him watching me sleep makes me shudder, and I curse myself for leaving myself vulnerable to him. He doesn't say a word as he joins the group of men waiting by the gathering area, ready for the hunt. They all stand there, sorting through their weapons.

After a while, I head down to the floor below. I need to wash, then find Corin—check that he really is okay.

There are a few women and girls already there, and some watch me with narrowed eyes. I hear the words *Enhanced spy* more than once. I tell myself to ignore them. I'm used to doing that. Having grown up with a highly prejudiced leader, I've learned to ignore a lot of comments.

It mustn't have rained that recently because the waterfall is a trickle, and the waterwheel is barely turning. One woman wonders whether the spirits have decided to cut the rainy season short, and several agree. Then another woman arrives, says that Barlee's gone into labor, and many leave quickly.

I wash myself as best as I can under the water, but

end up using too much of the soap-root, and it takes ages to wash it off.

I scrub at my sides, and I—

I freeze, stare at my skin there, then twist around, try to see it closer, clearer. My eyes widen as I touch my side again, feel the indentations above my left hip. They're close together, so close, that at first I think it's one wider mark, starting at my lower ribs and extending down, but it's not. The marks are slightly different. The ones in the middle are squarer. The ones around the edges are rounder. I wince, slight pain there. I poke at my skin more, until the whole area's sore. I think I can see specs of blood, but I'm not sure, the light in here's not great.

I frown, try to remember catching myself there. Then I remember the prickliness I felt before, when I fainted those times and when we were trying to escape…as if an insect had bitten me. I was going to check the skin there later, but I never did.

Now I stare at it. It's the same place. I nod. Insect bites. Maybe the Zharat den is infested.

I poke at my skin again, then try and stretch it out so the marks disappear.

"We need you to help with food preparation," a voice says.

I turn, see Jed's daughter—Jeena—staring at me, and I immediately put my hand over the insect bites. I don't know why I hide them, it's just instinct. My engagement ring burns.

Jeena doesn't smile, but she doesn't glare. It seems like a small thing, but it makes me feel a bit better. Maybe not everyone still believes I'm an Enhanced spy then.

For a moment, I want to say I can't join her yet—I need to find Corin—but I don't.

"Come as soon as you can," Jeena says, then turns away, leaves.

I quickly finish washing and try to forget about the insect bites, then dry myself off, pull on some clothes from the nearby box, careful to make sure my top is of my new color. The only one I can find isn't a nice yellow—somewhere between flaxen and a brassy hue. The only shorts in my size are a dull brown, and I hope that they will do. I can't find any shoe-wraps—but most of the women here don't seem to wear them in the tubes.

I feel better as I walk now, since I'm clean. But I'm walking on my own, and, at every corner I turn, I expect to see Mart and his friends up ahead. Expect to suddenly be grabbed. It is not a nice feeling, and I brace myself.

I speed up a little, trying to look into all the shadows, all the dark areas. But no one jumps out.

It's quiet now. But the air's getting hotter, drier. Harder to breathe.

I frown. This is right... I think. This is the right way to the food preparation area.

I trail my hands along the walls, over the lava ropes, feeling the bumps and dips. There isn't much light in here, though the skylight helps. I start to notice color on the wall as the tube twists around, up ahead. Blocks of red and white, thick black lines separating them. And drawings inside each marked-out box.

The bison is the first one. The bison from the Dream Land. I'd recognize him anywhere. Seeing him here though—in the real world, not in a Seeing dream—makes me feel strange. His eyes still follow me, and there's something about the atmosphere here... something that makes me feel this is important. That it's not just a painting I'm staring at.

I start to feel lightheaded, hear a hissing noise. I look up, see something cloudy ahead. Like the air's been colored slightly. Volcanic gasses? I frown. Hadn't the Zharat said there were no volcanic gases in the cave before?

I shrug.

The bison watches me the whole time.

I move onto the next painting, my skin crawling a

little. My head tingles.

It's a man. The figure's a man. A dark cloak covers his hunched body, and the hood obscures his face, but I can tell he's not facing toward me. He's looking to my left, but he's turning—he must be—because his arms are sticking out. Thin bony limbs that twist the wrong way from his body. Behind his arms, the black rock's been painted brighter. Blocked out with something white that makes it look as if his elbows are glowing.

I freeze, stare at the drawing.

My mouth dries, and I think I hear a clicking, whirring noise in my inner ear. I start to back away, but my legs feel like lead. I try to turn my head—got to look somewhere else—but can't.

My eyes burn.

It is a painting of him. A painting of Death. Done in dark blues and oranges, yet somehow I see other colors—a whole spectrum, twisting before me.

At the foot of the image are lumps of rock. Dark, sparkling gems. And a crudely carved, wooden doll with sparse straw-hair and a red-dyed face. Its mouth is a yellow half-moon, and its eyes watch me.

And then—

And then everything disappears. There's nothing—just blackness, emptiness.

I'm falling, arms and legs jerking out, trying to catch onto something—but there's nothing.

The air whizzes past me, moving too fast, and then—

Then it's gone.

No air.

The scream whirls inside me, can't escape. I try to turn, try to—

As quickly as it started, it stops. Air rushes into my throat, makes me choke. I look up, and I'm back in the Zharat tube, enclosed in the painted lava walls.

But it's different. It *feels* different. Everything looks the same, but dissimilar. Shimmering. Yes, it's shimmering—but only a little, as if there's a thin, watery glaze over my eyes.

I stare at the painting of Death.

It moves.

I leap back.

He turns toward me, and though I can't see his face—his hood holds a pit of darkness—I'm sure he's giving me a malevolent grin. His cloak billows, and he unfurls his back as he stands straighter, his head extending beyond the edge of the painting. He raises one bony arm and points a long finger at me.

"Death will be watching you… A traitor's soul is never free. A traitor's soul is Death's soul."

I flinch at the words, as if they've been cut into my skin, and jerk my gaze away from him. My breath comes in heavy bursts, and I lean forward, brace myself with my hands on my knees. But my arms shake, and I feel something fold around me, like the air's made of millions of threads, and they've formed a blanket, a blanket that wraps around me, tries to drag me down so Death can—

I turn back to him, look up and—

My heart speeds up as I stare at the…at the *image*.

It's just a painting. It hasn't moved. In it, Death isn't facing me like I thought he was. He's still looking to my left, still hunched over, so he fits in the box. His arms are still twisting the wrong way from his body, neither pointing at me.

The *painting* is all that is here. Just a painting—a flat, non-moving image.

Death isn't here, it's not like before—when Raleigh was… I try to calm myself. It's *just* a painting. The words were the same—an echo, a memory. That's all. I'm scaring myself. And I'm hallucinating—the image can't have moved. It's a painting, for the Gods' sake! I'm going mad. And the air's getting thicker, thicker with color, stronger. Something hisses. Pressure forms in my ears. As if I'm underwater.

Volcanic gasses. It's got to be. I'm hallucinating, reliving memories….

I take a deep breath, then touch the painting, spread

229

my fingers wide over it, and—

"No, this is the Dream Land, Seven Sarr."

I yank my hand back and look. The cave shimmers.

Death's elbows glow brighter as he pulls away from the wall again. The light gets brighter, and he starts to turn so I can see his face—and I know I will, it won't just be in darkness this time. But I mustn't see his face. No one must see it.

I swivel and run. And—

"*Obey* the Dream Land warnings, Seven Sarr, else Death will not be pleased. The mask of betrayal fits you well enough already—do you want it to be a permanent fixture?"

The voice is loud, and it's *his* voice. He's behind me. The man in the black cloak with the glowing elbows. Death, himself.

"Death knows all. Death sees all, and Death may be drawn to you, but Death will not give many more chances."

I stop. Blood pounds my ears. I won't look. I won't turn around.

I *won't*.

"The Dream Land exists for a reason, Seven Sarr. Do not ignore the Dream Land warnings." His elbows glow brighter, and his voice gets more severe. "Raleigh still has your eyes. Do *not* give him the chance to use them again."

My body jolts. Raleigh? He's been using my eyes all this time…*still*? I press my hands to my stomach. Is there another kavalah in me?

Death glares at me. "The stench of a traitor may cling to your skeleton, but *do not* let it become you. Do not let the gold cobwebs grow and rust further."

There's a long pause, and I hear rushing sounds in my ears.

"Your soul is already Death's soul. You will *always* belong to Death. You do not want to give him another reason to hate you."

TWENTY-NINE

I RUN, AND THE CAVE goes back to normal, no longer shimmers. It's a relief, but oh Gods—Death knows I didn't follow what the Gods told me. Knows I showed Raleigh the part of the Noir Lands where the Zharat live—that I showed him *twice*, because I looked through the grid at the end of that tube…. But I thought it was safe then, I thought my eyes were only mine!

But I was wrong.

Raleigh still had them. Or had got them again…

And Death knows I betrayed them.

You are marked for what you are. The mask of betrayal hangs over your aura, like gold cobwebs, rusting. Your body will rot under Death's command, long before your soul is allowed an escape from the decaying flesh of your ribs.

I flinch, then shake my head, paw at my temples, feel sicker than ever. When I die—when my death ends the suffering, like he said it would—he'll have my soul. A traitor's soul is never free.

You do not want to give Death another reason to hate you.

I try to remain calm, but that feels impossible. Raleigh's still got my eyes, can still use them. Maybe that kavalah spirit was just the start of it all, maybe it left a tracker or something... A way for Raleigh to *always* be able to see through my eyes....

Oh Gods.

"Sev?"

Suddenly, Corin's standing in front of me, in the tube. He stares at me, and I stare at him.

"Are you okay? No more fainting?" He peers at me, and I'm sure I should be asking after his health—not the other way around. He looks awful—sallow skin, covered in what looks like a sticky sheen of sweat.

I start to reach out for him, but stop.

Jed.

We have an appearance to keep up. You do not want to make me unhappy.

"I—I..." I shake my head, don't know what I'm saying. I need to tell him everything.

"Sev?"

Concern flashes into his eyes, and I want to tell him about Death—how I saw him when Raleigh tortured me, how I've seen Death again, and how he knows I went outside, that Raleigh could've seen—

That Raleigh *didn't* see... If he had, Death would've told me just now. He'd have been even more angry, *furious*. No. Death told me not to give Raleigh the *chance* to use my eyes again... So Raleigh *didn't* take that chance before...or either of them. No, this is a warning. A warning not to do it again.

But did Death really say that? Aren't you twisting it? Twisting it to make you feel better? Death didn't say Raleigh didn't *use your eyes either time...just that you mustn't allow him the opportunity again.*

Oh Gods. No. I shake my head. No. If Raleigh *had* seen anything, Death would've made sure I knew.

I take a deep breath. I'm still shaking. I stare at Corin, wonder how he'll react if I tell him about Death... Because no one speaks of Death, *ever*. I press my lips together, taste salt. What if Corin thinks I'm going mad, that it's all too much for me?

"Look, don't worry," Corin says. "I've been making plans. This will all be over soon. We're going to wait a week, then the three of us can escape. You, me, and Esther. Oh, and Clare—she's coming with us. We'll go out a proper exit this time. I've been talking to the other men, and they've got other lorries. They keep them a few miles from the lower tube exits, and I know where the keys are. It'll be easy."

There's a slight spark in Corin's eyes—something I haven't seen in a long, long time.

I stare at him.

Raleigh still has your eyes. Do not *give him the chance to use them again.*

"No. We can't…" My voice is too high, I'm sweating. "Corin, we'll get caught—and killed this time, Jed's not going to save us again. And we're not allowed to leave."

I can't leave. Death's made sure of that. If I left, Raleigh would use my eyes this time. And he'd find out where the Fire Mountain is… He'd come here, convert everyone. Nyesha and Soraya, and all the others—the ones I actually care about. And the children, the babies—there are so many of them.

Corin takes hold of both my hands in one of his. I stare at his fingers. They're bruised, look painful. And there are more bruises too, ones that go up his arms.

"We won't get caught," he says. "I've told you, I've made plans. This isn't like before, we were too hasty—this is going to work."

I breathe hard, shake my head again. Pain flits over my left eye.

Raleigh has your eyes.

My chest tightens. The warning: don't betray the Untamed. And it *was* a warning. Seeing the bison and Death in the cave—no the *Dream Land*… A proper warning.

I mustn't betray the Untamed again, I mustn't go outside.

I look at Corin. "I can't go. Can't leave."

"Of course you can leave."

"No. Raleigh—that warning, Corin. The one I told you about. Raleigh's got my eyes…."

His eyes narrow. "But I thought—"

"He's got them *again*—or still." My chest tightens, and I shake my head. "Corin, I can't put all the Zharat in danger, just because I want to get away."

Corin's face darkens. He lets go of my hands. "You were going to get away before."

I look around, and my tears threaten to fall. "I thought Raleigh didn't have my eyes then…but he did."

"Oh." The look in Corin's eyes changes. "It's true then."

"What?" I frown.

He looks away. "What those women were talking about this morning… You saying you're happy with Jed. That you're pleased he won you because he's a Seer…" His tone darkens. "*The greatest protector.*"

"What? No! *I* never said that, Corin—I'm not happy! You know I'm not happy! I wanted to escape—"

"*Wanted.*" His eyes seem to flash. "Past tense."

I stare at him, hug my chest. "Corin, I—"

Corin's arm jerks out, but he doesn't touch me. Then I realize it's our old gesture to be quiet—the one we used on raids. I look past him, see two very young girls, holding hands. One has three pale pink flowers in her hair, the other has one tucked into the belt on her dress.

We wait for them to pass; they watch us curiously.

"But you're not fighting it now," Corin hisses a few minutes later. "It was *me* who proposed, *me* who tried to find ways around it. And we can escape, we can, but *you* don't want to try."

"Because it'll lead the Enhanced here, Corin! There are hundreds of Untamed here, I can't do that to them."

"You didn't mind before."

I shake my head; he's not listening. I didn't think

Raleigh had my eyes then! And Death's watching me. Waiting for me to slip up. I rock back on my heels.

"You just don't *want* to try." Corin wipes the back of his hand across his mouth, shakes his head. Then he looks at my hands, at my ring. "It's him, isn't it? Jed."

"What?"

"He's making you say this, getting in your head. Controlling you—just like Manning's doing with Esther."

"No!" I try to reach for him, but he moves his hand. "No, Corin, Jed's not."

He turns away. "Look, if this is what it's going to be like—him just…controlling you like this… Well, I can't do this anymore. It's too painful, when I want to be with you—when I'd do *anything* to be with you— but you won't because you're scared of him. You won't even try anymore. And we've got a chance here, to get away, to be together, but you don't even want to *try* because of your fear."

"Corin, you're not being fair. This isn't about me, it's about all the Zharat, all the—"

"No, Seven. This isn't about them—I don't care about them. I care about *us*. And it's always *me* who's trying. You've given up on us. I don't know what's going through your head—maybe you think you deserve no quality of life because you took augmenters before and wanted to join the Enhanced, and this is your punishment—but you've obviously made your mind up and decided you have to be with Jed—that it would be easier or something—and not fight for *us*. So, I won't either."

I stare at him, aghast. And I want to tell him that it's okay, because Jed's not interested in me in a romantic way. But I can't get the words out. I just stare at him.

"How can you—" I break off. "Corin, we can't fight them! Look at what they're doing to you!" I grab at his arms, make him look at all the bruises.

The light goes out of his eyes.

"Look at what they're doing to *me*?" He shakes his

head. "You're not the girl who arrived here, Sev. She would've fought this. As pathetic as she was at times, she *would've* fought this."

My eyes blur over. My body jolts. *No.*

Corin meets my eyes slowly, but his gaze isn't strong. "I can't do this. Not anymore, Sev. Not now. You've changed, given up. I don't know what he's done to you, but you're getting farther and farther away from the girl I fell in love with."

THIRTY

JED COLLECTS ME FROM THE food preparation area when he returns from the hunt, and he seems to know Corin and I have argued. He smiles—and I know this was what he wanted, wonder if he got those women to talk about me being happy with him in a place where he knew Corin would overhear. Or did he say something to him last night? When he said he was taking Corin to have his head checked after he hit it? My shoulders tighten. I should've asked Corin about his head.

Jed takes me to his room and smiles with a softness I didn't know he had. Still, I don't speak. He goes out for a minute, returns with hot drinks—one for him, one for me. He hands mine to me, along with his questions. I sip at the drink, stare straight ahead. My eyes are playing tricks on me because, for a moment, I think I see the snake spirit watching me from the far wall, next to the water bucket. But I blink, and it's gone.

Great. I'm going mad.

After a while, Jed stops asking questions, starts talking at me. Tells me about a couple of the men

237

who have annoyed him today, how they're acting differently. How they seem to have forgotten all the rules of the Zharat lifestyle.

"He didn't even know how to hold a spear properly," he says. "It was as if he was using it for the first time."

I just stare at the wall, bring my knees up to my chest, rest my chin on them. Everything looks glassy. I swallow hard.

It didn't even take Corin *a week*. Not even a week to give up on me after the Zharat engaged me to Jed. Just—what?—a day. How can it *only* have been a day? All that stuff…all those things that have happened….

But Corin's right… I didn't fight it. Not like how I should've.

And now Corin's going to leave. Why would he stay when he hates it here? He's just going to go. Or get caught? Killed? I drum my fingers against my shins, the rhythm of hoof beats.

Maybe he's just angry. Maybe Corin didn't mean all that. Surely he knows we've got to be careful? And I can't leave and let the Enhanced know where the Zharat live—I'd thought Corin of all people would understand since his parents died in a conversion attack.

"Come on, S'ven. It is time for bed."

I stare at Jed. Is it nighttime already? My stomach rumbles a little, I can't remember whether I've eaten today, but I'm not hungry anyway.

I feel Jed's hands on me, pulling at my clothes. The flaxen-brass yellow shirt comes off, over my head. I don't do anything. Feel cold, empty. He puts a yellow gown or something on me, buttons it up, then pulls back the covers on my bed. I get in, still wearing the brown shorts underneath.

I lie down, shut my eyes, but I won't let myself sleep. Not this time.

Darkness.

For a second, I think I smell cigarette smoke. *Corin*. My chest aches. I roll onto my side, the blankets make crinkly noises.

I don't sleep. Hours pass, and I don't sleep. I just lie here, thinking. But I can't think. There's too much fog to swim through. So I listen to Jed's breathing, Jed's stirrings, Jed's snoring.

My *husband*.

I swallow awkwardly. I start thinking things— things that don't make me feel any better. So I think of other things. How the bison said I was the key to the Untamed, how if the Enhanced have me they'll have *all* the Untamed.

Then I freeze.

They've already got part of me—Raleigh's got my eyes. And I don't know how I didn't realized that before…how I didn't connect it… The Enhanced *have* got part of me…and if they have me, they'll get all of us.

Oh Gods. What if it's enough? Can they get all the Untamed by just having my eyes?

I try to remain calm—try my hardest, but my breathing increases its speed, and my head pounds. I try to think.

The Zharat are still here, safe, and—as long as they are—the Enhanced can't have all the Untamed. A *part* of me isn't good enough. The Enhanced must need *all* of me to get *all* the Untamed….

But the bison told me before—what seems like ages ago—that Raleigh would always be able to find me. But he can't. Not if I don't show him where I am. Not if I stay here. And staying where I am—making sure Raleigh doesn't know where we are—is the only thing I can do to make sure Raleigh doesn't get all of me, doesn't get all the Zharat…all the Untamed? Because I'm the key to the Untamed.

My eyes widen. Are we—the Zharat—the only ones left? Is that what this means?

The question burns my insides, because I know the answer—I feel it in me—and I realize now I should *never* have tried to escape. Should never have gone outside with Jed. It's not just the Zharat I'd be ending if Raleigh saw where we lived.

Because we're the last ones.

If Raleigh and his armies find us, we'll get converted.

And the Untamed will be extinct.

I press my lips together and try to breathe out through my mouth at the same time, feel my ears pop. My chest makes a funny noise as I hiccup. I am doing the right thing staying here.

I have to keep us safe, have to keep the Untamed race alive.

The next morning, I watch Jed as he leaves. He says he'll be back in ten minutes to take me to the gathering room. That he has Seer business to attend to first.

After a few seconds, I pull myself away from the warmth of my bed, find some fresh clothes apparently waiting for me: a yellow strappy top, a button-up outer shirt—also yellow—that will cover my Seer pendant, and a pair of tight, black jeans that are a little too short. For some reason, the outer shirt reminds me of one Corin once wore, and I struggle to blink back tears, tell myself to get a grip.

Then I peel off my nightdress, and—

For seconds, I can't move.

I let my nightdress fall to the floor, horrified.

The marks—the insects' marks. There are *more*. They're… I stare at my skin; they're joining up, the bites, making shapes. Slashes in my skin, four of them down my left side, stretching from just under my breast, angling toward my hip bone. It looks like writing now—crude letters, but I can't make them out.

I take several deep breaths. These extra bites weren't here yesterday, were they? I try to remember, but

I can't. Still, I don't think they were. There must be mites in the bed.

I touch the bite marks. They are raised, jagged, and feel strangely oily. I frown. There are smaller dots around them, individual puncture marks? I run my fingernails over them, trying to scratch them away, but all I do is aggravate my skin. Tiny, raw bumps appear, too painful to touch now.

I rush to the water bucket in the corner of the room, dip my hand in, then splash it onto my skin. I scrub at the little marks, until they're bleeding. But they won't go away. Of course they won't, they're insect bites. And I feel stupid for trying.

Taking a deep breath, I hold a rag to my side until the bleeding ceases.

Then I get dressed and change the bedclothes.

Jed returns a minute later. He looks better now. A lot better. "We shall go and get food now."

I try to hide my shaking. They're just insect bites, I tell myself. Just insect bites. And I keep telling myself that as Jed and I leave the room.

In the gathering room, Corin barely looks at me as we all prepare to eat. But just seeing him makes me feel better. He hasn't left.

Jed puts his arm around me, and his lips briefly press against my left temple. I crane my neck away from him, watching Corin as he limps across the room, joins a small group of people, including Esther, on the other side.

"We are going to be very happy," Jed says, his words pulling me back to our circle.

A Zharat man in front of us nods, smiling a semi-toothless smile. He is sharpening an arrow, and shards of wood and splinters fly from his lap. Something about the pattern the splinters land in on the table reminds me of my insect bites, and I shudder, try to distract myself.

Nyesha is next to the man with the arrow; she's preparing more food, and her seven-year-old daughter sits next to her. I'm not sure where her youngest baby is, but this girl's eyes watch me, make me feel uneasy.

And, looking around at Jed, the Zharat man, and Nyesha, I realize just how out of place I am here. They're all so much older than me. I'm still a child, according to my old culture. But here, I've been an adult for over three years. The Zharat even think I'm old to be getting married; before, when Nyesha was helping me change into my wedding gown, she told me how she got married on the eve of her fourteenth birthday. I'll be close to eighteen by the time of my marriage in a month's time.

I gulp, look across at Corin, but he still won't look at me. He's looking anywhere except at me. I keep glancing at him—when I think Jed's not watching me—imploring Corin to meet my eyes. But he doesn't.

A few minutes later, I see Esther sneak several glances at me, and I drop my gaze.

Nyesha's voice makes me jump. She's standing now. "Come on, Seven, we must go and sew now. There are clothes that need fixing."

I follow Nyesha. She exits by the smallest less-well lit tube, and we have to walk right past Corin and Esther. Neither looks at me. Corin is now intent on rolling some sort of cigarette. I notice Esther's short hair is now in tiny, stubby braids.

And, as I look around, I see other women are leaving too. In fact, *all* the women are leaving. Even the female children are getting up, following their mothers and sisters and aunts.

Apart from Esther. She doesn't move. She just smiles toward the opposite doorway, where Manning now enters. He returns her smile.

I quicken my pace, catching up with Nyesha. She leads me into a wide cave room where several other women are now sitting.

We join them on the floor, and Nyesha shows me how to use the needle more efficiently, scolding my poor, uneven attempts.

"Where's Soraya?" I put the sewing down a little while later and look around, can't see her. A small child climbs onto my lap. I'm not sure which one of the women is the girl's mother, but no one says anything. They just act like it's normal.

"Neither she nor Miles joined us at breakfast. They're probably together," says Nyesha.

"Unless they've run away too," a voice says. "Clare says we should all run away."

"What?" I look around.

Nyesha frowns at the woman who spoke, then she turns to me. "You know that first group of girls who went fishing on the day of the fight for you—the ones getting fresh fish for the wedding feast? They never returned. Our men went to look for them, but found nothing. And another group went out yesterday to fish. Different lakes though. And they should have got back within the last hour at the latest, but they're still not back. Many people think that's two lots missing." She turns her eyes on the other woman. "But they will return. They haven't run away—Clare's wrong. She shouldn't be listened to—there's a reason she wears violet now."

She nods, seems confident.

"They could've got in trouble. You know what the spirits at the lakes are like. They could all be dead," another voice says. "Or it could be the lions again. They'll be hungry at this time of year, and that group was all young girls, wasn't it? Easy prey."

Nyesha frowns at the new speaker. "They'll be back soon. All of them. Unharmed."

"Mummy?"

Nyesha's daughter suddenly crosses the room, stops in front of us. She looks at the small child I'm still holding, then at me.

"What is it, Kyla?" Nyesha asks.

The girl continues to regard me with her big eyes for a few moments, then shrugs, turns to Nyesha. "I had another bad dream this morning. But I was scared to tell you."

Nyesha kneels down by her, places her hands on her shoulders. She glances at me for a second. I'm the only one watching them—the other women are talking again.

"You were scared?" Nyesha asks, pulling her daughter closer to her.

The girl nods. There's water in her eyes, it nearly brims over the edges. She sticks her bottom lip out. It trembles.

"Why, sweetie?"

"Because of Daddy. He told me if I had a dream with it in I mustn't say because it would upset him. But this one was scary, and it felt real, Mummy. And I'm scared." She lowers her voice so her words are barely audible. "The bison looked like a *real* bison."

My body jolts. My chest tightens. I'm stepping nearer, holding the small child in my arms, before I'm even aware I've got up.

The bison.

Nyesha stands up quickly, shoots me a warning look, and grabs her daughter's hand. "Come on, Kyla."

She marches her daughter straight past me.

"Nyesha—" I race after her as best as I can, still holding the smaller girl.

Nyesha turns back to me, raises one hand. She looks around, eyes fierce. "Not a word of this to anyone," she says. "Forget this happened, Seven. Promise me."

Her eyes get even fiercer as she waits for me to nod, to agree.

"I promise," I say.

Nyesha nods, then turns, pulls her daughter from the room.

Not one word, Seven. Don't betray anyone else.

THIRTY-ONE

I TRY TO FORGET IT happened, but I can't get Kyla's words out of my head—or maybe I don't want to because it's a welcome distraction from my situation with Corin *and* the other situation with Raleigh and my eyes. But either way, Kyla saw the bison. And it felt real, that's what Kyla said. It's got to be a Seer warning. It *has* to be important.

But I wasn't warned. And I'm a Seer. If there was something we needed to know, the Gods and Goddesses and spirits should've told me. Could Kyla's dream have been a normal one that just happened to have a bison in it?

But Kyla said her dream was scary. And I remember how shaken up she was. Is that how a normal nightmare would affect her?

An hour later, I finally decide I need to find out what the girl saw.

But the moment I step out of Jed's room, he's there, eyes blazing.

"You did not listen." He leans forward until his face is right in front of mine. The dark circles under his eyes make him look dangerous, make me wonder if he's sleeping at all.

I look at him, uncertain, then tighten my hands into fists. "What?"

"I told you I did not want you outside. Yet you went out—and you had taken your ring off. I saw you." He leans in even closer. "I saw you down by the tree line. And, believe me, if I had not been up to my shoulders in animal guts, I would have marched straight over and dragged you back myself."

I stare at him, look down at my hand. The ring is definitely there. I've been trying to ignore it. "I didn't go outside."

The muscles around Jed's eyes tighten. "Do not lie to me, S'ven. I saw you, you disappeared through the trees. Thought you'd sneak out and meet Corin?"

Just his name—his name spoken by *Jed*—makes me flinch, but I lift my head higher.

"No."

"Do not lie to me."

"I didn't go outside! I was with Nyesha...and the other women. We were repairing clothes. You can ask them."

He makes a low sound in his throat. "I shall be lenient this time." Then he steps back, looks at me. His pupils seem to rotate as he looks me up and down. "Where are you going now?"

"To find Nyesha."

Jed glares at me. "But you should not be walking around the caves on your own, S'ven. I told you that."

I feel my temper rising. I fold my arms. "Then come with me. I'm just going to see Nyesha. That's all."

But if Jed does come—and he waits with me—I'm not going to be able to speak to Kyla. And what if Nyesha thinks I've told Jed? Or what if Jed suspects something?

"I am tired." He flicks his hands in an irritated manner, then steers me back into his room—our room. He indicates for me to sit down, and I do, on the edge of my mattress. "Stay here with me. I have to prepare for tomorrow."

"Tomorrow?"

"A Seer meeting." He looks up, and his eyes meet mine. Shivers run through me.

"Oh." Questions burn me, but I know I can't ask them.

Jed lets out a long breath, then he too sits down. Next to me.

I watch him from the corner of my eye. He's close, too close. I sit up straighter, fold one leg over the other. Then he puts his arm around me, rests its weight on me in such a way that pulls on my neck.

A minute passes, then his arm slips down, his hand curls around my waist. I flinch.

"What are you doing?"

"Comforting you."

"I don't need comforting."

I try to stay calm, try to stop my chest from shuddering. I need to keep a clear head. I look toward the doorway. The drape has been drawn across, and I'm not sure when that happened, but there's a slight gap. If someone walked past, they might see us. But I don't even know where I'm going with this thought. Everyone thinks we're together.

"You feel thin." Jed's fingers press into my left side, intruding, against my ribs.

I flinch, the skin there is still tender, and I don't want him to feel those bites, to ask questions.

Jed frowns at me. "I have hardly seen you eat here. Why are you not eating?"

"I am."

"You are not." He removes his hand from my body. "If this is some kind of protest against our marriage, starving yourself, then know that it is not going to work."

"It's not." I try to keep my voice neutral, but my words are too high-pitched.

"Good. Because you are obviously not happy about this, and you know I am not going to force myself on you—so there is no point dragging your health down too. That is just attention seeking, and I do not like attention-seekers."

Jed leaves early the next morning for his Seer meeting. He didn't speak to me any more that night, and I didn't speak to him either. Still, I caught him watching me though, when he thought I wasn't looking.

I stay in bed a little longer, but there's no point in just lying here—a baby's crying not far away—so I get up. It is cold, but the air is dry, rough. Unlike some of the other tubes, which are damp, there's no humidity here at all now, and it makes my throat feel tickly.

I sort out new yellow clothes to put on, then peel off my nightdress. I'm relieved to find there are no more marks. The insects must've gone. The old bites are healing now. Changing the bedclothes solved it.

I head off for the gathering room, and although I pass a few groups of men, none of them say or do anything. Still, I don't feel comfortable walking on my own, because they stare. Their eyes burn into me. And I already feel self-conscious enough as it is.

The moment I arrive in the gathering room, Corin corners me. He smells of smoke. My heart speeds up, relief floods me—he's been waiting for me, wants to talk to me, to see me.

I reach for his hands, and he lets me hold them. "Corin, I—"

"No, Sev. No." He yanks his hands away from me, as if he's only just realized he let me take them a moment ago. His eyes are on me, but he seems to have difficulty swallowing. "I need you to… I need you to watch Esther."

I stare at him. The insect bites start to itch a little. "What?"

He purses his lips for a few seconds, then drops his gaze to the floor as he wrings his hands together. "Something's not right. I'm worried. This isn't like her at all. She spends too much time with that man. She says nothing's going on, but I'm—I'm not so sure. She reminds me that he's married, every time I say it, but that doesn't mean anything." He shakes his head again, and the light catches the healing cuts on his face.

I want to touch his face. The sudden realization surprises me, makes me feel strange, and I have to actively think about not moving my hand. But his skin looks sore, and I want to make it better. I bite my lip.

"Sev?" His eyes are back on me now, and I watch his Adam's apple move a little.

A jolt runs through my body. "What… Which man?"

"Manning."

My eyes widen a little, and I know I shouldn't be so surprised. All the signs are there—they have been for a while, and I feel bad I haven't really been paying attention to what's going on with other people.

Corin rubs his hands together in front of his chest. "He's been doing way too much for her, more than a chief should." He shakes his head. "You must've noticed. He *personally* oversaw her healing, made sure she didn't get branded as a spy, and now he's… There's something going on, Sev. I don't like it. Keep an eye on her. She disappears on her own a lot. When she does, follow her. You'll be less noticeable than me."

I nod, because it seems like I haven't got a choice.

"Thank you," Corin says. He starts to turn away.

"No, Corin, wait—we need to talk."

I try to get his hands again, but he avoids me. His eyes meet mine, then he shakes his head.

"There's nothing to talk about."

And he walks away, to the other side of the gathering room, his gait uneven, limping.

I stare after him. It's back to the way it used to be: he only spoke to me because he wanted something. My chest caves in.

I turn back, toward the center of the gathering room. I look around, looking for a friendly face. The sudden need to talk to someone hits me hard. But I have no friends I can confide in here. None at all, not really. No one's on my side: Nyesha and Soraya are still Zharat, and if they knew I was a Seer, they'd be horrified.

"S'ven."

I turn, Jed's suddenly behind me, marching toward me with swift speed. He's back from the Seer meeting, so soon.

"Why were you talking to *him*?"

My cold fingers burn as I stare at him. My lips start to move, try to make sounds, but I don't know what I'm saying. My shoulders hunker a little.

"*Why*?" Jed repeats. His hands find their way onto my shoulders. "*I* will be your husband. You do not need to talk to other men."

His eyes are narrowed, waiting for me to agree or something.

"*S'ven*?"

I swallow hard, lift my head up higher.

Suddenly Jed's hands slip down to my wrists. I turn, try to pull my hands away, but can't. His fingers are concrete.

"Do you understand me?" His voice is darker, darker than I've ever heard it.

"Let go." Somehow, I keep my voice steady.

Jed's grip only tightens. "Do you understand me?"

I turn, and people are watching. Everywhere.

Corin's watching. I see him, see the tightness in his face, recognize the way he's breathing; he's angry. But he doesn't do anything.

Jed's grip gets tighter.

"*Do* you understand me?"

I nod. He drops my hands a second later. I pull my wrist up, see the imprints from his fingers on my skin.

My stomach tightens. But I don't say anything.

We don't speak for the rest of the day. Or the night. Which suits me fine. I don't want to speak to him. When we're not talking, it's easier for hope to grow within me, hope that says somehow I will get out of this marriage…that Corin might still rescue me. Somehow. I hope.

Then I feel silly.

I don't need Corin.

I can't afford to need anyone.

THIRTY-TWO

THE NEXT MORNING, I DO my chores. Soraya is back now, and I help her make flour from sorghum, grinding it into a fine powder. She introduces me to her two-year-old son who's playing with a piece of animal hide on the floor behind us, and I'm surprised I haven't already met him—or known of his existence. But there are so many children here, because of the rules about marriage and reproduction.

"Did those girls come back?" I ask. "The ones who went to the lakes? Or the first lot?"

Soraya shakes her head. "No. The men have gone out looking again, and Manning. That's what that Seer meeting yesterday was about. The Seers all asked their Gods, but didn't find out anything. They say Gods only see and foresee things in our world relating to their chosen Seers, but even then, they see a distorted version, or only fragments. The Dream Land only works because so many Gods put what they've seen into the warnings—it builds a picture. Sometimes, good spirits will help with the warnings too—maybe add a few small details if they can—but it is the Gods who are the strongest. Still, the Gods don't foresee everything. They never can. Not really." She sighs. "It was a long shot our Seers just asking a few Gods anyway. But there's no sign of them, the girls." Soraya pauses and rubs her stomach. "Evil spirits have probably got them, and in that case, the Gods might not know anyway. But it's best not to talk about the girls, in case their parents hear. Anna's not doing well."

I nod, because I don't know what else to do, and carry on with the work. A few minutes later, it's my turn to knead the dough that Soraya's made from the sorghum flour. I find it therapeutic, in a strange way, and I gradually work through the many batches.

I've no idea what time it is when we finish, and I head off to the gathering area, alone.

"Kyla!"

I spot the child sitting with a group of other girls and race over to her, look around. Nyesha's not in sight, but I'm sure she must be close by.

The girl eyes me warily as I approach. I try to smile, try to appear friendly, but I don't think I'm good with children. I sit down next to her, crossing my legs. The other girls immediately leave. Convenient.

"Hello, Kyla." I try a bigger smile this time, manage it.

She watches me, eyes large and round. She looks a lot like Nyesha.

"So, that nightmare you had," I begin, keeping my voice low. Then I wince, wonder if I'm being patronizing. I lean in closer. My stomach rumbles. "I need you to tell me about it, tell me what you saw."

Kyla shakes her head. She's got some dried food around her mouth, and my eyes are drawn to it. "I didn't have a bad dream."

I look around, keeping an eye out for Nyesha. "Kyla... This is really important. I won't tell anyone, I promise. You're not in trouble. I just need you to tell me."

She shakes her head, starts to stand up. I rise up

onto my knees, sit back on my heels.

My heart quickens. "I'll let you in on a secret, Kyla. I get bad dreams like that too."

Oh Gods. I shouldn't have said that. I look around quickly, but no one else is looking.

Kyla's eyes widen. "With a bison?"

I nod, feel my chest tighten. "Yes. This can be our little secret." I wince as I repeat back the words Marouska—that traitor—once said to me. But it's too late, I can't undo it now.

"You won't tell anyone?" Kyla looks doubtful.

"No. Of course not. I promise. But we've got to stick together. We can tell each other our bad dreams. Talking always helps—"

"Seven?"

Nyesha appears out of nowhere and grabs me. Her eyes burn as she puts herself between her daughter and me.

"What *the hell* are you doing?" Her words are cold and sharp.

She's waiting for me to speak—a lot of people are, I realize; the women have all stopped serving the food, and several men are watching. Oh Gods. What if someone heard me?

"Nyesha, I—"

"Get away from her!" Manning suddenly yells.

I look up, see him march through the doorway, heading straight for us, three men either side of him— his brothers, must be, the familiarity is so strong. And they all carry weapons: axes, knives, sharp blades.

"Get away from that child. Both of you. Get away from the fraudulent Seer."

Nyesha screams, throws her arms wide, shielding Kyla. I look toward Manning, feel blood rush to my ears. Kyla shrieks, and then other children are crying. Women herd them out the room as quickly as they can.

Manning and his men get closer, blades flashing. The Seer from our welcoming ceremonies joins the group, a wooden bat in his hands.

"Stop it!" I scream, and then I'm next to Nyesha, grabbing her hand, making a human wall, Kyla behind us.

Nyesha wrenches her hand from mine, hisses something I don't catch, then starts shouting. Her words fog my ears, I can't make them out, but I hear Kyla scream, "Mummy!"

"Get out the way," Manning snarls, looks at Nyesha and me. "That girl's tainted."

"She's just a child!" Nyesha screams. "She hasn't done anything wrong!"

Everyone's stopped now, looking at us. I twist around. We're too out in the open. Someone could go behind us, grab Kyla. Oh Gods.

"The corner!" I hiss to Nyesha, and I try to pull her along.

We need to get to the corner, but she doesn't understand. Her hand flies out, and her nails scratch the back of my hand. A string of saliva flies from her mouth as she screams, tears running down her face.

Manning advances. He bares his teeth. The axe is big. Bigger than the ones the executioners had.

"Seize them."

The nearest Zharat man lunges for me. I sidestep, crash into Nyesha, fall backward. My back hits something hard on the floor, and I grunt. Then I'm rolling over, tasting blood at the back of my mouth. I force my head up as I move, see her. Kyla's there, a foot away, eyes wide. I fling myself at her, grab her arm, push her behind me.

Two men have hold of her mother, wrestling her to the floor. I hear something crack—something like a bone—and a high-pitched scream fills the room.

I try to tell Kyla it's all right, but she's screaming because her mother's screaming. Nyesha's kicking out, and more men are going to her, holding her down. I keep my hand on Kyla's shoulder, feel her shaking.

"Get over there, that corner." I try to say the words quietly—but my voice cracks, and it's too loud. But

Kyla and I are moving, heading backward, toward the corner.

There's no one else there. The women have all moved to the other side. Kyla trips on something, and I yank her up.

"Get away from her, woman!"

Manning and four men. In front of us. My breath comes in short, sharp bursts. The chief lifts his axe up, and the blade refracts light about, reminds me of the Enhanced—dizziness tugs at my edges.

"No!" Nyesha screams, the sound drawing out, on and on and on and on.

"She hasn't done anything!" I look around. Need help. Corin? He's not here. Nyesha's still struggling against three men. "You can't hurt her!"

She's shaking, Kyla's shaking and crying, screaming, but my brain is tuning out her sounds.

Manning regards me with a venomous look. "We can and we will. Step aside."

I scream as the axe swings down toward us, duck, and push Kyla to the right.

"You can't hurt her! She's a child! She hasn't done anything!" My voice is hoarse, and the sounds aren't right. I'm not making sense.

"She's a fraud, the evil spirits be controlling her, and now she be controlling you, making you stand up for her." Manning spits the words at me. "Step aside now, woman, else I'll kill you an' all."

No. I grit my teeth, feel pain in my jaw.

I am not letting her die.

I am *not*.

"Step aside now. I won't ask again."

I don't move.

Nyesha screams. I hear another *crack*. She screams more and—

Something hits me in the shoulder. Hard. Throws me off balance. I stumble, fall to the right before a hand wrenches me back. Jed. He's here. For a second, I think he's going to help, and I see something warm in his eyes, something that makes me certain and—

He hits me.

I fall hard, and—

"Kyla!" Nyesha screams. "No! No! Kyla!"

I see the Seer strike the girl.

I see an axe head plunge into her ribcage.

I see another blade slice into her skull, as if it's not made of bone, but jelly.

And blood.

Too much blood.

Nyesha screams.

"Take the body away. Yanugh, prepare a group to go to the Falls."

Jed shoves me into the floor, leans over me. I hit the back of my head, cry out, see spots everywhere, all over Jed's face. I smell alcohol on him, see how dirty his teeth are as he presses his face up to mine.

"Never do that again."

Then he moves away. I roll onto my side, a hand pressed against my lower ribs on each side. Pain. I try to breathe, try not to look at Kyla's body… But I can't *not*. It's there. Right in front of me. The blood. A sea of blood. Looks black in the light.

My stomach flips. I throw up bile; the lurid smell wraps around me, squeezes me.

I cough, shudder, try to wipe the back of my mouth, and then Nyesha's right in front of me, free.

She slaps me, throws her weight onto me, punching, kicking.

I scream, try to fight back, try to push her off me, but I can't. And we're covered in blood. Both of us. And the men aren't doing anything. I see Jed, not far away, his head bowed.

"This is your fault," Nyesha screeches into my ear. "You've killed my child."

THIRTY-THREE

NYESHA'S RIGHT. IT IS MY fault. Kyla's dead, because of me. Someone must have heard me. It is my fault.

Or was the timing too quick? Manning and those men appeared almost straight away, as if they already knew....

I groan. I know what I'm doing—trying to make myself feel better, trying to pretend that Nyesha's daughter isn't dead because of me.

"Hold still." The woman cleaning my face grabs at my hand, waves a wadded bit of bloodied cotton wool in the other. It smells strongly of antiseptic.

She frowns at me. I can't remember her name, though she's told me three times already. She thinks the bad spirits have got me too. She told Jed that. He told her to shut up, that I wasn't the one pretending to be a Seer. Then he said something else to her, quietly though, too quiet for me to hear.

I try to hold still, but I can't.

It takes a long time, but the woman eventually sends me away. Jed is waiting by the door, and he leads me toward our room. He breathes hard the whole way, clenching his fists and flaring his nostrils. His eyes are too wide as well, he's showing too much of his sclerae, like an angered bull.

As we get nearer to our room, I feel my heart rate get higher and higher. Too high. Until it's pounding. But it's not beating regularly. It's stomping. I try to breathe more evenly, but I can't. Because Jed's here. And he's angry. I can't take a breath, not a proper one.

It's too hot. The tubes are too hot today. I'm sweating too much. My hands are slippery, I wipe them on my clothes, but that doesn't help, just makes the tiny pieces of debris that were on the fabric stick to my palms. I stare at them, at the specs of dust, the tiny nylon hairs.

I need to run. I need to get away. My legs are burning. I glance up at Jed, but he's not looking at me, he's focused on the end of the corridor, where our room is.

Our room.

Oh Gods.

I try to work out how fast I think he is—probably not fast, he's still limping. Because of his leg. But my knees are shaking, trembling, they feel too weak. Far too weak.

My throat starts to close in. My next breath squeaks against it. Jed looks down at me, frowning.

He pulls me into our room. No—we can't be here already!

But we are, we're here.

"What the hell do you think you were doing? Defending that child!"

His words echo off the walls around me, repeating themselves, over and over. I still can't breathe. Pain, in my throat, like the muscles are spasming and there's no room for them and they're crashing into one another and all I can see is the blood and Kyla's body with her cracked skull and broken ribcage and—

I sink to the floor.

Jed grabs me, but I'm only vaguely aware of his

hands.

"Breathe," he says, and I see one of his eyes, suddenly close to mine.

But I'm trying to breathe—doesn't he realize that? Only there's not enough air, not enough… I can't….

"*Breathe*, S'ven. Slower. Stop panicking." He sounds angry.

Oh Gods.

"S'ven." Jed crouches in front of me, cups my face in his hands. "It is okay. Just breathe."

But he doesn't sound like it's okay—and it's not okay, I know that; how can it ever be okay? But I try to breathe because it's Jed and he's angry and I don't want to make him angrier.

But it's too hot in here, the sweat's pouring off me, and I start to see blackness around the edges of my vision….

He shakes my shoulders, hard. I scream, and then he's telling me to breathe again.

It's a routine—one we settle into. Me trying to breathe, him telling me to.

But after ten minutes, I can breathe. Properly, again.

He swears then grunts. "It is out of your system now."

"What?" I press a hand to my chest. The engagement ring seems to have a pulse of its own.

"The evilness that fraud planted within you. Manning said that might happen." But his voice is different, and he doesn't sound like he believes it… My stomach tightens.

He snorts. But then the look in his eyes changes. It gets deeper somehow, softer, more intense, like he's really looking at me. Like…and I freeze. That look. If it was Corin who was looking at me I'd think he wanted to kiss me.

I shudder, try to look away from Jed, but at the same time I know I mustn't look away. It's dangerous to turn your back to a predator.

Jed turns away. "Get some rest."

Then he's gone, pulling the drape closed behind him. And I realize I'm never going to be able to forget what I've seen.

The bad spirits get me in my dreams, give me nightmares.

Raleigh's face. Big and huge, in front of me. Glistening eye-mirrors—but they look different. Not quite as reflective. I move, and I'm standing in front of him, in front of his face. And his face is getting bigger, until his eye is as big as I am, and I can see myself—my whole body—in his eyeball, but…but there are other lines too. Slashes and crosses and curves, all at different angles. Like the insect bites on my skin. They look like words, but they're not, they can't be words. Unless they're a language.

An ancient language?

I'm staring into his eye, which can't really be an eye because it's so big, and then he blinks—the rush of air sends me backward, like a dried leaf in a whirlwind.

I fall heavily, on my back. On the floor. Gray floor. Smooth and cold, but it's not stone.

"My dear little Shania."

The words make me feel sick.

He's watching me. That gigantic eye. I press my elbows in, try to tuck them into my sides, but they're suddenly too big, and he's laughing.

"You meant to kill her, didn't you? That innocent child. Poor Kyla, thinking you were her friend."

My throat tightens, my eyes water.

"You just threw her to the dogs," Raleigh says. "Look at you, Shania. You don't even care. All you're upset about is that boyfriend of yours, how he doesn't care. How he's left you, even though he said he'd always be there for you. And now he's going to replace you—with Clare. He's going to take her away from here, in your place. Face it, Shania. No one likes you, no one trusts you. You betray everyone."

I gulp, and then I'm screaming. But I know there's no point, because I know this is a nightmare. There's no bison.

It's just my mind. The ground wobbles, softer still.

And suddenly she's here. Kyla. Her body. On the floor, in front of me.

I smell her blood first. Rusty and salty and sharp. It's pooling out toward me, and her skull is in two. A clean break, down the front. Can see dark purple and gray tissue inside, and the blood's still coming out, seeping toward me. Trying to get me.

You let her die, Seven.

Bile rises in my throat. I try to swallow it down, end up spluttering. I turn away. But Raleigh's eye moves around, and—wherever I go—I see Kyla's reflection.

Blood. Too much blood.

Run, Seven.

I turn and run, and the room changes. It's getting longer, a corridor. And the floor's stickier…much stickier.

She's following me.

Kyla's following me. She's standing—no running—and her head is broken, and blood gushes out her chest, like a jet. It sprays toward me, splatters on my skin, soaks me, marks me for what I am.

"Seven!"

A female voice. but I don't know whose… No, I do. But it can't be. No. I don't want to see her.

Run, I tell myself. Got to keep running. It's the only way. But Kyla's blood is everywhere. Dark and slippery, and I'm in it, ankle-deep already. It's lapping against me, waves. Darkness.

I start to choke, and I try to turn to see Raleigh's eye. But it's gone. He's gone. And the walls have gone. I'm not inside, I'm outside.

In a lake of blood.

Only the blood isn't red. It's black.

A black lake.

I start to choke, my insides heaving. Got to get out. But every step I take I'm going deeper, I can't find the way out. It's up to my knees, my thighs. Sticky and thick, pulling me down. I scream, shrieking in a voice that isn't mine, and—

"Seven! Don't go here!" Five yells, and suddenly she's in front of me. Right in my face, standing inches from me. And—and she just appeared. In a second.

I recoil, my hair whipping around in the wind, but the black water holds both of us together, inches apart. I stare at her again, then look up at the sky. The action's instinctive. But there's no bison. The Gods aren't controlling this vision. No, of course, this is a nightmare. My sister's dead, I can't see her.

Only in nightmares.

This is a nightmare. Not real.

I try to move my feet, but the black lake won't let me get away. Oh Gods. I have to look at her. I have no choice.

My stomach squeezes.

My dead sister. The ghost of my dead sister.

I try to form words, but can't.

I'm going mad. I'm seeing things. But is it madness if you see them in your dreams?

Except before, with Five, that wasn't a dream….

"I haven't got long!" Five cries. "Two's said it's still going to happen—you haven't changed the future yet, you're still on the same path!"

I taste grit in my mouth as I stare at her. My dead sister. I shake my head. No. I was grieving for Three before when I saw her, and I was in shock—that's why I was susceptible to the spirits' hallucinations. When I saw her ghost. But I'm not now, am I? I've been calm. That was, what, a week-and-a-half ago?

You can't have finished grieving in that time!

"Don't come here!" Five screams. She still looks real,

solid. I don't understand.

But none of it's true, what she's saying. She was a lie, she is a lie. I'm seeing things. The evil spirits, messing with my dreams.

"Don't come here! He'll try and make you, and he'll—"

Darkness. Everywhere. It's a blanket, huge, vast. It presses down. Fabric over my mouth, my nose. I breathe in, suck it in, and then I can't—

"S'ven!"

I jolt awake, breathing hard; every breath makes a raspy noise.

Jed. Standing over my bed. He looks strange, like he's asleep but awake at the same time.

I can still see Five every time I blink. It's… That was different. That nightmare was different. That felt like before, when she said she contacted me through Two….

No, that's stupid. It didn't feel like that. My head pounds. It was just a dream. The first one was a hallucination. And the other times I thought I saw her can't have been real either.

Jed steps nearer, makes a clicking sound in the back of his throat.

"Kiss me," he says.

I stare at him, feel my chest tighten.

My eyes widen as he advances.

"Kiss me *now*."

No. No. *No.*

I shake my head.

"S'ven!" And then he's nearer, grabbing my wrist. "We have to kiss—we have to keep up this appearance that we are husband and wife."

He leans into me, and I try to twist around, but can't. There's nowhere to go, the wall's too close; there's only the bed and him.

Oh Gods.

I'm awake, I'm awake, I'm awake. The words run through my mind, the only thing I can truly comprehend.

Jed makes another noise in his throat. My eyes snap back toward him.

He pulls me to him, fiercely. His mouth goes for mine, and I push him away. A second later, his hands are under my nightdress, on my spine. I freeze. His hands move around to my front, over my hips.

Over the fading insects bites.

I tense up. His eyes are on me; he's stopped trying to kiss me. Because he's felt them, the marks… He must have, they're raised—less than they were, but still raised. I stare at him, swallow, wait for him to react.

His eyes don't change, but the corners of his lips pull up a little; a sly smile. For a second, I think he's going to try and kiss me again, but he doesn't.

"You are strong, S'ven." He pulls back, takes several steps, a strange look on his face—one I can't quite fathom. "It is hard to control you. But I like a challenge."

THIRTY-FOUR

I'M SHAKING, STILL SHAKING, WHEN I see Soraya a couple of hours later—and shaking like this is ridiculous. I need to be strong.

I swallow hard, my eyes on the lantern behind Soraya's head; the flickering light makes me feel sick.

"It's not your fault," she says. "Nyesha didn't mean it, she's just upset. Come on. It's best that no one's on their own when the men are on a disposal, else the evil spirits get tempted."

"Disposal?" I gulp, blink quickly.

"Yes," Soraya says, dropping her voice a few tones. "For Kyla's body… It has to be done quickly." She pauses, then puts my arm in hers. "The men are going to the nearest drop-off point, so they could be back today though, if the spirits are nice to them. It's all right, Seven. Jed's gone with them, you know, to contain her devious soul within her body, stop it possessing anyone—we're lucky that he's got his powers back. A powerful Seer like him. Before, Iro was the Seer who did the containing on disposals, but he was killed when you were rescuing them."

"Oh." I hadn't realized the dead man was a Seer.

None of the Zharat had said. And I don't think I saw a bison tattoo on him…though I never really *saw* him. Still, the tattoo doesn't seem to be a reliable way to identify Zharat Seers anyway. "So has another Seer gone with Jed?"

"No. You only need one."

I frown, and I don't really know why I'm asking. "But Jed was on that first one too…for Clare's sister." I wince as I say the words. "So, there were two Seers?"

"Oh, Jed wasn't active then." Soraya shakes her head. "His powers were blocked. No, he was just there because he likes the kill—well, the dissecting. She was already dead. But he's a proper hunter."

He likes the kill… He's a proper hunter.

I shudder, try to remain calm, but I can't help thinking of earlier. It could've been worse. I know that. It could've been a lot worse. It was just a kiss.

Just a kiss.

And his hands on my body, feeling the fading insect bites.

I swallow hard and try to keep my breathing even. But it's near impossible. Because the more I think about those marks on my body, the more I *feel* them. It's like they're burning, tearing holes through my clothing. I swallow hard again, check my garments. The material's fine. I've just got to remain calm.

And then I feel selfish thinking of myself when Kyla was *murdered* earlier. Only hours ago. How can only hours have passed since then? Time doesn't seem to be working properly.

Soraya thinks it will do me good to see others, so she takes me to a large room. We sit down on the far side, with some other women, and start repairing several patches on a huge blanket—or, at least, I try. I just keep thinking of Kyla—and my burning insect bites. And then I think of the coming night—and I'm sure I'll have more bad dreams. I don't want to go to sleep.

The rest of the room's mainly empty, apart from a few women sitting by a cold hearth. Among them is

Esther. She's wearing an ornate, green Zharat scarf, wrapped around her neck and shoulders, draping over her brighter green strappy top. She looks tired and worn out, her posture is stooped. Every time I see her, she seems shorter.

Corin's request comes back to me, seems like weeks ago… But it can't have been… Only days, back when Kyla was alive.

I gulp, look across at Esther again. She's now sewing something onto what looks like a deer hide.

Follow her.

That was what Corin said. But she's not going anywhere. I'm doing what Corin said, I'm keeping an eye on her. Esther's frowning, concentrating hard on her work. That frown, it's just like Corin's. A slight pain jabs my chest.

"Do you think that too?" A large woman jabs her finger in my direction. Her needle sticks out of her mouth, and several pieces of sinew hang from her dry hair.

"I, uh—" I look around at Soraya, for help. She nods, looking amused, and I tell the woman that I do think that too, whatever *that* is.

The woman looks satisfied.

And then Esther's getting up. Her movement catches my attention. I tune out Soraya's fast chatter, and I watch Esther. Her scarf starts to slip off one shoulder, and she pulls it back up quickly. She's approaching the nearest door, fast.

I need to follow her.

I stand up slowly.

"Seven?" Soraya looks up at me.

"I… I just need to get some more fabric from the store."

I walk quickly to the other side of the room, to the door, after Esther. I swallow hard, really hope that I'm *not* following her to some secret place where she'll meet up with Manning for the night. Just the thought makes me shudder.

It's colder out here, and I'm not dressed warmly. The tube gets narrower, and the ceiling swoops down until I'm having to be careful of my head. Strange. Not a lot of people must need to go down here, not when it's so low. Whatever this leads to—wherever Esther's going—it can't be that important.

A smaller passageway branches off down the left, and I pause at its entrance. It's even narrower down there. I listen carefully, trying to detect Esther's footsteps. But I can't hear anything. Only my heart pounding with adrenaline and my own anxious breathing.

I make my decision quickly, and I keep going, stick to the main pathway. I run faster, faster. The slapping of my feet gets louder and louder, but now I don't care. Something is wrong. I can feel it. Under my yellow shirt, my Seer pendant flashes hot, then cold. I clutch at my side, feel the tiny raised marks on my skin. But I keep going.

After what seems like hours, when I'm just about certain that Esther must've gone down the narrow side-tube, I see her. She's right at the end of the tube, pushing back a drape. She turns back, and I step up against the wall, breathing hard.

Slowly, I turn my head, craning my neck, trying not to breathe. I look back down the tube. The torches flicker; if she saw my movement, maybe she'll think it was the shadows?

Esther turns her back on me. I watch her push through the fabric. The drape falls back down behind her, a shield.

I approach the doorway. I try to think hard, remember whose room it is, but I can't remember. I'm not certain. Remembering how to get to the different rooms I need to go to, and where they are, is hard enough for me.

I creep forward, until I'm by the drape. Until my fingers are only inches away from the soft, velvety textile. I examine it carefully. It looks well made, valuable. Nothing like the tartan curtain in mine and Jed's room.

I listen carefully. So carefully, I feel like my head will explode. I can hear movement. Someone walking around. And whispers—Esther's? But the sounds are too quiet, and the drape's obscuring the sounds; I can't make out individual words. And I need to. It seems important.

I touch my mother's pendant through my shirt, then lift the weight of it by the sinew cord, until I can see it, test it. The crystal shakes, reflects some of the yellow I'm wearing onto the shiny floor. Then I make sure it's hidden safely under my clothes, and I—

"How dare you! I'm *Chief*. You can't just say you don't want me no more—not after all I've done for you, woman—how much I've cared for you, looked after you when you was on your own—when your own brother didn't want you no more. It was me, woman. *Me*."

"Manning, please—"

"Listen, woman. You be alive because of me, no one else. I gave you extra food when you wanted it, allowed you to ask me questions when it's against our rules. And this is what you do? You just ain't thinking straight, woman."

I inhale sharply, feel pressure in my ears, as if all my blood's rushed there.

"But, I—" Esther's voice trails off, and I hear her crying.

"You *do* want me. I know you do. Otherwise bad stuff happens, don't it? But I can keep the bad stuff away, ain't I been doing that for you? I kept your nightmares away. *Didn't I?*"

I freeze, strain my ears, eyes widening.

Then I hear the unmistakable sound of someone being slapped.

Esther shrieks.

And I don't stop to think. I don't make a plan.

I just charge in there.

THIRTY-FIVE

"GET AWAY FROM HER!" MY voice is uncharacteristically low.

Before I realize what I'm doing, I've put my own body between the two of them, my back to Esther, and I'm facing Manning. Staring him down. I'm taller, a lot taller, and that fills me with a little confidence.

Manning swears at me, his face red and burning. "Get out my way."

"No." I clench my fist, remembering Corin's instructions for how to get a punch in. With my other hand I try to reach out behind me, for Esther—but my hand bats at thin air. I turn my head, see her on the floor. "Esther, get out of here. Go and get Corin."

"Seven, no—" Her voice is quiet, but jolty. She's crying.

Manning steps closer to me. "How dare you, woman." He points at me with one short finger, and I smell the alcohol on his breath. "How dare you come in between me and *my* woman."

Your woman? My eyes widen, but I don't move. Because that's what he wants, for me to move. The moment I do, he's going to go for her, I know that. At

271

the moment, I'm what's separating her from him.

I shift my weight a little from foot to foot, tread on Esther's scarf which is now on the ground. I try to keep eye contact with Manning, show that I'm not scared, but my heart's pounding.

"Esther, go." I try again, but my voice is higher this time, shaky. I try to move a little, so that I can see the exit, but it's behind me, and I can't move too far without giving him access to Esther.

Manning growls at me. "This don't concern you, woman. Leave, now."

I swallow hard, my skin prickling. "No."

"I ain't gonna ask again."

"Seven, just *go*," Esther says, her voice is a whine. Doesn't sound like her at all. "I don't need your help—Manning's the only one who helps me, the only one who cares about me."

"What?" My eyes widen. "No, he's—*we* care about you. Me *and* Corin, Esther."

I risk a glance behind me; she's crouched on the floor, one hand pressed against the side of her face. The skin there's reddening, almost the same color as—

My mouth dries.

Her neck.

I gasp, stare at the marks. Fingermarks, red, around the base of her neck. They're turning bluish at the edges, bruises.

And I see him. I see Manning with his hands around her throat, squeezing, shaking her. I hear him shouting, his mouth inches from her face, see his braids smacking across her skin as he turns.

I turn on him, feel sweat forming in a line down my spine. Don't know what I'm going to say, what I'm going to do, I just—

"*Get out*, woman." He punctuates each word by slamming his fist into his hand. "Get out *now*, and don't speak a word of this, else you'll pay."

I turn, so the door's in my peripheral vision. My eyes tighten, I feel sick, my stomach twists and turns.

"Come on, Esther." I reach out a hand to her, but she doesn't take it. "You're coming with me."

I swallow hard, wait for her to take my hand. But she doesn't. She's hurt. That's got to be it, why she's not taking my hand. But I can't leave her here. Not with Manning. Not alone.

Manning slams a hand onto my shoulder. He wears several rings, and they dig in. "I told you to get out, woman. This ain't concerning you. You think you're so special, because you rescued me and my men, but you ain't Chief here. And you're fast losing status, woman, with what you're doing now, let me tell you that. Here, you obey *me*. So, do as I say, and get out."

I twist my shoulders around, feel pain in them, then—then I punch him. Get the soft fleshy bit under his chin with my fist, feel my knuckles burn.

Esther screams, and then suddenly I'm on the floor, so quickly—on my back, and Manning's on top of me.

His fist, my face.

Pain.

Something cracks.

I feel something move in my face, my jaw. More pain, white dots in my vision. I try to move, try to twist around, try to throw his weight off me, but he's strong, holds me down.

Esther's screaming, still screaming. Too high-pitched, and Manning's snarling something at me, but I can't make his words out because of her screams.

Movement. To my right. I turn my head, see a block of wood as it falls down—no as it's thrown—toward me. I twist around and—

It hits Manning's back. I see his eyes widen, feel his body jolt on top of mine. But he doesn't fall. He gets up, turns, and—

Esther flies across the room. Something rips across my skin, and I'm free. I scramble to the side, my shins scrape along something sharp—I wince, grit my teeth. But the doorway's there, need to get to the doorway. Have to get to the doorway. Need help.

"Oh, I don't think so, woman." Manning's voice is slow, deliberate. "You ain't going nowhere now. Not after you tried to turn my woman against me."

Cold fingers close around my ankle, yank hard. I scream as he drags me back across the floor. My hands fly out, looking for handholds, or anything. Weapons, I need weapons. Need to defend myself.

I kick out, screaming, screaming at the top of my voice, so loud my lungs hurt. Something sharp digs into my ribs as he spins me around, onto my back. For a second, I see Esther to my right, but then she's falling. Something's hit her, he's hit her? I don't know.

"Seven, go! Just leave!" Esther's voice is strange, off—doesn't sound like her. "You're upsetting him!"

And then—

Then he hits me. Hard, across the face. Something's in his hand, because it hurts, snags my skin. I feel it tearing, ripping. Pain. My eyes go blurry, and I feel his hands on me. I try to fight him off, but suddenly he's everywhere.

Manning's face is everywhere. Laughing. I hear him laughing.

Adrenaline floods through me. Need to get away.

I try to get one knee up, try to push him away.

"Oh no, woman." Manning punches my shoulder. "You ain't going nowhere."

"How dare you punish my wife," Jed growls.

Wife-to-be. My lips burn.

I'm in our room. Jed's shouting at a third figure.

I try to sit up, try to see him, but there's too much pain. The insects have been biting again, they're back… I need to change the bedclothes, find some new ones, but I can't move.

"She is my property. Not yours," Jed carries on shouting, then switches to the Zharat language, but I catch a name in the yells the other man sends back.

Esther.

Dread fills my body until there's nowhere else for it to go, and I feel like I am going to be sick. But I can't be sick. Because then the nausea would be gone, and I would be more comfortable. And I *can't* be comfortable in a place like this. It's when you're comfortable, when you're at ease, that you make mistakes.

I try to remember… Try to remember last seeing Esther… Images come back to me: Manning striking her… Esther screaming, saying she's sorry.

And I hope the next bit is my dark imagination. I really do.

"So, it's true? Not only has that bastard got my sister believing she's in love with him, and hurt her, but he's attacked Sev too?"

A man, shouting.

I open my eyes. Shapes blur around me.

"Sev, is it true?" Corin's in front of me. His figure. Strong. Broad. *Corin.* He's looking toward me, hovering despite Jed's shouts, waiting for confirmation. "They won't let me see her—Manning's got her away somewhere, and I don't know what the hell he's doing to her… Is it true?"

But I can't do anything. I can't think of what to say. All I can think is that it's Corin. That he's here.

"I am not going to ask you again." Jed's voice is low as he squares up to Corin, forcing him back toward the hanging drape.

I stretch up, trying to sit up straighter, and meet Corin's eyes. I nod.

Corin leaves.

"Who the hell does that man think he is?" Jed slams his fist into the wall.

He turns on me, and I try to shrink farther into the bed. Try to get away. Try to escape another beating... No, that's not right... This is Jed... That's not right, is it? Jed's nice... He wouldn't, would he?

No. I frown. Can't think... Everything's too... It's like...a bit like when that kavalah spirit was in me. I suck in my next breath too quickly, feel my stomach twist. Is one inside me now? But it doesn't feel the same, I don't think—not like before, not really... This disorientation, it's just because I'm hurt. Must be.

"I warned you what would happen," Jed says. His voice is flat. "I told you the other men are not as nice as I am. I told you." He walks toward me.

"But..." My voice comes out as a squeak. "Esther... It's abuse."

Jed shrugs. "What goes on between a man and his woman, behind the drape, is no one else's business. Whatever it is."

It sounds like a warning.

Jed steps up to the bed, looking down at me with a tenderness that is so sudden I think I must have gone mad. This can't be happening. This can't be real.

"I dressed your fingers as best as I could."

He looks down at my right hand. I look too. Each finger has a bandage, with a splint of some sort, around it. Some of the bandages are redder than others. But I can't really feel them. Can't feel any pain. Any hurt.

And then I notice what I'm wearing. A violet gown. *Violet*. I've lost more status. Because I challenged Manning.

"They might set a bit unevenly," Jed says, talking about my fingers. "I had Soraya dose you up on some strong plants. But you will feel the pain later." He turns away and walks to the door, then looks back at me. "I am sorry I was not there to protect you. I will not fail you again. But I have to go now."

"What?" I stare at him.

"There is another fraud to dispose of."

My chest tightens, and I feel the blood drain from my face. "What?"

He lets out an exasperated sigh, shakes his head. That's when I see the marks on his neck. The marks that look like the ones on my body. The insects have bitten him too.

I frown, get a bad feeling in my mouth.

Do not ignore the Dream Land warnings.

I flinch. Don't know why I remember Death's words now.

Jed turns his collar up, shakes his head again. "I should have gone straight there, but I came for you when I heard. Another girl has revealed herself as a fraud. It is a shame, as we are getting short on girls now... More have gone missing during hunts when you were unconscious. It must be the spirits. They want our girls." He pauses. "I am sorry, S'ven. I have to go." He bends down, presses his lips against my forehead. "Sleep now. When the painkillers have worn off, it will be harder."

THIRTY-SIX

FOUR HOURS LATER, ALL I can feel is pain. It rushes at me. Throbbing pains that scratch and tear at me, clawing their way inside, until I'm screaming dry tears. Until I can't breathe. Until I'm sure I'm dying.

It hurts with every breath. It wasn't only my hand and my face Manning hurt. My chest, my ribs, my legs. They're all *screaming*. I can't move. Can't do a thing to stop any of it… And the dreams are bad—Kyla's murder and Esther's attack play over and over in my mind—and when I awake, the bite marks are everywhere. But not just on me and Jed; they're on the walls, the bed, and the floor too. Everywhere I look, they're there…getting bigger and bigger. Until there's nothing else left, and I'm just here, crying, scared, alone….

At last, Jed returns with Soraya. She gives me a drink of bitter-tasting liquid, doesn't say anything to me though.

After a while, the pain subsides. I become more conscious of who I am… And the bites, the puncture marks, I'm not covered in them, after all. It was just my mind. There's still the same amount as there was before, just on my side, my ribs and my hip. And it makes me feel better. I just imagined them—imagined the ones on Jed's neck? I shake my head, try to think clearly, try to push the pain and confusion away.

Soon, I begin to feel things that aren't pain; the covers over my legs are heavy, the air is cold, but my mother's pendant against the base of my throat is colder.

My mother's pendant. I inhale sharply. *The Dream Land….*

There's a thickness in my head, like murky water, and it tries to obscure my thoughts… But I won't let it.

Why wasn't I warned of this? Why wasn't I warned of what Manning's capable of? No… He's Untamed. Of course I wouldn't be warned… The Dream Land is only to warn of the conversion attacks—Enhanced attacks.

But then I frown, trying to think of the last time I was there. Truly there, not just when Death pulled me there to threaten me, to warn me… When was the last time I had an actual Seeing dream?

I shut my eyes, try to fight through the pain. Try to think. I need to think.

But the throbbing in my head doesn't stop me from realizing it's been too long. That it's been far too long since I visited the Dream Land…since I visited it properly.

But that's because it's unnecessary here. Because we're safe. Jed's told me that so many times… I think. Their own Seers don't get warnings anymore, because there's no need for warnings here.

Yet two girls were made Seers recently. *Two.* Kyla saw the bison. She had a vision. And the other girl would've too, the one Jed's now disposing of.

I frown.

And both were killed—by the Zharat.

My frown gets deeper. *Two* girls became Seers.

My mouth dries. It's almost as if the Gods and Goddesses are trying to warn us of something. But if they don't warn *me*, why not use the Zharat Seers—the male Seers? I frown. Unless their access to the Dream Land has been permanently blocked, like the Enhanced Seers' access—after all the Zharat *kill* the female Seers, and their male Seers don't do anything to stop it, they even encourage it, take part. And killing an Untamed Seer would be justifiable grounds for blocking that Seer's access to the Dream Land, just as if the individual had converted to the Enhanced… wouldn't it?

I breathe out slowly. I'm onto something. I know that. I need to discuss this. It's been too long. I've had no Seeing dreams recently—the last was that one of Three, if it *was* one—yet the Gods and Goddesses are trying to get a message across. I think of the two dead Seers, the two dead girls. My stomach curls.

There are only two other Untamed people here who know about my powers. And Esther will still be recovering. And Manning will be with her, watching her carefully, I know that. I can't tell her, no. Can't risk any Zharat finding out. And I feel guilty for thinking about my problem when she's in danger.

But it still leaves one person I can tell.

Corin raises his eyebrows, and the movement highlights a new bruise on his face.

"You're asking me—someone who, not long ago, didn't trust Seers—Seer-related stuff?" His eyes are cold. If there'd been just a tiny hint of warmth, and if I'd been feeling like I wasn't dying, I might have laughed and we'd have got on fine. But there isn't any warmth at all. His eyes are as cold as the depths of the coldest river, with icy fragments protruding out of them, trying to scratch me.

"Corin, please."

I try to hold his attention, but he's already looking down at the crude piece of flint he's working on. He's shaping it into a sharp point. I'd managed to catch him alone, for once, in the men's workroom, but it had taken me awfully long to get here, having to pause and lean against the wall every few seconds, and several women gave me very strange looks on the way, but I made it here with no one stopping—or hurting—me.

I try again, press my hands flat against my gown. The violet color screams back at me, reminds me of my drop in status. "Something's wrong."

He shrugs and picks up his blade. "Oh, really? You've only just realized, after you and Esther were beaten, and Esther's—"

I drop my gaze. My insect bites burn. "I meant with the Dream Land."

He shrugs again. "You have no evidence for that assumption." I see him glance down at my bandaged hand, but only for a second.

"Corin, I haven't had a Dream Land vision in ages." I pause as a sharp pain shoots around my chest. I shake my head. "It's been too long. I can feel it." I frown. Maybe it's grief...my grief... Because grief stopped my mother's visions before... No. My back aches, and I'm sure it's not my grief at play here; I had a Seeing dream after the battle, before we even knew the Zharat. *And* Death told me to *obey* the Dream Land warnings—he'd have known if it was grief, he wouldn't have threatened me. No. Something bad is happening here. "I can feel it, Corin. Something's wrong."

I shiver. It *is* wrong. I know it is. I feel the marks down the left side of my torso as they begin to feel more raised, prominent.

Corin looks up at me, and our eyes meet for the briefest second. But there's no spark between us. And he doesn't place a reassuring hand on me, or tell me it'll be okay.

"So?"

I let out an exasperated sigh. "Are you not listening to me at all?" Corin doesn't answer, so I continue. "Don't you think it's odd? Since we've been here, I haven't been summoned. Not properly—there was only that one of Three, if it even *was* one."

And, Death summoned me to make it clear I must *obey* the Dream Land warnings—yet I haven't had any.

He shrugs. "We're safe here then, that's what that means. We're safe. Well, at least from the Enhanced." His eyes darken, and he strikes his piece of flint again. A shard flies off, and I watch as he tests the sharpness of the point with the fleshy pad of his thumb.

"So why were two others made into Seers? Those girls." I flinch a little. "Corin, I'm *telling* you, something's wrong."

He strikes the flint with his blade, making a shrill sound.

"I think it's fine," he says. "But, then again, what do I know?" His tone takes a dangerous turn. "I'm just the man who couldn't save his sister from that disgusting creep, and the man who was too *weak* for you to be with."

"That's not fair," I cut in.

"Isn't it?" He throws his arms in the air, dropping the flint and blade by his feet, showering us with loose stone flakes. "I didn't see *you* fighting for *us*. I didn't see *you* in Manning's chamber begging him to let us be together. No." He laughs sarcastically. "You just swanned off to that Jed bloke, happy as can be."

"Happy?" I shake my head. "You think *I'm* happy with this?"

He glares at me. "You're not trying to get out of this marriage," he says. "You spend so much time with that man and his friends. You even smile when you see him now. What else am I supposed to think? You're getting like Esther. Neither of you can see what these men are really like, and it's as if you're happy being treated like…" He shakes his head, then pushes past me. "And I can't do a bloody thing about it. Not for either of you... Look, I've got to go, Sev. I've got better things to do than worry about Seer matters with you."

"Better things?" I echo his words, and, for some reason, I think of Clare, picture them together. My shoulders tighten, and I breathe a little harder.

"Yes," Corin snaps, picking up the flint. Its point looks sharper than before. "Like making sure Manning knows exactly what I'll do if he ever touches my sister again."

I watch him leave, my eyes glassing over.

He doesn't care about you anymore, the voice in my head says. *He doesn't care if anyone else hurts you*.

THIRTY-SEVEN

OVER THE NEXT FEW DAYS, I begin to feel better, even despite more insects biting me last night; but it's okay, because the older scars have nearly gone, and I've changed the bedclothes twice more. At least, I feel better until I see Mart blocking my way.

I swallow hard, look around. It's just the two of us in the tube. Nearly everyone else is outside. Jed said the spirits have granted us some unusually sunny weather within the rainy season, and people are making the most of it. He even said he'd take me out, show me the gardens where they grow food, but I told him I was too tired.

I can't go outside. I can't let the Enhanced find us. Can't let them have all the Untamed.

But what are you going to do? Make sure your people survive by hiding here all the time? That's no life.

I push that thought away and concentrate on Mart, see his eyes narrow. The lantern just above him casts long, jagged shadows across his face.

"I know what you are." Mart steps closer, until he's right in front of me. I try to move, but my legs won't work. "I heard you, Seven. You don't fool me."

I twist my head, try to lean away from him, but he just presses himself closer to me, until his head is an inch from mine, and I'm engulfed by the foul smell on him—rotten vegetables and stale body odor.

Mart's blue eyes flash. "I know you're an Enhanced spy, and I *know* you're planning an attack." He bares his teeth slightly, and I swallow hard. "I'm watching you. So are my men. You won't get away with this."

I try to hold my head higher, but he can see I'm shaking.

"Run along, Seven." His tone is nasal. "Run along while you can. Because it's only a matter of time. A matter of time before I have proof of what you are. A matter of time before I slice your neck open with my axe, spill your blood."

Mart's lips twitch slightly, and then he steps back. I feel my nostrils flare as I watch him, try to work out what he's going to do next. But he just stands there.

"Run along, Seven."

My chest pounds. I push past him, gulping back tears. I try to keep them at bay, but I can't. So, I run. I run out of the room, down the corridor. Don't know where I'm going. I alternate left and right turns, until the walls are just blurring past me.

Until I'm—

Until I'm standing in front of Death.

That painting. Next to the bison. I stare at the wall, waiting for Death to move, waiting for Death to warn me about betrayal again. But he doesn't move. Of course he doesn't. It's just an illustration, not the Dream Land now. But I need it to be. I need to get there, find out what's wrong, receive the vision that Kyla had, that the other girl must've too.

But nothing happens.

My tears only make Death blur as I stare at the wall. I slide down, onto the ground.

I'm going mad. I'm actually going mad. It's just a painting. And I'm sitting here, waiting, expecting it to move, to transport me to the Dream Land.

Oh Gods. I'm not normal. I'm like that woman my mother told me about. One who went mad after she was rescued her from the Enhanced. She said the woman never was the same again, that she saw things, talked to people who weren't there.

And I've been doing that—talking to my dead sister's ghost. And Death.

I swear loudly, then I punch the ground next to me with my bad hand, feel my scarred knuckles split open; pain shoots through my crushed fingers. Feel the blood oozing out, bursting around the bandages on my fingers, the splints. I watch it, watch the redness make little trails down the dry skin on the back of my hand. It's like a map, a living map on the back of my hand. New rivers forming.

I pull the bandages off, one by one, and—

"Seven?"

I look up, see a girl heading toward me. Jeena. Jed's daughter. Another girl trails her.

"There you are!" Jeena's eyes widen as she sees my hand, the blood.

I try to hide it, try to wipe the redness away on my violet shirt, but I can't. There's too much. My worn, black denim skirt soaks some of it up, but not enough.

"Are you okay?" That's the other girl. They're both staring at me.

I nod. Then I point at the wall with my bloody fist, at the painting of Death. "Have you ever seen it move?" And I don't know why I'm saying it, because I know last time it *was* because of the Dream Land, not my madness.

Jeena looks uncomfortable. "That's a painting. Paintings don't move."

More tears roll down my face.

"Come on, we shouldn't be here," the other girl says. She's looking around. "The Seers don't like females to be alone in the Gods' Corridor."

Electricity springs through my body. I jump up, feel a strange pressure in my ears. "What? The Gods'

Corridor?"

The girls recoil.

"These are depictions of the Gods." Jeena points at the one of Death, then farther down to where there are more paintings—paintings I didn't get a chance to look at last time. "We shouldn't be here."

My chest tightens as I stare at the painting of Death. "He's a *God*?" My hand shakes as I try to point at him.

The other girl nods. "Yes, that's Waskabe, the God of Death."

The God of Death.

My lips move slightly. I shake my head. And I've seen him. Jed's words come back to me, about how Seers meet their Gods. About how his father met the God of Life.

My skin starts stinging, all over.

I've seen Death.

I've seen *the God of Death*.

"The stories say that he is drawn to those who are the most powerful," Jeena says, "those who will become the most important Seers, because they are the ones who are most easily tempted by the Enhanced—he wants to stop them converting. He makes them his Seers of Death, and he threatens them if they think of converting; and those Seers listen, because as their God, he owns their bodies and souls. No one wants to be trapped with *him* forever and never make it to the New World when they die."

I freeze. Trapped with Death? Never make it to the New World?

My chest rises and falls sharply. I feel a tightening in my throat, as if all the muscles are constricting. I take several deep breaths. No. It can't be. These are just stories. That's all. The Zharat are full of stories.

Just stories.

Except I know it's not a story. Because Death told me—that first time I saw him, he told me.

Death will collect what belongs to Death… And that means *me*. I belong to Death. *I'm* never going to make it to the New World. *A traitor's soul is Death's soul.*

I step back, try to breathe, but every breath gets stuck. I press my lips together; no, it can't be.

The mask of betrayal hangs over your aura, like gold cobwebs, rusting. Your body will rot under Death's command, long before your soul is allowed an escape from the decaying flesh of your ribs.

I gulp. That's what Death said to me. Permanent pain after I die... My soul stuck in my rotting body... And when my soul is free, I'll still belong to Death... I'll always be his.

A threat. A promise of what will happen to my body and soul because I wanted to join the Enhanced.

Because he thinks I will betray the Untamed again, because he knows I already thought about it... *Most easily tempted.*

Because I'm powerful.

Powerful.

Raleigh said that. He's said that loads of time, said that's the reason he wants me.

Because I'm the most powerful Seer? Because I'm most easily tempted? I frown. No. I'm strong. I resisted the pull of the Enhanced lifestyle. I'm still Untamed.

Because I'm the key to the Untamed? Does Raleigh know that? He must... He seems to know everything, more than I know.

I shake my head.

Death is watching me. Death chose me, because I am easily tempted—and I was.

Death chose me because he believes I'll betray the Untamed again.

I'm a Seer of Death.

THIRTY-EIGHT

"SEVEN? WE REALLY NEED TO go. If the men catch us…" Jeena touches my arm gently.

I stare at the painting of Death, of Waskabe, try to remember everything he and the bison and the spirits have ever said to me. But my head is heavy, fuzzy. I can't think.

My death.

He said the day of my death is marked to end the suffering. But how? I don't understand. If I'm a Seer of Death, and I'm powerful—very powerful—and the key to it all, does that mean I'll kill people? A whole side? I gulp. Is that why Death was so adamant that I mustn't betray my people again… Because if I'm Enhanced I'll kill all the Untamed? Because I'm the *key to it all.*

But how? I don't understand.

No. I shake my head. That's not right. Can't be. It's to do with *my* death. That's what Death said. My death would end the suffering. Because I'm going to kill people, bring death about… And I'll die to end it all, end the war? I'll be the last death?

Or because if Raleigh finds me, the Enhanced will

289

get all the Zharat—all the Untamed—and somehow, then, I'll die?

"Seven, *come on*, we need to go. We shouldn't even be here. It will upset the Gods, and they will punish all of us," Jeena says. "Manning wants you in the council area. If we're not there soon, he'll come looking for us."

"And he'd better not find us here," the other girl mutters.

Manning. The hairs on the back of my neck stand up, and I shudder. But then Jeena and the other girl are marching me away, and I don't try to stop them.

It doesn't take long to get to the council area. Manning and two other men are already sitting there.

"Seven." Manning grins. "How lovely of you to join me again."

I glance at Jeena, pray that she and the other girl aren't going to leave me. But there's another woman here too; she's in the shadows. *Clare.* The only person I've seen who wears violet…the same shade I now wear. Because we've both challenged the men. Maybe violet isn't just for marking us as being of the lowest status. Maybe it's also to single us out as the dangerous ones… The ones who need to be watched.

But no one's doing a good job of watching Clare now. She's in the shadows, and something tells me only I have noticed her there.

"We've had a request to put your marriage date forward," Manning says. "To next week. The request has been granted."

My jaw drops.

Manning looks amused for a few seconds. "The ceremony will be held in six days' time, woman. You better prepare." He looks across at Jeena. "Ain't that lovely? Seven will be your new mother."

Jeena looks away, and Clare steps up to me. She stands next to me, hands behind her back.

"Congratulations," Clare says, smiling.

"Who requested it?" I ignore her, stare at Manning.

Clare moves a little, and then something brushes against my hand. I feel the sharpness of it; right away I know it is a blade. I wrap my fingers around it, hold it behind my back, confused. Clare moves closer, and her words are a whisper that's lost among my fast breathing. I start to turn to her, but then she moves—leaves the area so quickly.

And I'm left holding—hiding—a knife.

Manning's lips curl. "I think you know who requested to have your marriage date put forward, woman," he says.

I turn my attention back to him. He's right.

I do.

I stare at Jed, head still pounding. There's too much going on in it, I can't think clearly.

"Why?"

The corners of Jed's lips tug up. "Because I want to be with you in *all* the ways."

I cross my arms, try to stop myself shaking. I shake my head, try not to let his words affect me.

"You said you weren't interested in me—not in that way." I swallow hard. Clare's knife is under my shirt, tucked into my belt, out of sight. But my fingers start to burn; they're yearning for it.

Jed's voice is heavy. "I've changed my mind." He moves toward me, touches my waist. "It will be all right, you will enjoy the wedding," Jed says. "And there is no point in waiting all this time. Look, my leg, it is almost healed now. We can have a proper ceremony."

I look down, but there's nothing to see but his trousers. Jed's not like some of the other men here. He covers up as much of his skin as possible, doesn't show off his tattoos—because he's comfortable in his own power, his status, that's what he said before. But I suppose he *is* putting his weight on his bad leg. And I haven't seen him limping much lately—he even went out hunting before.

Jed reaches across, touches my face. His hands tilt my head back so I look into his eyes. Dark eyes, like Corin's, but not as… Something's different. I want to say Corin's are truer, but that doesn't make sense. They're just eyes. Untamed eyes.

"You are beautiful."

I try to lean away, but his hands on my face stop me. Before I know what's happening, he's trying to kiss me.

Déjà vu.

I shove him backward.

My breath comes all at once, and I take several deep gulps, nearly choking. My head feels too hot. I pull at my left ear, tug it.

Jed smiles an unkind smile.

"I must go and prepare with the other Seers," he says. "We have another meeting tomorrow, to find the missing girls—girls and women now." His eyes meet mine. "More have gone missing." His tone is dark, and there's something about it that makes the words sound like a threat.

I stare at him. My stomach starts to hurt.

He crosses toward the doorway, pulls the drape back. "I will not be long."

I collapse onto the leaf mattress, feel Clare's knife press into my back. My head spins, pounds. Tears come to my eyes again, and then I'm looking at my fist, at my cracked knuckles. I run my fingertips over them, flinch a little. The blood has dried now, but it feels unstable. Like more is trying to gush through.

I press on the broken skin harder, harder, until I feel it.

Pain.

I welcome it. Feels good. I take deep breaths; feel

tears pierce the corners of my eyes. But they're good tears. Good tears.

Waskabe.

The name suddenly flashes in front of me. Then I see Death, in my memories. I take deep breaths. Need to concentrate on that, not Jed. On Death. Waskabe.

I'm his Seer. I'm a Seer of Death. That's why I'm the key to the survival of the Untamed. Because I'm his Seer.

And my death will end the suffering. That's what he said the very first time I saw him: *The day of your death is marked to end the suffering.*

I try to clear my head. That's what I know. But it's not enough. I need to know how my death will end the war, and what being a Seer of Death means I will do. Because suddenly I don't think it means that I'm supposed to stay here—holed up with the Zharat—so Raleigh can't find me. No. It means I'm going to do something, something *active*. Kill a whole side? Kill all the Enhanced? But how… There are too many. I can't kill millions of people….

But the Enhanced isn't the smallest side, is it?

I gulp, and then I don't know where my thoughts are coming from. They're just there.

The Untamed has the smallest number. It would be easier to kill all of them. End the war that way, with the Enhanced victorious. End the suffering of the Untamed… Isn't that what Waskabe said my death would do? End the suffering. And then I'd kill myself—the last Untamed person? And the war would end.

And I could do that here….

Stop Raleigh and the Enhanced from ever getting all of us.

No.

I flinch. Feel my insides start to get jittery. I rub my hands together, watch my legs as they tremble.

Or maybe being a Seer of Death doesn't mean I'll kill anyone after all. I reach for my Seer pendant, twist the crystal around, over and over in my hand, as if by doing it I'll suddenly get all the answers I need.

But the answers don't come, and I know they won't. The Gods and Goddesses work in strange ways. I know that. They're probably never going to tell me how I'll end the war, just that I will. Somehow.

Oh Gods. I feel the pressure on me, a weight pressing down on my neck. I take several deep breaths, let go of the Seer pendant. It slams into my chest with a little too much force, as though a magnetic field's pulled it back.

I take several shaky breaths, then I cover my face with my hands, breathe deeply. So deeply that it sounds as if I'm hyperventilating.

"Sev?"

The voice makes me jump. I bolt upright, the edge of the mattress pressing against my ankles.

Corin. In the doorway. My heart races.

Then I get ready for his instructions, what he wants me to do.

But they don't come.

"What do you want?" I shift my weight a little.

Corin looks at the ground. I look at his shoes. They're the ones that we got on that raid back at New Repliza, together. We both got a pair. But I've no idea where mine are. I don't seem to wear shoes anymore. I stare at my bare feet.

He pulls a hand through his hair. "I don't know." He exhales. "To see that you're all right, after Kyla… and Nyesha?"

"Nyesha?"

Corin's eyes widen a little. "You don't know?"

I get a very bad feeling in the pit of my stomach. "What?" My voice is a whisper.

He turns away slightly, and I see his profile. "Women have gone missing too now."

I nod. Jed said that.

"Nyesha's one of them."

At first, I don't understand his words. It's like he's speaking the Zharat language, and his words are butterflies that just glide over me, singing sweet songs that I'll never know. Then I touch my head slowly.

"Missing?" The corners of my eyes sting. "What? Out fishing?" I try to remember what Jed said.

Corin shakes his head. "No. They seemed to disappear straight from the cave. Haven't you heard the talk about it? Manning thought at first the group had run away, but they haven't taken anything with them. No weapons, nothing. And some of their babies have been left behind. He says it's the spirits."

"The Noir Lands are bad," I say, and I don't know where the words come from, or how I manage to keep my tone so neutral.

I wring my hands together, try to scrape the rest of the dried blood off, but the movement just makes me sweat. Makes my hands go clammy, damp, horrible.

Nyesha's gone… I blink hard, shake my head. I feel my breathing get sharper, feel the panic rising, know that I need to distract myself.

"How's Esther?" And I feel awful that *that* question is my distraction, that I haven't asked sooner.

Corin looks grim. "She's been better." He pauses. "Manning's not been hurting her anymore now. She's safe. You haven't seen her?"

I shake my head and—

"My wedding's going to be next week." My body jolts as I blurt the words out.

Corin's face darkens. "What?"

I press my hands down onto my thighs, dig my nails in until I can feel sharp points of pain. I try not to look at him. "He's moved it… Jed…wants it sooner."

Your wedding is going to be next week.

Next week.

I gulp, get a prickly feeling in the bridge of my nose. And—and I can't do it anymore.

I turn away from him, don't want him to see me cry, don't want him to see how weak I am. I stare at the cave wall. The black-gray lava.

"Sev?" Corin's voice is full of alarm.

I hear him step closer—*feel* him step closer, the air changes. Then his hands are on me, turning my head back toward him.

I hesitate, force myself to look away. "Jed will be back soon, he'll be looking for me. Someone will see us."

Corin shrugs—I see the movement from the corner of my eye. Then his hands pull me up, and I'm standing in front of him. His arms catch me, hold me, and I stare over his left shoulder. I feel his warm fingers pressing against my waist, and he makes a noise deep in the back of his throat. Part of me is aware the knife's still in my belt—I need to move it—but my body feels strange, like I can't control it.

He shouldn't be here… You shouldn't be touching him… Jed will be back soon… He'll be angry if he sees Corin with you… Bad things happen when Jed's not happy.

But I'm not supposed to be with Jed. I'm *supposed* to be with Corin. I press my lips together, feel tears run.

Corin's breathing deeply, and I feel his body shake with every breath. He starts to say something, but changes his mind. His fingers splay out along my back, touching more and more of me, and he presses his hands flat against my sides, as if he needs to touch me.

I lift my head up, focus on his full lips. They look the softest I've ever seen them.

"What's this?" His voice is sharp and sudden. He's pulling up my shirt farther, and I think he means the knife tucked in the back of my belt, but then I realize he's looking at my skin.

"I—"

The marks. He felt the marks, and now he's looking at them. Looking at my side, my hip. Dread fills me. I go cold. No. The *room* goes cold.

"Sev?"

I look at him carefully. "I don't know, insect bites?" And I'm about to say Jed's got them too, when I realize that would anger Corin, make him think Jed and I have been naked together.

But the insects have bitten him too. That wasn't a hallucination, what I saw on his neck before he turned his collar up, was it? Oh Gods. I don't know.

"They're *not* insect bites, Sev," Corin says.

He pushes the hem of my shirt up more, squints at the skin across the left side of my ribcage. His fingers brush against the bite marks; I shiver. My breath catches in my throat. But still he's touching them, touching me. He doesn't stop. He lifts my shirt higher still, and I see his eyes get wider and wider.

"They're all over you, all up this side," he says, his voice almost too low to hear. "Those ones… They're like snake bites. Tiny, tiny snake bites. But they're not…" He shakes his head. "Have you told anyone?" There's a strange lilt to his voice, a lilt that makes me wonder if he knows what they are. But it's a lilt that stops me from asking him.

I shake my head, gulping. My hands are clammy, and suddenly I'm sweating loads.

His fingers smooth my shirt back down, back over the knife in my belt. Then he takes hold of my shoulders softly. His eyes stare into mine. My heart feels like it's going to burst. "Don't tell anyone about them," he says. "I've got a bad feeling."

I nod, take a deep breath. I look up at Corin, a thousand words on the tip of my tongue—words I can't say. And—

He kisses me.

A deep kiss. A kiss that isn't like our others. This is faster, harder, more…desperate?

I kiss him back, press myself closer, taste the smoke on him. Part of me is surprised I'm doing it. That I'm grabbing him, like an animal. But I want him.

I hate Jed.

I want Corin.

I need Corin.

I feel different. Older. A lot older—the realization slaps me, and, for a second, I see myself as Five. For the first time in my life, I don't feel like a weak, little girl. I feel strong, confident, empowered. A woman.

And I want him.

Corin's hands move around my body, my arms, my shoulders, my waist. Then his lips move down, to my neck, to the soft skin there. I breathe deeply. His hands press against my lower back, pulling me in toward him. Then he pushes the back of my shirt up again. His fingers touch my searing skin, burn me. But he doesn't care about the insect bites this time.

"Sev...."

He pulls away, just enough so our eyes meet. His pupils are dilated, more dilated than I've ever seen them, and the rim of color around them glows, more amber than usual.

The question in them burns, then he whispers in my ear.

"Yes." I nod, my head's pounding. Adrenaline. I pull Jed's ring off, throw it behind me into the dirt and dust, and reach for Corin's hands, press them against my skin again, want to feel him close. Need to feel him close.

I pull him down onto the ground, with me. We miss the leaf mattress, but it doesn't matter. Isn't important. My fingers pull at his clothes, but they shake too much, and I can't undo the buttons.

No, you don't want this....

No. I do. I *do*.

Your wedding is going to be next week.

I want to be with Corin. I need to be with him first, before the wedding, before Jed. I *have* to be with Corin. If I've been with him, it will make it more bearable. I can think about Corin when I'm with Jed, remember it all. It will make it better.

It has to.

My fingers work at the buttons on his shirt, one of them falls off. His hands are on me, pulling at my top, exposing more and more of my skin. Skin he touches, skin he kisses.

I get his shirt off, throw it into the corner. I press my hands against the strong planes of his chest, his stomach, his muscles, feel something inside me respond. Then my eyes fall on his belt, his shorts. For a second I don't know what to do, what I'm supposed to do. Do we go straight for it? Or more kissing first?

I hesitate for a second, then I lie back, feel the rough stone against my spine, digging in.

Corin climbs over me, makes a deep sound at the back of his throat, hands either side of my chest. Then he shakes his head.

"Sev, this isn't like you—*you* don't behave like this."

Corin's right. You know he is.

"You're wrong," I cry, and I don't know whether I'm telling him or myself.

I reach up, pull him down, kiss him, hard. Half a second later, he responds: kissing me, feeling me, a hand slipping down to my thigh.

Then he pushes me away again.

He breathes hard, looks at me. A slight line appears between his brows. His hands go to his belt. "Are you sure?"

"Yes!"

He swallows, apparently with some difficulty. "But this isn't you," he says. "Something's not right… Sev."

And I don't know why he's protesting so much. Doesn't he want this too?

Corin frowns. "I've no idea what you're thinking anymore. But I *know* this isn't you."

"It is!" I pull his hands toward me again, stretch up, kiss his neck. My heart speeds up, it's like a countdown's ticking, always in the background.

But Corin's right. This isn't you.

No. It is. It *is* me. He doesn't know me like he thinks he does—no one really knows me.

So *I* reach for his belt. I undo it, keep my eyes on him the whole time. I watch as his pupils dilate again. I watch as the amber in his eyes gets stronger, as—

"What the hell are you doing with my wife?"

THIRTY-NINE

FOR A SECOND, WE FREEZE. Then Corin and I spring apart as Jed storms into the room. The Zharat man's face is angry, his eyes dark. He grabs Corin and pulls him farther away from me.

I cry out, straightening my shirt and checking my skirt as I stand.

"What the hell are you doing with *my* wife?"

"We—we were just talking." Corin looks back at me. His face is red now, redder than I've ever seen it.

Jed slams a fist into the wall, and I flinch. His eyes travel to me. To where I'm standing, shaking. I glare at him, feel something building up within me. Feel heat rush to my face, fire in my veins.

"You were *talking*?"

"Look," Corin says, fiddling with his belt. A second later, he glances toward the corner where his crumpled shirt is on the floor. "You don't have to worry—"

"*Worry*?" Jed steps right up to Corin, gets in his face. "Why would I have to worry about you? You are no threat to me." He looks at me, eyes narrowing. "S'ven knows her place. We do not play games. She knows she will lose and I will always win. Women are weak."

And that's when it happens.

That's when I punch Jed.

I catch him off guard. He stumbles backward, and I—I leap at him. I claw at his skin. I am like a cat. And suddenly all I can think of is *him* kissing me, all I can feel are *his* hands on me. And something inside me snaps.

I scream and hit him again. My fist impacts with his arm, but my strength's gone. And—

Jed swears at me, shouts at me, face contorting. I see his hand a half-second before he slaps me. I start to fall back, but his hand closes around my arm.

"You should not have done that, S'ven."

And then Corin grabs me; for a moment I'm stuck between the two men.

"I have won her. She is mine," Jed snarls. "So back off. Get your own wife."

Corin punches him. It is a much better punch than the one I threw.

I jump back, away from Jed as he falls. I turn and see Corin, nostrils flaring, fists still clenched in front of him.

"You deserve more than that!" Corin yells, stepping over Jed, bending down so close that his face is mere inches from Jed's. He punches him again.

"Corin!" I scream, leap forward. Electricity bolts through me. I grab his arm, try to pull him back, but he's too strong. Just shrugs me off, yells something I can't make out.

And then—then he's falling, hits the ground hard. I spin around, just as Jed kicks Corin again, uses the movement to lever himself up.

"You really want to do this again?" Jed snarls, his finger jabbing into Corin's face. "After I nearly killed you last time? I was kind, leaving you alive, but not this time."

"Stop it!" I scream, and I'm getting in between the two of them. My hand's on Jed's chest, and I'm trying to push him away, but he just bats me aside.

I fall, but I get up and—

White light flashes from Jed's hand. It hits Corin hard, just as he's trying to get up.

My mouth dries. *No.*

I scream, lunge for the two of them again. My hands drag against Jed's shirt, and I try to pull him away, but I can't. Another bolt of white light flashes, hits Corin, but Corin's still moving, still trying to fight him, though he's lying on the stone floor.

"You really want me to kill you?" Jed snarls, kicks Corin. He's wearing boots, thick heavy boots.

Corin shouts something, but there's blood pouring from his nose, and his words get lost in it. He rolls over, hands pushing toward the ground, ready to get up.

"I do not think so," Jed says.

More white light.

Corin screams.

I scream.

That's when I see the knife. The one Clare gave me. It's on the floor, partly under the mattress. Must've fallen out my belt when Corin and I were….

My ears hum as I retrieve the knife. It feels heavy now.

I turn. Corin's flat on his back, Jed's standing over him.

I line the knife up with Jed's back.

One quick movement, that's all it takes.

I stab Jed.

For a second, I can't understand the scene in front of me. There's too much movement, not enough light. But I still see it all.

Jed falling, blood spurting over Corin. Jed gurgling. Corin shouting—at me?—his face red.

Blood. Everywhere. The floor, Corin, the walls. But not me. No blood is on me, and that seems significant, but I don't know why.

I stare down at Jed, start to bring a hand to my mouth as I feel the bile rise, but then I see I'm still holding the knife, and blood is dripping from its blade. And then Corin's moving, getting up. He grabs his shirt from the corner, rushes back, kneels at Jed's side, pressing his hand and his shirt over the wound—the wound that *I* made—over the gushing blood, trying to stop it, trying to save him. And I don't understand. He hates him.

And it's so quiet suddenly.

"Is he—is he dead?" I struggle to breathe. The cave's closing in on me. The walls are moving. Squashing me. Stone, against my skin.

Oh Gods.

I stabbed him. I *stabbed* Jed.

I've killed him.

I've killed a man. An Untamed man. Jed. My husband.

No, fiancé.

But I've still killed him.

I watch Corin, watch as he searches for a pulse, but I know. I know he won't find one. Because I've killed him.

I'm a Seer of Death.

I kill people. I hurt them, and I kill them.

"He's alive," Corin says, and the walls move away from me.

But I don't react, feel detached from it. This isn't happening. Can't be.

He pulls the bloodied mass that is his shirt away from Jed, puts it behind him. "Give me the knife, Sev." Corin's voice is low, reminds me of a panther.

"What?" I look down. Blood drips from it still, adding to the small pool of red next to my left foot. There's a surprising amount of blood coming from the blade, like *it's* the one bleeding.

"Give it to me." Corin's reaching up toward me, for it. But he doesn't take it. "We need to finish this."

What?

I stare at him. Don't understand. Finish it… No, he can't mean that. He was just trying to stop the bleeding, only a few seconds ago… Unless *that* was instinct, and this is….

"We need to finish this," he says again.

"*We*?" I stare, my eyes glassy. I feel movement inside my chest, like something's rotating. It makes me gag for several moments. When, at last, I can speak, my voice is all scratchy, like there are holes in it. "I didn't mean… We can't kill him…."

Corin stands. "If Jed's dead, it solves all the problems. You won't have to marry him. We can be together."

"They won't let *us* be together." I shake my head. "No, they'll—"

"But I was the second strongest man—"

"But they'll kill us, Corin! If we've *killed* one of them…" My breaths are ragged, and my mouth is too hot, burning. "We—we can't just kill him."

"*You're* the one who stabbed him." Corin's eyes flash.

The knife twitches in my hand. "No, we can't kill him…just… We need to go."

Corin grunts. "That's what I've been telling you all along—we can't stay here."

"No." I grab at my head; my thoughts are all over the place. Nothing makes sense anymore. "We can't leave. I can't. We have to—"

"Sev. No. Listen. Just breathe," Corin says. Blood trickles from his nose, makes a trail down his bare chest.

He puts his hands on my shoulders, looks into my eyes. His pupils are back to normal now, and I can't stop looking at them, can't stop remembering how dilated they were before. How Jed stopped me from being with Corin. Anger flares within me.

"Sev, we're going to *have* to go. Whether we kill Jed or not, we have to leave. You're right. If Manning finds out what we've done—even if Jed lives—he'll kill us. We can't be *here*. We *have* to leave. Now."

Oh Gods.

I drop the knife. It clatters by my feet, and more blood sprays over my ankles. I reach down, try to get the blood off, but I just smear it onto my hands.

We have to leave?

Raleigh has your eyes.

I flinch.

Don't betray the Untamed again.

I swallow hard, feel sick. I look across at Jed, lying on his front, face down. The blood's pooling around him now.

If I kill him, I'll have to leave right away, before Manning finds out and kills me. But, if I leave, Raleigh will find me and bring the Enhanced here; the Zharat tribe will be no more—and, if we're the last Untamed, then I'd have ended our race.

If I let Jed live, the Zharat will still want to kill me. They'll know what I did. I'd still have to leave. And cause the end of the Zharat.

But if I stay here—whether Jed lives or not—I'll die, and then Raleigh won't be able to use my eyes, he won't find the Zharat. But, if I die at the hands of the Zharat, Death's prediction will be useless—my death won't end the suffering. The war would continue—for ever? Raleigh wouldn't find the Zharat without my eyes, but I would die.

It's death and destruction, whichever scenario we choose.

Jed's death.

My death.

The end of the Zharat—the end of all the Untamed?

And I know what I have to do. I have to stay here. If I stay here—and die—the Zharat will live. Death said my demise would end the war—and maybe it would've done, if things had happened differently. But they haven't. The future's changed.

And I've got to let the Zharat kill me. My death here will save them.

But then I swallow hard, grab Corin's hand. His fingers are slippery, bloody. I let go, wipe my hand against my skirt.

I have to stay here. The Zharat will kill me, but it will save them.

Those are the words I try to say…but I can't get them out; I'm shaking too much, every part of me trembling.

My head pounds, and then *it* comes to me—what we need to do.

Corin can blindfold me when we leave—if I'm blindfolded, Raleigh won't see where the Zharat den is. I'll be protecting myself—and them. And I don't know why I didn't think of it earlier. It's obvious, so obvious I start smiling.

No one needs to die.

My smile gets wider. "Let's go."

Corin looks at me for the briefest of seconds. Then he nods.

"You go and get Esther. I'll meet you at her room."

"What? Where are you going?" I look down at Jed. At his body. He's going to die soon anyway, I can tell.

I'm a Seer of Death.

Corin squeezes my hand, then he pulls away. "I need to wash this blood off, find another shirt. I'll be two minutes. *Go.*"

I do.

My heart pounds in my ears the whole way. I pass several Zharat men, all their eyes follow me as I run, and they're talking. I can hear them. I try to cover up the blood stains on my clothes, really try, but I can't do it. My hands aren't big enough, and there are too many dark patches on me.

I speed up, hear a pounding in my ears.

I can't remember where Esther's room is, not sure if I've ever known—unless it was where she was recovering when we first got here—but then she's in front of me. For a second, I can't do anything but stare at the bruises across her face. Orange and yellow and blue. I start to feel sick.

Then, I pull her to the side, looking around quickly.

But there are people about. I can't tell her here that we're going to escape.

Esther frowns, then pushes me into a room. I look around. Store room. Small.

"You came back?" Her eyes are wide.

My heart pounds. I feel weaker than ever. "What?"

"I saw you," she says. And I can't read her expression at all, don't understand what she's thinking, whether she's still angry with me. "You packed a rucksack, and you left. I followed you down the slope, but you went into the trees. You were running, you were quick. And you'd left us. Me and Corin."

"What?" I stare at her, my temples throbbing. "I didn't go outside."

But people *are* seeing me outside. Jed. And now Esther.

Oh Gods. I'm really going mad. I'm doing things, going outside, and I can't even remember. And does that mean I've already shown the Enhanced the way here?

Esther's eyes narrow. "I saw you, Seven. Look, I know you got out, so don't lie to me. But why'd you come back after you'd obviously already decided to leave me and Corin here?" She pauses, and she looks around quickly. "Did you come back for us?" Her voice gets lighter. There's hope in it, and she looks at me differently. She looks at me like how she used to, like I'm her friend. Then she shakes a little.

"Esther, I've no idea what you're talking about." I shake my head. "But we have got to go. The three of us."

"So you did?" Her eyes get wider. "You did come back for me and Corin?" Her bottom lip quivers. "Because I *do* want to come with you."

"What?" I squint at her.

She looks around quickly, and when she turns back her expression is completely different—tenser somehow, but her eyes are lighter, more earnest, more *her*. "I'm scared, Seven. And I don't know what to do, because of him… Corin told me it isn't right—what he's doing… And the way he said it he *sounds* right… He said if it was you being sucked in by some older, violent man then I'd do what I could to protect you, and I know I would… But it just… I can't see it like that because Manning's nice to me… Well, I mean, he *hurt* me, but…" She looks away and pulls on her short braids so they stick up even more. "I'm just all messed up. I can't think, and if Manning hears me saying this then…."

I reach for her, but she flinches.

"I miss Three." Esther gulps. "I *really* miss him, Seven. And I just want what you and my brother have, and I thought I'd have it with Three, but then he's not here and Manning is, and Manning loves me." She wrings her hands together, and her eyes take on a far-away look. "You've not seen what he's like—what he's really like—how nice he can be, how nice he is. He told me I love him too…and he's right. A part of me *does* love him because he was the one who was there for me. And I know it's wrong because he hurt you, and he's not a nice man, but…."

And then she's crying—Esther's *crying*—and I don't know what to do, what to say.

I reach out for her, take hold of her hands.

"You really came back for us, so we can all go." She tries to smile through her tears. Her lashes look sticky, and she gulps. "We have to get away from this place… before I see Manning and change my mind… We just have to go…like those other women who have gone… The ones who left too, on their own accord." Her voice is loud, too loud, and I raise my hand in our *silence!* motion—the gesture that we always used when we were on the run, on raids.

Esther nods, presses her lips together, and then—

"Is that blood?"

Her eyes are wide, and she grabs my hands, turns them palm up. The light in here's poor. But I look at my hands. The blood's still there. I should've gone with Corin to wash it all off and—

I dropped the knife. I left it in the room.

My head jerks up. I look at Esther. "Corin's going to kill him."

My hands freeze. Oh Gods. That's why he got me to leave. He wasn't going to wash blood off. No. He was getting me out the way, getting me—

"What?" Esther says.

I turn to her, heart pounding too fast. "I stabbed Jed…and Corin's going to…going to kill him."

Esther's eyes get even wider. "What? You stabbed him?" She looks uncertain. "What did Jed do?"

"Come on!" I grab her hand, pull her out of the store room. "We've got to stop him!"

The corridor's even busier now, and we try to weave through the men and women and children, but they're stepping out in front of us, and I can't get past them quick enough. And Esther's slow, pulling on my arm, making it ache.

My feet pound the ground. I feel dizzy, lightheaded. Can feel pressure in my ears. But I see the room up ahead, on the left. The doorway with the swinging, tartan drape.

I barge in, Esther right behind me, and—

The room is empty.

I look around, clutch at my chest, at my mother's pendant. It's burning.

But the room is empty. Jed's not here.

Neither is Corin.

"Is that more blood? Is this where—where it happened?"

I look up, see Esther on the other side of the room. She's standing over the pool of blood. It's glistening. And there's so much of it. More than I remember.

"What's that?" Esther's hand starts shaking. Then she bends down, picks up my engagement ring.

Footsteps. Heavy. Quick. Someone running. A man, probably.

Seconds later, Corin bursts through the doorway.

"I thought those were your voices." He's got a clean shirt on, but he doesn't look happy. "What the hell are you doing back here? I told you to stay in Esther's room!"

I stand up shakily. "Where's Jed?" My voice wobbles.

Corin looks around, his face whitens. "I left him here."

"Alive?"

"Yes!" he yells. "Oh, shit."

Jed's not here now… He's gone. My chest hitches. He's gone, walked out? Gone to tell everyone? Oh Gods. The Zharat'll be here in a matter of seconds.

I look at Corin, then Esther as she walks toward us. "We have to go *now*."

But Corin's not moving. He's just standing there in front of me. And then—*then* I see what he's holding, what's been in his hands the whole time.

I go cold, feel all the air rush out of me.

"What…" I begin, but I can't say any more, won't say any more. I swallow hard, feel more bile rise in my throat.

The colors wink at me. Pale blue and neon orange. They flash under the burning light, jolt as Corin lifts them up.

I look at him, try to keep my breathing normal. "Why… Why've you got them?" I swallow hard, can't say their names. Mustn't say their names.

My thighs burn, burn with energy.

Go on. Take them.

"What's going on?" Esther steps forward, steps in front of me, blocks them from my sight.

Corin grunts, steps closer. "Sev? Want to explain?"

I try to move my lips, try to say something. But I can't make a sound, my voice, it just won't work.

And then Corin's stepping around Esther. He thrusts the vials at me, expects me to catch hold of them eagerly. But I don't move, force my arms to stay by my sides. Wince as the glass smashes on the floor, as the liquid runs out, toward me, begging me. I feel it against my bare feet. Cold.

Corin steps up to me, his face right against mine. "How long this time, Sev?" he asks. "How long have you been using augmenters?"

FORTY

I TAKE A STEP BACK. The Calmness—and whatever the neon orange ones are—runs over my toes, and I grimace, have to get away from it. But it's sticky, it's holding me down. I swallow hard, and Corin's still in front of me. No one's moved, no one's doing anything.

"You're Enhanced?" Esther says at last. She's looking at me strangely, head inclined as if she's trying to see mirrors in my eyes.

I shake my head, try to keep my breathing even.

Remember how good it felt to be Enhanced?

My back stiffens. I mustn't look down.

"They're not mine… I don't…" I turn my head as much as my neck will allow, can't risk looking at them. "Get them away from me."

But they don't move. Neither of them moves.

"Promise me." Corin touches my shoulder. I jump. "Promise me you're not lying."

"I promise. I'm not lying." My voice is weak.

Then his arms snap around me, and he lifts me up over the sticky mess, and I try not to look, I really do. But I can't help it. I see the colors on the floor, swirling together in an intricate pattern among the broken glass.

Pain flits through my chest.

"Where did you find them?" Esther asks.

"The edge of the washing zone. Hidden under some clean towels," Corin says.

I swallow hard. "Whose… Whose augmenters are they?"

"One of the Zharat?" Esther suggests. Then she frowns. "One of the Zharat's been taking augmenters? One of them's *Enhanced*?"

Corin's glare gets deeper. "Whoever it is, I'm going to catch him, and I'm going to take him to Manning. Expose the monster."

"We need to go to Manning *now*," Esther says. "We can't go and confront someone who's secretly Enhanced."

"We did with Rahn," Corin says, a dangerous look in his eyes. "And Manning wouldn't believe us, not if it was just our word against whichever Zharat it is. No, we're taking the traitor to his chief."

The thought of seeing Manning—when he'll most likely know I stabbed Jed—makes me go cold. I press my tongue against the roof of my mouth for a few seconds. "I thought we were all leaving."

Corin turns on me in an instant. His eyes flash. "*I'm* not leaving when I know there's a Zharat who's Enhanced here. Gods, he could do anything—he could be in contact with other Enhanced, or…or converting children. Innocent children." He wipes the back of his hand across his mouth, and I think of how his parents died in a conversion attack.

Corin stoops, picks something off the floor. It's the knife. The knife I used to stab Jed.

"It's just a question of waiting him out down there. He'll go back for his augmenters at some point. And I'll get him, threaten to kill him if he doesn't confess to Manning, show what a monster he really is—pretending to be one of us. Huh. Manning will probably slit his throat anyway." He pauses and breathes hard. "You two, you better get out of here now. I'll join you once I've sorted this out."

Esther reaches for my hand. Her face is ashen.

I shake my head, eyes on Corin. "You're not dealing with an Enhanced Zharat on your own. Safety in numbers."

It doesn't take us long to get there, down the tubes to the washing zone. Corin goes first—he's got the knife, and he holds it out in front of him. Esther and I walk side by side after him, trying to keep a lookout on all directions. Esther squeezes my hand.

I swallow hard, look around. It's the exact same place where I fell in the river before, where the kavalah came out of me. I try not to look at the water, but there's not a lot of it anyway now. Not a lot at all. There hasn't been much rain, so the Great River's starving, and the generators aren't creating much electricity.

Corin points to two baskets near the far wall. They're next to where the fold-up chairs are now stacked. "That's where I found the augmenters. Behind the baskets, I was getting a shirt out, but the basket moved, and I saw there's a groove in the wall there, with some towels stacked in it. But I pulled them out, thought there might be some shirts there too, and the augmenters were under the bottom towel." He crosses over to them, stepping over the narrowest part of the water channel in one stride. "No, there aren't any left now."

I scratch at the back of my neck as Esther and I join Corin by the baskets. The skin there feels sore, rough, broken. "So, we just wait here?"

Corin nods, then points to the nearest corner. "We'll wait over there. Better if we're hidden."

I feel sick as I follow him, and a glance at Esther tells me she's shaking. We shouldn't be doing this. If one of the Zharat is Enhanced, we should be telling Manning. Or *someone*.

Corin pulls me closer to him as we reach the corner, but then lets go. It's not an embrace, and, for a moment, I feel upset. Then I get a grip on myself. I breathe out steadily, my eyes trying to pick out shapes on the far wall. It's the darkest part of the washing zone there, and I can just about make out an animal hide hanging up against the rock. An antelope's hide. No. I peer at it, leaning forward slightly. There's more than one animal's hide there—several sewn together to make a larger covering that sways very slightly where it hangs. And there's another one, bunched up on the floor at the bottom of the wall.

"Here, Seven."

I turn, see Esther picking something up off the floor, a few feet away. A white, sleeveless dress. She holds it out to me.

"You'd better change—it's best not to walk around with blood on your clothes."

I nod and take it from her, then strip off my violet shirt and the denim skirt—aware that Corin is so near, but he's not watching me now. His eyes are on the baskets where he found the augmenters, a hard look in his face. I slip on the knee-length dress. Part of me feels strange as I wear it. I've never seen any women wear white—we're supposed to wear colors. Maybe it's white because it's ready to be dyed. I shrug.

"Do we just wait?" Esther whispers a moment later.

"Yes." Corin's voice is curt. A muscle throbs in his jaw. The knife in his hand glistens strangely. "He'll come."

"Why'd you think it's a man?"

"Because he's had to get the augmenters somewhere," Corin says. "And the women don't go on raids—I asked."

Esther clears her throat. "What if it wasn't a Zharat?"

I look at her. "What?"

She pales. "We—we assumed that the augmenters belong to a Zharat. What if they don't? What if proper Enhanced Ones are here? Non-Zharat."

"If the Enhanced are here, we'd all know about it," Corin says. "They'd have started conversion attacks. That's what they do. No, this is a Zharat thinking he can get away with it and still pretend to be Untamed."

I know he's right—we would know if any Enhanced Ones, ones who *weren't* Zharat, were here—but as we wait, I can't help but think about what Esther said. If there's a chance those augmenters could belong to an Enhanced Ones—a *fully* Enhanced One—then we should be warning everyone. We should be doing it now.

"Who do you think it is?" I ask, mainly to distract myself.

"I'd love it to be Jed, love to see *him* die," Corin mutters. "But my heart says it's not. He had that leg injury, didn't he? Augmenters would've cleared that up faster, right? And he never seemed *calm* ever."

I shrug and look down; the Zharat mark on my arm, from when I was welcomed officially into the tribe, seems smaller.

"There are hundreds of Zharat here," Esther points out. "It's probably going to be someone we don't know."

I breathe deeply. The room is still, the air heavy. There's no breeze in here. Then I frown and look back toward the patchwork animal hide on the opposite wall.

It's *moving*.

The whole hide is swaying.

Tingling sensations run down my spine.

I step toward it.

"Sev, what are you doing?" Corin's voice is low.

I point at the joined hides as I swallow. "It moved… There's…."

I frown, try to work out where exactly in the

mountain we are. I think we're near the edge, not deep in the lava tubes.

The hide moves again. Corin swears, then he's lunging forward. He grabs the leather, pulls it down, and—and we stare.

The wind rushes through, catches my skin, makes the bottom of my dress ripple.

"It's an *exit*?" Esther says the words slowly, looks first at me and then at Corin.

I step nearer, look through the gap. The walls are thick. Very thick. But I can see long grass and the sky at the end, about ten feet away. I look away quickly, my heart racing.

"That wasn't there before," Esther says.

I turn to her slowly.

"What?"

"Before—I was here. Manning took me here. We… It was this wall we sat against so he could purify me—it was after we'd tried to escape, and he thought you were spies," she says quickly. "He said he had to purify me." She points at the tunnel. "I am absolutely sure it wasn't there then." She shakes her head then. "No. It *wasn't*. Neither was the hide. It's all new."

I frown, try to remember if I've ever seen that tube before. I can't remember there being an exit here, but would I have noticed it, especially if the heavy hide *had* been hanging up? I can't remember.

Corin pushes past me, a little roughly, then touches the inside of the tube wall, runs his fingers over it.

"It's sharp, uneven," he says. "Like it's been knapped really recently. The walls aren't smooth like all the other tubes. And this opening is man-made—you can see the marks."

I reach forward, touch the walls. The lava would be brittle enough to knock a new tube through it—to the outside world. On the floor of the new exit, there are several stone flakes. I pick one up, turn it over in my fingers. There's still dust on it.

"So it's been made sometime in the last week?"

Esther's voice sounds thick. "Because it definitely *wasn't* here when Manning was purifying me. And they've tried to disguise it with the hide."

"But we would've heard someone knocking an exit through here." I wipe my hands on the white dress, try to get the dust off my fingers. "Making a tube like that would be noisy. Everyone would hear, wouldn't they?" I frown. "Or would the mountain absorb it?"

Corin shrugs. "Things work differently here, in the Noir Lands. The normal rules don't always apply, especially with so many spirits about."

I frown. "But *why* would someone make an exit here—why not just use one of the others? Be a lot less work."

"Maybe someone wanted their own exit. One only they know about," Corin says.

The Enhanced would want their own exit. They'd want to be able to come and go undetected.

I inhale sharply, push that thought away. I'm wrong. There aren't any Enhanced here.

But there are augmenters.

Yet they belong to one of the Zharat, don't they? I touch the bridge of my nose, frowning hard. They've got to. Corin was right earlier—there can't be any Enhanced here because we'd know already.

We'd have seen them.

Yet you didn't see the Marouska-imposter for who she really was. And she was Enhanced.

But she was posing as one of us—to keep me addicted to augmenters, she wasn't there to convert the others herself as Raleigh must've thought he'd get all of us once Marouska lured us to him, and—

And then I go cold.

An Enhanced was *posing* as Marouska—as one of us. That's how we didn't spot her for who she was.

And—

Oh Gods.

My chest tightens.

Mart. Jed. Esther.

My eyes widen—it can't be… But they all said… They all *accused* me of… Oh Gods!

I look at Corin, then Esther.

I gulp. My stomach feels heavy, and my mouth's dry. Like I'm going to be sick.

But I've got to tell them.

I have to.

"They're here," I say. "The Enhanced are here."

Corin shakes his head. "They can't be. The Enhanced don't know where the Zharat live—and we'd have seen them if they were."

"People have," I say.

Esther frowns.

And suddenly it's so obvious now. And I think of the words—those accusations…how certain each person was. How I even considered *I* was going mad.

"I know what they look like…" My mind whirs faster and faster, until I think I'm going to explode. "The Enhanced. They're here, and I know who they are." The words drags against my lips. "Or, at least, who one of them is."

"What? Who?"

I take a deep breath. "It's me—there's a clone of me here."

FORTY-ONE

FOR A SECOND, NEITHER OF them reacts. They stare at me. Then the corners of Corin's lips twitch.

"What?"

"There's a clone of *me*." I tug on my hair, feeling sick. "It makes sense. People are seeing me where I'm not—and Mart said he heard me planning a conversion attack, with a radio, or something. And after that, he said something to me too that confused me—that he knows what I am, or something." I point at Esther. "And *you* said you saw me outside. And Jed did too, before. He thought I'd been outside."

Still, Corin and Esther just stare at me.

"*Did* you see Sev outside?" Corin asks her after a long pause.

She nods. "I—yeah. It looked like her. I was... I was sure it was her."

I nod. "It's the only explanation. That's who the augmenters belong to—not a Zharat." The words taste strange. "The Enhanced *are* here—and they've made that exit, so they can get in here."

Esther frowns. "But Mart... He accused you of planning a conversion attack...a *week* ago. So, that

320

means there's been an Enhanced One hiding among us *here* for a week. And no one realized."

I bite my lip for a second, feel the hairs rising up on the back of my neck. "There'll be more than one, then. Maybe not in the tubes as well, but somewhere about—outside... They always work in packs...."

"More clones of you?" Corin clears his throat suddenly, eyes narrowing at me. "Tell me something only *you'd* know."

"What? Why?" My eyes narrow. Then I realize it. I know what he's thinking—about how I was acting, how forward I was with him before... *He* even said I wasn't behaving normally... Oh Gods... He might think... But if I was, why would I tell him about the clone I think's here?

"I've got to check, Sev. Especially after what you've just said."

I stare at him, my mind going blank. *Think*! But I can't think of anything—and I need to. Find something that'll prove it... Something only we know about... Something that isn't common knowledge....

"Before, you said you didn't like me...that it would be revolting," I blurt out the words as they come to me.

Corin looks at me sideways. "Right. Okay." He nods. "But if it's true, shouldn't you have seen something like this happen, had a warning or something? You're a Seer."

I swallow hard. We shouldn't be talking. We should be acting—doing something. Telling the Zharat. "I told you before, I haven't had any Seeing dreams here, not for days—not after that one of..." I take a deep breath. I don't *know* that the dream I had of Three was a warning, but something stops me from saying his name in front of Esther. I focus on Corin. "I told you something was wrong—that it didn't feel right. No visits to the Dream Land."

"Wait," Esther says, and, for a moment, I think she's going to ask what the last Seeing dream was of. But she doesn't. "If the Enhanced have been here a while, *why* hasn't a conversion attack happened already?"

"Because the Zharat are a big tribe—and the Enhanced are scared of them, I don't know!" The answer comes to me quickly. "They ran away when they heard the Zharat's lorry coming, didn't they?"

And I think of how the Zharat jumped on the Enhanced Ones' bodies, destroyed them. Any Enhanced who found that mess would be worried about facing the people who did that. The *wild* Untamed.

Corin nods quickly. "So when they found out where the Zharat live, they didn't immediately launch into a conversion attack like they normally do…because they think this tribe is dangerous. So they put a spy in here, instead. Gather information first. Decide the best way to do convert us all with the minimum loss of life for them."

Esther pales. "But the spy's been here a *week*. Maybe even a day or two longer. That's plenty of time to work out things, prepare… Shit. We… We need to tell Mann—we need to tell the Zharat *now*. They're all in danger, and the Enhanced could attack any moment now. We have to raise the alarm, get everyone out, and—"

Voices ring out and cut Esther off.

We freeze.

Angry voices. A man and a woman. Shouting. Arguing.

And then—and then they're stepping into the washing zone.

Two Zharat. They see us. I recognize them. I've seen them about in the gathering room before, I think. The man stares at me, and his eyes go to the uncovered tube behind us. He takes a step forward.

"What are you doing?" His question is slow, careful, but it's not: *How is there an exit there?* No surprise at all. Are we wrong about that? Was it there all the time?

Are we wrong about the clone too?

But Jed and Esther and Mart all claim to have seen me. And I definitely believe Esther.

"We think there are Enhanced Ones in here," Corin says, and then he's explaining about my clone.

"What?" the man says, glancing at the woman. He turns back to us, a strange look on his face.

And that's when I recognize him—he's the man Jed went hunting with, the man Jed was complaining about. He *didn't even know how to hold a spear properly*.

I stare at the newcomers. At the man. He's Zharat. Zharat men *should* know how to hold spears properly.

It was as if he was using it for the first time.

My eyes widen as it clicks, and I draw my next breath too quickly.

Because it was.

It *was* the first time.

"*They're* Enhanced too!" I yell. "Imposters!"

The man looks at the woman, throws his hands up in the air. "This—"

"What?" Esther's face fills with alarm.

The man snorts, and I'm sure he's going to deny it—or do something to prove me wrong—but then he turns to the woman. "And this is exactly *why* you're supposed to be guarding this exit—keeping it hidden—since we're not using the other one now." He grabs something from his pocket. It's a radio. "Now we'll have to export these three, but we haven't got enough people waiting. *Great*."

I take a sudden step back. Esther grabs my arm. She's trembling.

Get out. Get out. Get out.

"Just kill them," the woman says. "Either export or kill if they're going to draw too much attention. That's what Raleigh said."

I go cold.

And then another one's coming. Light footsteps, fast. And—

I come face to face with myself.

I stare at myself—at the girl who looks exactly like

me. At the clone.

For a second, the girl who looks like me seems shocked. Then she laughs. Her laugh even sounds like me. Tension pulls through my body.

Esther shouts something, but her words get lost.

Corin lifts his head a bit higher, but nods. Then he throws me behind him, just as the *Enhanced me* comes toward us. I trip on the patchwork hide, fall, end up sitting, dazed.

"Stay away from us!" Corin shouts. He raises the knife.

"Just get them through there!" my clone screams at the other two—the two Zharat who aren't really Zharat. The two *imposters*.

"There's no one out there—we weren't scheduled to take the next lot until tomorrow!" the man shouts.

"But they know we're here. We've got to get them out before they tell everyone."

I stand up slowly, lean against the wall. My vision blurs a little.

We weren't scheduled to take the next lot until tomorrow.

My eyes widen.

Girls and women have gone missing, *and* there are Enhanced Ones here. They weren't gathering information while they were waiting to start converting us after all. They've been taking us all along…in small groups. Cutting our numbers down slowly…until we're a manageable size to mass-convert all at once?

Nyesha's missing.

I make a small choking noise, remember Mart's words… Oh Gods—he heard me *planning a conversion attack*.

And the next day—that was when that second group of girls went missing, wasn't it? Because of my clone? I picture her lying in wait with more Enhanced Ones, grabbing the girls as they leave the safety of the Fire Mountain, dragging them away, ready to be converted….

And that other group—the first group who went

missing when they were fishing, getting food for my wedding feast—they never returned either. Was that my clone too?

I gulp, feel sick. Then I see a hand closing over Nyesha's mouth, right here in this room, see her struggling against the Enhanced Ones, just before they knock her unconscious and take her out their new exit.

I gulp.

Oh Gods.

"Just kill them," the woman says.

And suddenly there are guns out. Semi-automatic pistols. They're going to kill us? Not even try and convert us? Unless the bullets in these guns aren't lethal…and she only said *Just kill them* to scare us?

A barrel is shoved into my face before I even see it coming. I twist around, see another one go to Corin, and to Esther. Corin fights with the knife, but then it's kicked from his hand; it clatters onto the floor several feet away.

It's the man who holds the gun on me. The man who looks so much like a Zharat. My head whirs. How many of them are here? How many have been living among us, replacing the Zharat? Have I spoken to any?

And why didn't the Dream Land warn me? Because I'd already ignored their warning about not going outside—even though I didn't mean to go out there with Jed? Do the Gods and Goddesses and spirits no longer trust me? I swallow hard. Death—no, Waskabe—told me I wouldn't be given many *more* chances. But I didn't go outside after that, did I?

"Hey!" Corin shouts. He's holding his hands up, and I see the whites of his eyes flash. "Hey, we'll walk. We'll go willingly with you. Just put the guns away."

My gaze jerks to him, alarm fills me. Join the Enhanced? *Willingly.* I shake my head at him, no, we can't!

"Not a chance," my clone screams. She's holding the gun on him, and it makes me feel strange seeing her in front of Corin. She's dropped the imitation of my voice, my accent now. She just sounds annoyed, and her words are heavy. "Not a bloody chance. You really think we're stupid? The moment you're out there, you're going to run."

"All together. On the count of three," the woman says.

Esther whimpers.

"One." The woman smiles.

The man in front of me moves the gun closer, until its barrel is an inch from my forehead. It seems to get darker, something's blocking the light, or my eyes aren't working.

"Let us go!" Corin shouts. But he doesn't move. "You're not actually going to kill us!"

My clone steps closer to him, and I see her whispering something into his ear. Something I can't hear. The skin on the back of my neck prickles.

"Two."

Cold metal, against my skin.

"If you kill us, they'll hear the gunshots—they'll know you're here," I say quickly.

But the Enhanced just smile, they don't even seem worried about it. Yet the shots *will* make a noise— there are no silencers attached to the firearms, not that I can see…

And they're going to kill us.

My throat squeezes a little. "You can't *kill* us."

"We're tranquilizing *you*," the man says to me. "We know who you are."

Of course they know who I am. My clone's one of them.

I breathe deeply, taste darkness behind my front teeth, try to work out what to say next, how to make them listen. I take several deep breaths, feel my heart stutter, and—

My clone screams.

I jerk forward, movement to my left. The tube. The dark shape and—

"Get out of here!" the Enhanced man shouts, but his words aren't for me.

The gun moves away from me, toward the tube entrance where a bulky, dark shape fills the gap. My heart starts racing, my eyes narrow. Can't see what it is.

Corin swears, then suddenly he's by my side, grabbing my hand. He pulls me to the right, behind the Enhanced—the Enhanced who have turned away from us. Their guns are on the new shape. That's when my eyes finally work.

And I see it.

I see the silverback mountain gorilla a second before he moves right into the room.

For a second, I just stare, can't comprehend it.

The silverback's big. Massive. Huge, domed forehead and dark eyes. Light flits around him, makes his silver fur look darker and—

He charges.

I throw myself backward, drag Corin with me. My hand reaches for Esther, but I can't see her. Someone screams. An Enhanced. And then there's dust, flying up. So much dust and—

"Get out!"

A gun goes off.

The gorilla screams—strangely high-pitched. Then he grunts, low, throaty. Sounds that echo off the lava walls. Then he's moving again, stretches up slightly. Got to be at least six feet tall, fills the cave.

"Get out!"

"Not that way! Could be more!" the Enhanced woman shouts.

I look up, see my clone going for the tube. The exit's clear now, as clear as we can see. She gets there, and then she's blocked from sight as the silverback swings his weight around. He's big. So big.

"Don't look it in the eye!" the man shouts, and then I can't see him, and there's more movement.

Angry barking fills my ears.

"Sev!"

Corin pulls me to him, pulls me across the channel of running water. I trip, step into it, end up soaked up to my knees, but he drags me out.

I see Esther, not far away. She's got the knife now, and a Luger—from one of the Enhanced, must be.

Another gunshot goes off, but it's not from hers.

"No!" she shouts, and she's turning. "Don't shoot it!"

But the Enhanced One's aim isn't good. The bullet bounces off the lava wall, fractures into pieces that fling back. The gorilla turns, eyes on the man. Charges again. Slapping sounds fill my ears.

I can't look away. Blood pounds through me. The gorilla grabs the Enhanced man. He screams, and the silverback—

"Sev, we've got to get out now!"

And then we're running. I can barely breathe; we're going too fast. Behind us, the Enhanced man screams. Proper screams. Last screams.

"Are you all right?" Corin looks from me to Esther, starts to slow down. She nods, and then Corin's reaching for my arm. "Sev?"

I nod, feel bile rise in my stomach.

"Come on." He pants, face red and shiny. "We need to warn the Zharat *now*."

FORTY-TWO

MANNING BLINKS AT US. "IMPERSONATING?"

His gaze goes to me, and I wince, expect him to say something about Jed and the attack—but he doesn't.

He just shakes his head, then laughs a strident laugh for exactly three seconds before stopping abruptly. His eyes cross to Esther, and a strange look takes over his face for a second.

I step closer to Esther, and Corin barges in front of us, puts himself between the Zharat leader and us. I swallow hard. We shouldn't have brought Esther to him like this, I know that. But we had to find Manning, he's the leader—he can spread the word sooner among the Zharat than anyone else. We *had* to see him.

And give him the opportunity to kill you for stabbing Jed.

But he hasn't said anything about that. And I don't think the chief's treating me differently. Something tells me he doesn't know...yet. So where's Jed? He'd moved from our room. But he hasn't come to Manning?

Corin snarls. "Just listen. They've infiltrated. They've been in here...*ages*. Those girls that went missing—the Enhanced have been converting them." He breathes hard, looks at me for a second, and I nod—I told him and Esther on the way here what I'd worked out, and they both saw it too. "They were taking the girls when they were outside, but those latest women weren't on a hunt. They were taken, straight from the den. The Enhanced even said something about scheduled conversions—that there are certain times when they take us. And there's a bloody great hole in the wall of the washing zone where they took the women through." Corin grips the back of his neck, rubs it hard. I know he's having a hard time controlling himself in front of this man. "You have to raise the alarm—they know we know about them now. They're not going to leave it any longer; it's going to be a conversion attack, a massive one—starting any minute. They'll call backup."

But Manning shakes his head again. His eyes are still on Esther, and his lips twitch. I step even closer to her. "If the Enhanced *was* here, our Seers would know. And my men ain't heard nothing."

"But those girls did!" I shout. I don't even know if Kyla or the other girl saw this, but the words just fall out my mouth. "And we've *seen* them, the Enhanced—you've got to do something!"

Manning bares his teeth as he steps nearer. Corin straightens up, pushes Esther farther behind him, leaving me more vulnerable to Manning. "You do not mention those beings ever, those frauds. They have contaminated—"

"Are you even listening to us?" Corin shouts. "No, don't come any closer. And stop looking at my sister. There are Enhanced in the cave, living among us, using Zharat bodies, pretending to be us. And you're not doing a thing about it?"

"Because you're lying—"

"You believed us about the gorilla," Esther says. Her voice wobbles, and I glance at her quickly. "You sent your men down there, no questions asked. And you've sent them right down into the heart of the Enhanced

Ones' plan—they're using that room as a base. And one definitely got away—she'll be getting backup, and then they'll come here and convert you all. They're not going to waste time, not now we know about them."

Manning laughs. "Gorillas in the caves be quite *common*." He cracks his knuckles. "They like licking salts from the walls. But if an Enhanced One was here, we'd know. There'd be signs."

"But you're not listening!" And then I'm shouting and I'm filled with so much rage and my whole body's shaking and he's just *not listening*. "We had no idea until Corin found augmenters."

Manning looks at me with a strange look, taking in my white dress? Then: "Given how you seem to have lost all status, I don't think you're in any position to tell me what to do."

I start to shake my head. This is a waste of time. If Manning won't raise the warning among his own people, we'll have to.

"What the hell?" Corin shouts, balling his fists. Then he steps closer to Manning. "Are you Enhanced too?"

"How dare you," Manning says. "How *dare* you suggest such a thing."

"Then bloody *do* something! Protect your people."

A dangerous look crosses Manning's face, makes me think of blood and death. "If there're Enhanced Ones in that washroom where the gorilla be, my men will see them. If I get confirmation—either from them, or from one of my Seers—I will act."

Corin swears loudly, spits at the floor. "Don't ignore the facts. Ignorance is not bliss. Ignorance is death." It's Rahn's survival lesson, number five.

"But this is giving the Enhanced more time," I say. "You need to find out which of your people are really Enhanced Ones, and you need to get rid of them—not give them a chance to regroup and make plans—"

Corin slams his fist into the air. "This is stupid. We're going now. We're not staying to be converted and killed."

He turns, grabs Esther and me, pulls us out of the room with surprising strength, and—

We crash into men.

I scream as I'm pushed away, against a wall. And I'm trying to turn, trying to get ready to fight the Enhanced. But they don't come at us. They're not— they're Zharat, I think. Aren't they? No. We don't know. Don't know anything anymore. My head pounds.

The men go straight for Manning's room, ignoring Corin who's shouting at them. I recognize one of them. *Mart.* My blood burns.

"He's been made a Seer!" the man at the front of the group shouts, pushes Mart forward. "He says we're about to be attacked by Enhanced men who are using our images for disguise."

Manning's out in the tube in an instant. He grabs Mart.

"Finally!" Corin shouts. "You know, you could've saved a lot of time—a lot of lives if you'd just listened to us and what *we* were saying."

"Get everyone to the gathering room," Manning says. His eyes narrow as he looks at us. "Everyone. Now."

And then the men are pushing past us again, running.

"Now!" Manning shouts at Corin, Esther, and me.

We run.

Esther's still got the gun and knife, and Corin takes the Luger from her. She keeps the knife.

"Stay right by me," Corin says to both of us. "Don't ever leave my side."

It's the fierceness in his eyes that makes me go cold inside.

The Zharat are wasting too much time. It seems ironic, really, given Manning's earlier speech about how good leaders make quick decisions.

We're in the gathering room, but no plan has been made. Nothing at all. Everyone's panicking and trying to find their families, but there are just too many people.

We stand at the end, by a wall that has water trickling down it. Corin's hand is on my shoulder, he seems to have forgotten it's there. Esther's next to us, and a couple of children have attached themselves to us, saying they can't find their mothers. They're all crying.

And it's my fault.

I realize it as I watch the toddlers cling to one another. It's my fault the Enhanced are here. Raleigh has my eyes, and I went outside—my trip out there with Jed, on my second day here, must have done it. It was only after that when the Zharat girls started going missing. I showed Raleigh the way here. When I had that kavalah in me, when I couldn't think properly.

But it's *still* my fault.

Yet, I can't help thinking I should've been warned about this. The bite marks on my body start to burn, and I think of Death's words: *Do not ignore the Dream Land warnings.*

Ignoring them? Is that what I've been doing? But no, I haven't had any. Yet I'm a Seer. I should've been shown something. Instead it was Mart—Mart, who wasn't even a Seer before.

Yet he was the one who was shown.

I get a bad taste in my mouth. I'm a Seer. It's *my* job to protect people. These people. And I haven't. I've failed. I worked out the problem through actually seeing the evidence—the augmenters—like any normal person would've. Not because of my abilities.

What's the point of me being a Seer if I can't use my powers to work out atrocities before they happen?

I grimace, clutch my side. The marks are cold. Ice cold. They make my mother's pendant feel hotter under the high neckline of the sleeveless, white dress. The crystal tells me I should have known about this, I should have been warned, I should have been able to save the lives that are going to be lost.

Corin clicks his tongue, stands up straighter as he looks over the others' heads. "People are turning on each other," he says.

As if on cue, in front of us, a man hits another, accuses him of being Enhanced. Shouts that there's no way he can know for sure that his brother's still Untamed, because the Enhanced use violence now. Our enemy breaks the one rule we had for them for so long. And that's the problem. That's the—

Seven!

My body jolts, and I start to feel strange—that's the bison… That's his voice….

I turn quickly, looking. The sky… I need to see it… But it's not like normal… This is… Everything shimmers. For a second, I think I'm moving… And time's passing, and I'm falling. Pain rebounds through my head…and my skull—something's squeezing my skull.

I fall backward, darkness. So much darkness.

And, for a long time, nothing happens. I wait.

I wait for the bison. But he doesn't come. There's just… It's dark and….

My skin starts burning, over my ribcage. Sharp pricks, and I know the strange marks are increasing, spreading. *Know* they are, and I don't understand. But they're connected—to the lack of Seeing dreams, the Dream Land visions—they have to be… They only started, the marks only started once the Seeing dreams stopped….

"Sev?" Corin's voice, in the darkness. And he's saying more words and….

I open my eyes, he's holding me against his body. I breathe hard.

Oh Gods.

"What did the Dream Land say?" Corin's words are soft in my ear. "What's going to happen?" His eyes are wide, alert.

I stare at him, start to frown. "Nothing… There was nothing. Just darkness. It was just dark… There was nothing there."

Corin frowns.

I taste grit on the roof of my mouth as I look around. So many people in here.

We shouldn't be in here. We're all cooped up, like animals, like prisoners. My mind whirls. The Enhanced, if they're all coming, they could surround us easily, launch a mass conversion attack. No, we need to get out of here.

Don't ignore the facts. Ignorance is not bliss. Ignorance is death.

I look at Corin. Then Esther. "We need to get out there, outside."

It doesn't matter now. Raleigh and the Enhanced are already here.

"You *did* see something, what we need to do?" Esther's face pinches in.

"No. But we need to go. It's obvious." I pause for a second, hear Rahn's voice. *Lesson seven: If attacked by the Enhanced, save as many people as you can, and get as far away as possible.* I press my lips together. *Get as far away as possible.* "Come on."

I try to lead the way out, but there are just too many people. I can't get straight to the exit, so I sidle around the edge, Corin's hand is in mine, and Esther's behind him. I look ahead, trying to work out how close we are, but can't see a thing. Just people, squashed together. Their shouts fill my ears and—

A figure staggers toward me. My chest tightens. It's… No. It can't be. But it *is*. It's him. And there's so much blood. He's still bleeding.

It's Jed.

He's seen me; I see the look in his eyes. He's coming

for me, raising one arm, pointing. There are two men behind him, men who I distantly recognize.

I come to a complete stop, feel Corin press up behind me.

"What's happening?" His voice is low in my ear, but the sounds of his words mingle with all the other sounds. Everything pounds in my ears. Too much going on.

And I can't speak. I can't do a thing, feel my body lock up. And then—and then *Jed's* here, right in front of me, and—

He slaps me.

I fall back, but Corin and Esther are there, and there's no room to fall. Corin pushes past me, Esther's hands grab me.

"Hey!" Corin shouts, menace in his voice. "Don't touch her."

Jed growls something, and I notice the blood that's all over him. His clothes, his skin. His eyes narrow as he points at me again. "She did it."

The men either side of him start toward me. The blades in their hands flash.

I gulp, feel tingling down the back of my spine, down my legs, down to my feet. My knees shake. I try to turn, try to get away, but there's nowhere to go.

"She stabbed me! Tried to kill me! I managed to get away, but I passed out somewhere, came 'round to men shouting about Enhanced Ones in here—but she did it! She did this to me. She stabbed me!"

"No!" Corin yells. "That wasn't her! That was one of the Enhanced clones—one they made look like Sev! Jed, that *wasn't* her."

Corin pushes me behind him. I trip over something, accidentally jab Esther in the ribs with my elbow as I struggle not to fall. And then I'm turning, facing Jed, and I see the way he's looking at me.

"You are lying, protecting her."

"I'm not!" Corin shouts, but the room's louder now. Not just voices, a deep rumbling too. Hard to hear his words. "Sev's not violent like that! It was an Enhanced clone, not her. Look, they're wearing different clothes—the one who hurt you had a violet shirt on. Sev—the real Seven—has a white dress, *see*. We realized afterward, when the real Sev came in and there were two of them. That's how we knew they were among us."

I swallow hard, don't know where to look. Esther squeezes my hand.

Jed's eyes narrow. "Surely she's the clone if she's not wearing the right color?"

"No," Esther says, and then she's pressing something into my fingers.

I look down. It's my ring—the one Jed gave me. And I remember, distantly, her pulling it out of the puddle of blood. I take it from her, put it on quickly.

"She was with me," Esther says. "The real Seven was with me but I spilled some water on her clothes, and she had to change. It was all we could find, the white dress. She's the *real* Seven. Look, the engagement ring. Proves she's the real one."

"Yeah, the Seven I was with didn't have that on," Corin says quickly. "So that wasn't the real Seven. Proves it wasn't her."

Jed glares at Corin. "You seemed pretty happy to undress the clone, thinking you were contaminating my woman, stealing her purity."

The rumbling's getting louder—and I don't know how anyone can hear anything. The air is too thick, too heavy with voices and humming and rumbling.

Esther nudges me again. "Act shocked that Corin thought he was going to—"

Jed screams.

I whirl around, hands braced, see him fall against the men. He turns, eyes open but unseeing, and then his weight sags. The two other Zharat men shout words I don't understand.

Jed's body jolts. The men are holding him up. He looks at me. I go cold. And then he's *really* looking at me. His hands reach out for me, but there's something in his eyes, something that's not him.

Enhanced? Is *he* a clone?

I try to back away, but there's no room.

"We have to go now, Seven," Jed says, and his words wrap around me. "I have to save you. We have to go *now*!"

But it's not his voice, isn't deep enough, and the words aren't spoken with the guttural tones he normally has. They're clearer, there's no accent. His lilt has gone, gone completely, as if his voice has been stripped back.

Something hisses near me. Something—the wall? But it does it again, hissing—like something's going to happen.

I frown, turning, and—

Hands grab me. Corin's. His eyes catch mine, and then he's pushing me away. Away from what? Can't tell.

The pounding in my head speeds up.

"S'ven!" Jed screams—his own voice now.

I turn, pull away from Corin, see Jed's hand. His blood-covered hand, and then I see the rest of him. And—

"He's told me to save you! It's the only way!" Jed's eyes are wild, on fire. And something's happening to his body—it's…it's shimmering. And I see how the blood stops pouring out, how the wound starts to heal. Seer powers—I know it is. "He told me the augury—"

"Sev!"

And—

That's when the gunshots go off. One after another. Quick succession. Thumping, in my ears.

The Enhanced. They're here.

No. Oh Gods.

Blood.

I scream. Others scream.

Hands grab at me. Corin's? Esther's? Jed's?

There's a loud crack, above. I jerk my head up,

look. Dust falls, gets in my eyes. Stings. I cry out, rub my eyes, but there's blood, and everything's red and sharp and gritty.

Another round of bullets. Someone next to me falls. I hear someone shriek Manning's name in a voice that sounds too much like Esther's.

And then there's stuff falling, and something hits my head—hard. Too hard. I scream, hunker down, arms over me. Hissing fills my ears. Too high-pitched and—

"Get out!"

People are screaming. Zharat and—

Manning's body.

Blood.

Clare—a blaze of violet—with a knife.

I shriek, and then I'm moving. Running, faster and faster.

Corin.

I turn, eyes bleeding as I look for him, for Esther. But the air's hazy. It's thick, it's going opaque. And the hissing's getting louder, and everything tastes funny, smells funny. And—

Burning steam sprays over me.

I shriek, turn, feel my skin blistering, wet. I push through people, stumbling, need to get away from the jet of steam.

"Volcanic gases!" someone screams.

"What?"

"The Gods are angry! They've activated our Fire Moun—"

"Elmiro! We're sorry, we worship you—"

"Get out!"

People are screaming. Red, blistering faces loom up in front of me. People push past me. I trip over something hard, manage to keep my balance.

I turn.

"Corin! Esther!"

Can't see them.

Oh Gods.

And the air...it's... The hissing's louder. I look up, see part of the lava wall on the far side break. Actually *break*. Cracks appear, run down and—and a whole section blows out. Steam and vapor and water jet out, toward us. Hot.

"Gas eruption!" someone screams.

"But it can't be—the Gods keep us safe! These are their caves!"

"We've angered them! Just get out, they've turned on us!"

And then a man shrieks as he's soaked by the scalding water. His skin turns red, bright red, and it's all welting, blistering, puckering up with white bits that stand out from his crimson flesh as he falls, and he's still screaming. Just screaming. Screaming. Everyone's screaming.

"Get out—"

I try to move, but everyone's trying to get out. Bodies press against me, and the air's too thick. No one can see. People are shouting, yelling, crying. Sweat runs down them, runs down me. It's hot. Too hot. The air is burning, scalding.

"Get my baby!"

The words are screeched into my ear, and I turn, strain my neck, try to see a baby. But I can't. It's just men and women. I can't see the floor...and...no children. Can't see any children and—

I fall. My face crashes into the ground, the hard floor. Stone. Hot and wet.

I scream, try to get up, but feet kick me, press down on me. I try to move, try to protect my head as they run past me—over me—but I can't. Can't move my arms. Suddenly a face appears in front of me. One of the dolls with the straw hair and painted features. It grins at me.

And I can't do a thing as the burning steam reaches me, soaks me, scalds me, burns me. Burns me until there's nothing left.

FORTY-THREE

I'M SCREAMING, SCREAMING, SCREAMING. Too hot, burning. Too hot, white. Pain. Burning.

I try to move, but there's water, hot water.

Nothing's left. Nothing's left. Nothing's left. The words play over and over in my head, and that one phrase is all I can think of.

I cry out. But opening my mouth just makes more of the bad air enter. Burning, in my throat, my lungs. Too much burning.

It's eating me…eating me…*eating me*.

Hands. I see hands. Fingers. Coming for me.

I scream again, try to call out, because he's coming. He's coming for me. Not going to leave me behind.

I'm screaming…writhing…but he's there. The cage. My cage…around me. All that I know, all I can feel as the darkness comes down because the air's too heavy… No something's too heavy…and they can't stop it.

No one can.

No one wants to.

They like it like this… It's beautiful.

Dazzling colors.

And I'm free. At last, I'm free. No longer trapped. Not a prisoner.

Not anything.

I shut my eyes, but I don't feel them. Can't feel anything. No body. I'm free, not trapped in a vessel—a body that doesn't work, a body that's broken. A body that's useless. But I haven't got it now, and it's okay.

It's more than okay. Because there's nothing to hurt—

Something hits me.

I feel it.

I am awake. And I *feel* it. I start to cry. I've got a body. I'm vulnerable again, only free for a second. Two seconds. Three seconds.

I look around. He's gone. My cage. Where has he gone?

I try to see, and I'm standing up. I'm walking but the pain is there. It wraps around me, squeezes me. I push my wet hair behind my ears, and it's hot, burns my skin. I start screaming and try to push the scalding heat away, but I can't.

Seven.

I jump, flinch, turn. Look around. Barren landscape. My scalp crawls. But there's no one here.

I continue walking, don't know where I'm going now I have my body back... He's still not here... Corin's still not here. And we're....

I frown. This isn't the cave. The Zharat cave...it's gone.

The Noir Lands?

I look around, but there's nothing to distinguish this place. It's just flat. Scrubland. Grass.

It starts to rain. I speed up, hunch my shoulders. Haven't got a hood. The droplets get heavier, pounding my skin. And—

I remember. The cave, the debris, the people, the screaming, the gases. My eyes widen, and then I'm shouting at the bison, because he's here. He's right *here.*

"Help! Tell me what to do! Show me!"

But he's turning away, running, hooves pounding. Running away from me, getting smaller and smaller in the sky. The far-away sky. Until he's not there. A black dot that's disappeared.

Gone....

He's gone....

Your mother's gone....

The bison's gone....

My mind reels. The Zharat have gone too? Everything's gone? Destroyed?

Coldness wraps around me. I start to call out, but there's no one here. But I don't understand. If this is a Seeing dream, how can the bison just *go*? Just leave me?

And you shouldn't be here.

I shake my head.

Suffer.

The word pulls through me. I shudder, feel my neck crick.

I turn my head, and that's when I see them: four figures.

The women are all dressed in white. Three of them, in long white dresses that seem to flow and flow and flow. They're standing with their backs to me, and their red hair billows out.

The fourth figure also has his back to me, and he stands a little way off from the women—the Goddesses, because that's what they are.

The man is Death. I know it's him instantly, and the realization makes me feel strange. But hopeful. He'll help me, tell me what to do.

Blood. Blood. Blood. We want your blood, the land says.

I swallow hard and walk closer to them, my heart fluttering. They haven't seen me, don't know I'm here. As I near them, I hear their words.

"Sever the connection, sever the contact, sever the warnings."

"Revoke the access now."

343

"Complete the banishment."

Flames emerge from the Goddesses' fingertips, and dark, black smoke shoots from Death's fingers. The flames and the smoke meet, start to sizzle then shoot upward twenty feet into the sky. The sky that's now a swirling mass of purples and navies and oranges. *Spirits*.

"It isn't working!" one of the Goddesses screams.

"It has to work!"

"It isn't! She's too strong!"

"It *will* work," Death's voice booms out. "The banishing will work. She may be strong, but she is not *that* strong."

Banishing? My eyes widen a little, and a part of me wants to run. But I don't. I take a step forward, feel something crunch under my feet. I look down, see gravel. And I'm wearing shoes. Rubber soles. I stare at them—but I felt the gravel, as if it had been against my skin....

"She's there!"

My head snaps up, and—

They grab me. So quickly. Hands everywhere, and white light and threads that wrap around me, against my blistered skin. I scream, but Death's right by my head, and he turns, and then there's pain, so much pain and I can't...can't breathe.

"That's why it's not working! She's sensed it and is trying to stop us!" one of the Goddesses cries, and suddenly her nails are on my face, scratching, pulling as she turns to glare at Death. "How is it possible? You said she wasn't that powerful! That no Seers can sense the moment they're being banished, let alone try and stop it!"

I *can't* move. I'm rooted to the spot. My legs...they won't work, and—

"Finish the banishing! Get her out of here before she lets the others in and they kill us all!"

I stare at them, try to breathe, but the air's too heavy. It's not right. I start to move backward, still sitting on the ground, hunched up so my spine's curved too much, and pain shoots down it.

"Banish the Enhanced Seer!"

And…and my chest tightens. The world stops. The land screams, and all I can do is stare at them. Stare at them and try to speak, speak words that won't come out, that don't have any substance.

They…they think *I'm* an Enhanced Seer.

Me. *Me.*

I stare at them—keep staring at them—the seconds dragging, then I start screaming, telling them I'm Untamed, but they don't listen. Or maybe I'm not saying the words.

Death bares his teeth. "You're on their side. Do not lie. Death knows all. Death sees all."

He's wrong—he hasn't—he doesn't—he's *wrong.* "But—"

Death roars at me. "You ignored Death's warnings. You ignored Dream Land visions—"

I gasp. "What? No!" Coldness runs through me. "I didn't… I didn't know that was going to happen, the attack! I haven't had any warnings!" I cry. "Not about this! Not anything… Something's gone wrong, the warnings—I haven't—they're—I don't understand… There was that one of Three, my brother, but I don't even know if that *was* one… But the marks on me, here, they're—"

And I'm trying to show him the marks, because I know they're important and he'll understand even when I don't—because he'll *know.* He'll know something's gone wrong because these marks have to be linked to my lack of Seeing dreams, and then he'll know it wasn't me.

They say Gods only see or foresee things in our world relating to their chosen Seers, but even then, they see a distorted version, or only fragments. Soraya's words turn me cold.

The look in Death's eyes gets sharper. "Do not lie to your Gods and Goddesses. You *are* an Enhanced Seer,

Seven Sarr. Death is very disappointed in you. Death warned you that he sees all, knows all. You can hide nothing from him."

But he's wrong! He hasn't seen all—he doesn't believe me! He hasn't seen what's really happened—that I've had no Seeing dreams, no Dream Land visions.

And, before I can say or do anything, another Goddess steps right up to me. She reaches out, and then suddenly—too quickly—her hands are on my face, and—

I scream.

The world goes dark, and there's pain. So much pain. Under my nails, digging in at the soft flesh. And in my nose, the delicate tissue. And—

My neck. The noose… There's a noose. A noose around my neck. There, now.

My hands claw at it, frantic. I feel the rope, tough, fibrous.

The world moves, lifts me up, higher. I'm suspended in the air, and I make the mistake of looking down. The Goddess screams and the rope tightens and the darkness gets—

"Banish her!"

"We've not got enough power, not now she's here."

"Get her out of here and complete the banishing!"

"Throw her out!"

"Waskabe, we need your power—join us!"

I fall, crash to the ground, gasping. A deep ache in my chest, an ache that spreads and spreads, numbs me. Dead? No. I try to turn, try to see where the Goddess has gone, but can't. And then—then there's a flurry of movement. Something washes over me, makes my insides squirm. I throw up bile.

Sudden heat pours over me. Too hot. Burning.

I pull myself to the side, just as the flames leap out toward me.

I scramble backward, shaking. The smell of burning flesh fills the air, and I scream, try to turn, but can't.

The eyes are on me, the glowing eyes—another God. A short man with a gold cloak; he's just appeared. And more are coming. More and more Gods and Goddesses, more and more power, directed against me.

And the spirits? I look up, see more flashes of angry colors, swirling and mixing together, only feet above me. I shriek, and they shriek back.

"Get her out of here!"

"But I'm Untamed!" I cry, and I leap up, somehow manage to get to my feet, fight it all. A flash of angry red light dives toward me, and I jump out the way. "You've got it wrong!"

Death's in front of me now, and he watches me with eyes that bore far too deep. "No true Untamed Seer lets innocent people be converted without at least trying. But you ignored the warnings—multiple warnings. You let your brother be converted."

My heart sinks. That was *real*… That was a warning after all… My brother….

"And then you allowed multiple conversions to take place after that. You let this large-scale conversion attack happen." He points at me, and smoke erupts from his hands, dives toward me, stains my dress with gray patches. "*You* are a traitor." He punctuates each word with a snarl. "Death does not take kindly to traitors. Your soul will suffer for this setback."

A bolt of fire zigzags toward me, from the hands of one of the Goddesses.

I cry out, try to move, but my legs won't work. The fire hits me. I barely feel the pain, and then the Goddess is in front of me. Her hair strikes me, strikes me hard—and it's metal. Her hair's metal. I start to fall, and my arms jerk out, but the metal rods just get me, and—blood, so much blood….

I fall, hit the ground hard, taste grit. Spirits shriek. My head jerks up, but I can't see them. They've gone? And then…then the Goddesses stand over me. Their faces get bigger, eyes, noses, mouths…all stretching.

FRAGMENTED

They start chanting again. All the Goddesses. *"Sever the connection, sever the contact, sever the warnings! Send Seven Sarr far away! Block her access! Sever the connection, sever the contact, sever the warnings!"* And they shout it over and over again, and they're looking at Death, waiting, and I don't understand.

One of the Goddesses breaks away, points at Death. "Waskabe, complete the banishing now! You're giving her too much time; she'll summon the others, and they'll kill us and—"

"The others?" I blink. And I imagine Raleigh suddenly storming in here, killing the Gods and Goddesses, and I start to choke. "No! I'm not bringing anyone—I don't understand! I'm Untamed!"

"Prove it then," Death says. "Make sure the Untamed win the war. "

"What?" My word is a squeak. Make sure the Untamed win the war? How? I don't understand, don't get why *I'm* so important. I know I'm the key to one race's survival—the bison told me that—but I don't *understand.*

"It is your choice," Death says. "The winner—the surviving side—it is *your* choice. It is written in the augury: *the Seventh One, born of Light, holds the strongest Seer powers. Her side will win the War of Humanity. The rest will be destroyed, and Death will call Seven Sarr back to him at the end of the war.*" He looks at me pointedly. "*That* is the only way this war will end. You are the Seventh One, born of Light. Prove you're Untamed and make sure the Enhanced do not survive."

He pauses, and his elbows glow a deep purple. I stare at him, feel my eyes glass over. And I hear what he's saying, but there's too much... My head... *My* Seer powers are crucial... *I'm* the strongest? I start to choke. *My* side will win the war...and the other side will be destroyed?

Because I'm a Seer of Death....

"Seven Sarr, you will always belong to Death, and Death will have your soul when you die. You'd do

348

well to give Death fewer reasons to hate you. If the Enhanced win, Death will make sure your soul is trapped in your rotting body *for an eternity*—and when an eternity is up, Death will find another way to punish your soul when your body can no longer contain it. There would be no escape. Only pain. Death would torture you *forever*."

Oh Gods. I try to clear my throat, but can't. I stare at my hands, my tingling fingers, and try to concentrate. The Goddesses are shouting, telling Death not to talk to me like this, that I can't be given another chance. And I don't understand. I try to step backward, but my legs won't budge. I move my arm, pull my sweating fingers through my matted, bloody hair. My breaths come in a series of short bursts.

Me. It's me. It's got to be me who ends the war? I squint. My powers? And I look at them—so powerful compared to me.

"Why can't *you* do it? You're Gods and Goddesses— can't you kill the Enhanced? Why's it got to be me who—"

Death growls and fury lights up his eyes. His elbows glow even brighter. "Gods and Goddesses cannot kill mortals nor walk the mortal planes—*you* cannot get out of this. It has to be you, else the war will never end and the suffering will continue. You were born to end this war—"

"Stop it!" a Goddess screams. "Waskabe, she's buying time with her questions. She understands this perfectly! She's stalling, trying to get the Enhanced Seers in here! We must complete the banishing before she kills us all."

Death's eyes narrow, and his face pales rapidly. He turns back and joins hands with the other Gods and Goddesses. And then they're all chanting those words and—

I scream at them, I shout. Tears pour down my face. "What are you doing? I'm not… I'm Untamed!"

"Prove it, you know what to do. The Untamed must

win," Death snarls. "Give Death one less reason to hate you when he collects you at this war's end."

The green fire appears out of nowhere.

I don't see it in time.

It slams into my body.

Traitor, a voice screams. *Be gone, and never return.*

FORTY-FOUR

I GASP AS JOLTS RUN through my body, forcing me awake, coughing and spluttering. Eyes flutter open. I'm lying on the ground. In blood. Steam's everywhere, but not as much as there was in the caves. I hear screams. Bright light. All around me. Above. The sky. I'm outside. And I'm on my own.

I look around, head pounding. Too much stuff in it, foggy. Can't think.

You're a traitor. You didn't stop the conversion attack. You didn't even try.

I gulp and narrow my eyes against the bright light. The cave entrance is to my left, the trees are in front of me. The air's foggy with steam. Somewhere, I can hear water....

But I'm alone. Left behind. No one's here....

Dread fills me. Corin, Esther... Did they leave me? Did they think I was dead? That I'd died from the steam eruption when I was....

When you were being exiled from the Dream Land?

My breath drags in, hurts my throat. And...my mouth, it tastes different. My teeth aren't... I frown. Something's different.

Exiled.

I stare at my hands. I've been exiled, banished. *I'm a traitor?*

What? No. No. No. I shake my head, and then I see it all. See the memory, but it's all mixed up. The Goddesses in white, and the falling. The flames and the glowing eyes. Death's threats and his anger. The voices, the words…the pain.

I shake my head. Oh Gods. I've got to get back there.

And I *try* to get back to the Dream Land but I don't know what I'm doing, how to do it, yet I'm climbing something, and nothing feels real anymore. It's like I'm not here, not in my body, and I'm getting higher and higher, and I don't understand, start to feel sick, and—

Something hits me hard across the chest.

I fall.

Your access to the Dream Land has been revoked and destroyed.

I start shaking, looking around again, trying to peer through the steam.

I touch my head. My temples throb, and I can feel something pulsing under my skin, like a heartbeat. *My* heartbeat. Too fast. My chest's going to explode. Pain.

But I'm alive.

And I've been blocked from the Dream Land.

No true Untamed Seer lets innocent people be converted without at least trying. But you ignored the warnings— multiple warnings.

I shake my head. No. Something's gone wrong. The Dream Land's gone wrong, it's mixed up. They didn't summon me, not for Seeing dreams—I haven't had any, not after the one of my brother! The marks on my skin prove that! Something's gone badly wrong. I would've known if they'd summoned me. It's a mistake. It's all a big mistake.

I swallow hard.

I need to move. I try to think logically. The Enhanced

could find me….

Raleigh will always be able to find you.

My skin crawls. *No*—that's not right, is it? My head hurts. I can't think about Raleigh. No, I need to get away, somewhere where I'm safe. Once I'm safe, I can sort out this Dream Land mess.

I manage to pull myself to my feet, holding my bleeding hip. I gasp, crying loudly as I tense my leg. I put my weight on it. Just about holds.

Then I hear footsteps. Crashing through grass. Behind me.

My head whirls… They've come back for me. Of course they would! They wouldn't leave me! They wouldn't!

He said he'd always protect me, he wouldn't leave me.

A figure moves toward me, blurry.

I try to see him, but the light's too bright. He's just a figure… A figure that gets clearer, clearer.

I blink, blink again, feel my mouth dry up completely, until there's no saliva, and everything's just dry and cracked and—

No.

I shake my head. My eyes are wrong. It can't be him. Not *him*.

"You are badly blistered," he says, and he's holding something out to me. A cup, a cup with liquid in. "Drink this, you need painkillers."

I take the cup. It is heavy, and the water swirls round and round on its own. I look up at him, and his face wobbles a little, makes him look like he's not really here.

Then I look around. The others….

"They are regrouping, just up there," he says, and his arm goes around me. "I need to move you. It will be easier if you do not feel the pain."

I try to turn, try to look. Need to find Corin, Esther… I blink against the harsh light. For a second, I think I see murky figures but then the shapes dissipate until there's nothing there.

Gone….

"Drink it now, S'ven."

I drink it. It tastes bad, too strong. I start to gag, but he holds the cup at my lips, tips it up more. I try to press my lips together, try to seal them, but can't.

"All of it, S'ven. You are badly blistered. It will heal you." His tone changes, but I can't concentrate, can't work out what it means. "Quick, drink it. We have not got time for this. The Enhanced Ones will get us."

I swallow a few more gulps.

Jed's talking to me, telling me how he's going to heal my burns. My blister burns. Says he can use his Seer powers, but all of a sudden I can't focus on his words.

The sky is gray and dark. I stare at it; my eyes feel strange, too heavy.

Jed lifts the cup back to my lips, tells me to drink more.

My eyes start to close again. I blink several times. My head rolls forward for a second. Something's happened to my neck.

Traitor, another voice says.

My eyelids are too heavy, they make my vision blur. I blink, trying to….

Prove you're Untamed.

Something pulls at my chest.

"Drink it, S'ven. Come on, hurry up."

He's holding me upright, trapping me against his body with one arm, and I stare at the last dregs. Only it's not dregs. It's half a cup full. And the colors are swirling… Round and round and round and round….

Banished.

I'm sweating. Sweating so much, can feel it… It's pouring off me. I'm shaking… The cup, I'm going to drop the cup… And my eyes… I try to keep them open, but there's something stopping me….

"It will be all right if you drink all of it," Jed says. His voice is strange, too fast, too high-pitched.

But it won't be all right… It's him. *Him.*

Jed. It's....

The thought slips away.

Don't drink it. Just get away. Get away now.

I blink, look up as I hear the words. And for a second, I think I see him—Corin. He's standing there, in front of me, sunburnt and angry. Staring. Just staring.

Staring's rude, but he's staring at me. Makes me—

Then he's gone.

Jed's moving, speaking. He's got something else now. A small water-skin. He hands it to me. I don't know where the cup's gone.

"Drink this."

I frown, my head's too heavy. I sniff the drink. It smells the same as the liquid that was in the cup... The cup... Where's the cup now? I look around, but the scenery looks different, as if we've moved, as if we've walked, but I don't remember it.

A muddy pathway leads farther up, among rocks and trees The air is thick, alive. The cave entrance is nowhere in sight now. Neither is anyone else.

We're on the side of a mountain. I see it now, look around. Halfway up? I try to focus on the nearest plants, wait until my vision clears again.

No Untamed Seer does that.

Nettles. They're nettles. And the trees... They're short, with thick branches, thick trunks. I reach out for a branch, touch the peeling bark. I stare at it. I should know its name. I *do* know its name... I reach for it, reach for the word....

"Drink it, S'ven. Be a good girl." Jed's voice pulls through me, and there's something about his tone, a quality that makes me want to obey him. A quality that—

No.

I rub the back of my neck with my free hand, and the ring catches on sinew. I freeze for a second, but it's just the pendant. My mother's pendant. It's under the top of my dress, against my left breast, the crystal has twisted around. It feels cold, like ice.

"Drink it," Jed says. His hand presses against my lower back. "Drink it now."

I look around again. We're *alone.*

I'm wearing the white dress still, and it's perfect. But that's not right… Death got his smoke on it, made it go gray and….

"Drink it, S'ven." His voice is more insistent. Deadly.

Something jolts through me. I look back down at the water-skin. My whole body stiffens.

I shake my head, try to hand the drink back.

"I… I don't want it." My voice wobbles, still doesn't sound right. Not like me.

The light in Jed's eyes disappears. "What do you mean you do not want it? Of course you want it."

His hands grab me. I try to move, but can't, my limbs are like lead. And then Jed has the water-skin by my mouth. I try to twist away, but liquid splashes over me, over my face, and I swallow some. His fingers go for my lips, like clamps. He tries to pull them apart.

I whirl around, head pounding. I try to kick him, punch him, but my movements aren't right. My arms and legs aren't doing what I want them to do, they're ignoring me. My shoulders tighten, my spine stiffens. Everything's locking together.

Your soul will suffer for this setback.

The scream builds up in me, and then I'm reaching out, my fingers grabbing him. My feet are slipping, it's muddy. Too muddy. I'm falling, manage to latch onto his shirt. Beads of sweat drip into my eyes. I try to slam my body into him. But can't do it, can't—

A snake spirit suddenly appears, hovers in front of us. A kavalah.

I freeze, feel my breath get pulled from my body. Jed stops.

I stare at the spirit. The air around it is damp, but too bright. I can't focus on it, yet I know what it is, that it's watching us. And Jed… He's watching it. He's absorbed by it. His eyes have dulled, and—

I run.

I run uphill, because Jed blocks the route down. It's steep. Slippery. Thick mud, the kind that grabs you, tries to bind your ankles.

"S'ven!" Jed screams.

I flick my head back, try to see where the spirit is now, but can't. It's just Jed. Just Jed, after me. Oh Gods.

My heart flutters, my head bangs. I feel more bile rise, spit it out, see the strings of phlegm fly across. Got to get away.

My feet slam the ground, my heels are already bruised. Low creepers grab at my ankles, yank me backward. I fall heavily. The air's knocked out of me. I hear him yell something at me, turn and twist, see him: a looming figure, silhouetted by the sun.

Oh Gods.

Adrenaline propels through my body, and I roll over, under a low tree branch. Its thorns catch my skin, ripping through it like paper. Blood, everywhere. I taste it as I push myself up, my hands closing around a stick.

Weapon. Yes. I need a weapon.

"You won't get far!" Jed shouts. "Not with that in you!"

Mud and water spray over my legs. Fine bits of grit stick to my skin. My arms flail out. My left one—my hand—burns. It's the ring.

Keep going!

"S'ven, I *will* catch you!"

I shriek, try to turn, try to see him, feel his hot breath on the back of my neck.

Oh Gods.

Faster, faster—I need to be faster. Have to be.

I force myself onward, but my thighs are burning. Burning into a sticky mess. And it's just more land, getting steeper, steeper. More of those thick trees—*hagenia*. The name flashes into my mind, and—

Jed grabs my shoulder.

I scream, feel my voice grate, drop the stick.

He slams me onto the ground.

357

My eyes blur for several seconds, pain in my head. I try to get away, I kick out, but there's blood everywhere, and suddenly all I can look at is the blood and—

He points a gun at me.

"Get up. Drink this. Do not disobey me again."

He pulls me up. My legs jerk out. He's still holding the water-skin. After all that, he's still got it. Or it's another one, I don't know.

I try not to show fear. "Where are the others?"

I swallow hard, but my voice was stronger that time. And it feels like an accomplishment, something to be proud of.

Jed bites back a laugh. "You do not need the others. You only need me. *We* will survive." He tilts his head to one side, glares at me. "But not if you fight me. He has told me. He has told me what to do. We have the knowledge, S'ven. We are going to use it. Drink this."

The pouch is thrust into my hands. I grab it. My hands just do it, without me telling them.

"Drink or I shall shoot you." He moves the gun closer to my head.

I gulp, don't understand where the semi-automatic pistol came from. He didn't have it before, did he?

"Drink it all."

The water-skin seems to get heavier. Sweat runs down me, soaks my shirt as I stare at it. I move my lips, try to think of something. It's not an augmenter. Just a drug, to make me sleepy. Right? It's not an augmenter, because augmenters are in vials.

Unless this is… I press my lips together, shift my weight a little. I try to look around. The hagenias close in. I weigh up my options again. Drink it or run.

The gun flashes.

Drink it or get shot.

Shaking, I bring the water-skin to my lips. And it's not an augmenter. *Can't* be augmenter. I tell myself that over and over again, as if it will make a difference. As if it will help.

Jed's eyes narrow, watching me. "Drink it *all*," he says again.

I drink it all.

FORTY-FIVE

THE BLACK WATER LAPS AT my bare feet, and I watch it through half-closed eyes. The water feels warm, nice. Jed tells me it's good.

I'm lying on a slope, a steep slope. The ground above the dark waves is dusty, dry. Strangely dry. The air above me is mist, water vapor.

"It is all right, S'ven," Jed whispers. He's next to me, sitting, and his voice makes me shudder. I feel sick, but the nausea's good—I remember that. If I feel sick, that liquid wasn't an augmenter. Augmenters just give positive emotions. Nothing bad. Jed smiles. "Go back to sleep. We will be safe soon."

I nod, feel fuzzy. There's too much stuff in my head, I can't think, don't want to think because there's something bad there, but it's something I need to remember. No. Jed is right. Sleeping does sound better. And I am tired. So tired.

You let this large-scale conversion attack happen.

I frown; that's not right.

The black water blinks at me. It's moving, hissing. Steam rises from it. I try to shut it out, because it looks bad, and I don't want to think of bad things before I go to sleep. I roll onto my side, so I'm facing Jed. I need to watch him. Mustn't turn my back to a predator.

Jed's smiling as he looks up at the sky. He's been watching it for ages. Staring at it. But it's just white, there's nothing there. Just mist.

I pull my feet out of the water, and the cold breeze washes over them, makes my skin tingle. I move my head, so I can't see the black water because it looks bad.

Don't go to a black lake. If you see it, you run. If you go to this black lake, you'll die. But he's going to try and get you to go there. He'll trick you.

The words jolt through me, make me frown; I don't know why, and I can't remember who said them. Every time I try to think, try to sort through everything in my head, the pain starts.

It's small at first. Little beads of pain that dive into my brain. But then the beads get bigger, push my thoughts out of the way, to make room for them—for the beads of pain. And the pain's all I can concentrate on.

Traitor!

I try to sit up. After a few seconds, I manage it. I twist my head around, look at Jed. He's sitting calmly, face up to the sky.

"It will be over in a minute," he says. "All over and done. And we will be safe."

I rub at my bare skin, try to ignore the puncture marks. My bare arms.

I go cold.

I am naked.

I drag in air, struggle to breathe.

"My clothes…" I look around, can't see the dress or my underwear, can only see the steep banks of the lake, rising up above me, higher and higher. But I still have my mother's pendant on…and the ring. The engagement ring…*my* engagement ring. "Jed… What's happening?"

"We are being saved."

My skin starts to tingle. I look at him. That's when I notice he's naked too. And—and he's covered in the marks. Covered in the puncture marks—the insect bites? But his are everywhere, covering every ounce of skin, tattooed or not. There's no part of him that hasn't got the bites. Even his face now.

And his bites are *bleeding*.

I blink, and then his blood's pouring out of them, pooling toward me, scorching my skin.

I start screaming, shouting at Jed. And I'm trying to get away, but I can't, can't move.

Jed's eyes are still on the sky, and the angle of his head emphasizes the bites on his skin. "Any minute now."

Pain flits down my spine; I don't understand. My shoulders tighten. I try to wrap my arms around myself, try to do something. My gaze focuses on the bites on his lower back, how they're distorting the tattoo there—

It's the bison. The bison tattoo. Like that other Zharat Seer had, just a different place.

I swallow hard and stare at my hands.

"Where are we?" My voice still shakes as I pull the ring off my finger, as I try to press it into the bloody ground, get the redness to swallow the jewelry up. But the ring doesn't disappear, it's moving, buzzing against my fingertips.

"The crater lake at the top of our Fire Mountain," Jed says. He's still looking up, as if he's waiting for something.

I look up. But all I can see is the mist. Thick, white, hazy.

"Why?"

"He told me. Told me what to do, how much energy to give the spirits."

"The spirits?" My voice cracks.

Jed nods. "The spirits… He told me…" He trails off, frowning.

He? I blink hard, think I remember something… Jed

said something about a *he* before, didn't he? I grimace, can't remember. But I need information.

"What *are* these marks?" I ask, and a voice in my head tells me that that isn't the question I should be asking.

Jed glances at me. I see the gun behind him, but it's out of my reach. At the moment.

"Scars," he says. "Kavalah spirit scars."

I stare at him, echo his words. The whole world seems to stop. Oh Gods.

"What have you done?" My voice stutters. I flex my fingers, need to get up, need to get away. I take several deep breaths, push my hair back from my face. It is wet, warm. "Jed! What bargain have you made?"

But he just shakes his head, looks up at the sky again. Oh Gods.

I need to get out of here. Something bad is going to happen. I look around again, but my clothes aren't here.

"Do not worry." Jed's hand darts across, and his fingers close around my wrist. His skin burns. For a second, I think he's seen I'm not wearing his ring. But he doesn't say anything about it. "Come on. It must be time now."

"Time?"

But he doesn't say anything else. Just pulls me up. And, the moment I'm standing, I feel the full effects of the drug in my system. My legs weaken, and I feel all my blood rush to them. Dizziness starts to overtake me, but Jed's holding me up.

"Lean against me. I will help you walk."

Run! the voice in my head screams, uses Five's tone.

But Jed's got my arm; he's right next to me… And he's strong. I can't run. So, I do as he says. I lean into him, and he tells me what a good girl I am. But I don't like the way he says the words, or how his voice shakes.

I shudder. "Where are the others?" My words are slurring again; I hadn't realized they were so clear before.

"I cannot save the others," Jed says. "I can only save you."

He steps forward again, pulls me with him. I stumble, force my legs to work. But they're still not right. Nothing is right.

If you go to this black lake, you'll die. But he's going to try and get you to go there.

Five's voice.

I whimper.

The Untamed part of you will be killed.

I try to turn, don't know where those words came from…not Five's voice now. I try to speak, but my words don't sound like words. They're just sounds.

"It's all right," Jed says.

But it's not. It's not. It's *not*.

Oh Gods.

He marches me forward more. I can't stop him. We're suddenly waist-deep in the thick water, and there are stones under my feet. I frown… Time—I'm losing time. I shake my head, try to feel something beyond the pain. Something important, it's right on the edge of my mind.

The black water laps against my body, swallowing me. I look down, can't see anything below the water's surface. My hips, my legs, they're completely obscured by the dark liquid. The water…it *is* black. Thick, and gloopy, the kind of water that has weight.

The kind of water that can pull you down, trap you.

My body jolts. I look at Jed.

He knows I'm a Seer.

He's a Zharat man.

He's going to drown me.

He's finally going to kill me, after waiting so long—tormenting me.

Soraya said he likes the kill—but he likes the chase too.

He's a proper hunter.

"No…no…no…" I shake my head, try to pull away

from him, away from the black water.

But his arms are around me, and the water's around me. Everything's around me, and it's pushing.

And—and I can't die now. My chest tightens. My death, it's important… I try to fight through the fog in my head, try to remember why….

"Please… Don't kill me…" I cry, turning, facing Jed.

A muscle pulsates in his neck. "I am not going to kill you."

But it's a lie. Oh Gods. Yet the gun's still on the bank. He's not going to shoot me, because it's too far away now, glinting. I frown, the light isn't—it shouldn't be glinting. It's still foggy here, still—

The spirits drop from the sky.

I scream, try to duck but I'm suddenly too deep in the lake. Water invades, the darkness dives down my throat. I jump back up, feet slipping on the rocky bed, splashing. Water sprays from my mouth, I'm choking, and Jed—

Jed is….

He's not here.

"This is her! Do it now," he yells, but it's just his voice. *He's* not here. "Save her!"

I turn around again, and again, and then I can't stop moving. I'm just going round and round. Nausea squeezes my throat, then I see a spirit in front of me. An evil snake spirit, like the one I saw before… The one in the cave? I frown… That feels right…doesn't it? I saw one…a snake spirit….

And then Jed's voice is everywhere again. "Do it! I fed you all, I gave you the energy, my blood has run for this—so do it!"

The nearest snake spirit moves closer to me.

I stare at it. It's looking at me. Its eyes are bigger than before, so big. Its whole body's bigger. Fatter. The thin line of its mouth gets longer.

Get out!

My body jerks, and I turn, and—

Something slams into me. I don't see it, just feel it.

I fall back, my head underwater. I kick out, but the water's thicker now, heavier…and it's hotter. So much hotter. It's holding me, burning me.

My skin…blistering, too much pain…can't….

I try to kick out, but can't find anything. Try to move my arms, but they're too heavy. The water's wrapping around me, and the silver lines—the silver lines that are suddenly there—are wrapping around me too. They're ropes, tiny ropes that pull me down.

And—oh Gods.

I can't breathe.

Can't—

"Do it!" Jed's voice is different, lighter. "Spirits! Let them save us! Give control of our souls to the Enhanced!"

FORTY-SIX

THE BLACK WATER BURNS MY throat all the way down. I feel it in my stomach, my lungs. I'm choking, choking. Heat forces its way up my esophagus, mixing with bile and rancid tastes and—

I take another breath, breathe in more water, more pain....

No... No... No... I'm drowning. Actually drowning. Oh Gods.

I can't die! Not now... Not like this... I'm supposed to die at the end of the war...when Death calls me back....

I try to move, to swim, but my arms won't work.

Jed... It was him. That's all I can think. That kavalah spirit that was in me before...it was *him*. He sent it. Not Mart, not Raleigh. *Jed.*

My mind reels. Why? Why would Jed—

Do you want to be safe?

A kavalah spirit appears in front of me, smiles at me. For a moment, it looks less like a snake.

We can make you safe, Little One. Tell me yes, *and we'll make you safe.*

Its face elongates as I stare at it. Safe? The Enhanced?

367

"No!" But more water invades me, and my word doesn't come out… Just more pain… No… Too much pain. I'm dying, dying, dying….

Poor little Seven. You don't want to die, do you? But you are dying. You're dying right now. Only we can save you. He gave us the energy to do it, Seven. Gave us our new instructions.

I try to get away, need to swim—but the water's too heavy, and my arms are still trapped, useless. And the spirit smiles again.

So let us save you, Little One. Just say the word. Give us access to your soul. Let us get you a nice, strong soul-commander.

The silver threads around me tighten, and I scream again, more water in my body, lungs burning. The black water gets hotter. I raise my arm—somehow manage it—see my skin, see the top layer twist and peel off, wrinkling at the edges.

My stomach twists.

No. No. No. I need to get out. Have to get away.

I try to look up, try to see the sky, but the water's too dark. Can't make out a thing. It's all just black. Black and gloopy. All black and gloopy apart from the spirit in front of me.

You're not supposed to die like this…drowning… Let us save you.

I shake my head, feel thousands of pins dive into my flesh. I scream, see flashes of white everywhere, and—

You can't beat us, Little One. We always get what we're sent for.

Something cackles next to me. I flinch, try to turn, try to see….

They swim at me, all at once. Hundreds of them. The snake spirits. But they're smaller. Tiny. An inch long, and they get to me—crash into me. *Through* me.

My skin—more marks, more punctures, more kavalah spirit scars. Everywhere. Like Jed… Everywhere.

I scream, more black water in my lungs.

We took your Seeing dreams as you slept… And you had no idea… You thought we were gone, after you expelled our mother. You couldn't detect us: us who she'd so carefully laid inside you.

You didn't even know… Couldn't feel us coming and going… Free access.

And Jed gave us enough energy to be invisible.

We stole your warnings from the Dream Land when you fainted once, twice, three times….

Three times? I blink—then I remember. Earlier, before the Enhanced attacked *and* on the day of the fight… I fainted twice then. Corin thought the second time, when we were trying to escape, looked like a Dream Land summoning. Oh Gods. Two summonings, close together on that day… But what were the Gods and Goddesses trying to warn me about? I struggle to think….

You allowed multiple conversions to take place.

The conversion attacks! The girls going fishing… The girls who never returned… *Two* faints, two summonings to the Dream Land—warnings that were stolen away from me before I even saw them. Oh Gods. And Death warned me about obeying the visions soon after that, said he wouldn't give many more chances.

Oh Gods. How many other Seeing visions have I missed… The dreams, when I was sleeping… How many?

And I look down at my body, my left side, see all the kavalah spirit scars—all the marks, the bites, the older ones that were so prominent before. And, oh Gods… It works… The timings work… I'm sure of it… Every time new marks appeared, it was after a Dream Land vision I never received…and something bad followed—girls went missing, were converted… Several times… And the last summoning, right before the Enhanced attacked: deaths and conversions I could've prevented if I'd seen the vision…deaths and conversions that the Gods and Goddesses *needed* me to prevent....

We took your Seeing dreams as you slept. We stole your warnings from the Dream Land when you fainted.

And every time, it marked my body—wrote on it that something bad was going to happen.

My body jolts. My Dream Land visions... Jed—Jed arranged for me to forget... Put the mother kavalah inside me... How? I blink, then I think of the drugs... and the other drinks he's given me, how after the first drink—when he'd just rescued me—I'd felt ill, because of the kavalah... It was in the drink? My head pounds; I don't understand... Why? Why would he do this? Block my Seeing dreams?

Because he's Enhanced? He must be... Jed's Enhanced... Got to be... Stopping my visions...so I couldn't prevent conversion attacks... But what about his visions? His Seeing dreams? No—he's on the Enhanced Ones' side. He won't get visions... So he made sure I didn't either, so I couldn't stop the conversion attack and—

Pain lashes through me, tries to stop me from thinking.

But I push through... Got to... Know I... The other Zharat Seers... Do they have bite marks too... The baby kavalahs... Did Jed target the other Seers too? I don't know, can't think, can't remember. But they had no warnings, did they? Oh Gods. No Zharat Seers had any warnings...because they let female Untamed Seers be killed...and they kill them themselves...and so the male Seers were traitors...good enough Enhanced—and that explains why they don't need their own Seer pendants, or how they didn't recognize mine... They can't get lost in the Dream Land...not after they've been banished from it....

My head... *no*—I scream as something burns me, my back, my neck....

We were with you...all the time.

And it was fun...so much fun....

I blink, feel my body get lighter. Can't understand

how I'm still conscious, how I'm still alive. I can't breathe. But I'm alive.

A snake laughs. Then it moves closer, touches my stomach with its nose for a second.

And now we have a new assignment.

We have to bind you now, Little One. Change the governor of your soul.

Just say the word, Seven Sarr. Give us access. A simple yes *is needed for such a big task.*

Bigger than stealing your dreams....

Let us do our job.

Let us save you.

I reach out for the nearest spirit, try to grab it, but I can't reach. It slithers out the way, waiting until the last second, and I can't move fast...not fast enough. And they're all the same.

I scream, more pain in my chest.

But I know I can do it, can get away, can avoid this. I'm stronger than they think—than Jed thinks... They thought they blocked the Dream Land completely... But I saw Death, he called me there, I spoke to Death... And I got to the Dream Land when the Gods and Goddesses started to banish me....

But neither of those showed you the future, showed you conversion attacks, Seven Sarr...

But my brother! I saw him, *saw* him—

That was before we were employed!

We did our job, Little One. Jed didn't want you seeing the future.

And you didn't, not once we were onboard.

I feel empty. Seeing my brother—that was my last Seeing dream. My last vision. And I didn't do anything—Death was right. I ignored it. Because I didn't see the bison. But we were indoors. I wouldn't have seen him.

But it was my *last* vision.

The snakes hiss, and I see fangs. Fangs so sharp they cut the black gloopy water, leave slashes.

We'll make you agree... We always get what we come for.

So make it easier for yourself.

Just one word. Just say it.

The pain in my chest sharpens, spreads down my left arm. I gasp, but there's no air. Just more black water, and then—

Then I see Corin.

He's suddenly here.

He's swimming toward me, reaching for me, pushing the snakes aside.

I'll help you, he mouths, and his hair looks longer, floats in the water around his face. His eyes are wide open, staring at me. *Sev?*

His hands reach for me. Our fingertips touch. Electricity races through me, stirs the adrenaline, the energy. And I'm kicking out behind me, propelling myself closer to Corin. I grab his hands, ignore the heaviness in my stomach.

Let me help you, let me save you, Corin says. *Do you want me to save you?*

I nod.

Sev?

And I know it isn't him, because it can't be. But my lips aren't listening to what I'm thinking.

My mother's Seer pendant burns, tries to remind me that it's still there, but the water cools the burning, and then the sensation's gone.

Sev? Say the word!

"Yes."

Corin changes instantly. His face pinches in, his body gets longer… The contours of his face become sharper…sharper…sharper…   And   something happens to my face, my neck, my arms, my body… I look down, see something gold splash onto my skin.

The snakes all smile.

We'll deliver your soul's access safely. Jed gave us the name of your new master.

This one's said to be a strong soul-commander.

No!

Goodbye, Seven Sarr.

FORTY-SEVEN

A LONG TIME LATER, SOMEONE grabs my arm. I feel my body moving, swaying, floating, as the hand pulls me along, flips my body over.

My eyes are open, stinging, and I make out blurry shapes. But nothing else. I can't do anything else.

"S'ven?" The voice is weak, but frantic.

Access to your soul has been delivered to your new soul-commander.

You will now be under the control of the Enhanced.

At first the words don't make an impact. Then, what little contents is left in my stomach starts to shift. My body sways faster. My skin starts to burn. A flash of gold, *there*—and there.

More movement. Floating. The water's cooling down now. My skin burns, hurts, aches. But there's too much pain, so I shut it out, what I can. Just push most of it away.

"S'ven?"

Sudden hard gravel, rocks, beneath my shoulders.

He needs to lift me over the gravel, not drag me. But he doesn't lift me, and the sharp rocks cut into what's left of my shoulders.

I stare at the sky, can't blink. The steam above me makes everything shimmer. The sky is purple and red and orange and navy. Little streaks. But there's blue too.

The Turning.

Yet there's no sound. It's silent. Except for his voice, saying my name, over and over again.

My arm twitches a little.

You will now be under the control of the Enhanced.

"Oh, S'ven! Thank the Gods! I thought the kavalahs had disobeyed...."

I don't like his voice—don't like him, hate him—so I shut my eyes, and I drift away.

I dream of Corin, see him running on the forested slopes with Esther, Clare, Soraya, and three Zharat men. One of them carries a child, but the girl will be dead within minutes. The adults are screaming, crying, and they're covered in blisters.

"We need to find them!" Corin yells.

But Jed doesn't like Corin, and he doesn't like me dreaming of him, so he wakes me up, leans over me, his wet hair dripping into my eyes. He's got splashes of gold on one side of his face; they merge with his black tattoos, make the goat look as if its horns are golden.

I sit up slowly. My underwear and dress are back on now, and the thought of him touching me makes my stomach twist. My mother's pendant is still on too, and I hold it, try to get some comfort from it.

You will now be under the control of the Enhanced.

Then I retch and spew out what little was still inside me.

"S'ven?"

I jump up, anger hot in my veins.

"Why?" I demand. My hands shoot out. I want to strike him, but don't want to touch him. "What the hell have you done? My Dream Land visions... My *soul*... The Enhanced! Why? Oh Gods, stay away from me."

I look around. I have to get away. He's one of them. And I'm trying to talk to him, understand him... No. I can't. I need to get away. You can't reason with an Enhanced One.

But his eyes are still Untamed. That unsettles me.

Jed's lips lift up at the corners. The movement reminds me of someone. "To save you."

"*What*?"

I'm breathing hard, too hard. My fingers click as I clench them into fists. I turn slightly, look about again. His gun. He hasn't got it, so it must be somewhere. Must be. And I need it.

But I can't see the firearm, no glint of metal.

"He said I must keep you safe. All of it was done to save you," Jed says, louder. "If you did not remember your Dream Land visions, you could not tell anyone. Therefore, my people could not kill you for being a Seer." He pauses, and my upper lip trembles with disgust. "As for your soul-commander, he will keep us safe, he has promised. We are on the right side now... The Enhanced will be around here somewhere, come on." Sweat glistens off his brow. "They will not have sent only a few to the cave. We shall find them. I did all this to save you, to keep you alive."

I shove my finger at Jed. Part of it is gold—gold like the splashes on his face—and the brightness of it shocks me.

"You gave an Enhanced One *access to my soul*—to command me?" I swear loudly. "Why? Oh Gods. How—how can you do this?"

For a second, I entertain the idea that Jed doesn't know how powerful I am, how I'm the key to the survival of one race, but then I forget it. He'll know. *Of course* he'll know.

Jed breathes hard. "To make sure we are on the winning side. He told me. He is not supposed to share the augury but he did. To save us. The Chosen Ones survive. Now, we are on the right side. We will survive too."

You will now be under the control of the Enhanced.
If they have you, they'll have all the Untamed.

I scream, and I go for him as rage fills my veins, hot and desperate. I shriek as I punch him, catch him off balance.

"It is the only way," Jed cries, and he catches my hands, holds them together, stops me and I just—halt. Freeze as if someone's made me.

Oh Gods—the Enhanced? I'm now under their control… I look around quickly, expect to see hundreds suddenly surrounding us, but there's no one there. It's just us.

"S'ven, I *have* to protect you. He promised me he would keep us both safe if we gave him access to our souls. That was the deal."

"I am *not* joining the Enhanced!" I shake my head, spit at him. I don't care if I'm under their control—it's not happening. Just—not.

"You already have." His fingers push against my face, tracing what? Some sort of pattern? Another gold streak? But I don't care. I try to bite those fingers, but can't. "You have a Promise Mark here. We both have them. All over us. We are theirs now."

"No," I say. "No. *No*." I look at Jed, look at the gold patches on him among the many kavalah spirit bites. "Undo it," I scream. "Undo it now!"

"I can't," Jed says.

"Call the spirits back!" I shove my hand at him, as if expecting white light to shoot out, like it seems to for all other Seers, but nothing happens. I curse. "Get the spirits back here, and stop it all! The Enhanced can't have access to my soul, Jed. They *can't*. Call the kavalahs back."

Jed shakes his head. "Only a powerful God can take a soul away from a soul-commander by destroying the Promise Marks."

A powerful God—Death? My eyes widen. But he's… banished me… I can't contact him… And I think of what he said about my soul, how it will suffer even more if it is the Enhanced who survive. And now I'm *bound* to them, to my enemy?

I swallow hard, then decide exactly how I'm going to kill Jed. I want him to suffer. I want him to suffer greatly. He has to feel pain, he has to know what he's done.

"S'ven, I am sorry I tricked you." Just seeing Jed's eyes on me nearly makes me vomit. "But he told me. And he said you would not agree, that you wouldn't understand. That's what my father said, why I had to—"

My legs turn to stone. "Your father?"

My eyes widen. I feel something moving inside me, inside my chest. I'm shaking.

No. No. No.

It can't be.

Just *can't.*

Coincidences like that—they just don't happen.

But who else? And—oh Gods. Suddenly I know, don't know how I didn't realize before. Jed looks like him in this light, this angle. He looks just like him. Younger, but *just like him.*

But appearance means nothing! Their appearances are artificial!

But….

I turn, and I run. Because I know. Oh Gods, I *know.* I know who my new soul-commander is.

My legs don't feel numb anymore, and I can't feel the pain in my hip. I am devoid of everything. I pant, pumping my limbs.

Jed's behind me. Always behind me. Can hear him shouting. But I'm getting away. How? He's faster. I'm injured. Yet, I *am* getting away… The distance between us is growing. Brown grass gets crushed beneath my feet. I skid on a rock. Something scrapes my ankle. I can see the valley. It looks dark down there...eerily dark.

I crash through more undergrowth. Thorns rip at my ankles, tear the skin there. I feel blood, wet and sticky and—

He's there, in front of me. Feet away.

No. Can't be.

But he is.

He grins at me.

I skid to a stop.

No. No. No.

He will always be able to find you.

I go cold, feel my body tighten up, tighten until it's stone.

Oh Gods. *No*.

"Shania, how lovely to see you once more. Then again, I knew you'd run toward me, because I made you do it." Raleigh pauses, and his mirror eyes flash. "We're going to do great things together."

FORTY-EIGHT

I SHRIEK, ARMS JERKING OUT, but there's nowhere to go—he's everywhere, everywhere I look. Raleigh is everywhere. I throw my hand out, my fingers catch against rubbery bark, try to stop myself. Slow my momentum down, and—

Jed crashes into me, grabs me.

"S'ven, I am sorry, but it is the only way! My father told me the augury, that only the Enhanced survive, and he said if I love you, I had to save you, give him control of your soul because it is the only way to make sure you are safe and—"

I see the exact moment on his face when he sees his father. His eyes widen, his mouth drops open, his temples pulse.

Raleigh smiles at Jed, takes out his gun. A revolver. "Thank you," he says. "Thank you for giving Shania to me. Thank you for ensuring the Chosen Ones will be victorious."

I barely hear Raleigh's words. All I can do is look at him, try to see him as older. Because he's a grandfather—and suddenly that's all I can think about. Jeena is his granddaughter. Oh Gods. But he doesn't look old enough, Raleigh doesn't look old enough. He looks *younger* than Jed.

I feel sick, see myself in Raleigh's eyes and quickly look away.

Jed stares at Raleigh. "What... *Ensuring*? You said..." He looks at me, then back to Raleigh. "You wanted her? *She* makes the difference..." He shakes his head, frowning. Then his arm goes around me. "Where is this safe house you have for us?"

Raleigh laughs. "Oh, yes, there's a safe place. A safe place for each of you."

He lifts his arm up slowly. So slowly I almost don't notice the action. Almost don't see him lining up his aim, almost miss the small movement of his finger going to the trigger.

But I don't.

I scream, throw myself at the ground. Dust flies up, all over me. I taste blood at the back of my mouth, hear my heart pound in my ears. The gunshot echoes, over and over again. And I look up. I see it. Somehow, I see it all, even though I shouldn't.

The bullet gets Jed in the chest.

He falls. Just like that. Jed's eyes latch onto me. And I want to run, want to run to him, and I don't know why because I hate him, because he's done all of this. Because all of this is *his* fault.

"S'ven..." His voice tries to grab me.

I swallow hard. My body tenses up until every inch of me hurts.

Jed's gurgling. His throat is... And the blood, it's seeping out. Not gushing like it did when I stabbed him in the tube; it's a small trickle, what little energy he has left after the kavalahs.

My stomach twists. I try to point to Jed... Jed on the ground, still alive, barely... I try to get Raleigh to do something. To help him, because Jed needs help.

And Raleigh does.

The second gunshot fills my ears.

Raleigh laughs. "I do wish he'd kept my name

though. Maybe then I might've kept him. He never even knew how important you are, Shania. What a shame, he died not knowing the real augury. He believed me all too quickly, poor sod."

Choose your companions carefully, Seven. Some are not worthy… They will lead you down the wrong path… They won't mean to…but they cannot help it.

The bison's words flash through me—words he said before, when he told me Raleigh would always be able to find me—words I haven't thought of for a long time, words I didn't know I hadn't remembered. But now I go cold, and I know those words were about Jed. *He* led me down the wrong path—toward the Enhanced. He didn't mean to. But he couldn't help it. Not if Raleigh was playing him.

And now he's *dead*.

I clap a hand to my mouth. My chest pounds, I stare at Raleigh. His lips twist, and he leans into me, as if he's sharing a secret.

"It's a shame to kill him, really. Especially when he was in love with you. I could tell, by the way he looked at you when he was looking after you, after you were beaten. It was rather disconcerting really, looking through your eyes and having my son stare back at me like that."

My eyes….

My gaze jerks toward him. "How? My eyes—how?"

And I don't know why I'm asking, how I'm even managing to speak after….

Raleigh smiles. "I tried to get control of your soul myself, before that boyfriend of yours stabbed me. I didn't manage it, and we only get one attempt." He shakes his head. "But I did get a tracker on you, on your eyes, though I couldn't activate it for a few days—the one on your ears didn't work so well, but I heard some conversations—like that one in the Turning, when they mentioned killing that female Seer, poor girl."

I stare at him. No. This can't be happening.

"Really, though, Shania, you should thank me. I got Jed to protect you, keep you safe. Even got him to keep Corin alive when there was that scene with the executioners—I don't want you grieving, do I? No. You need your Seer powers, Shania. And wasn't Jed good? He followed my orders. You'd probably be dead, if it wasn't for him. It was a nice touch too, him finding a way to block your Seeing dreams—didn't expect that. But it worked—and he had the kavalahs in place for you before he even knew of the soul transferral that would require them. Brilliant. Saved time. Well, Jed always was *innovative*."

I stare at him, don't know how he can talk about his son so casually, keep his voice so light, not when....

That's when I make the mistake of looking at Jed's body. I see the blood, the lifelessness in his eyes. He needs sending off, sending to the New World. I start to cough, feel my throat squeezing together.

"You killed him." My lips start to burn, and I can barely speak. "He did what you wanted, and you *killed* him. You had his soul, and you...."

Raleigh leans closer. "It was too much of a risk. Advising his soul as well as yours would've used up too much energy—sending him the instructions was hard enough... But I managed to keep you safe and alive while I waited until Jed's powers were strong enough to bind you to me. It was extraordinary—the lava even seemed to help him heal his abilities quicker." He clicks his tongue.

I just stare at him, feel empty, hollow. Jed's body... Nausea rises in me.

"I *was* worried though, Shania, leaving you with the Zharat, letting you suffer so long. I am sorry. But the timing had to be right—there were so many variables—it was best to leave you there. If I'd gone in and got you both out as soon as I knew where you were, many things could've gone wrong and it would've been much longer before you were bound to me—and there's *always* a risk of death when we launch a rescue, for the Untamed *and* us. I couldn't risk either you or Jed dying *before* you'd been bound to me—that's why I didn't want a mass-conversion operation on the cave until you were safe with me…in case you got killed. But I knew my men would launch one after you discovered the infiltration, and then the gas eruption started, and the shock of it increased Jed's powers further."

He turns and looks at the body of his son, a fond expression on his face.

I try to turn away—to move, to run—but I can't.

Just—can't.

My body…pain…sudden pain….

"And I knew I had to act then, Shania." Raleigh grins euphorically, and he seems lost in his own world. "Jed was strong enough! And I had to make sure Jed saved you, my darling—because the timing was getting tight, and the steam was coming through and guns were firing. I had to tell him the augury—well, I adapted it a bit—make him bind you to me as soon as possible. And what a good boy he was—eager to follow my instructions, to get you out of there. Protect you from everything. He really believed he was saving you. His love, his desperation was quite sickening." He shakes his head, a slight look of amusement on his face. "Well, it worked perfectly, the timing in the end. It's all fine now. And you and me—we'll achieve wonderful things."

My stomach tightens as I stare at Raleigh.

Fine?

My eyes glass over.

"Your son is dead, and you think this is *fine*?"

Raleigh leans in closer, then looks back at Jed's body. "Well, he would've had a heart attack soon." He shakes his head. "All that sleep deprivation while he commanded the spirits to block your Seeing dreams, it wasn't doing him any good. High blood pressure, irregular heartbeat—not to mention the effects of the kavalahs feeding from him every night before they went to you. And they would've continued to drain him." He purses his lips for a few seconds. "No, it was kinder to kill him. He's free now. He served his purpose."

He served his purpose.

"But you're not violent," I say, and the words sound stupid, but it's what I was taught, growing up. Even if it is wrong now.

I start to choke, eyes streaming.

Raleigh looks at me. "You know now, don't you? Why I've wanted you for so long, why I had to let you go—become Untamed again—when I had you at New Kimearo?" Instead of waiting for an answer, he continues. "Playing the long game was worth it. If I hadn't, you wouldn't have become the Seer the augury, the Gods, speak of—you know the augury, yes? It's your powers. You're the most powerful Seer, and you're mine. It's a shame really that Waskabe will claim you at the end."

Waskabe. The name makes me go cold.

You will now be under the control of the Enhanced.

I look at Raleigh. Under *his* control.

Every part of my body tells me to run. Every single part. My muscles are twitching, yet I can't—my body is locked.

I go cold.

"Oh yes," Raleigh says. He leans forward, until his face is a mere inch from mine. "Your soul is mine to advise, mine to control. And I'm a good advisor. If you resist my direct control, it'll only hurt you. "

I try to pull away from him, but I can't move—still can't move.

Raleigh smiles. "You are mine. You're not getting away, Shania. We're going to do great things together. First, we'll work out what your amazing Seer powers are. Then, we'll work out how you'll convert all the Untamed—or kill them—and finally end this war."

He grins at me, and the world stops.

I stare at him, then I'm falling, crashing into the

ground. My powers. My Seer powers… How *I'll* use them to end the rest of the Untamed?

Me.

Sweat breaks out across my face; I feel it, sticking to me. I try to pull away, but can't. Try to just flex my fingers, but—

Pain lashes through my body. I scream.

You will now be under the control of the Enhanced.

If they have you, they'll have all the Untamed.

I'm the key, and they've got me.

I will wipe out the Untamed….

No.

I scream.

I won't. I can't.

It will *not* be me who destroys the Untamed.

My arms jerk in front of me, and then I'm getting to my feet. My knees knock into each other.

"No, Shania. I don't think you understand. You're under *my* control now. You can't just go where you want, you can't just try and leave."

But he's wrong. I manage it. I take a step backward, feel him fighting me. I feel it in every muscle of my body, every part of my brain, every part of my soul that is still attached to my body.

But I do it.

I turn, I fight through the pain.

And I run.

FORTY-NINE

I MAKE IT TWO STEPS before the real pain starts in: my ankles, burning. The heat spreading up. Hot, white flashes. I start to fall, twisting around.

I scream, try again. But… My legs—they're…not working. Not mine. Not my legs. Not my—

More pain. It's like—like the torture… Just pain. Pain. Pain. Pain. I'm crying, feel the tears. No, it's sweat. Sweaty and horrible—my skin. My skin. Something's not….

Breathe, Seven!

I drag in more air, start to choke.

"Get back here, Shania! Obey me, and the pain will stop."

No. No. No.

Another step, just about manage it. I try to look up ahead—need to fix on a landmark, aim for that. That's what I do when I'm running, and I'm the fastest runner the Untamed have.

The Untamed.

I gulp, start to choke as more pain wraps around me. But it's not like normal pain. It's getting worse. Not numbing. Eating me.

But I do it, lift my head higher, force myself to see through streaming eyes, and—

I inhale, sharp.

They're all around me. The Enhanced. They're everywhere.

Hundreds of them. Men and women. They each look different. Not the automatons that chased us before. They're each individual. Like Raleigh. But they're not coming for me, not stepping closer. They're stepping away, in all different directions but me. And they're shouting: *More over there, getting away!* and *It's too late for them, convert what you can.*

The mountain rumbles, something hisses near me, and heat splashes against my skin. I skid on loose stones, feel tension rip through my leg, feel my muscles burn, swell, getting ready to burst. I look down the mountainside, steep. Orange, everywhere, in rivers. Too bright, my eyes.

Get away. Keep running.

I take more steps. But there's nowhere to go!

"You're only hurting yourself, trying to fight my control!"

A second later, I hear him grunt, and something sizzles. Then there's wet spray over my back. I scream.

"You can't get away, not when I control your soul, your actions, your body, Shania! You can't resist my plans for you now," Raleigh screams. "You will do as I say, and I'll teach you how to use your Seer powers. We'll save them all, Shania! You're going to find them all, Shania! Find all the elusive Untamed, across all the lands, the ones who've been hiding. And you'll covert—or kill—them all: every single last Untamed creature."

Pain drips down my spine, and I want to smile— there are still some Untamed out there, the Zharat wasn't the last tribe.

But I'm going to find them, the others. And that's what stops my smile; the end of the Untamed, it's going to be because of *me*. It really is.

If they have you, they'll have all the Untamed.

And they've got me. The Enhanced have finally got me—*all* of me. And I can't get away.

I retch, bend over, watch the vomit spew from my mouth. Smell its acidity as it burns.

I manage a few more steps before more pain lashes. White hot pain, it goes up my legs now, shredding my thighs, my hips, my stomach. And the gold marks on me, burning. My chest tightens, gets too tight, and—

I fall, smack my head on something hard. See darkness dance around me, like mist. And then—then I'm getting up. I think I am. Put my hand down on something sharp. Thorns. Feel my flesh tear. I see red. Blood.

My stomach curls.

I push myself up, panting.

But this. Raleigh? This pain. How?

Something snaps within me as I manage a few more steps, but I'm crawling. So they're not steps; I don't know what they are. But I feel it snap. Hard and quick and—

"You won't get far!" Raleigh yells. "You can't resist this, not when I can control you. And my men are all around here. You won't get past us. You can try if you want, but you'll still do as I say."

I turn, but it's not me moving. It's my body. Rotating back to him. He's farther away than I thought. I've made it farther than I realized.

I have to try. Can't give up.

I force myself to stand, grab my leg, try to turn my foot around and—

"Seven."

The man appears in front of me. Four hundred feet away. The man who—

I freeze, feel my chest tighten. No. No. No. It can't be. But it *is*.

It's *him*.

I shake my head. A clone. A clone. Just a clone. Because there are more behind him. More dark figures, but I can't see their faces.

But they're clones. I know that. They have to be.

But he called you Seven. Esther's words dive at me. I feel sick as I look at him, as he walks toward me.

He's smiling. Smiling broadly. Smiling how he never smiled before. His teeth flash, his eyes throw more light about.

"Stop it!" I turn back—turn away from the man—and shout at Raleigh, tell him to stop it. "You've already got me!"

But Raleigh's laughing.

And—and the Enhanced man is here.

He's *here*. Right in front of me.

It's *him*.

No. He's dead.

But he isn't. He's here. Esther was—oh Gods. And that dream, that warning, the conversion....

"Get the augmenters in her, Tomas," Raleigh shouts to him. "We need to get back to the base."

My body jolts. I look at the *Enhanced man* in front of me—because I have to just see him as another Enhanced man, as *Tomas*, now. That's who he is.

He's got a gun. But it's not like anything I've ever seen before. Because I can see the bullet. Except it's not a bullet.

It's a vial. A murky concoction fills it, but the color's changing.

And the pistol is aimed at me.

"Oh dear," he says. "You're not *still* resisting this, are you? Why didn't you tell me how much better it is to be a Chosen One?"

His voice even sounds the same.

"No... no... no..." But I'm mumbling, my words are barely audible.

Thr—no, *Tomas*—steps up to me. His eyes make me feel sick, but I force myself to look at them. To try to see *him* under the mirrors. To hope that maybe he's still in there. I survived it, so he can. He doesn't have to be Tomas.

But all I can focus on is the iron sheet under his left eye. Facial reconstruction? That's what the Seeing dream said… The last vision I had… But that isn't… This isn't reconstruction.

"Just one short, sharp prick," he says, and he moves the gun closer to me, drops it down about a foot, so it's lined up with my right thigh. "You'll feel so much better then, when you wake up. All the fear will be gone, and then we can save everyone. And we have the Eriksens too—my dear Esther, and her cocky brother. You won't be alone. Raleigh said he'll convert them, as soon as possible—we'll all be together again."

My muscles seize up as my gaze jumps back to his face. I try to focus on him, but can't. They've got Corin. Esther and Corin. They've got them.

No.

He steps toward me, the pistol gets closer. The vial—the murkiness—gets closer.

My chest shudders. "What—what augmenter is it?"

His smile is so like mine that it hurts. "A mixture. Mainly Sleepiness. But there's some Compliance, Calmness, and Tranquillity for when you wake."

My mouth dries. I start to try to form words. "What… No…. You—"

I hear the click of the trigger. Too loud.

The augmenters get me in the upper right thigh. I scream, try to move back but something stops me. The air stops me. It presses against my body, won't let me move.

Heat floods my veins. My muscles start to burn, but then—

I struggle to keep my eyes open. My eyelids are too heavy.

I start to fall.

Three's face is the last thing I see.

END OF BOOK TWO

ACKNOWLEDGEMENTS

As always, writing a book isn't a completely solitary process, and there are a number of people I must thank for helping me with *Fragmented*. Without you all, this book wouldn't have been possible.

Thank you to my wonderful editor, Deelylah Mullin. Working through the editing process with you has been so much fun. Thanks must also go to Molly Phipps, my amazing cover artist and interior designer. Thank you so much! *Fragmented* is definitely one of my favorite books I've written, and it's been so wonderful seeing it come to life.

I'd also like to thank T.A. Maclagan, E. Mitchell, and Rachael Bundy, each of whom read an early draft of this book and provided feedback. Your insightful comments were invaluable and really helped strengthen this book. Equally, many thanks must go to my writing groups: the YA Story Sisters, AAYAA, and the NaNoWriMo group. Your support has been amazing and your enthusiasm unwavering. And to Lizzie Colt: thank you for your encouragement, help, and support—even when it meant workshopping the same sentence with me for (literally) an hour and a half! I don't think I've ever written quite so many variations of one sentence!

Additionally, special thanks must go to T.A. Maclagan, Marissa Kennerson, Sue Wyshynski, Heidi Sinnet, Pintip Dunn, Jen Knox, Dr. Jessie Voigts, *A Drop of Ink Reviews*, *Readcommendations*, *The Literature Hub*, and *The Story Sanctuary*. Thank you for blurbing my books and/or permitting the inclusion of pull-quotes from your reviews of my Untamed series for use in this book. Your support means a lot. Thank you.

This book required an incredible amount of research, and I'd like to thank the team of volcanologists who kindly gave up their time to help me in my research: Dr. Jessica Ball, Dr. Rebecca Williams, Dr. James Hickey, Dr. Erik Klemetti, and Professor David Rothery. Thank you for answering my (many) questions about volcano formation, volcanic rock, lava tubes, and the composition of volcanic gases. Equally, thank you for providing me with countless diagrams and guiding me in my research around Mount Bisoke, an active volcano in the Virunga Mountains of the East African Rift, which became the basis for the Zharat's Fire Mountain. Extra thanks must also go to Dr. Jessica Ball, for reading an early draft of *Fragmented* and kindly fact-checking my volcano sections, and to Dr. Rebecca Williams, who provided me with copies of her own photographs of the Thurston Lava Tube in Hawaii. It was so much fun learning about volcanoes, and any mistakes in this book are mine.

Next, I must also thank my family and friends: you've all been brilliant. Countless times, you've blown me away with your enthusiasm and support. So, thank you.

And, finally, I wish to thank my parents and my brother, Sam. Thank you for believing in me, and for your support. Thank you for not getting too mad at me when I kept asking you the same questions over and over again. And thank you for being so enthusiastic about this book. It honestly means the world to me, and I'm very lucky to have you.

ABOUT THE AUTHOR

MADELINE DYER lives on a farm in the southwest of England, where she hangs out with her Shetland ponies and writes young adult books—sometimes, at the same time. She holds a BA Honors degree in English from the University of Exeter, and several presses have published her fiction. Madeline has a strong love for anything dystopian, ghostly, or paranormal, and she can frequently be found exploring wild places. At least one notebook is known to follow her wherever she goes.

Find Madeline online:
Twitter: @MadelineDyerUK
Instagram: @MadelineDyerUK
Facebook: MadelineDyerAuthor
Website: www.MadelineDyer.co.uk

Sign up to Madeline's Newsletter:
http://madelinedyer.co.uk/newsletter/

THE STORY CONTINUES IN . . .

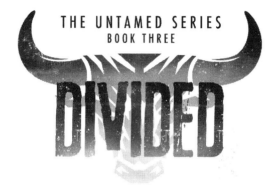

THE UNTAMED SERIES
BOOK THREE

DIVIDED

Having been tricked into binding herself to the Enhanced Ones in the War of Humanity, Untamed human Seven Sarr has never felt more exploited or used. When Raleigh forces her to develop her Seer powers and use them on a most innocent target, Seven knows it's only a matter of time before the Enhanced Ones use her to wipe out the rest of her people.

Certain that the only way to save the Untamed would be to get back full control of her soul, Seven must get the Gods and Goddesses to trust her again. Only they can destroy her Enhanced Promise Marks, and prevent her enemy from controlling her.

But these are the same Gods and Goddesses who have already branded Seven a traitor and exiled her from the Dream Land, fearing she will cause their deaths. With no way to contact the Gods and Goddesses herself, Seven needs help. And she needs it quickly, before the war is over and she loses Corin, and the rest of the Untamed, for good.

Yet, in a world as dangerous as this, only one thing's for sure: no one trusts a traitor twice.

AVAILABLE FROM JULY 11, 2017